DEATH, TAXES, AND A SKINNY NO-WHIP LATTE

"Readers will find Kelly's protagonist a kindred spirit to Stephanie Plum: feisty and tenacious, with a self-deprecating sense of humor. Tara is flung into some unnerving situations, including encounters with hired thugs, would-be muggers, and head lice. The laughs lighten up the scary bits, and the nonstop action and snappy dialogue keep the standard plot moving along at a good pace."   —*RT Book Reviews*

"Readers should be prepared for a laugh fest. The writer is first class and there is a lot of humor contained in this series. It is a definite keeper."   —*Night Owl Romance*

"A quirky, fun tale that pulls you in with its witty heroine and outlandish situations… You'll laugh at Tara's predicaments, and cheer her on as she nearly single-handedly tackles the case."   —*Romance Reviews Today*

"It is hard not to notice a sexy CPA with a proclivity for weapons. Kelly's sophomore series title…has huge romance crossover appeal."   —*Library Journal*

"An exciting, fun new mystery series with quirky characters and a twist…Who would have ever guessed IRS investigators could be so cool!"
          —*Guilty Pleasures Book Reviews*

"Kelly's novel is off to a fast start and never slows down. There is suspense but also laugh out loud moments. If you enjoy Stephanie Plum in the Evanovich novels you will love Tara Holloway!"   —*Reader to Reader Reviews*

ST. MARTIN'S PAPERBACKS TITLES BY DIANE KELLY

PAW
ENFORCEMENT

Diane Kelly

St. Martin's Paperbacks

This is a work of fiction. All of the characters, organizations, and events portrayed in this novel are either products of the author's imagination or are used fictitiously.

PAW ENFORCEMENT

Copyright © 2014 by by Diane Kelly.

For information address St. Martin's Press, 175 Fifth Avenue, New York, NY 10010.

ISBN: 978-1-250-04834-9

Printed in the United States of America

St. Martin's Paperbacks edition / June 2014

St. Martin's Paperbacks are published by St. Martin's Press, 175 Fifth Avenue, New York, NY 10010.

10 9 8 7 6 5 4

To Schultz. You chewed my shoes, shed on my bed, and picked fights with dogs ten times your size, but I loved you anyway. Thanks for eighteen good years as my BFF—best furry friend.

ACKNOWLEDGMENTS

It takes a village—or a pack—to bring a book to readers, and I am grateful to the many people who made this new series possible.

To my amazing editor, Holly Ingraham. Your suggestions and insights are always spot on. Thanks for making me a better storyteller!

Thanks to Cassandra Galante and everyone else at St. Martin's who worked to get this book to readers. You're a fantastic team!

Thanks to Danielle Fiorella and Jennifer Taylor for creating such a cute book cover!

Thanks to my agent, Helen Breitwieser, for your hard work in advancing my career. I appreciate all you do!

To my inner circle of talented writer friends—Ceyla Bowers, Cheryl Hathaway, Hadley Holt, Angela Hicks, and Kennedy Shaw. Thanks for your encouragement, feedback, and friendship!

To Liz Bemis-Hittinger and Sienna Condy of Bemis Promotions. Thanks for your work on my Web site and newsletters. You ladies rock!

ACKNOWLEDGMENTS

To the many wonderful writers I've met through Romance Writers of America, as well as the national office staff. RWA is an awesome organization. I am glad to be part of such a supportive and powerful group. Go, RWA!

Special thanks to Detective Rick Castro of the Fort Worth Police Department for giving me insights into the fascinating life of a detective. To Officers J. Alejandro and Brandon Kramer of the Mansfield Police Department, as well as their K-9 partners. Thanks for all of the great information about K-9 operations and for putting your lives on the line to keep the rest of us safe. Thanks also to Officer Phillips and the other officers and volunteers who put on the Mansfield Citizens Police Academy. I learned so much while attending the program and am proud to be a graduate.

And, last but not least, thanks to my readers. Because of you I have my dream job. Enjoy your time with Megan and Brigit!

ONE
JOB INSECURITY

Fort Worth Police Officer Megan Luz

My rusty-haired partner lay convulsing on the hot asphalt, his jaw clenching and his body involuntarily curling into a jittery fetal position as two probes delivered fifteen hundred volts of electricity to his groin. The crotch of his police issue trousers darkened as he lost control of his bladder.

I'd never felt close to my partner in the six months we'd worked together, but at that particular moment I sensed a strong bond. The connection likely stemmed from the fact that we were indeed connected then—by the two wires leading from the Taser in my hand to my partner's twitching testicles.

I didn't set out to become a hero. I decided on a career in law enforcement for three other reasons:

1. Having been a twirler in my high school's marching band, I knew how to handle a baton.

2. Other than barking short orders or rattling off Miranda rights, working as a police officer wouldn't require me to talk much.
3. I had an excess of pent-up anger. Might as well put it to good use, right?

Of course I didn't plan to be a street cop forever. Just long enough to work my way up to detective. A lofty goal, but I knew I could do it—even if nobody else did.

I'd enjoyed my studies in criminal justice at Sam Houston State University in Hunstville, Texas, especially the courses in criminal psychology. No, I'm not some sick, twisted creep who gets off on hearing about criminals who steal, rape, and murder. I just thought that if we could figure out why criminals do bad things maybe we could stop them, you know?

To supplement my student loans, I'd worked part-time at the gift shop in the nearby state prison museum, selling tourists such quality souvenirs as ceramic ashtrays made by the prisoners and decks of cards containing prison trivia. The unit had once been home to Clyde Barrow of Bonnie and Clyde fame and was also the site of an eleven-day siege in 1974 spearheaded by heroin kingpin Fred Gomez Carrasco, jailed for killing a police officer. Our top-selling item was a child's time-out chair fashioned after Old Sparky, the last remaining electric chair used in Texas. Talk about cruel and unusual punishment.

To the corner, little Billy.

No, Mommy, no! Anything but the chair!

I'd looked forward to becoming a cop, keeping the streets safe for citizens, maintaining law and order, promoting civility and justice. Such noble ideals, right?

What I hadn't counted on was that I'd be working with a force full of macho shitheads. With my uncanny luck, I'd been assigned to partner with the most macho, most shit-headed cop of all, Derek the "Big Dick" Mackey. As implied in the aforementioned reference to twitching testicles, our partnership had not ended well.

That's why I was sitting here outside the chief's office on a cheap plastic chair, chewing my thumbnail down to a painful nub, waiting to find out whether I still had a job. Evidently, Tasering your partner in the *cojones* is considered not only an overreaction but also a blatant violation of department policy, one that carried the potential penalty of dismissal from the force, not to mention a criminal assault charge.

So much for those noble ideals, huh?

I ran a finger over my upper lip, blotting the nervous sweat that had formed there. Would I be booted off the force after only six months on duty?

With the city's budget crisis, there'd been threats of cutbacks and layoffs across the board. No department would be spared. If the chief had to fire anyone, he'd surely start with the rookie with the Irish temper. If the chief canned me, what would I do? My aspirations of becoming a detective would go down the toilet. Once again I'd be Megan Luz, aka "The Loser." As you've probably guessed, my pent-up anger had a lot to do with that nickname.

I pulled my telescoping baton from my belt and flicked my wrist to extend it. *Snap!* Though my police baton had a different feel from the twirling baton I'd used in high school, I'd quickly learned that with a few minor adjustments to accommodate the distinctive weight distribution I could perform many of the same tricks with it. I began to work the stick, performing a basic flat spin. The repetitive motion calmed me, helped me think. It was like a twirling metal stress ball. *Swish-swish-swish.*

The chief's door opened and three men exited. All wore navy tees emblazoned with white letters spelling "BOMB

SQUAD" stretched tight across well-developed pecs. Though the bomb squad was officially part of the Fort Worth Fire Department, the members worked closely with the police. Where there's a bomb, there's a crime, after all. Most likely these men were here to discuss safety procedures for the upcoming Concerts in the Garden. After what happened at the Boston Marathon, extra precautions were warranted for large public events.

The guy in front, a blond with a military-style haircut, cut his eyes my way. He watched me spin my baton for a moment, then dipped his head in acknowledgement when my gaze met his. He issued the standard southern salutation: "Hey."

His voice was deep with a subtle rumble, like far-off thunder warning of an oncoming storm. The guy wasn't tall, but he was broad shouldered, muscular, and undeniably masculine. He had dark-green eyes and a dimple in his chin that drew my eyes downward, over his soft, sexy mouth, and back up again.

A hot flush exploded through me. I tried to nod back at him, but my muscles seemed to have atrophied. My hand stopped moving and clutched my baton in a death grip. All I could do was watch as he and the other men continued into the hall and out of sight.

Blurgh. Acting like a frigid virgin. How humiliating!

Once the embarrassment waned, I began to wonder. Had the bomb squad guy found me attractive? Was that why he'd greeted me? Or was he simply being friendly to a fellow public servant?

My black locks were pulled back in a tight, torturous bun, a style that enabled me to look professional on the force while allowing me to retain my feminine allure after hours. There were only so many sacrifices I was willing to make for employment, and my long, lustrous hair was not one of them. My freckles showed through my light makeup. Hard to feel like a tough cop if you're wearing too much foundation or more than one coat of mascara. Fortunately, I had enough natural coloring to get by with little in the way of cosmetics. I was a part Irish-American, part Mexican-American mutt, with just enough Cherokee blood to give me an instinctive urge to dance in the rain but not enough to qualify me for any college scholarships. My figure was neither thin nor voluptuous, but my healthy diet and regular exercise kept me in decent shape. It was entirely possible that the guy had been checking me out. Right?

I mentally chastised myself: *Chill, Megan.* I hadn't had a date since I'd joined the force, but so what? I had more important things to deal with at the moment. I collapsed my baton, returned it to my belt, and took a deep breath to calm my nerves.

The chief's secretary, a middle-aged brunette wearing a poly-blend dress, sat at her desk typing a report into the computer. She had twice as much butt as chair, her thighs draping over the sides of the seat. But who could blame her? Judging from the photos on her desk, she'd squeezed out three children in rapid succession. Having grown up in a family of five kids, I knew mothers had little time to devote to themselves when their kids were young and constantly needed Mommy to feed them, clean up their messes, and bandage their various boo-boos. She wore no jewelry, no makeup, and no nail polish. The chief deserved credit for not hiring a younger, prettier, better-accessorized woman for the job. Obviously, she'd been hired for her mad office skills. She'd handled a half-dozen phone calls in the short time I'd been waiting and her fingers moved over the keyboard at such a speedy pace it was a miracle her hands didn't burst into flame. Whatever she was being paid, it wasn't enough.

The woman's phone buzzed again and she punched her

intercom button. "Yessir?" She paused a moment. "I'll send her in." She hung up the phone and turned to me. "The chief is ready for you."

"Thanks." I stood on wobbly legs.

Will the chief take my badge today?

Is my career in law enforcement over?

I turned the knob and stepped into the doorway, a dozen eyes on me. Two of the eyes belonged to Chief Garelik. The other ten were lifeless glass spheres inserted into the various animal heads mounted on the wall, including a sixteen-point buck, a mountain lion, and an enormous gaping trout. Given the abundance of wood paneling and taxidermy, the room looked more like a hunting lodge than a government office. Two long windows looked out on to downtown Fort Worth, the clock tower of the Tarrant County Courthouse visible a block away. Situated between the windows was a bookcase boasting framed snapshots of the chief in camouflage coveralls crouched next to a fresh, bloody kill. In another, the chief held a dead duck by the neck while the Big Dick stood next to him, his red burr cut flaming in the sunshine, his arm draped over the chief's shoulders.

No doubt about it. The chief was a man's man.

I'd met Chief Garelik only once before, at the induction ceremony for the officers in my training class. After administering the police officer's oath, he'd made his way down the line, shaking hands, pinning badges on uniforms, giving each new officer a stiff salute. Today he sat in an oversized leather chair behind an enormous oak desk, a collection of hunting rifles mounted in a rack behind him. The chief was broad and bulky, with a complexion best described as Spam-like, red and ruddy, with visible lines of broken capillaries on his cheeks and around his nose. High blood pressure would be my guess. Serving as police chief in a city of three-quarters of a million people wasn't exactly a low-stress job.

He ran a hand through his silver hair and locked his steely eyes on me, shooting me the same look one would give an aluminum siding salesman who'd appeared uninvited on the doorstep. "Get your ass in here, Officer Luz."

Not exactly a polite invitation, but I was in no position to take offense. I stepped into his office, closing the door gently behind me. The latch caught with a resounding *click*, as if sealing my fate.

He gestured to one of the wing chairs covered in genuine fake leather courtesy of the city's taxpayers. The stretched-out fabric on the seat evidenced decades of butts' having perched on the chair. My ass was obviously not the first that would be chewed out here.

Before I could even settle in he snapped, "Good God a'mighty, Luz! What the hell were you thinking?"

No working up to the subject. No pussyfooting around. Then again, the chief was a busy man with no time for niceties.

"I guess I w-wasn't thinking, s-sir," I said, disappointed to hear the stutter in my voice. I was a cop, dammit. I needed to sound professional, tough, competent. Instead, my voice sounded feeble and fumbling, the way it had back in school when a teacher called on me in class.

No.

I'm not going to let myself down.

I can do this.

"I'm sorry. I lost my t-temper." Carefully choosing my words and using as few as possible, I explained to the chief that Mackey and I had arrested a woman for driving under the influence. "We found a bag of what appeared to be crystal meth in her car."

I'd cuffed the woman, turned her to face the cruiser,

and patted her down. Mackey had suggested I perform a body cavity search, further proposing I lick my finger first, not only to make insertion easier but also "to make things more fun" for the woman. The perverse comment had been bad enough, but when he offered to lick my finger clean afterward it was the last straw. I had put up with his disgusting, sexist bullshit all day, including him positioning his erect baton between his legs and rubbing it up and down while making moaning sounds.

Grrr. An uncontrollable rage had seized me. An instant later Derek lay twitching on the asphalt, his hands cupped over his crotch, his eyes rolling back in his head, and drool oozing from his mouth. Then came the urination, as disclosed earlier.

Repeating the exchange was embarrassing. But I had to tell the chief the filthy things Mackey had said. I had to defend myself.

When I finished, the chief shook his head. "Mackey's a prick. You'll get no argument here."

I wasn't sure whether to be offended by the chief's vulgar language or to be glad he was treating me like one of the guys. I didn't want him to treat me differently because I was female. I wanted the same respect—or disrespect—he gave the male officers.

The chief sat back in his chair and exhaled loudly. "Ironically, the fact that Mackey's a prick is what makes him valuable to this department."

Mackey not only had a reputation for being a sexist pig, but he was also known for his extreme, bordering-on-insane bravery. He'd recently rescued a woman dragged into her apartment by an abusive boyfriend who'd already taken several shots at officers with a sawed-off shotgun. While the other cops shielded themselves behind their cruisers and waited for the SWAT team to arrive, Mackey had snuck up the side staircase, kicked in the door, and stormed the place. Of course Mackey claimed afterward that he'd never have risked his life if the woman didn't have such a "ginormous rack" and "smoking-hot ass."

The chief put his feet up on his desk and his hands behind his head. A good sign. He'd be in a more formal posture if he was going to fire me, right?

His chair squeaked as he rocked back. "You shouldn't have Tasered Mackey. Especially in the balls." He cringed involuntarily, as if the mere thought caused him pain. "But he had it coming."

Frankly, when considering what the Big Dick deserved, electrified gonads was a drop in the bucket.

Chief Garelik wagged a hairy-knuckled finger at me. "You're lucky Mackey brought this to me rather than Internal Affairs. I'm going to keep this incident off your record and let you slide this time."

Thank God.

"But *only* this time," he added. "You'll be booted off the force and face criminal prosecution if you pull a stupid stunt like that again. You hear me?"

I swallowed hard, forcing down the lump that had formed in my throat the instant the word "stupid" registered with my ears. I was *not* stupid. Impatient, sure. Short-tempered, hell yeah. Maybe even impulsive.

But not stupid.

My jaw clenched so tight my teeth threatened to crack. "Understood, sir."

The chief retrieved a paper pouch of chewing tobacco from his breast pocket, pinched a bit from the package, and slid it into his mouth between his cheek and gum. He returned the pouch to his pocket and picked up a Diet Coke can, putting it to his lips and expelling tobacco juice into it. *Puh-ting.* I tried not to show my revulsion.

"I'm assigning you a new partner." The chief's eyes gave off a wicked gleam, like the glint from a freshly polished revolver. "She's a real bitch. You two will get along great."

I ignored the implication that I, too, was a bitch. Unlike stupid, though, being called a bitch didn't really bother me.

"A female officer?" Teaming with a woman could be fun. Mackey had kept the cruiser's radio tuned to a sports channel all day. With a female partner, we could listen to NPR or a book on tape, maybe a good detective novel. A female partner would smell better, too. Mackey was a big guy, producing sweat by the gallon in the Texas heat. By the end of each shift, our cruiser became a BO gas chamber. Of course the jerk never seemed to be bothered by his own stench.

The chief retrieved his handheld radio from his desktop and squeezed the talk button. "Send in Sergeant Brigit."

So my new partner was a sergeant, exceeding me in rank. Typical, as rookies like me were generally paired with a more experienced officer. But *Brigit?* It sounded more like a first name than a last name.

A jangle sounded outside the door, likely Sergeant Brigit's keys or handcuffs. The door opened and she walked in.

Whoooa.

The chief hadn't been lying. My new partner was a real bitch. As in four paws and eight tits. Huge, too, with thick fur in black and tan. The jangling came from her tags, a city license and a rabies tag, hanging from a studded black leather collar that made the bitch look butch.

A cry of, "No!" spurted involuntarily from me. Remembering my manners and the fact that I was in the chief's office, I turned back to him. "I mean, *no, sir.* I c-can't partner with a dog."

The chief cocked his head. "You allergic?"

"No, sir."

"Then she's yours. You'll be responsible for caring for her after hours, too."

No. No way. I didn't want that kind of responsibility. Don't get me wrong. It's not that I had anything against dogs. Problem was, as I was the oldest of five children, any jobs my parents couldn't handle had been outsourced—or should I say *down*-sourced?—to me. I'd been responsible for dressing, feeding, and generally riding herd over my brothers and sisters. The only thing my parents had never asked me to do was tutor my siblings.

Things had been no better when I went off to college. I'd gone potluck for roommates in the dorm and the computer had paired me with one irresponsible roommate after another, girls who partied every night, forgot to set their alarms, left their dirty panties and socks all over the floor. They counted on me to wake them for class, to maintain a stock of tampons and rolls of quarters for laundry.

When I'd moved back to Fort Worth after college graduation last May, I'd immediately signed up for the fall police academy and rented a tiny apartment in an older complex in East Fort Worth. It wasn't much. Three hundred square feet with worn blue industrial carpet and a tiny rectangle of rippled linoleum in the kitchen nook. But, as management loved to remind disgruntled tenants, the place came with free cable television. Most important, though, I'd been finally free of responsibility for anyone but myself. I didn't even own a houseplant.

Someday I'd want a husband, kids, maybe even a cat or dog.

But not yet.

Not now.

The handler holding the dog's leash ordered the animal to sit. The dog obeyed, turning her big brown eyes on me in what could only be described as a death glare. She seemed no more excited about being partnered with me than I was about being partnered with her. It was almost as if she'd understood what I'd said, that I didn't want the responsibility of taking care of her.

But a dog wouldn't be smart enough to understand that, would it?

I tried to think of another viable excuse. I glanced over at the dog. The beast had to weigh close to a hundred pounds. I turned back to the chief. "I drive a smart car, sir. She won't fit inside."

He waved his hand dismissively. "Sure she will."

He still wasn't biting.

"My apartment management doesn't allow pets. They're forbidden by my lease." *Good thinking, Megan. He's head of the city's law enforcement. He can't argue with the law.*

"We called the property manager," the chief shot back. "He said he'd make an exception for a police dog. Figured it might reduce crime at the complex."

The place had suffered a rash of vehicle burglaries lately. Nonetheless, "I—"

Chief Garelik cut me off with a raised palm. "No more excuses, Officer Luz." The chief spit another gooey blob of tobacco into his soda can. "You messed up good and I've gotta make some cutbacks. You either partner with Sergeant Fluffy-butt or you're off the force."

TWO
A BIG WHIFF OF ROOKIE

Fort Worth Police Sergeant Brigit

Megan had no way of knowing, of course, but Brigit didn't set out to be a hero, either. She became a K-9 officer for three other reasons:

1. Her original owner was too irresponsible to take proper care of her. The dipshit left her in the backyard for days on end in freezing weather while he and his equally dipshitted friends went on a bender of Jack Daniel's and Northern Lights, a species of cannabis that he cultivated himself under grow lights in the garage.
2. The frostbitten dog was forced to dig under the chain-link fence, working until her paws bled, to go in search of water before she died of dehydration. She mustered up one final tiny turd—her aforementioned dipshit owner had forgotten to feed her, too—and left it on the back step as a parting gift before taking off.

3. Animal Control picked her up five blocks over after an elderly woman reported a bear licking the frozen water in her birdbath. The officer freed the dog's frozen tongue from the ice, gave her some water from the bottle in his truck, and brought her to the city shelter.

Brigit didn't stand a chance of being adopted by a family in search of a pet. She was an adult dog by then, no longer one of those adorable puppies who drew an *ooh* or an *aww* or an *ain't you the cutest thing?* A shepherd mix, she weighed in at a whopping ninety-seven pounds. Not much of a market for a dog that size. To make matters worse, her fur was long and thick, sure to shed all over the place and require regular brushing. Few people would take on such a high-maintenance pet.

The dog was doomed.

She wagged her tail vigorously when families came in looking for a pet to adopt, showed them how well-behaved she was, that she could sit, shake, even play dead. Occasionally someone would remark about how beautiful her coat was or how smart she seemed. But nobody wanted to take home a beast that would cost a fortune to feed.

Brigit watched carefully through the steel mesh of her enclosure and quickly caught on to how things worked at the shelter. Volunteers would occasionally come to take the dogs for a walk outside. Those dogs would come back happy. But dogs didn't return to their cages if they went with a man wearing a dingy lab coat. The man smelled of mint gum and cheap aftershave. But most of all he smelled of death. He smelled sad, too, as if he didn't like having to do what he did, as if he wished people would stop letting their pets reproduce willy-nilly so that his services would no longer be needed.

Brigit spent her nights clawing desperately and futilely at the concrete floor, trying to dig a hole and escape.

One day, the same animal control officer who'd picked her up off the street bent down to look at Brigit through the steel mesh. "Sorry, girl," he'd whispered, his eyes cloudy, his soft voice cracking. "I'm really, really sorry."

Brigit could smell the man in the lab coat coming down the hall, could smell the mint gum, the cheap aftershave, *the death.*

He was coming for her.

She panicked, spinning, spinning, spinning in her cage. *Woof!* she cried. *Woof-woof! Woof!*

Before the man in the lab coat could reach her, up walked another man in a dark-blue uniform.

"I need a dog," he told the animal control officer still kneeling in front of Brigit's cage. "A smart dog. One with lots of energy that can be trained to serve as a K-nine officer."

Brigit didn't hesitate. *Me! Take me!* She jumped on the door of her cage, her long tail slapping the sides of the small enclosure as it whipped desperately back and forth. *Please!*

"Got just the dog for you," the animal control officer said. "Right here."

He pointed into Brigit's cage and the man in the blue uniform bent down to take a look.

Brigit stopped barking and sat. She held out her paw to shake. She fell to the floor, rolled onto her back with all four paws in the air, playing dead. If there were an Academy Award for animal performers, she would've won, paws down.

She showed the man in the blue uniform every trick in the book, then turned her big brown eyes on him and gently licked his hand through a hole in the chain-link mesh.

The man showed his teeth, a bad sign on dogs but, as Brigit had observed, a good sign on humans. "I'll take her."

Thus, Brigit became an officer in the Fort Worth Police Department, her salary paid in dog biscuits and belly rubs.

The cop who'd picked Brigit out at the shelter had taken good care of her and she'd enjoyed working with him for the two years they'd been together, but he'd recently resigned from the police force to work for a private security firm. Half the risk for twice the pay. Who could blame him?

He'd told Brigit he'd miss her, given her a big pat on the head and a chuck on the chin when he'd turned her over to the chief. He couldn't keep Brigit. She wasn't his pet. K-9 officers were considered tools, pieces of equipment, no different from a gun or a baton or a Taser. Brigit belonged to the Fort Worth Police Department.

So here she was, being reassigned to a new partner, Officer Megan Luz. Brigit could tell Megan didn't like the idea of being partnered with her. When Brigit walked through the door of the chief's office, Officer Luz hadn't shown her teeth. She'd also emitted short, loud sounds. Brigit knew those short, loud sounds meant Megan wasn't happy.

Well, Brigit wasn't too crazy about being partnered with Megan, either. Officer Luz smelled like a rookie. Too fresh, too clean. Her uniform lacked the stench of terror-induced sweat that no detergent could ever quite wash out. Luz hadn't seen real danger yet, that was certain. It would take some training to get her up to speed.

Fortunately, Brigit was up to the task.

THREE
LESSONS TO BE LEARNED

The Rattler

He never set out to be a killer, exactly. Like a rattlesnake lying coiled up in the grass shaking its tail, he, too, simply wanted to issue a warning, to shake things up, to force people to change course. A bomb seemed the best approach to achieving his aims for several reasons:

1. Bombs are easy to make. Hell, you could find detailed instructions on the Internet.
2. Materials needed to make a bomb were cheap and readily available.
3. A bomb would not only get attention but also destroy evidence. He could execute his plan with little risk of being identified. On the other hand, the low risk of capture almost took the fun out of it. . . .

FOUR
MY NEW ROOMIE

Megan

The handler who'd brought Brigit to the chief's office gave me a brief training session, just enough to hold me over until I could begin the full K-9 course next week. He showed me how to make the dog sit, stay, heel, and lie down, as well as how to order her into her cage. The dog followed each of my orders perfectly. I still didn't like the situation, but I had to give her that.

"Got it?" the handler asked, tentatively holding out the leash.

I just as reluctantly took the leash from him, fighting the urge to sigh. "Got it."

Our tutoring now complete, the handler left. After a little more ass chewing, Chief Garelik dismissed us, too.

I fumed as I walked down the hall, the dog's nails giving off a *click-click-click* as we went. The chief had not only saddled me with a partner who was sure to be a pain in the ass but also ordered me to take a six-week anger management course. At least the class was offered online.

If I had to sit in a classroom with some overly cheery teacher telling me to *turn my frown upside down* I'd have to punch somebody.

As I stepped out of the headquarters building, the afternoon June heat enveloped me like an unwelcome hug from a creepy uncle. Brigit trotted ahead of me as we made our way out to the employee parking lot, pulling me along by her leash, virtually dislocating my wrist. I had thirty pounds on the furry beast, but with four on the floor she had better traction. The fact that I had a gym bag over one shoulder and her enormous crate in my hands didn't help, either.

"Heel!" I barked.

The dog, who had been the epitome of obedience inside, ignored me now.

I shifted the cage in my hands the best I could and jerked back on the leash. "Listen up, dog! I t-told you to heel."

The dog glanced back at me. If I didn't know better, I would swear she rolled her eyes.

"Well, well, well." Derek leaned back against his shiny black pickup, causing the pink rubber testicles hanging from his trailer hitch to sway. He crossed his meaty arms over his chest, a nasty grin on his face. "The bitches are on the beat."

Ignoring the Big Dick, I continued three spaces down to my tiny two-seater metallic-blue smart car. Why was I taking the dog and her things home with me? Because she and I were to form our own pack now and cohabitating was evidently an essential part of the canine bonding process. I now had to think and act like the alpha dog. Perhaps I should lift my leg and take a pee on my back tire.

I set the cage and bag down on the asphalt and bleeped the door locks. After depositing the bag containing Brigit's bowls, brush, and flea shampoo in the small space behind my seat, I rolled down the windows, opened the passenger door, and gestured to the dog. "Get in."

Sniff. Sniff-sniff. The dog performed an exploratory snuffle along the floorboard, dash, and seat before attempting to climb into the car. No luck. Her furry hindquarters hung out the side. She turned on the seat, but that wasn't much better. There wasn't enough room for her.

I waved her back out of the car. Grabbing the lever under the front seat, I moved it back as far as it would go and leaned the seat back to the rear until the headrest met the back window. "That's as good as it gets," I muttered.

The dog climbed back in, fidgeted for a moment or two, then settled back. The tips of her ears touched the ceiling and she was forced to rest her front paws on the dash, but at least all of her was in the car now.

As I struggled to lift the dog's cage to the roof of my vehicle, nearly dropping it twice, a sharp corner of the metal dug into the paint. *Screee.* My roof now bore a five-inch scratch. *Fantastic.* The cage was nearly as big as my car, and I had to turn it sideways for the best support.

If the Big Dick had been half the man he thought he was, he would've offered to help me, maybe even put the cage in the bed of his pickup and delivered it to my apartment. Instead, he just kicked back against his truck and watched, a smirk on his face. *Asshole. Who needs him? Not me, that's for sure.*

I ran a rope through the bars of the cage and looped it through the windows. I tied it off as taut as I could and silently pleaded with whatever deities might be observing that it would hold.

With the rope through the windows, it was impossible to open the door. I had to slide into my car through the open window like a NASCAR racer. Once I was seated, I looked over at the dog. No two ways about it. She was going to be a total nuisance, an enormous burden, an impediment to my career plans. "I really don't deserve you."

She gave me a look that said she felt the same way about me.

I cranked the engine. Finding the gearshift among the dog's long fur wasn't easy, nor was backing up with her enormous body blocking my line of vision, but eventually we managed to make our way out of the space.

Two other male officers had gathered with Mackey to watch, shaking their heads as I drove past.

"For someone who drives a smart car," the Big Dick called after me, "you sure look stupid!"

Grrr. It took everything in me not to hook a quick U-turn and run the guy over. If I'd thought my car was up to the task, I might've done it. Unfortunately, a strategically placed sneeze could probably blow me over.

Don't let him get to you, Megan, I told myself. *He's not worth it.*

When guffaws broke out behind me, though, I changed my mind. He *was* worth it.

My tires emitted a short squeal as I slammed on my brakes, shoved the gearshift into park, and wriggled out the car window.

"Uh-oh," one of the other cops teased as I stalked toward them. "You're in trouble now, Mackey."

I ripped my baton from my belt and extended it with a flick of my wrist. *Snap!*

Derek straightened and instinctively turned sideways to make himself a smaller target. His hand rested on his gun.

"What the fuck is she doing?" said the third cop, taking a few steps back.

My baton down at my side, I stomped up to Derek's truck, bent down, and delivered a solid *whack* to his truck's rubber testicles.

Damn, that felt good.

That first whack had been for Derek, but I delivered a second one for the jackass who'd invented those disgusting rubber truck nuts. *Whack!* The nuts swung back and forth, just like the real thing.

Standing, I collapsed my baton, gave the men a smile and a nod, and walked back to my car.

Derek's voice came from behind me: "Told you that girl is crazy."

Glancing over at the enormous beast as I drove, I cursed my short temper. If only I'd been a little more patient, if only I hadn't pulled my Taser, I wouldn't be in this situation now, paired up with a dog for a partner. This would not be a career-enhancing partnership. What could a dog teach me about being a cop?

The air conditioner blew at full power, fluffing the dog's fur as she sat panting on the seat, drops of drool falling from her tongue to my dashboard. Having so much thick hair had to be a bitch in the Texas heat and, since it was only early June, the worst was yet to come. She'd be miserable in July, when we'd have day after day of one-hundred-degree weather.

Wait. Was I actually feeling sorry for the dog? How ridiculous. Why should I? This dog would tie me down and shed all over my tiny apartment.

Brigit glanced over at me, her eyes narrowed as if she'd read my mind.

Blurgh. The dog was right. This wasn't her fault. It was mine.

Didn't mean I had to like it, though.

As we waited at a red light, a beat-up black Mustang pulled up beside us. Two pimple-faced boys sat inside, the *thump-thump-thump* of a hip-hop bass line shaking their car and reverberating off mine. The driver glanced our way, did a double take, and rolled down his window. "What the hell is that?" he hollered. "Sasquatch?"

The two hooted with laughter. The light turned green and the driver floored the gas pedal, tires squealing as he sped off. Evidently he hadn't noticed my uniform. I supposed I could call him in, report him for exhibition of acceleration, but why bother? The kid was right. The dog did look like a 'squatch.

On the way home, I stopped by a Target store. Brigit came inside with me. A dog in a store with a grocery department probably violated the health code, but what would they do, call the police? I *was* the police. Besides, I couldn't very well leave the beast in the car in the ninety-five-degree heat. If she didn't die of heatstroke she'd probably eat the seats.

Brigit padded along behind me as I made my way to the automotive department. Shoppers watched as we passed them, their eyes going from Brigit to my uniform. Not likely to be any shoplifting going on while the two of us were in the store.

I grabbed a lemon-scented air freshener to hang from my rearview mirror. My smart car wasn't much, but I didn't want it to smell like dog. We headed to the pet section next, where I loaded my cart with a twenty-pound bag of dog food, a box of dog biscuits, and the largest fleece dog bed the store carried.

Brigit stuck out a paw and put it on top of a cardboard canister of doggie beef jerky. She looked up at me and batted her big brown eyes.

I checked the price. *Nine bucks?* This dog had expensive taste. Heck, I didn't pay that much for my own fancy organic snacks.

"No," I told her, using my foot to nudge her paw off the canister.

Brigit stiffened, stared up at me, and emitted a low warning growl: *Grrrr.*

Time to let this bitch know who was boss. I bent down,

got in her face, and narrowed my dark-brown eyes at hers. "'No' means 'no.' I'm the one in charge and don't you forget it."

The dog stared back at me, unblinking, her lips pulled back in a silent snarl. I returned the sentiment, my eyes locked on hers in a primal power play, waiting to see who would blink first. After twenty seconds or so, my eyes began to water, but damned if I'd let this dog best me. I'd keep them open until my retinas burst.

A woman rolled a shopping cart up the aisle, stopping next to me. "'Scuse me. I need to get to the cat litter."

My watery eyes still locked on Brigit's, I motioned with my arm. "Circle around the next aisle."

The woman made no move to back up her cart. "Can't you just scooch over a bit?"

"No." My eyes tingled painfully. "Official police business going on here."

The woman harrumphed. "Looks to me like you're just making goo-goo eyes with your dog."

Had this woman failed to notice the weapons on my hip? I was tempted to whip out my baton and give her toes a nice *whack*. That would teach her to give a cop some respect.

When the woman still made no move to back off, Brigit began to growl again: *Grrrr.* Though the dog kept her eyes glued on mine, she turned her snout toward the woman, curling her lip back even farther to expose her ready fangs. The cat lady gasped, turned her cart around, and made a swift retreat down the row.

When Brigit turned her snout back my way, I pressed my warm, dry nose firmly against her cold, wet one and reached a hand out to cover her eyes. It was a low-down, dirty move, but there was no way I could keep my eyes open any longer. "We'll call this one a draw," I whispered.

When I removed my hand, Brigit gave me an unmis-

takable look of disgust. After my flagrant cheating, I supposed I deserved it.

Our battle for dominance over for the moment, I stood,
turned my attention back to my cart, and pushed it down
the aisle, pulling Brigit along behind me.

When we reached the front of the store, I rolled into
the express line and began to unload the items in the cart
onto the belt.

"What the—!"

Brigit clenched the canister of beef jerky in her mouth.
She jumped up, put her front paws on the countertop, and
dropped the can onto the end of the moving belt. *Klunk.*
She sat down and looked up at me, her tail moving up and
down, slapping the floor in what had to be canine language for "screw you." *Slap-slap.*

I eyed the canister as it slid by on the belt. The darn
thing bore holes from Brigit's pointy teeth. I couldn't very
well expect the store to put the damaged container back on
the shelf, could I? I glared down at my partner. *You win
this time, dog.*

I paid for our purchases and headed back out to my
car. It took a bit of wrestling to get the oversized dog bed
and food into my car's tiny trunk, but eventually we were
on our way to my apartment.

My complex was called Eastside Arms, appropriate
since the buildings were pocked with bullet holes from
drive-bys and the tenants, the majority of whom were single males, likely packed heat. The place was nothing to
brag about, obviously, just a trio of three-story concrete
bunkers painted in a peeling pastel-blue hue reminiscent
of a beachside souvenir shop. Never mind that the closest
beach was a five-hour drive away.

The buildings formed a U around a common area that
contained the parking lot and a rectangular pool only
marginally bigger than a bathtub. The pool, in turn, was

surrounded by cracked concrete and a chain-link fence. If
you wanted a lawn chair, this was strictly a bring-your-
own situation. Not much landscaping to speak of unless
you counted the dandelions that had cropped up in the
gaps between the sidewalks and buildings. The rent was
cheap, though. One of these days, when my student loans
were paid off, I'd find better digs. Until then, I'd power
through.

I pulled into a spot and retrieved the food, bed, bones,
and jerky from the trunk, clutching them against my
chest, leaving the cage for a second trip. Circling to the
passenger side, I found the window fogged from Brigit's
breath and smudged top-to-bottom with doggie nose prints.
Wonderful. There went the twenty-five bucks I'd paid to
have the car detailed. It was my turn to growl now: *Grrr.*

My next-door neighbor, whom I knew only as Rhino,
sat on the side of the pool in a pair of cutoff jeans, his
skinny legs dangling in the water, his bare shoulders sunburned. His bleached-blond hair was swept up and glued
into a single pointed horn standing up stiffly on his scalp,
directly above his forehead. The guy had three gold rings
through one eyebrow, randomly placed teeth, and a can of
Bud consistently clasped in his hand even when, as now,
he was fooling around on his bass guitar. He played in an
indie punk band called Crotch Rot.

Charming, no?

Rhino gestured to my car with the can. "You win that
big dog at Six Flags?"

I shook my head. "She's not stuffed. She's real."

His mouth fell agape. "You're shitting me, right?"

If only. Alas, my assertions were excrement-free.

I opened the passenger door with my free hand. "Come
on, dog."

Before my fingers could round up the leash Brigit
leaped from the car and bounded toward the fence sur-

rounding the pool, hurdling the four-foot enclosure with the case and grace of a gazelle. If I hadn't been so enraged at her disobedience, I might've been impressed by her agility.

"Get back here!" I ordered. It wasn't the official command the other K-9 handler had instructed me to use, but I wasn't yet accustomed to using the formal charges. I racked my brain for the command word and said that, too. I could tell you what the word was, but then I'd have to kill you. Would I be correct to assume neither of us wants that?

I might as well have been talking to a rock. The dog ignored my orders and jumped into the pool, her belly flop causing a tidal wave and sending up a splash that doused Rhino and his guitar. Good thing the instrument wasn't plugged in or the guy would've been electrocuted.

"Hey!" Rhino scrambled backward, grabbed his towel from where it hung draped over the fence, and dabbed gently at his guitar.

I might've been inclined to apologize to Rhino if the guy hadn't been jamming until 2:00 AM in his apartment last night. Every note was audible through the walls, which I suspected were made of cardboard. I'd debated reporting the offense to the on-site manager but decided to cut Rhino some slack. After all, if he didn't practice his bass he wouldn't get better and if he didn't get better Crotch Rot wouldn't get the gigs that would enable them to move down to Austin, which had a better live music scene. Rhino couldn't control when his muse showed up, and if I went down to complain to the manager I would've had to put on something other than panties and a tank top. Besides, with my meeting with the chief hanging over me, it wasn't like I was dozing peacefully last night anyway. So I'd let the offense slide and instead stuffed toilet paper in my ears and put my pillow over my head.

After circling the pool three times with her leash trailing in the water behind her, my new partner and roommate paddled to the steps and climbed out. Leaving a wet trail, she trotted back to the fence, jumped over it, and returned to my side, chlorine-scented water pooling at her feet.

The dog looked up at me, an evil gleam in her eye.

I pointed a finger down at her. "Don't you dare!"

Again my words fell on deaf ears. Brigit's hindquarters began to gyrate, slowly at first, then faster, working her body into a full and frenzied shake that would've registered a 9.8 on the Richter scale. Before I could back out of range Brigit sent up a shower of dog-scented spray that doused me head to foot and left my car spotted with droplets from the headlights to the back bumper.

Wiping the spray from my face, I glared down at the dog. "You know exactly what you're doing, don't you?"

She did the up-down wag again. *Slap-slap. Screw you.*

I grabbed the soggy leash and headed up the steps with Brigit trotting along beside me. The leash had wound under her belly and between her back legs, giving her a wedgie, but I didn't bother fixing it. After drenching me the darn dog deserved a little discomfort.

Halfway up the steps sat an elderly black tenant sporting a dingy once-white tank top, wrinkled boxer shorts, and house slippers with holes in both toes, exposing long, thick, yellowed nails. *Edward Scissorfeet.* He took one last drag on his cigarette before stubbing out the butt on the step and flicking it over the railing. "That's one big-ass dog you got there."

He had a tremendous grasp on the obvious.

Brigit stopped, gave the man's shoes a quick sniff, then continued on, dripping on the stairs. In the excessive heat, the droplets evaporated almost as soon as they landed.

My apartment was in the middle of the second floor, which meant I had neighbors not only to my left and right but above and below me as well. Maximum neighbors, maximum noise. Upstairs lived an older Latino man who flushed his toilet approximately twenty times a night. Prostate problem, evidently. To my left was a fifty-something leftover hippie with stringy hair and tie-dyed T-shirts. A series of elongated "ohhhhhs" routinely emanated through his wall, though whether they were a meditation mantra or the sound track from porn movies was up for debate. To my right was Rhino. The tenant below me was a grumpy Congolese emigrant who constantly banged with a broom on his ceiling—*my floor*—to protest the noise my other neighbors made. You'd think growing up with constant machine-gun fire would've desensitized him. Perhaps he wasn't so much protesting the noise as exercising his newfound freedom of expression. At any rate, there were few neighborly days in this neighborhood. Were he still alive, Mister Rogers would be sorely disappointed.

I unlocked the door to my unit and stepped inside what felt like a sauna. *Blurgh!* The air-conditioning was out, yet again. Some home sweet home. More like home *sweat* home. First I get stuck with the damn dog, then I get sprayed with pool water, and now my AC was out. Could this day get any worse?

I unclipped the dog's leash, tossed a handful of bones onto the kitchen floor to keep her occupied for a few minutes, and clunked back down the steps, past my elderly neighbor, to the apartment manager's office.

Dale Grigsby had inherited Eastside Arms from a spinster aunt years ago and ran the place from the lower floor of Building A. The walls between the three first-floor apartments had been knocked out and the space remodeled into a combination office and living space. Dale lived in relative luxury, the only one at the complex with two bedrooms and a separate living area.

I made a fist and, though I was tempted to put it *through* the door, merely banged on it instead. *Bam! Bam! Bam!*

A voice came from within: "Hold your horses. I'm comin'."

A few seconds later the door opened. Grigsby stood there wearing a stained pair of elastic-waist shorts and a T-shirt not quite long enough to cover his paunchy belly. At least three inches of pasty, pimpled gut was visible. His bulbous nose twitched, the bristly hairs inside reaching out like tentacles as his nostrils flared. "That you giving off that funky smell?"

I didn't bother to explain that Brigit had doused me with dog-scented pool water. "The air-conditioning is out in Building B again."

"I know," Grigsby said, lifting a chin to indicate the roof. "We're working on it."

I glanced back at my building, noting a guy in coveralls up on top fooling around with the enormous HVAC unit.

"Working on it's not good enough," I said, turning back to the manager. This was the third time the air-conditioning had gone out this month. The unit must have been twenty years old or more. "It n-needs to be replaced."

The rust on the unit was visible from the ground and the system gave off a nerve-jarring rattle every time it cycled on.

"Don't get your panties in a bunch," Grigsby snapped. Such professional service, no? "He'll get it fixed. And remember, you're getting free cable."

Free cable. That was Grigsby's answer to any complaint. The roof could cave in and he'd suggest any complaint was rendered moot by the free cable.

I glanced down at the baton on my hip. Seemed a shame I couldn't use it to persuade Grigsby to replace the AC. One solid whack to his pudgy ass—*swish-swish-whap!*—and he'd surely be convinced.

"I've got a police dog living with me now," I told him. "She's got to have cool air. Dogs can't sweat, you know."

He scowled. "I made an exception, letting you have a pet. You should be thanking me and instead you're complaining."

I made no attempt to hide my eye roll. "The dog isn't my *pet*. She's my *partner*."

He scratched at his exposed belly. "She's still a dog. I did you a big favor by letting her stay here."

Some favor. I didn't want the damn dog in the first place!

I gave up the debate at that point, knowing further efforts would be futile. When Grigsby ran out of excuses, he'd shrug and say, *You get what you pay for.* If we tenants wanted peace and quiet, hot water for our showers, or AC units capable of cooling below eighty-four degrees, we could go on down the street and pay five times as much in rent.

I didn't bother bidding the jerk any form of adieu but merely turned, collected the cage from my car, and stormed back up to my place.

FIVE
NEW DIGS

Brigit

Brigit ate three of the crunchy bones, then hid the others in the corners of the tiny room for later. She would've liked some water, but her new partner hadn't left her any. Didn't that woman know how to take care of a dog?

Brigit sniffed around the edges of the lower kitchen cabinets, her nose picking up scents she translated into a mental inventory. Whole-grain bread. Roasted almonds. Granola cereal. No cookies or potato chips. She sniffed the seal around the refrigerator next. No hot dogs. No ham. No baloney. Only fruits, vegetables, and soy milk. What kind of fresh hell was this?

The dog moved along the wall, snuffling her way past the television and stack after stack of books. She reached the closed door of the bathroom, noting the unpleasant scents of lavender and jasmine. Why humans wanted to smell like flowers was beyond Brigit. She'd take the natural smell of a rotting rat corpse over lilacs any day.

She continued on until she reached the closet. Though the door was closed, Brigit could tell exactly what was inside. *Shoes.* And lots of 'em.

Maybe this new partnership wouldn't be so bad after all. . . .

SIX

IT'S NOT ROCKET SCIENCE

The Rattler

Only a few people meandered around the small hobby shop, most of them men, either alone or with their young sons in tow. Amazing any of these nerds had managed to get laid.

The Rattler headed past the model trains to the rocket section near the back. Though no security cameras were visible, he was careful to keep his head down just in case. The San Francisco Giants baseball cap, mirrored sunglasses, and loose-fitting long-sleeved button-down shirt would go far in making identification difficult. Still, one could never be too careful, especially when one would soon be the subject of a manhunt.

Of course he had to get his ducks in a row first. Buying supplies was duck one.

He selected the largest-model rocket the store offered, a bright-red one nearly four feet tall. Next, he gathered up a half dozen of the F50-4T 29mm engines, some of the most powerful on the market. The engines contained ammonium perchlorate, or APCP, a solid fuel mixture that acted as a propellant and could send the rocket up to two thousand feet into the air.

But it wasn't the rocket that he planned to propel. Oh, no. He had much more creative uses for these little engines that could.

These little engines that *would*.

Atlanta may have burned back when the Confederacy's Rebel army had fought to maintain their exploitative economy, to hold on to their precious cotton plantations and their elitist ways of thinking, their racism and arrogance and riches. But soon a new southern rebel would arise, a solitary, righteous rebel who would set this fucked-up world straight.

He waited on a nearby aisle, pretending to look over the selection of remote-control airplanes, until there was no line at the register where a teenage boy was working. A sixteen-year-old would likely be less suspicious and less observant than the older man working the second register, especially a geeky boy like this one wearing the Yoda T-shirt. *An idiot must be he is.*

The Rattler forced his lips into a smile and stepped up to the counter, quietly laying his purchases on the countertop.

The boy picked up the rocket in both hands and looked it up and down. "Wow, this is a big one."

The Rattler knew it would be a mistake to talk, yet some type of audible response was called for. To remain silent would be odd and awkward. He forced a grunt of agreement. "Mm-hm."

The boy rang up the engines and put them into the bag with the rocket. "That'll be three hundred eighty-nine dollars and sixty-seven cents."

The Rattler pulled a stack of twenty-dollar bills from his wallet. He'd carefully added up the total earlier after looking at prices on the store's Web site so he'd know exactly how much cash to have ready. He didn't want to be in the store any longer than possible or to make a spectacle out of counting the cash.

Unfortunately, the boy didn't share the Rattler's concerns. After the teenager took the stack, he counted through the bills, laying each twenty on the counter. "Twenty, forty, sixty, eighty—" The kid might as well be yelling, *Hey, everyone! Look at all this cash!*

It took everything in the Rattler not to reach across the counter and grab the kid by the throat. *Dumb little shit. Couldn't he count in his head? What did they teach in public schools?*

In his peripheral vision, the Rattler saw the older man at the other register glance over. Luckily, a customer in a scoutmaster's uniform stepped up to the old man's register and inquired about dragsters, drawing the man's attention away.

The boy finally finished counting. "Three-hundred-eighty. Four hundred."

The kid slid the bills into his register's till, then counted out the change. He handed the change to the Rattler and ripped the paper receipt tape from the register. "Would you like the receipt in the bag?"

Shove it up your ass for all I care, the man thought. But he said, "Sure."

He took his bag and headed out of the store, fighting the urge to throw his head back and laugh.

Soon they would learn.

Soon he would have them trained.

SEVEN
BEDTIME FOR BRIGIT

Megan

When I opened the apartment door after my futile chat with Grigsby, I was hit not only with the sweltering heat but also with the overpowering stench of wet dog.

Inside, Brigit had finished the treats and was sniffing around the apartment, familiarizing herself with her new home. It wouldn't take her long. I supposed I could call the small place a studio, but that would sound pretentious. Truth was, it was a minuscule efficiency apartment, barely three hundred square feet. A closet and narrow bathroom were situated on the right wall. The kitchen, which ran along the left wall, consisted of a small fridge, a two-burner stove/oven combo, a stainless-steel sink, and three feet of counter space covered in scratched powder-blue Formica. A coffeepot, toaster, and microwave rested on the counter.

My decorating style could be called minimalist, but such a term would imply the décor was a conscious choice. The fact of the matter was that I had neither the money nor need for much furniture. A card table with a single metal folding chair sat on the rippled linoleum, serving as a dinette set for one. No need for more chairs. I never had friends over, because I had no close friends. My only other furniture was a cheap metal-framed futon with a bright yellow cover and a 17-inch television that sat on an upended plastic milk crate.

Feng shui? No way.

I threw open the vertical windows that flanked my door, as well as the wider window on the back wall, hoping to create a cross breeze that might relieve the heat and the smell. No such luck. Too bad I hadn't had the foresight to buy an electric fan and some room spray when we'd been at the store earlier.

I settled for rubbing some lavender-scented lotion on my hands and windmilling my arms around in a desperate attempt to freshen the place and create a breeze. All I managed to do was make myself warmer with the exertion.

By then, Brigit had determined that the kitchen linoleum was the coolest place in the apartment to lie down. She'd settled in front of the fridge. I filled her bowl with water, adding a couple of ice cubes from the freezer, and set it down in front of her. She stuck her snout into the bowl and noisily lapped up the water. *Slurp. Slurp. Slurp.*

I looked down at her. "You could stand to learn some manners."

Her eyes looked up at me as she continued to drink.

I fixed myself a glass of ice water, too, gulped it down, and walked to the bathroom, where I peeled off my uniform and changed into my black bikini. I left my hair up in the bun, grabbed a towel, and slid my feet into my dollar-store flip-flops.

Leaving the dog inside, I stepped out of my apartment, locking the door behind me. I'd made it down only three

steps when Brigit bolted past me. I turned back to see
the window screen bent and hanging at an odd angle. A
second later it fell to the concrete walkway with a tinny
clatter.

I turned my eyes back to Brigit. Stupid dog! She was
out of control. What was I going to do? If I couldn't learn
to make her behave, they'd reassign her to another officer
and I'd be out of a job.

"Brigit!" I yelled.

She ignored me, continuing down the stairs. Discon-
certing, given that she was a potentially deadly weapon
and I would be held liable for her behavior.

"Get back here!" I screamed. "Now!"

Again, ignored.

Effing dog.

As I squeezed past him on the steps, my neighbor lit
another cigarette and took a deep drag. "That dog don't
listen too good."

No shit, Sherlock.

Down on the ground now, Brigit turned and looked up
at me. She didn't come back up the steps, but at least she
wasn't running off anymore.

I closed my eyes and took a deep breath, tamping
down my anger and saving it in storage for later use. It
might come in handy someday.

I continued down the steps to the gate that surrounded
the pool. Rhino had evidently gone inside. I had the place
to myself now.

I let Brigit into the fenced area and followed her inside,
shutting the gate behind us. Tail wagging, she made her
way to the edge of the pool, turning back and *woof*ing
softly as if inviting me to join her. She slid into the water
more gracefully this time, foregoing the belly flop. After
hanging my towel over the fence and sliding out of my
flip-flops, I hurried across the hot concrete—"Ow! Ow!

Ow!"—and stepped onto the metal ladder, easing myself down into the pool.

The water was a mere four feet at its deepest point and only slightly cooler than the outside air, but I'd take what I could get. I swam back and forth doing the breaststroke while Brigit dog paddled up and down the pool, swimming laps along with me.

I had to admit, it was nice to have company for a change, even if it was furry, four-legged company. Thanks to my childhood stutter and the resulting teasing, I'd learned early on to be very careful in choosing my words and even more careful in choosing my friends, which meant I spent a lot of time alone. While the other kids had played tag at recess, I'd sit by myself under a tree with only a book from the school library to keep me company. Although I sometimes had groups to hang with—the kids from church when I was young, the band geeks in high school, the girls from my dorm in college—I'd always been the quiet tagalong on the fringes, never part of the core clique. I'd never been close to anyone in particular, never had a BFF, a bestie . . .

And you know what?

I'd been just fine.

My experiences had taught me to be self-reliant and resourceful. Good traits for a cop. Besides, I'd learned lots of things from all the books I read. I could name more than twenty of Japan's six-thousand-plus islands, quote the entirety of "The Raven" by Edgar Allan Poe, and tell you all you'd ever want to know about Emily Morgan, otherwise known as the "Yellow Rose of Texas," a young mulatto slave woman who was captured by Mexican general Santa Anna and distracted him sexually while Sam Houston's army moved in to defeat the Mexicans in the battle of San Jacinto. If Santa Anna had kept it in his *pantalones,* the southern border of the United

States might be the Red River rather than the Rio Grande.

Half an hour later, the AC repairman climbed down from the roof and went to Grigsby's door. He held out a clipboard for the manager to sign and accepted a check from him. Looked like the air-conditioning was working again, at least for the time being. We tenants could only hope our luck would hold out and the unit would keep chugging away until the outdoor temperatures cooled off in October.

When we finished our swim, Brigit followed me back up the stairs. I retrieved the bent screen from the walkway and wrestled it back into place in the aluminum frame. Inside, I closed the windows so the dog wouldn't be able to escape again and cranked the AC down to sixty.

I pointed a finger at Brigit. "Don't eat my couch while I'm in the bathroom."

She cocked her head and wagged her tail, looking contrite. Almost cute, even. Reflexively, I ruffled her head. *Oh, God.* Was I being sucked in by this mischievous beast?

Noting how shiny Brigit's hair looked, I retrieved her flea shampoo from the bag the other K-9 handler had given me. The bottle contained a creamy peach-colored solution and promised *a shiny, well-conditioned coat that will make your dog the envy of the pack!* Why not give it a try myself? Besides, given the sleazy people I dealt with every day, it couldn't hurt to have some protection from parasites.

I stripped out of my bathing suit and took a cold shower, though even the cold water was lukewarm in this heat. Somewhat refreshed, I left my hair wet. Not only would it help keep me cool, there was no way in hell I'd crank up a blow-dryer in this heat. I wrapped the towel around me, tucking the end under at the chest to hold it in place, and stepped out of the bathroom. A rush sounded in the ducts overhead and a burst of cool air gushed from the vent. I stood under it and raised my hands in the air. "Hallelujah!"

Brigit barked as if in agreement: *Woof!*

After slipping into panties, a tank top, and a pair of knit shorts, I went to the kitchen. Bridget stood on the linoleum crunching on dog food that poured out of a hole she'd torn in the side of the bag while I was in the shower.

"Bad dog! Look at the mess you've made." I scooped what kibble I could into her metal food bowl, taped the hole in the bag closed with duct tape, and shoved the bag of food into the cabinet under the sink.

I opened the fridge, hoping to scrounge up some dinner that didn't have to be cooked. Even though the AC was back on, it had only managed to cool the place down to eighty-five degrees so far. The last thing I wanted to do was turn on my oven. My choices were fruit, bagged arugula salad, or granola cereal with soy milk. As you've probably guessed, I'm a bit of a health nut. To stay safe as a cop it was important to keep yourself in shape. Especially for a female officer. Who knew when I might have to outrun a crazed wife beater wielding a hunting knife? Eating well made staying in shape easier, though I admit to an occasional fall off the wagon for raspberry sorbet. Everybody deserves one guilty pleasure. Am I right?

Sitting on the couch with my granola and the remote, I clicked the television on. Normally, I liked to watch the History or Discovery Channel, programs that were both entertaining and educational. One can never be too smart, after all. But tonight, as I scrolled through the stations, Brigit gave a bark when Animal Planet came up. *Finding Bigfoot* was on, the sound of wolves baying in the background drawing her attention to the set.

I conceded. "Okay, fine. You can watch this show. But

if anyone wants to find an oversized, hairy beast, all they need to do is visit this apartment."

Ignoring my insult, the dog plopped down on her bed in front of the television, where she lay, rapt. When her show was over, I switched to the ten o'clock news, which contained the usual reports of murder, rape, and drug violence, as well as details of political unrest in various foreign countries and the latest evidence of global climate change. I liked to be informed, but did the news always have to be so damn depressing? Was it too much to ask for the world to break out in peace for a change? For everyone to put down their guns and join hands for a round of "Kum Ba Yah"?

I switched off the set. After brushing my teeth, I lowered the back of the futon to convert my couch into my bed. Brigit looked up at me, growling softly, as I tugged her bed out from under her and placed it inside her cage.

"In you go." I motioned with my hand for her to go into the cage.

She looked up at me but didn't move.

"Come on," I said, jerking my head. "Get in."

Her handler had assured me she slept in the kennel every night, yet here she acted as if she didn't recognize it. Of course my apartment was new to her and so was the cushy dog bed I'd put inside the cage. Maybe she just needed a reminder.

I got down on all fours and crawled backward into the cage. "See," I said once I was inside. "This is where you sleep. Comfy, comfy, comfy."

The dog glanced at me with a look of disinterest and I could feel my Irish temper reaching the red zone.

"I paid forty dollars for this bed!" I barked. "Get your furry butt over here and sleep on it!"

Brigit stood and walked over. Finally, she was getting it. Rather than attempting to step inside the cage, however, she bumped the door with her nose. It swung closed, smacking me in the forehead as I attempted to crawl out. The dog plopped herself down against the closed door and did the up-down tail wag. *Screw you.*

"Hey!" I pushed on the door, but it wouldn't budge. "Move, you stupid dog!" I poked my fingers through the cage and jabbed Brigit in the butt. She lay there, unmoving, refusing to even give me the *screw you* wag now.

My mind ran through the list of basic commands the handler had taught me. *Sit. Stay. Heel. Down.* None of them would work in this situation. I needed a command for *move your fluffy ass!*

I twisted around in the cage until my feet were braced against the door. I pushed with all my might but managed to get the door open only an inch or two before Brigit turned sideways and blocked the door even more effectively. Her mouth hung partly open and her chest moved as she breathed. She glanced back at me through the bars, a look of loathing in her brown eyes.

A loud rattling sound came though my vents and the cool air that had been streaming through them stopped. A moment later, hot hair began blowing through the vents, carrying gray smoke in with it. The AC had given out again, just as I'd expected. From the look of things, the unit had caught fire, too.

I closed my eyes, which stung with tears only partially caused by the smoke.

This was it.

I'd taken all I could take.

Tomorrow morning, I'd give my move-out notice to Grigsby and move back in with my parents across town. I'd resign my job, return the dog to the chief, and give up on my plans to become a detective. I'd tried being a cop and failed. Time to accept that and move on. Right?

HELL, NO!

The name-calling and the heat and this crappy apartment and my nasty partners who enjoyed making my life hell . . . it was all too much. Something in me broke—*I felt it snap*—and I exploded in rage. My eyes popped open and, with a primal scream, I threw my body against the side of the cage, knocking it over onto its side. Brigit leaped to her feet and darted to the other side of the room, her ears back. The dog might not respect me, but at least she feared me a little now.

I kicked the door open, crawled out of the cage, and stood. My downstairs neighbor banged his broom on the ceiling. I grabbed my twirling baton from under my futon and banged right back. *Whomp-whomp-whomp! Take that, jackass!*

Baton in hand and Brigit on my heels, I stormed downstairs to Grigsby's office. Three other tenants were already at his door. My upstairs neighbor held a frying pan with a steaming pork chop still in it. Rhino had his bass guitar aimed at Grigsby's door as if it were a machine gun. One of men from the first floor had a crowbar. A more proactive tenant had pulled the garden hose up to the third floor of Building A, where he stood on the walkway, his thumb on the nozzle as he directed a stream of water at the flaming HVAC unit on top of my building.

When Grigsby opened his door, we brandished our various weapons of choice.

"Replace that air conditioner!" I demanded, my fist tightening around my baton. "Now!"

The other tenants backed me up with murmured agreements while Brigit backed me up with a low growl: *Grrr.*

Grigsby glanced at the various weapons in our hands, looked up at the flaming system on top of our roof, and raised his palms. "I'll make a call first thing tomorrow morning."

"No refurbished equipment," I snapped. "Get us a brand-new unit. One with a warranty."

"All right, all right."

When I was sure the fire had been thoroughly extinguished, I returned to my apartment with Brigit, turned off my AC, and threw open the windows again. I plunked down on my futon and sat there, twirling the baton until I calmed down.

Brigit padded over to the mangled cage. Her bed lay halfway in, halfway out of the kennel. She settled down on the cushion, took one last glance in my direction, and, with a shuddering breath, closed her eyes to go to sleep.

I turned off the light and lay down, still twirling my baton in the dark. *Swish-swish-swish.* Though the motion provided both a calming effect and a soft breeze, it was no match for either my emotions or the temperature.

Tomorrow would be my first day of training as a K-9 officer.

I needed a good night's sleep.

It wouldn't be easy.

...

EIGHT
YOU CAN'T KEEP A BAD DOG DOWN

Brigit

Her new handler thought she was the boss. How naïve. It might take some time, but Brigit would set her straight. From the tenacity Megan had shown so far, Brigit knew she had her job cut out for her.

She lay on her doggie bed, listening as her new handler's breathing became slower and steadier. Brigit heard a mouse in the wall scratching at the drywall, hoping to find a way into the apartment. Brigit didn't know why the mouse would bother. There wasn't anything worth eating in the place, unless you counted the shoes. Megan, with her inferior senses, couldn't hear the noise, of course. *Humans.* They thought they were so superior to other animals. What were they smoking? Catnip?

Gradually, Megan's breathing grew slower, deeper. Brigit noticed Megan's jaw go slack, her fist uncurl. The baton rolled off the bed and onto the floor with a soft *thunk*. The woman was out.

Slowly, carefully, so as not to make noise with her tags,

Brigit crept toward the futon. She paused at the end of the bed and listened again. No change in Megan's breathing. *Good.* Brigit gingerly placed one paw on the bed, then another. Waited again. Again no change in breathing. Third paw. Fourth paw.

Home free.

Brigit settled in and panted softly, a dog chuckle.

Sleeping in a cage was for suckers.

NINE
SHOPPING SPREE

The Rattler

It was after 11:00 PM when he ventured into the twenty-four-hour Walmart. Too late for mirrored sunglasses but in Texas it was never too late in the day to wear a Texas Rangers baseball cap. After all, the caps were as much about pride as they were about keeping the sun out of a person's eyes. He pulled the brim down, casting his face in shadow.

Given the hour, the store was relatively quiet, just as he'd hoped. Fewer people around, fewer potential witnesses who could identify him. Not that he thought anyone would be able to trace his purchase to this particular store on this particular night. Nonetheless, one could never be too cautious.

He swung by the home goods department and picked up a travel alarm clock before making his way to Sporting Goods. He picked up a container of BBs and selected an assortment of fishing hooks, including a box of Ultra Points that, according to the label, were chemically sharpened for maximum performance. Who knew there were so many types of fishing hooks? Certainly not him. But he was going to give the detectives a run for their money, make them earn their paychecks, prove their mental moxie. Yeah, he was going to use these fishhooks to plant some red herrings. He chuckled softly to himself at his unintentional pun.

"Where you headed?"

The Rattler jumped at the voice. He'd been so absorbed in his thoughts he hadn't heard the overgrown bearded guy approach. He'd have to pay more attention to his surroundings from now on.

The guy rocked back on his boot heels as he looked the Rattler up and down, clearly sizing him up. Fury heated the Rattler's blood. Who the hell did this redneck think he was?

"Excuse me?" the Rattler said, forcing calm into his voice.

The redneck gestured to the alarm clock and hooks in the cart. "Looks like you've got a fishing trip planned. Where you headed?"

The Rattler shrugged. "Haven't decided yet."

"I caught me a fourteen-pound bass up at Lake Ray Roberts."

The Rattler knew nothing about bass other than that, thanks to exorbitant market prices, Chilean sea bass had been severely overfished, many of them caught illegally by poachers and devoured by consumers who either were ignorant of the crisis or simply didn't care. Yet more evidence that human beings were a selfish, self-centered species, thinking only of themselves. Of course these facts had nothing at all to do with the freshwater bass the redneck spoke of. But from the way the man stood, head cocked, brows lifted in anticipation of accolades, the Rattler could tell the fourteen-pound fish must have been an unusually large catch. "Fourteen pounds, you say? That's quite a catch."

The man's ego sufficiently stroked, he lowered his brows and returned his head to the normal, upright position. "You ever been up to that lake?"

"Can't say that I have." The Rattler turned back to the display in front of him, hoping the man would take a hint and mosey off. No such luck.

The redneck continued to eye him, even had the nerve to duck his head to get a better look at the Rattler. "What's your pleasure, then? Trout? Catfish? Crappie?"

Nosey son of a bitch, wasn't he? The Rattler couldn't help himself. This backwoods imbecile wanted to talk fish when all the Rattler wanted to do was pick up a few items and get the hell out of there. "I'm partial to piranha."

The redneck's brow furrowed. "Say what now?"

"Oops. Got a jiggle here." The Rattler pulled his cell phone from his pant pocket and pretended to consult the readout. "Looks like the wife needs me in the dairy aisle. Nice talkin' with ya."

With that, he offered a phony smile and walked away, leaving the bass fisherman floundering in his wake.

TEN
NATURE CALLING

Megan

Something heavy pressed down on my rib cage, threatening to suffocate me.

My eyes fluttered open to find Brigit standing with her front paws on my chest and panting into my face, as if she were performing some type of canine CPR on me. A quick glance at the clock on the microwave told me it was only 5:00 AM.

"Too early," I croaked, shoving the dog off me. "Go back to sleep."

Brigit jumped down to the floor and nudged my hand with her cold, wet nose.

I jerked my hand away and put the pillow over my head. My alarm wasn't set to go off for another hour and I'd be damned if I'd let this dog tell me when to get out of bed, even if my sheets were disgustingly damp with sweat. If Grigsby didn't get the AC running today, I'd beat him to death with my baton and enjoy every minute of it.

The dog grabbed the corner of the pillow in her teeth and dragged it off the bed. Still in denial, I pulled the sheet up over my head.

Brigit was quiet for a moment. I assumed she'd acquiesced to waiting. Alas, I assumed wrong. The unmistakable sound of liquid hitting linoleum had me bolting out of bed. I yanked the apartment door open and pointed. "Out!"

Brigit stood from her squatting position in the kitchen and trotted out the door. I left the door open and followed her in my bare feet as she made her way down the steps and onto a small patch of dirt behind the Dumpsters, where she finished relieving herself.

Tonight I'd remember to take her outside before bedtime.

Done, she trotted up the steps, tags jingling, and came back inside. I wanted to scold her, but it wasn't really her fault, was it? When nature called, nature called, and besides, she'd given me fair warning. These facts didn't keep me from shooting her dirty looks and grumbling as I used up the last of my paper towels to clean her pee off the kitchen floor. At least she'd had the sense to urinate on the linoleum and not the carpet.

As long as we were up, I figured I might as well get the coffee going. While liquid life gurgled in the pot, I refilled Brigit's bowl with food, freshened her water, and fixed myself a bowl of oatmeal.

For the next two months, Brigit and I would attend special K-9 training. Of course Brigit had already completed the course with her previous partner, so this round would be primarily for me. She'd come with me, of course, so the two of us could learn to work together, become a real team.

Looking down at the dog chomping kibble at my feet, I wasn't sure that was possible. She didn't listen to me, didn't respect me, didn't even seem to like me. And I wasn't sure I liked her, either. She was pushy, obstinate, insubordinate. But if our partnership didn't work out, I'd be screwed and my dreams of one day becoming a detective would go down the toilet. One way or another, I had to make this work.

I nudged the dog's butt with my toe. "You and me, girl. What do you say?"

She glanced up at me, loudly crunching kibble. Her eyes were wary, but her tail gave a small side-to-side wag. That was a positive sign, wasn't it? If we could get past our power struggles, maybe there'd be hope for our partnership.

After breakfast, I took a shower, brushed my teeth, and slicked my hair into its usual tight bun, noting my hair looked just as shiny as Brigit's thanks to her flea shampoo. After applying a soft pink eye shadow and a single swipe of mascara, I retrieved a freshly dry-cleaned uniform from my closet. I dressed and slid into my shoes and belt. Last, I clipped the leash on to Brigit's collar. "Let's go, girl."

Brigit let out a *woof,* which was immediately followed by a *bang-bang* from downstairs. I fought the urge to send a bullet through my floor. That would make the guy think twice.

As I loaded Brigit into my car, a large truck from an AC service pulled into the parking lot with three beefy men in the cab. Maybe it was a good sign. Maybe things were turning around for me. They had to, didn't they? They sure as hell couldn't get any worse.

A half hour later, my partner and I pulled into the parking lot of the canine-training facility in West Fort Worth and parked next to a blue muscle car with flames painted down the side. The car looked to be an early-seventies model and its front grill bore the Chevrolet emblem. A Nova, if I wasn't mistaken. The car looked like an overgrown Hot Wheel.

The training site comprised a central one-story administrative and classroom building, plus a barn-style structure that appeared to serve as a kennel. Surrounding the buildings were several separate fields enclosed by six-foot chain-link fences.

In one field, an obstacle course was set up and a trio of purebred German shepherds made their way up and down ramps, over walls, and through large concrete pipes, each of them following the directions of their instructors, who stood nearby issuing orders. Impressive. In another field, an instructor stood behind a line of puppies on extra-long leads, their handlers walking backward away from the pups with their hands raised to give the *stay* command. All but two obeyed. In the enclosure closest to the parking lot, a male yellow Lab scampered around stacks of wooden crates and cardboard boxes, apparently searching for something. Eventually, the dog stopped by a crate and sat.

"Good job, Blast," came a deep voice.

I turned to look for the source of the voice, surprised to see the blond member of the bomb squad who'd come out of the chief's office yesterday. He wore his T-shirt today with a pair of navy cargo pants and black ankle boots. He looked even hotter today, if such a thing was possible. A fiery heat detonated in my lower belly, radiating outward and downward.

The guy made his way to his dog with purposeful strides and rewarded the creature with a playful game of tug-of-war with a white towel. As he wrestled the towel from the dog, he turned my way and caught me watching him.

Damn! How embarrassing! I quickly looked down and pretended to adjust Brigit's collar. She glanced up at me, a quizzical look on her face. *What the fuzz?*

The yellow Lab trotted up to the fence and barked at Brigit: *Arf-arf!*

Brigit responded by dragging me over to the fence so she could sniff the Lab through the chain link. Both dogs wagged their tails. Looked like it was love at first smell.

"Hey!" the guy called, walking toward the fence.

Okay, now my *damn* became *hot damn!* I looked up and gave Mr. Sexy a small wave, not trusting myself to respond verbally.

"Gorgeous dog," he said. "She's got such a shiny coat."

His eyes went to my hair next, then back to Brigit, then back to me. *Oh, God.* I hoped he hadn't figured out I'd used her flea shampoo.

If he had, at least he didn't say so. "Haven't seen you two here before."

"First day," I replied. No stutter. *Thank God.*

He smiled. It was a soft smile, a sexy smile, the kind that could cause a girl's leg bones to turn into spaghetti.

"A newbie, huh?" the guy said. "You've got some hard work ahead of you."

No problem here. I'd never been afraid of hard work.

The bomb squad officer stepped closer, reaching his hands up and curling his fingers around the top of the chain-link fence. I tried not to notice the way his biceps bulged, how his broad chest tapered down to flat abs and a trim waist. I tried, but I failed. I noticed. Then I kept noticing. In for a penny, in for a pound.

He cocked his head. "I'm Seth Rutledge, by the way. I work for the fire department."

"So I figured," I replied, gesturing at his shirt.

He looked down, as if to remind himself what he was wearing. He chuckled, cocked his head, and flashed me a grin. "I can see why you're a cop. You don't miss any clues, huh?"

"Not a one."

His dog barked again, as if reminding Seth to introduce him: *Arf!*

Seth gave his dog a quick scratch on the head. "This loudmouth is Blast."

I tilted my head to indicate my dog. "Brigit."

One side of Seth's lips lifted in a half smile. Damn but if the guy wasn't even more attractive up close and personal. It's not that his face was perfect in that *GQ* cover model kind of way. His ears were slightly on the too-big side and his right cheek bore a light scar, a faint pink blotch the size of a small lemon that ran down to his jawline. But these traits only made him more enticing. He wasn't some airbrushed illusion, all makeup and camera angles, who would merely traipse around in a woman's fantasies. He was a *real* man. Flesh and blood.

Seth let go of the fence and took a step back. "Have fun with your training, Officer . . . ?" He quirked a brow in question.

"Luz," I said. "Megan Luz."

"Megan Luz," he repeated, saying my name slowly, as if committing it to memory.

Seth's dog grabbed at the towel in his hand, drawing his attention away from me. Stupid dog.

"See you later," Seth said.

I hoped he would. Maybe over a nice dinner and a bottle of wine. I could impress him with my recently acquired knowledge of Bigfoot tracking techniques.

Brigit and I went inside. The desk clerk directed us to a field out back, where we checked in with the instructor, a dark-haired man with an athletic build. He wore khaki shorts along with a bright-green knit shirt and matching baseball cap bearing the facility's logo, a white outline of a dog sitting up straight, its ears perked, its head held high. A shiny metal whistle hung from a chain around his neck. The instructor introduced himself as Hank and shook first my hand, then Brigit's paw.

"Wait a minute. I know this dog. Her name's Brigit, right?"

I nodded.

Hank formed a gun with his index finger and thumb, pointed it at my partner, and pretended to shoot. "Bang!"

Brigit immediately went limp, fell over onto her side, and lay there, her tongue lolling out of her mouth, playing dead.

"I taught her that trick," Hank said, pride evident in his voice. He bent down and ruffled her ears affectionately. "Brigit was one of the smartest dogs ever to come through the facility. She always paid attention and caught on quick." Hank looked up at me now. "It's rare to find a female dog on a police force. Males are normally preferred for their aggression."

Given the way Brigit had behaved so far, I doubted lack of aggression would be a problem. The bitch seemed to suffer a chronic case of PMS.

Hank ran his hands down her sides, groping her through her fur. Really, he should buy her dinner first. "Solid muscle," he said. "You've kept yourself in good shape, girl."

Brigit wagged her tail and licked his hand as if she knew she'd been complimented. What a suck-up.

Hank stood. "You may not realize it yet, but that dog'll be the best friend you'll ever have."

Surely he'd meant his words to be encouraging, but instead they struck a sad chord in me. I'd never had a best friend. Back in elementary school, nobody wanted to hang with the girl who stuttered. A couple of the mean kids had made fun of me, calling me M-M-Megan or Luz the loser. I'd been unable to defend myself, afraid if I said something back I'd stutter again and only add fuel to the fire. To make matters worse, I couldn't tell the teachers about the teasing. I couldn't manage to get the words out. The frustration was evident on the teachers' faces as they struggled to understand me, to help me form the words. The effort was likely futile anyway. Even if the teacher had scolded the other students or punished them, they would've just continued their torture when the teacher turned her back, maybe even amped things up.

Doctors don't fully understand what causes stuttering, but most children eventually outgrow the problem. As for me, though, no matter how much I practiced in private, I couldn't shake the stutter. While my speech problem had improved over the years, it had never gone away completely. I learned that my best defense was to limit my communications with others to essential speech only. I'd refused to do oral presentations in school, taking zeros on my grade reports rather than suffering the embarrassment of stuttering in class. I became used to keeping quiet, used to being a loner . . . even if being a loner meant being lonely.

Not all of my classmates had teased me, of course. But the ones who didn't tease me pitied me, which was almost as humiliating. None of them stuck up for me, either, afraid that doing so would make them a target for the bullies, too. Wimps.

All that is necessary for the triumph of evil is for good men to do nothing.

In retrospect, I suppose my childhood experiences are what led me to become a cop. I didn't want evil to triumph. I wanted to be a good person and do something.

With that thought, my resolve returned in full force. Here I was, doing something. And damned if I wasn't going to do it well, prove to the chief that I was much more than a rookie with a hair-trigger temper. I was capable, perceptive, and smart. I'd show him.

Hank stood, checked us off on his clipboard, and directed us to a group of four other students and dogs who had already arrived. I shook hands with the other students while Brigit and the other dogs took turns sniffing one another's butts. *Blurgh.* Glad I wasn't a dog.

The other officers were all male and all from various smaller police forces in towns making up the Fort Worth suburbs. All of their dogs were male, too. One of them was a Belgian Malinois while the other three were full-blood German shepherds. Not to brag, but Brigit was the best-looking K-9 among them. Not that looks mattered in her line of work.

When Brigit had finished sniffing the boy dogs' butts, she reared up onto the back of the largest shepherd, wrapped her front legs tightly around his chest, and proceeded to hump his hindquarters. Casting furtive glances back at my partner, the dog moved forward, trying to get out from under Brigit, but only succeeded in dragging her along with him. He turned his head as if to bite her but couldn't quite reach her face or paws. Finally, he dropped down in a last desperate attempt to throw her. She hung on for dear life, humping away on the crouched form helplessly immobilized in her clutches.

"Brigit!" I cried, horrified and embarrassed. "Stop!"

I yanked back on her leash and the shepherd finally managed to extricate himself from her grip. He darted away, scurrying over to hide behind his human partner.

The handler of the Malinois, a hulk of a guy standing at least six feet four, issued a snort. "Your dog has gender identification issues."

"Maybe she's a lesbian," said another.

I didn't bother to point out that in order for Brigit to be a lesbian she'd have to be humping another female dog.

This conversation was ridiculous enough already without me piling on.

Hank stepped up. "Brigit's just establishing her dominance."

Wonderful. My dog was a dominatrix. Perhaps I should buy her a leather whip and some thigh-high boots to go along with her studded collar.

Hank clapped his hands once to get everyone's full attention. "Give me one straight line, dogs sitting on your left unless you're a southpaw, in which case your dog should sit on your right."

We officers took our places in line. Brigit stepped into place beside me and sat, her head up, her ears pricked for further instructions.

Teacher's pet.

ELEVEN
LEADER OF THE PACK

Brigit

Her new handler had a lot to learn. Who did she think she was, pulling Brigit off that other dog? Didn't she know Brigit had to let him know who was boss?

Looked like her handler still needed to learn who was boss, too. Maybe Brigit would have to hump Megan next.

Brigit sat at attention next to her partner. Though she didn't move, her mind actively processed the scents picked up by her twitching nose. Fresh-cut grass. Shaving cream. Vanilla shower gel.

Raccoon.

Brigit lifted her nose and turned her head. The raccoon hid among the scrubby trees outside the perimeter fence. Lucky for him or Brigit would've eaten him for breakfast.

TWELVE
NOT YOUR EVERYDAY DIY PROJECT

The Rattler

With summer well on its way, Home Depot had discounted its remaining inventory of patio furniture and outdoor grills. The Rattler grabbed a set of barbecue utensils from a half-price bin. His bomb would not only be filled with a creative array of sharp objects, but it would be cost-effective as well. No sense spending any more than he had to. After all, he'd need to hang on to some of his cash for afterward, to put a down payment on a place near the coast.

He hadn't yet decided among Galveston, Port Aransas, and South Padre Island. Hell, he might even cross the border and find a nice little casita on a beach in Mexico. The country didn't have the death penalty and refused to extradite anyone facing a possible capital sentence in the United States. It couldn't hurt to set up south of the border for a little added protection. Not that the Rattler thought he'd ever be identified or caught, of course. He was much too smart for that.

He tucked the barbecue set into his handheld basket and proceeded to the nail aisle, marveling at the variety of nails offered. Galvanized steel nails. Vinyl coated. Bright finish. Smooth shank. Even something called a sinker nail, whatever the hell that was. Though the Rattler was a devout Marxist—he'd read *The Communist Manifesto* cover to cover seventeen times—he had to acknowledge that capitalism occasionally had an upside.

Though many of the nails appeared to be multipurpose, there were specialized nails for framing and drywall, even plastic-capped nails for roofing. *Why not get an assortment? Variety is the spice of life, after all.*

Now it could be the spice of *death*.

Some of the nails would go into his practice bomb, but many would be saved for the real event, along with one of those special nails he had at home in his bottom dresser drawer. That particular nail would put the investigative capabilities of local law enforcement to the test.

He slid several boxes into his hand basket before moving on to the screws. The screws, too, came in a variety of lengths and widths, with varying types of heads. Polymer-plated flat-head. Coarse phosphate-plated steel bugle-head. Hex-head concrete anchors.

He examined the screws, choosing the longest and sharpest to add to his basket. Why waste time with the smaller, shorter screws that would inflict only flesh wounds? He needed screws that would dig deep, tearing through skin and sinking into organs and bones, drawing blood.

On his final stop in the store, he picked up several short lengths of metal plumbing pipe, as well as caps for the ends. Seemingly benign materials used for a variety of purposes, nothing that would necessarily draw attention.

His basket full, he headed up front to the checkouts. Though he'd hoped to use one of the self-checkouts as he'd done at Walmart, none of the lanes were open. He was forced to stand in line behind a middle-aged woman with three gallon-sized containers of jasmine and a bag of composted cow manure in her cart. The sweet scent of the flowers and the reek of the bovine excrement combined to create a contradictory and nauseating aroma.

When it was his turn, he stepped up to the register. A stoutly built woman with a man's haircut and no makeup stood behind the counter. Her eyes flickered to his cap. "Hockey fan?"

The Rattler had never attended a hockey game, nor had he ever watched one on television. The only hat trick he knew was the trick he was pulling with his San Jose Sharks cap, trying to fool people into thinking he was someone else . . . *anyone* else. He forced a smile as he placed his basket on the countertop. "You got me."

"I'm a Stars fan myself." The woman cast him a pointed look that implied he'd betrayed the local team by wearing a competitor's cap. She pulled the boxes of nails and screws out of the orange plastic basket, running them over the scanner with a *beep* before plunking them into a plastic bag. "Looks like you've got a big home improvement project planned."

The nails and screws and pipes weren't for *construction;* they were for *destruction*. But this nosey bitch didn't need the details.

"Oh, yes," the Rattler said, offering her a sincere smile this time. "I've got very big plans."

THIRTEEN
TRAINING

Megan

Hank began our training by giving us an oral history of dogs and their uses in war, police work, searches and rescues, and as service animals for the disabled. I was amazed to learn that dogs had served alongside paratroopers, parachuting into war zones along with their handlers. Interestingly, Rin Tin Tin, the American canine movie star, had originally been a member of the German military but was left behind by soldiers in 1918 as they fled with their tails between their legs. No more bratwurst for Rin Tin Tin once the Americans took in the abandoned dog, but the dog did earn a star on the Hollywood Walk of Fame, along with fellow canine actors Strongheart and Lassie, and was paid a pretty penny for his acting roles.

I'd never realized how many things a trained police dog could do. Dogs were used to sniff out drugs, perform building searches, keep watch. Not only could they chase and restrain a suspect; they could also track and sniff out suspects who attempted to evade arrest on foot. Hank noted that a suspect will often surrender more peacefully when a K-9 is on-site, because the suspect realizes he can't outrun, overcome, or reason with a dog. Dogs were used to find missing children and elderly people who'd wandered off. Dogs were even being used now to find lost pets. Dogs could also be used for arson investigation and sniffing for explosives.

Unfortunately, about the only thing dogs couldn't do was clean up their own crap. I learned that lesson right away. We handlers were required to tidy up after our partners. *Yick.* At ninety-seven pounds, Brigit produced turds the size of cow patties.

As he wrapped up his history lesson, Hank noted there was a memorial at the police headquarters in Jacksonville, Florida, for dogs who'd been killed in the line of duty. At the thought of a dog giving its life to serve and protect people I felt a slight tug at my heart. Maybe I'd sold Brigit and her entire species short by considering her less worthy than a human partner. Maybe I should stop by the grocery store and pick up a T-bone for her dinner tonight.

We spent the rest of the morning learning how to control our dogs off leash. Hank taught us the commands to use to make them sit, stay, and return to our side. Each time the dogs obeyed, we were to reward them with praise or a pat or some playtime, along with an occasional treat.

After the lunch break, Hank moved us to an inside classroom where we could avoid the brutal afternoon sun. It was time for a lesson in sniffing.

"Dogs can be trained to sniff for all kinds of things," he said. "Drugs. Explosives. Blood. Cadaver dogs are used to find . . . well, I guess that's self-explanatory."

He went on to tell us that dogs had been trained to sniff out bumblebee nests, bedbugs, and termites. They could also use their noses to locate mold, mobile phones, currency, and polycarbonate disks such as bootleg DVDs. Dogs had been used to find an invasive species of mussel that often hitched a ride on recreational boats, and had even been used to detect cancerous tumors. Impressive, no?

Of course no single dog could be trained for such an extensive array of targets. Each dog would have his or her specialty. Our dogs would be what were known as dual-purpose dogs, trained to track a hidden or fleeing suspect and to locate illicit drugs. The blood, explosives, and dead bodies would be left to their canine coworkers in other departments.

Although all of us cops had been trained in building searches in our regular police training, Hank gave us a lecture on how to conduct a search with a dog.

"Sending a dog ahead into a building is less risky for the officers," Hank noted, "and a dog can locate a suspect more quickly." He mentioned that it was important for the officer to attempt to keep the dog in sight, so the cop could give the attack order if a suspect attempted to flee.

After a few more tips and pointers, Hank concluded his lecture and we moved to an adjacent area of the facility set up for search training. The place was divided into three rooms, each of which was filled with random pieces of furniture that appeared to have been picked up at secondhand shops or garage sales. A dining table with six mismatched chairs. A sagging sofa. A dented metal gun cabinet.

We started our lesson by playing a game of hide-and-seek with the dogs. The officers took turns hiding in the rooms, while the dogs took turns finding us. Brigit was the quickest of the bunch, hunting down the hidden officer in mere seconds. It took one of the shepherds a full two minutes to find me lying under a rug in the makeshift bedroom, and I only think he found me then because he tripped over me. Clearly this dog would not be the class valedictorian.

"Round up your dogs and wait in the other room," Hank said, pulling out a joint and a Baggie full of white rocks. "I've got some marijuana and crystal meth to hide."

We retrieved our dogs and stepped into the adjacent room. One by one, Hank invited the K-9 teams back into the search area. Brigit and I were last.

Hank grinned as Brigit and I stepped into the room. "I've made your search particularly challenging. Want to see what my star pupil is capable of."

I unclipped Brigit's leash, gave her the signal, and off she went. She put her nose in the air, her nostrils twitching as she processed the olfactory data. She scrambled through the first room and into the second, where a refrigerator hummed alongside a built-in countertop. Brigit first sniffed around the fridge, then put her paws on the countertop, sliding sideways down the counter, *sniff-sniff-sniff*ing until she reached a coffeemaker with a pot half-full of lukewarm coffee. She nudged the lid where the grounds and water were housed, took one last big sniff, then plopped back to the floor, where she sat at alert. She glanced over at me as if to say, *Come on, Megan! I've done my job. Now you do yours!*

I went over to the coffeepot and lifted it up. No drugs underneath it. None inside the pot, either. I lifted the lid off the top. All I saw was a chamber half-filled with water and a soggy filter filled with moist grounds.

I looked down at the dog. She *woof*ed, almost as if she was telling me to take a closer look.

I poked a finger into the grounds and stirred them up. *A-ha!* Buried in the grounds was a plastic Baggie with the doobie inside. I pulled out the bag and bent down to my partner. "Good job! Good girl!" She'd earned a nice scratch behind the ears for that solid piece of police work.

Now for the meth.

I gave Brigit the signal to continue her search. She put her nose in the air again, holding it there as she pranced into the last room. This room was packed solid with boxes and bags, buckets and bins, a virtual hoarder's paradise.

Brigit sniffed the floor around the perimeter of the pile. No luck. She raised her nose to the air, sniffed, and began to scale the pile.

Buckets and boxes and bins slid to the floor as she made her way to the center of the heap. She began to dig then, shredding through a couple of cardboard boxes until she reached a large blue plastic tub, the kind a person might store holiday decorations in. She sniffed around the seal, then sat back at alert, having to fight to keep her ground as boxes and bags slid out from under her.

I pushed the clutter aside and cleared a way to the tub. When I opened it, I found another, smaller airtight tub inside. I continued on until finally finding the bag of meth tucked inside a series of five airtight containers and wrapped in a towel doused with kerosene.

Hank shook his head in awe. "That's damn impressive. I thought surely the kerosene would stump her."

Evidently nothing could stump my partner.

After the hands-on training, Hank gave us a lecture on the legalities surrounding the use of dogs in building searches.

"Be especially careful when searching residences," he warned, telling us that in the case of *Florida v. Jardines* the Supreme Court had deemed a home search to be illegal when officers deployed a drug detection dog on the front porch of a suspected drug dealer. When the dog signaled the presence of drugs, police raided the house and found a marijuana-growing operation on the premises. The defense argued that the dog should not have been brought onto the private premises to perform the sniff test and that by so doing the officers violated the Fourth Amendment.

"However," Hank continued, "you can allow your dog to sniff trash at the curb or the outside of a vehicle that you pull over. People don't have a reasonable expectation of privacy in those cases." He informed us that this area of law was continually evolving and that we should take pains to remain up-to-date lest our searches be deemed unconstitutional and criminals go unpunished.

For the final lesson of the day, we ventured back outside, where we human trainees donned attack gear: padded suits and helmets with face protection. The suit was thick and heavy and hot and smelled moldy and ripe. Guess it wasn't an easy thing to clean.

One at a time, the instructor lined us handlers up on one end of a field, a dog on the other. Because it was imperative that each handler's dog view his or her human partner as the superior, none of us could be attacked by our own dogs. Given that Brigit was the biggest of the bunch, I thanked heaven for small favors. Or should I say *big* favors?

We played eenie-meenie-meinie-mo to determine which dog would attack us. My "mo" garnered me the midsized shepherd. The officer who'd earlier questioned Brigit's sexual preferences ended up with her. Karma's a bitch, no?

Brigit and her target went first. The officer jogged out into the field. Brigit crouched down next to me like a runner in the starting box, her body quivering with anticipation. When the guy was a hundred feet out, I gave Brigit the signal.

She tore out so fast she dug ruts in the ground and kicked up dirt and grass behind her. She bounded across the field, a black-and-tan blur, her feet barely touching the ground. When she made her final leap, her body arced through the air, strong yet graceful.

Smack!

On Brigit's impact, the cop buckled in two, his upper half snapping forward, his bottom half folding under him. Brigit rode him to the ground. Prone now, he wrapped his padded arms around his head, instinctively protecting his face and throat, as Brigit grabbed the back of his suit in her teeth and jerked him back and forth.

"Good girl!" I called, following the praise with an order for her to return to my side.

She gave the cop one final tug, then released him, putting her head in the air and prancing back across the field like the belle of the ball.

The other three officers took their turns, the largest one managing, somehow, to say upright, wearing the dog on his back like a canine cape until the handler called him off.

With a sweep of two fingers, Hank gestured me out onto the field. "Officer Luz, you're up!"

I glanced back at the shepherd. He crouched, his muscles shaking with anticipation and bloodlust. He seemed much bigger all of a sudden, his eyes more crazed, his teeth longer and sharper.

I headed out onto the field in the sweltering suit, trying to sprint as far away as possible in the hopes that the dog might be winded by the time he reached me. Wishful thinking, I know. I could barely jog in the lead suit, let alone run. Seemed I'd gotten only a foot or two into the field when I heard the handler give the command.

I'm no chicken, but when I glanced back and saw eighty pounds of furry, fanged beast tearing toward me with the intent to rip my limbs from my body I instantly regretted my decision to partner with a K-9. Should've turned in a resignation letter while I still had the chance.

Too late now.

Oomph!

The dog hit my back like a wrecking ball, sending me stumbling forward. Though I fought to regain my footing and stand upright where I'd have a better chance of defending myself, the impact made it impossible. Momentum carried me careening forward until I dove involuntarily to the ground, skidding forward on my hands. My chest slammed into the packed dirt, knocking what little air remained in my lungs out of me.

The dog grabbed the back of the suit between my shoulder blades and yanked with surprising force, lifting my upper body off the ground and whipping me helplessly back and forth, filling me with sheer terror from the top of my head to the tips of my toenails. I clawed at the ground, desperately and vainly seeking purchase. I'd never felt so out of control and powerless. Much more of this and the dog would give me whiplash or break my neck.

Had I been able to breathe I would've screamed. But while my lungs were empty, my bladder was not. My body released a short burst of urine before I was able to clench the stream to a close.

I knew this was a trained dog, that he should retreat when ordered. But Tilikum, that killer whale at SeaWorld, had been trained, too, and that hadn't stopped him from dragging a poor woman to her death. After years of performing with large cats, Roy Horn of Siegfried & Roy was attacked by one of his beloved white tigers during a show in Las Vegas, leaving the man in critical condition with severe blood loss. Circus elephants had been known to go on a rampage or take revenge on abusive trainers.

No matter how much we humans thought we could tame and control animals, some primal instincts would always remain. There was no telling what might trigger a sudden regression to their brutal, base nature. I could only hope that now would not be the time this dog chose to get in touch with his inner beast.

The dog pulled in only one direction now, dragging me around the field like a life-sized rag doll. The bottom of the helmet's faceplate dug a rut in the dirt, kicking up dust into my nose and eyes until it fell off completely, leaving my head, face, and throat exposed. I heard the

officers laugh from across the field, but I knew it was false
bravado. I'd seen the looks on each of their faces when
their turns were up. Each one had been rattled and hum-
bled, with a new appreciation for his K-9 partner.

After what seemed like an infinity of eternities, the
cop issued the order for the dog to release me. Instantly
the dog dropped me to the ground, where I lay bent, broken, and covered in dirt, my fingernails shredded, grass
and earth trapped under their jagged tips.

I stayed there, unmoving, until motion to my right
caught my eye. *Oh, God.* Seth stood outside the fence
watching me, Blast beside him, wagging his tail. *Blurgh.*
How embarrassing! So much for the fancy dinner and
wine. With all the dirt, sweat, and urine coating me, I'd
be lucky if Seth ever talked to me again.

After Seth gave me a good-bye wave, he and his dog
stepped away from the fence and climbed into the overgrown Hot Wheel. A minute later they disappeared out of
sight down the road. I wondered when or if I might cross
paths with Seth again.

"Class dismissed!" Hank called from across the field.
"See y'all tomorrow morning. Eight sharp."

Though I hadn't issued the order, Brigit loped across
the field, returning to my side. I rolled onto my back and
forced myself to a sitting position. When I tried to stand,
Brigit shoved her nose into the crotch of the suit. I shoved
her face away. "Stop it!"

While the others gathered up their dogs and headed out,
I ambled slowly across the field. By that point I'd worked
up such a sweat inside the suit that my entire body felt
wet. Good. Maybe the fact that I'd peed myself wouldn't
be so obvious.

FOURTEEN
THERE'S MORE TO FEAR THAN FEAR ITSELF

Brigit

Her new partner had urinated in the bite suit. Brigit could smell it. She knew what it meant. The same thing it meant when a dog rolled over on its back and peed on itself.

Her partner was scared.

Well, she should be. Police work was scary. When Brigit worked with her former partner, the dog had been shot at, had her paw slammed in a door, and nearly been run down by a car. The suspects they apprehended were vile, violent people. Virtually subhuman. Megan might as well get used to it now, learn to face her fears and fight through them. Because sooner or later the two of them would face something frightening.

And they'd have to deal with it together.

FIFTEEN
TEST RUN

The Rattler

He headed into the woods, dressed head-to-toe in camouflage, cheap canvas pants and a long-sleeved tee he'd pick up at a discount military surplus store. His backpack was slung over his shoulder, the same backpack he'd used when he'd attended college. He'd fired one up on occasion back then, and the bag still hung on to a faint scent of marijuana.

College. What an absolute waste of time that had been. What did he learn there? That people were shallow. Hypocritical. Horny. Not that he'd minded the horniness so much. He'd indulged himself in the pleasures of more than one drunken sorority girl's flesh. His only regret was that his actions had brought pleasure to those sickeningly self-absorbed, feebleminded young women, too.

Time to set those thoughts aside. Time to practice.

The sound of an explosion wouldn't draw much attention in the fall when it was deer season. People would likely just mistake the sound for that of a high-powered hunting rifle. But in early summer it might raise questions. Best to get as far from the neighboring ranches as possible.

This land was private, surrounded by barbed wire. But fences weren't always respected, as he well knew. How many times had he sneaked across fields owned by others, climbed trees owned by others, swum in creeks owned by others? Why shouldn't everyone get to enjoy the land, enjoy nature? What right did anyone have to own an earth they did not create? What happened to the grand ideals Woody Guthrie had sung about in his classic "This Land Is Your Land"?

Guthrie, who'd raised his first family in the Texas panhandle, had fought against oppression and injustice, stood behind the little guy. Deemed a radical, the singer-songwriter was targeted by alarmist anticommunist zealots in the fifties. His visions of equality and fairness proved to be mere grandiose ideals.

Pipe dreams.

This land didn't belong to "you and me." The United States belonged only to the rich and powerful. Democracy and capitalism constituted nothing more than legalized theft, allowing the *haves* to exploit the *have-nots*, to accumulate more property, more power.

The rich get richer. The poor get poorer.

Time to give the wealthy a wake-up call.

He continued on, stalking over the hard-packed, dusty ground. Once he was far enough into the woods, he found a small clearing and knelt down to unpack his bag. He pulled out the boxes of nails, screws, and fishhooks, as well as a rocket engine, a short piece of metal pipe, two end caps, and the alarm clock.

Once he'd perfected his skills, he'd work his way up to more sophisticated explosives. But this bomb, his first, would be a small, simple one. Cheap, too. The whole shebang would cost him less than seventy-five dollars. Lots of bang for the buck. Amazing how much destruction one could wreak for so little cost. Of course Timothy McVeigh and his cohort, Terry Nichols, had figured that out years ago. A few bags of fertilizer, a rented truck, and *KA-BOOM!* Over $650 million in damage. One hundred and sixty-eight lives ended.

Unlike McVeigh and Nichols, though, the Rattler wouldn't be foolish enough to get caught.

He donned his helmet, protective goggles, and the ballistic vest he'd ordered online under the name Huey Kablooey. The morons in customer service and shipping hadn't clued in. Not that he'd expected them to. The vast majority of humans had shit for brains.

He'd paid for his items with a money order purchased at a post office a six-hour drive away in Hot Springs, Arkansas. Though Texas law allowed anyone over the age of eighteen who was not a convicted felon to purchase Kevlar gear, he'd nevertheless had the items delivered to a cabin he'd rented for a week in Broken Bow, Oklahoma.

He'd splurged and treated himself to a Level IV hard-plated vest even though he didn't think he'd need it. Still, this was his first attempt at bomb making. One could never take too many precautions, especially if one had important plans to carry out.

The ground was hard, dry, and dusty. He spread out the business page from today's Fort Worth *Star-Telegram* and began assembling the bomb, consulting the instructions he'd printed from the Internet. This one would be a basic pipe bomb, controlled by a timer, of course. The model rocket engines would provide the ignition. The gunpowder would provide the power. The nails, screws, and hooks would provide the results.

As he looked over the paper, he kept an ear out for suspicious noises. A hawk flying overhead gave off a *caw-caw*.

Something small rustled in the nearby brush, most likely a squirrel, Nothing unusual. He slapped at a mosquito that had lit on the back of his hand, intent on drawing blood. He chastised himself for not having the foresight to buy bug spray.

Despite the shade from the trees, the woods were almost unbearably warm. There was no breeze this afternoon, as if the world were holding its breath. Sweat dripped from his chin as he carefully assembled the parts. He slid a cap onto one end of the pipe and filled the tube with an assortment of nails, screws, fishhooks, and gunpowder. Next, he slid the engine into the open end of the pipe. As he went to slide the fuse through the hole in the end cap, it slipped from his fingers and fell to the dirt. He picked the fuse up, blew off the dust, and slid it through the opening. After affixing the timing device he was finally done.

Tingling with anticipation, he started the stopwatch feature on his cell phone, setting the timer for nine minutes.

As he wound his way back through the woods, his pulse raced, partly from the physical exertion, partly from the excitement. He felt like a kid with a new toy.

After eight minutes had elapsed, he was a quarter mile from the site where he'd left the bomb, definitely out of range. He crouched behind a wide tree trunk and eyed the phone's screen. One minute left. Thirty seconds. Ten.

He swatted another whining mosquito away from his face.

Three.

Two.

One.

He held his breath and stayed perfectly still, waiting for the sound of the explosion.

He waited . . .

and waited . . .

and waited. . . .

It didn't come.

He stood and kicked the tree trunk. "What the fuck?"

Maybe his mother was right. Maybe he was nothing more than a good-for-nothing screwup.

A disappointment.

An embarrassment.

He put his hands to his head, unsure what to do.

Should he return to the site and attempt to assess where he'd gone wrong? If he went back, might the bomb explode in his face? He didn't want to end up like that dolt in Exeter, England, in 2008. The would-be suicide bomber fucked up royally when detonating a bomb in a restaurant. Not only had he survived the attack; he'd also been the only one injured in the blast. What an imbecile.

But if the Rattler left the bomb out here, would someone find it?

If someone found it, would it matter?

After several minutes of deliberation and a few choice expletives spit into the still air—"Shit! Damn! Fuck!"—he decided that it was too risky to return to the site. The likelihood of anyone finding the bomb in this remote area was slim to none. If someone did find the bomb, the chances of the bomb being linked to him were also slim to none. Most likely law enforcement would assume the bomb had been made by local delinquents.

He slunk the two miles back through the woods to his car. He felt disgusted and disappointed.

But by no means deterred.

SIXTEEN
THE BITCHES ARE ON THE BEAT

Megan

Though the six weeks of training were grueling, I was surprised to discover how much I enjoyed working as part of a K-9 team. Brigit and I practiced building searches in both daylight and darkness. My partner could find a person, no matter how well hidden, in mere seconds, the fastest among her training group. We practiced searching for drugs in buildings, cars, and on people. Again, Brigit shined. She found a tiny speck of cocaine inside the instructor's shoe. We practiced using our dogs to track suspects, to restrain those who resisted arrest. She proved herself to be faster, more nimble, and just as strong as her male counterparts. I felt proud to be working with the class standout.

Each day before training, we'd give the dogs a few minutes to play with one another, to burn off their excess energy so they could buckle down and concentrate during training. They chased one another around the field like schoolkids at recess, retrieved tennis balls, ran after

Frisbees, and caught them in midair. Brigit continued to hump the male dogs, who escaped only when I ordered my partner off them. When the male dogs attempted to return the gesture, Brigit easily threw them off. Good for her. If they wanted to mount her they should at least give her some foreplay first to put her in the mood.

By the end of the sixth week, I knew all the commands and could direct Brigit properly. She was the epitome of good behavior in class, obeying each of my commands instantly, exhibiting perfect self-control. Off duty was still a different story, but we were working on it.

While Brigit and I had been in training, Seth and Blast had come to the facility several times to practice their drills. Although Seth had raised a hand in acknowledgment, we'd had no chance to talk. Our near misses left me feeling discombobulated. An odd word, isn't it? I mean, you never heard about someone feeling *combobulated,* right?

I hoped to cross paths with Seth again. With my job once again secure, I was ready to work on improving my private life. After all this hard work, didn't I deserve to have some fun?

Not only had I completed my K-9 handler training, but I'd finished the online anger management course also. I'd scored only the minimum 70 percent required to pass, but that was all it took to satisfy my obligation. Why try harder? I'd printed the certificate of completion to turn in to Chief Garelik. The stupid certificate featured smiley faces in each corner. I had to fight the urge to crumple the damn thing.

Fully trained now and allegedly anger-free, Brigit and I headed out for our first day together on the beat. We rode over to the station in my smart car to pick up our cruiser. Derek's big-balled truck sat cockeyed in a parking spot as if he'd been driving too fast when he'd pulled in and hadn't bothered to correct the angle. After parking near the end of the lot, I let Brigit out of the passenger door, grabbed her leash, and whipped my baton from my belt. I flicked my wrist and my baton extended. *Snap.* As we passed Derek's truck, I swung my baton and smacked the rubber scrotum.

Whack!

Not a bad way to start the day.

My partner and I continued on to our specially equipped K-9 cruiser. Rather than a backseat, the rear contained a carpeted platform better suited for a dog. The front seat and rear area were divided by metal mesh to prevent the K-9 officer from jumping into the front seat and escaping when the officer opened the driver's door. The mesh also prevented the K-9 from being thrown into the front seat or windshield should the driver have to brake suddenly. To prevent the dog from breaking out a window and to prevent someone on the outside from breaking in to access the dog, the back windows were also lined with the metal mesh. The car had sensors that would automatically roll the windows down if the temperature in the vehicle rose above ninety degrees for more than ten minutes. This feature protected the K-9 partner from heatstroke if the human officer was forced to leave the dog in the car and was unable to return to the cruiser right away.

I situated Brigit in the back and climbed in, motoring off to begin our patrol. Though I'd been assigned a new partner, I'd retained my same beat—Western 1 Division, or W1 for short. W1 comprised approximately nine square miles and was bounded on the north by I-30, on the east by Hemphill, on the south by Berry Street, and on the west by the Trinity River. W1 included Texas Christian University, the quaint older neighborhoods surrounding the college, and Colonial Country Club, which hosted the

Crowne Plaza Invitational professional golf tournament, drawing huge crowds to Cowtown each year. Our beat also included Forest Park, the Fort Worth Zoo, and a new open-air shopping mall. A pretty sweet beat, even if I did have to share it with the Big Dick.

As a patrol officer, my job was to cruise my beat, keep an eye on the area, and respond to calls made to Dispatch. I would also serve as backup for other officers in my division when needed. Though our superiors might occasionally ask us to keep a close eye on a particular part of our division, we street officers mostly roamed freely and randomly about our beat, like balls in that ancient Pong game. All in all, not a bad gig for a mutt from the streets and a woman who sometimes had trouble speaking words with more than one syllable.

We spent the morning cruising around Mistletoe Heights and Forest Park without incident. Fine with me. While some police officers thrived on action and conflict and spent their days hoping for skulls to crack, I was not one of them. My plans were to lie as low as possible until I made detective. I'd do my job to the best of my ability, but I would not be at all disappointed if the people of W1 chose to behave themselves.

Around eleven, I decided to head over to the country club. I drove down Colonial Parkway, making my way into the exclusive neighborhood with the air conditioner cranked to full blast, the back windows of the cruiser rolled down so Brigit could sniff the air. Not exactly the environmentally conscious thing to do, but it was already ninety-six degrees outside, the sun was streaming through the windshield like an enormous laser beam, and my Kevlar vest was glued to my chest and back with sweat. My partner had clawed at the mesh on the back windows and whined incessantly until I'd rolled them down. She was probably bored back there with nothing to do. Brigit. Now there's an inconvenient truth for you. Al Gore and the ozone layer would just have to forgive me.

FWPD didn't require officers to wear their ballistic vests at all times, and few did. The vests were hot, heavy, and confining. I never went on duty without it, though. Perhaps I had less faith in humanity than my fellow officers, or perhaps I had less faith in my own abilities to survive a gun battle. When questioned, I told my coworkers that I'd promised my mother I'd always wear the vest and rolled my eyes at her alleged overprotectiveness. The truth was I was terrified to go out on patrol without it. Besides, I valued my life too much to be deterred by a little extra warmth and weight.

Brigit pressed her face against the mesh, her mouth open, tongue lolling out, the breeze blowing her fur. Occasionally she raised her snout up, her nostrils flaring as we made our way up and down the streets. I wondered what she scented. Flowers? Garbage? Cats? The sweet smell of success? Probably the latter. This place reeked of money.

Every house in the exclusive development was custom-built, each feature, from the porch lights to the doorknobs to the mailboxes, carefully designed and selected to be unique yet tasteful. The houses averaged at least four thousand square feet, plenty of room to ramble and roam. The residences ranged in style from redbrick colonials, to white plantation-style designs with black shutters, to modern asymmetrical structures of wood and stone. Many had three- or four-car garages, and all had lush landscaping. I spotted none of the driveway basketball hoops often seen in middle-class suburbia. The deed restrictions or homeowners association rules likely forbade them. Kids from this neighborhood were more likely inclined to play tennis or golf, anyway. Even the pets in this neighborhood were high-class, all purebreds with not a mutt—other than Brigit—in sight.

The country club was an idyllic place but, frankly, not one at which I'd aspire to live. Too many rules and restrictions, too much trying to keep up with the Joneses. My tastes tended to be simpler, my aspirations more intellectual and spiritual than material. I didn't fault the residents for their lifestyle choices, though. It takes all kinds to make the world go round, and many of these people owned businesses that provided jobs to the citizens of Fort Worth.

My eyes scanned the environment, looking for anything suspicious. Thugs in beater cars casing houses. Unmarked vans or delivery trucks backed up in driveways, being loaded with property that belonged to a homeowner away on summer vacation. Crazed murderers carrying bloody axes or ice picks or severed heads. Though I saw none of the above, I did spot a yard with its automatic sprinklers running, a blatant violation of the city's water-rationing ordinance. *Blurgh.* Why couldn't people just obey the rules and let us cops spend our time on more important matters?

"Mr. Cuthbert's at it again," I told Brigit as I eased to a stop in front of the man's house. Given the number of people a patrol officer dealt with on a daily basis, it was unusual for a cop to remember their names. Mr. Cuthbert was a different story. As much as I'd like to forget the jerk, he was branded into my brain. You don't forget a pompous ass like him.

"Stay," I ordered my partner.

As I climbed out and walked around the car, Brigit trotted to the other side of her seat. She stuck her nose up to the mesh, watching me as I headed up the driveway to the *ch-ch-ch* sound of the sprinkler. The sprinkler's range covered not only a quadrant of the yard but also the walkway from the driveway to the front door. I timed my dash in the hopes of missing the spray, but no such luck. A jet of water cut a wet path across my thighs, the force of the spray stinging my skin. Perhaps this was some type of karmic payback for making Derek wet himself.

I rang the bell and added a few slams of the brass knocker as well, taking out my irritation on Cuthbert's front door. A moment later the door opened. Mr. Cuthbert stood there in a pair of slippers, black dress socks, and a loosely tied bathrobe that exposed far more than I cared to see of his swarthy skin and moss-like chest hair.

"Yeah?" he snapped.

"Good morning, Mr. Cuthbert." I forced myself to remain polite but drew the line at forcing a smile. He didn't deserve it. "You may recall a couple of months ago I talked to you about the watering restrictions?"

Derek had remained in the car back then, finishing off a sub sandwich loaded with onion and banana pepper that had stunk up the cruiser and leaving me to handle the homeowner on my own.

Cuthbert shrugged. "I don't remember that. Must've been someone else you talked to."

"No"—I pulled a small notepad from my breast pocket—"it was definitely you." I flipped through my pages until I found where I'd jotted the date, his name, and his address along with the words "sprinkler violation" and "pompous ass." I put my thumb over the latter words to hide them and held up my pad. "My notes are right here."

He glanced at my pad and crossed his arms over his chest. "So? What?"

Did I really need to spell it out for this guy?

"It's not your assigned day." I gestured behind me at the sprinkler. "Yet you're watering. Again."

Cuthbert issued a dramatic sigh, as if I were some type

of pesky, persistent peddler trying to sell him a subscription to *Entertainment Weekly* rather than a member of law enforcement trying to serve the public good. He stormed outside, brushing past me to punch in a code on the keypad next to his garage door. Once the garage was open, he stepped inside and jabbed a button on the control box for the sprinkler system. With a final *ch-ch-ch*, the sprinkler spewed its last spray and turned off, the offending head popping back down into the ground like a groundhog who'd decided there'd be six more weeks of winter.

Cuthbert stepped into the driveway and raised his palms. "It's off now. You happy?"

Grr. "I'd be happier if you'd stop turning them on when you're n-not supposed to."

He turned and keyed in the number sequence to close the garage door. "Don't you have better things to do than harass homeowners who are just trying to maintain their property values?"

My mind briefly played with a vision of Cuthbert being crushed under the door, his black socks and slippers curling up and disappearing like the legs of the witch who was crushed by Dorothy's farmhouse when she landed in Oz.

"As a matter of fact," I barked back, finding myself instinctively toying with the handle of the baton at my waist, "I *do* have better things to do than deal with people who refuse to obey simple rules designed for the public good. I'd appreciate it if you won't waste any more of my time."

As I pulled out my citation pad, he brushed past me again, muttering something about the "public good" and "bleeding-heart liberal tree huggers" before stepping into his house and slamming the door. Awfully presumptuous of him. I'd given him no indication that our interaction was over.

I stood there, fuming, and debated my options:

1. I could write a citation, knock on the door again to deliver it to him, and hope I could refrain from whacking him upside the head with my baton.
2. I could make a note of this second infraction and issue him a citation if I caught him watering again.

As enraged as I felt, I wasn't sure I could trust myself not to give Cuthbert the whack he deserved. Tasering my partner in the nards had been risky enough, but my career would be over if I inflicted major head trauma on a citizen who'd committed a relatively minor infraction. Of course Brigit would be the only witness. She couldn't testify and if I hit Cuthbert hard enough he wouldn't remember anything. *Hmmm . . . tempting.*

Though it left me feeling somewhat dissatisfied, I decided to go with option two.

As I returned to the cruiser, my eyes spotted a sprinkler head that hadn't retracted. A swift but subtle kick was all it took to knock the head cockeyed and put it out of commission. I didn't even have to break stride. *Oops.* Looked like that anger management class hadn't quite stuck with me. At least I felt satisfied now. My frown had turned upside down.

I climbed back into the patrol car and Brigit and I continued on, driving through the country club and Tanglewood neighborhoods, noting nothing unusual. It was nearly one when we backtracked to University Drive. I pulled through a drive-thru and ordered myself a salad, along with a plain hamburger for my partner.

We ate in the car in the parking lot while listening to NPR. The *Think* program was on, today's guest a medical researcher discussing how germaphobia and the overuse of antibiotics, antibacterial soaps, and hand gels were creating superbacteria and turning the human race into a bunch of immunity-insufficient wienies incapable of fighting off diseases and infections. In some cases, doctors had been forced to resort to primitive, pre-antibiotic treatments, such as amputation, to rid a patient of infection. *Yikes.*

When my lunch break was over, I disposed of our trash and turned south onto University. Knowing the college students sometimes crossed the main thoroughfare against the lights, I slowed as we approached TCU.

Fewer students were on campus in the summer than during the long semesters, though a good number milled about the sidewalks and green spaces, some rushing to class, others stopping to speak with friends and classmates, still more braving the heat and sprawling on the grass with laptops, tablets, or books. I stopped at a red traffic light, watching students cross in front of the cruiser.

While I wasn't much older than most of these students, worlds separated us. I spent my days on the streets dealing with the dregs of society and hoping not to get knifed or pricked with a heroin needle during a frisk, while these students, the vast majority of whom came from upper-class families, spent their days on the pristine private school campus with other rich kids, their biggest challenge deciding between a caramel or vanilla latte at the nearby Starbucks.

Brigit let out a soft whine. I turned to check on her. She looked at me and wagged her tail before nudging the edge of the mesh screen at the window and letting out a single bark: *Woof!*

"Do you need to take a potty break, girl?"

This open lawn looked as good a place as any

When the light turned green, I pulled forward and turned down a side street that led into the campus. After activating my hazard lights, I exited the vehicle and opened the back to let Brigit out. As I bent down to attach her leash, her head snapped up and smacked me smartly in the chin. Damn, that dog had a hard skull!

Before I realized what was happening, Brigit sped off across the lawn, a black-and-tan blur as she hurtled toward a brown squirrel puttering around in the center of the grass. When he heard the trampling paws and jangling tags, the squirrel popped bolt upright, looked Brigit's way, and scampered over to the base of a large oak tree. He didn't ascend it, though. Rather, he stood there, flicking his tail as if taunting my partner. The squirrel was either extremely brave or extremely stupid, or perhaps he was simply suicidal.

I cupped my hands around my mouth. "Brigit!" I hollered, following it with the command for her to return to my side.

My partner ignored me. She was as bad as Cuthbert. Hot fury welled up in me again, and again I found myself toying with my baton. I'd never hit a dog, of course, but whacking the shit out of the tree would feel awfully good about now.

Brigit reached the tree, skidding in the grass and nearly colliding with the trunk as she attempted to slow herself down. The rodent issued one final flick and dashed up the tree in the nick of time. Brigit leaped repeatedly at the trunk, looking up into the branches and barking her head off: *Arf! Arf! Arf!*

While the students and professors looked on, I stalked across the lawn to my partner, who ran in circles around the tree, still looking up, trying to figure out where her prey had disappeared to.

When I reached her, she stopped circling, sat, and cut wary eyes my way. She clearly knew her behavior had been less than exemplary, which only made me all the more angry. This relationship would never work if she didn't respect me.

I clipped her leash on to her collar and wrapped the leash around my hand until it was taut. I knelt down, put my face in hers, and stared her in the eye in an attempt to remind her that, as far as our two-member pack was concerned, I was the alpha dog.

"Bad girl!" I hissed through clenched teeth.

She stared back at me for several seconds, refusing to blink or look away.

Forcing air up from the back of my throat, I began to growl: *Grrrrr.* Brigit growled right back. *Damn.* What was I supposed to do now? I pulled my lips back to expose my teeth. After all, that's what a dog would do next, right? Brigit opened her mouth, too, but instead of showing me her teeth she whipped out her tongue and licked me across the lips before I could pull my head back.

"Ew!" I stood and wiped my mouth with the back of my hand, gagging and fighting the urge to scream for disinfectant and iodine like Lucy did in the *Peanuts* shows when Snoopy kissed her. Oh, how I wished it were true that a dog's mouth was cleaner than a human's. Given that they licked their butts, I didn't believe it for a second.

My eyes scanned the area. While virtually everyone was watching us, nobody seemed to have their cell phones out taking video. *Thank goodness.* The last thing I needed was someone providing the footage to the chief or the local news or featuring it on YouTube in a video captioned "Kissing K-9 Cops Interspecies Love Affair."

Brigit did the up-down tail wag. *Screw you.*

Again I wondered whether I should've resigned when Chief Garelik gave me the chance.

I tugged her leash. "Come on, girl."

Brigit followed willingly now, trotting back to the cruiser with her head and tail in the air, happy as you please.

Once she was in her space and I was behind the wheel, I pushed the button to roll up the back windows and met her gaze in the rearview mirror. "You've lost your window privileges."

That'd teach her.

I headed south to Berry Street, the boundary of my division, then turned around and spent some time cruising through the Bluebonnet Place, Ryan Place, and Fairmount neighborhoods. Weren't nobody misbehavin'.

As the workday began to wind down, I drove north, aiming for the new mall. The Shoppes at Chisholm Trail was an open-air center of rough stone in a variety of light shades trimmed with dark wood, the effect tastefully rustic. The building was shaped like a large X, with smaller stores along both sides of each arm and larger high-dollar department stores anchoring the ends. In the center of the X sat a large glass-enclosed, diamond-shaped courtyard with a wooden façade over the glass roof to block out the brutal Texas sun.

The shopping center was named after the famous cattle trail that had run from South Texas up through Fort Worth and the plains of Oklahoma, ending at the rail yards in Kansas. A small herd of bronze longhorns greeted shoppers at the main entryway. Riding behind the steers was a bronze cowboy on horseback, his lasso poised over his head as he aimed for a willful maverick who'd strayed away from the herd and appeared to be aiming for the Abercrombie & Fitch store to check out the sales.

Despite the shrubbery forming a foliage fence around the metal cows and the Please Do Not Touch Statues sign, people inevitably squeezed through the bushes and climbed onto the back of the front-most steer to have pictures snapped with their cell phones. The joke was on them, though. The metal heated up in the sun and burned their lawbreaking asses.

Some offenses carry their own penalties.

The Shoppes at Chisholm Trail was built on the former site of an outdated strip center that had recently had a date with a bulldozer. Why the mall's owner had chosen to combine the British spelling for "shops" with the name of an Old West cattle trail defied both logic and grammar, but given my mixed pedigree, who was I to complain about the culture clash? The mall contained a mix of chain stores and specialty niche shops, catering to both locals and tourists who were in town to visit the nearby museums or attend events at the Will Rogers Coliseum.

The mall employed its own security team, of course, and I had no obligation to patrol the place on foot. But when a girl could get paid for window-shopping, hunting bargains on the clearance racks, and sampling testers at the Macy's perfume counter, she'd be a fool not to, right? Besides, I was afraid if I sat on my butt too long in the cruiser I'd end up with a case of flat ass. And it's not like my stroll would be entirely self-serving. After all, when Derek and I'd worked this beat together we'd arrested the occasional shoplifter and kept an eye out for gang activity. My new partner and I would do the same.

I bypassed the crowded parking lanes and headed straight ahead, grateful for my reserved Law Enforcement Only spot near the mall's main entrance. This time, I didn't let Brigit out of the cruiser until she was properly leashed.

We strolled down the sidewalk, making our way past Macy's. When we passed the pet store, Brigit tugged me over. She propped her front paws on the large aquarium that made up the store's front window, her head whipping comically back and forth and up and down as she attempted to follow a clown fish darting around in the water.

Woof!

The frightened fish fled to the back of the aquarium, earning me and Brigit an annoyed, though warped, look from the store's owner, who stood on the other side of the aquarium inside the store, stocking shelves.

"Sorry!" I called to the man. I pulled Brigit away. "C'mon, girl."

Next door at the bridal shop, a thirtyish redhead in a sleek satin wedding dress stood on a low platform in front of a three-way mirror under the watchful eye of an older woman, presumably her mother. The tailor, a white-haired yet surprisingly spry Asian man named Vu, flitted around the redhead, gathering the fabric along the sides of the woman's torso and slipping straight pins into place to guide the alterations he'd do later.

A few shops down at Williams-Sonoma, a woman in a mustard-yellow apron was conducting a quick course in fondue, offering samples of meats and breads dripping with melted cheese and encouraging those gathered around to take advantage of the sale on fondue forks and sets. While the cabinets in my apartment had no space for a fondue set, that fact wouldn't stop me from enjoying a free early dinner courtesy of the cooking supply store.

The woman handed me a long-handled fondue fork with a sizable piece of cheddar cheese–covered sourdough skewered on the end of the two pointy prongs. Grilled cheese on a stick as far as I was concerned. Maybe not the healthiest choice, but sometimes a free meal took precedence over a healthy one.

"Delicious," I told her when I'd finished eating the bite. I disposed of the fork in a metal ice bucket displayed for that purpose and she handed me another, this one containing a chunk of rye bread doused in a creamy white cheese.

Mmm. When I finished the rye, she handed me another fondue fork with a cheesy beef cube on each prong. I pulled the meat from the fork and fed the bites to Brigit, wiping my fingers clean on a napkin.

One of the owners from the adjacent wine store, a fiftyish woman named Stacy, stood in her doorway and held up a bottle of cabernet and a small plastic unicorn with a corkscrew for a horn. "Don't forget some wine to go with your cheese! Free novelty corkscrew with each fifty-dollar purchase!"

Several of the shoppers chuckled at Stacy's impromptu yet apropos sales pitch. Though I laughed along with them, I knew her pitch was far more desperate than it seemed. Shortly after she and her partner opened their wine shop, a discount liquor store opened only a block from the mall, causing their sales to plummet. I'd overheard them in the mall manager's office not long before I'd Tasered Mackey. They'd been attempting to negotiate their way out of their lease or, at a minimum, to secure a reduction in rent. The mall manager had turned them down. He'd paid for the installation of custom-made shelving in the wine shop and had yet to recoup the investment. The women had been forced to let their sales staff go, splitting the long shifts between just the two of them now. Working as many hours as they did had to be exhausting. But maybe their luck would turn around. The holidays and attendant festivities would be here before we knew it. Spending time with family led many people to drink excessively, too. Nothing like a crisp Riesling to take the edge off a critical aunt's comments.

Before I could snag a chocolate-coated strawberry, my shoulder-mounted radio crackled to life, the dispatcher's voice coming through. "K-nine team requested at David-son rail yard. Urgent."

While not technically located within the boundaries of the W1 division, the train yard was close by. As one of the few K-9 teams, Brigit and I were expected to handle calls outside our division when our special skills were needed. *Dang.* I'd been hoping to end my workday here at the mall.

I grabbed my mic and pressed the button, turning my head to speak into the device. "Officer Luz responding."

Brigit added a *woof* as if to remind me that she was at work here, too.

We scurried to the cruiser, hopped in, and backed out of our reserved spot. I turned on my siren and lights to signal the cars ahead of me to pull to the side. I sailed out of the mall parking lot and back down University, reveling in the feeling of power as the others yielded to me. I took a turn onto Vickery and pulled into the rail yard a minute later.

The yard, which was operated by Union Pacific, comprised a dozen or so tracks running side by side, along with a diesel maintenance area and a large asphalt lot where the boxcars or their contents could be transferred to tractor trailers to be moved to their final destinations. Today the tracks bore long lines of railcars, including engines, rectangular boxcars bearing dry goods, and cylindrical tank cars containing liquids. Some of the cars were shiny and new, others old and rusty.

Two cruisers sat on the asphalt near the outside track, both with their flashing lights on. A late-model pickup truck sat just ahead of the cruisers, both of its doors hanging open. It didn't take a genius to figure out that at least two people had fled from the vehicle. The only thing that was unknown was why. Drugs? An outstanding warrant? Stolen vehicle?

My former partner stalked down a line of railroad cars fifty yards ahead, his gun drawn. Officer Hinojosa, a Latino guy in his midthirties, was bent down low, attempting to spot feet moving among the trains.

I parked behind the other patrol cars and climbed out of my cruiser. "What's up?" I asked Hinojosa as I let Brigit out of the back.

"Stolen pickup," he said. "Mackey tried to pull them over for a traffic violation, but they took off."

Hot pursuit. That explained why Mackey was here, outside W1.

"The truck pulled in here," Hinojosa said. "The driver and two passengers bailed."

This was where Brigit and I came in. I unclipped her leash and gave her the order to find the trail of the people who'd fled from the pickup.

She put her nose to the ground, sniffing in first one direction, then another, before picking up the trail and following it. As she trotted along, Hinojosa and I trotted along behind her, our footsteps crunching in the gravel. While my fellow officer pulled his gun, I opted for my baton, whipping it from my belt and flicking it open with a *snap*.

Brigit's nose led her between two cars. While she could easily duck under the coupler, Hinojosa and I had to climb over it. We were sandwiched between two trains now. My partner continued on for three more cars before again cutting between them, taking us deeper into the yard.

My pulse pounded. With trains on each side, I felt trapped. If the car thieves were armed, if they took shots at us, would Hinojosa and I be able to escape? Or would we be gunned down, our blood seeping into the gravel? And if the thieves were armed, would they take a shot at Brigit? I found myself wishing my partner had a Kevlar vest, too.

One more cut through and Brigit took off running, the scent evidently much stronger now. We ran after her.

She stopped and turned to look between two cars ahead, barking to alert us to the presence of her quarry. She disappeared between the cars as the truck thieves apparently fled.

Thank God they're running instead of shooting.

Hinojosa and I crossed between yet another set of cars and turned up the row. Ahead were two white men and one black man, all running, Brigit on their heels.

I gave her the takedown signal and she lunged ahead, bringing down the front-most man. The slower car thieves sprinted past their cohort, who now grappled with Brigit in the dirt and rocks between two trains. As Hinojosa and I ran up, I ordered Brigit off the prone man.

"I got him!" my coworker said.

I gave Brigit the order to continue her pursuit and ran after her once again. She leaped onto the back of the black man and he stumbled forward across an empty track, hitting a knee on the metal rail. He fell to the ground, clutching his knee, rolling side to side, and issuing a howl of pain that echoed off the metal cars nearby: "Aaaaaaah!"

As I ran past the man I hollered, "Stay right there!" A moot point probably. He wouldn't be able to run off with a shattered kneecap.

Ahead, Derek stepped out from between two cars on the right. "I got him!" he yelled.

Spotting Mackey, the remaining runner turned to the left in an attempt to escape between two trains, but on my signal Brigit took him down in short order, too.

The Big Dick ran up, his face red with both exertion and anger. "I told you I'd get him!"

"And my partner beat you to it." I offered him a snide smile before calling Brigit off the man. I clipped her leash back on to her collar and stepped back, gesturing to the car thief lying facedown at our feet. "He's all yours now, Mackey."

Derek glanced down at the wet spot on the back of the man's shirt. "He's covered in dog spit."

"Not my problem."

I gave Brigit four liver treats, one for each of the men she'd taken down and one for pissing off Mackey. I followed the treats with a nice scratch and a, "Good girl!"

She wolfed down the treats and wagged her tail, side to side this time.

"Come on, girl."

We left Derek to stew and returned to our cruiser to head back to the station. As I pulled out of the rail yard, an involuntarily smile spread across my face.

A day that ended in besting Derek Mackey was a good day.

SEVENTEEN
GOOD COP, BAD DOG

Brigit

Okay, so maybe chasing the squirrel had been impulsive and disobedient. But that damn rodent asked for it, twitching his tail at Brigit, teasing her, daring her to chase him.

Brigit knew Megan had been none too happy about her behavior, but Brigit also knew that she'd more than made up for it by taking down the three men at the train yard. Besides, any day that ends in liver treats is a good day.

EIGHTEEN
TROUBLESHOOTING

The Rattler

Since he hadn't retrieved the bomb, he had no way of determining exactly what went wrong. Nonetheless, he attempted to troubleshoot the problem, carefully reviewing each step of the assembly process. Eventually, he reached the conclusion that either dust on the fuse had inhibited the ignition or the cheap alarm clock had malfunctioned.

No problem.

There was still time for a second practice session before his target date.

NINETEEN
SHOP TILL YOU DROP

Megan

It was early August now, and Brigit and I had been on duty together for two weeks. Brigit had quickly proved to be a much better partner than Mackey had been. She didn't talk smack, didn't force me to listen to sports radio, didn't make inappropriate sexual comments. Like Mackey she occasionally passed gas in the cruiser, but at least she didn't laugh about it and hold the window lock button down to prevent me from getting fresh air.

At 8:00 Friday morning, Brigit and I arrived at the W1 station in my smart car. There was only one parking spot left and it was next to Derek's truck. The Big Dick had parked haphazardly again, his pickup straddling the line, taking up two-thirds of one spot and one-third of another. What a discourteous jerkwad. Luckily for me, my car only needed half a spot. I pulled in next to him and parked with room to spare.

After letting Brigit out of her side, I took hold of her leash in my left hand and pulled my baton from my belt with my right. I flicked my wrist and my baton extended. *Snap.* I delivered a solid hit to the rubber testicles hanging from Derek's truck, my morning ritual.

Whack!

Oh, what a sense of satisfaction.

My partner and I continued on to our cruiser and took off to patrol our beat.

After a relatively uneventful morning, I decided to head over to country club, see if I could catch Cuthbert wet handed. The next time he violated the watering ordinance he was getting a citation. No ifs, ands, or buts.

My patrol car followed a shiny late-model black Lexus into the neighborhood. The car turned into the driveway of the clubhouse, but I continued on, past a long fairway bordered by a copse of trees.

Thunk!

A golf ball bounced off the hood of the cruiser, leaving a small dent in the black paint. My eyes went to my rearview mirror. No sense trying to figure out who'd hit the ball. All four men who'd been standing at the tee box had jumped into their carts and headed off down the cart path. *Oh, well. Wasn't my car. No sense taking it personally.* Besides, the humiliation of making such a crappy shot would be punishment enough for the offender.

I continued on, into the neighborhood. It was Friday, the day when cleaning and gardening crews swarmed over the upscale neighborhood, mowing and blowing and dusting and disinfecting, getting the houses and grounds ready for the homeowners' weekend entertaining. I slowed for a landscape worker standing in the street. He had a gas-powered leaf blower strapped to his back and waved the air hose back and forth at waist level as if it were a huge plastic penis and he were writing his name in the snow. As we drove past I raised a hand in greeting and Brigit offered him a friendly bark: *Woof-woof!*

Nothing unusual in the neighborhood. Might as well head over to the mall.

As I prepared to turn out of the neighborhood, a female dispatcher came over the line. "Got a report of a woman stealing trash on Park Hill Drive," she said. "Who can respond?"

I was only a few blocks away. I grabbed my radio mic and pushed the talk button. I was tempted to question the report. How could someone claim their *trash* had been stolen? By putting an item at the curb to be hauled away by garbage collectors hadn't the owner relinquished his or her rights? Forfeited ownership?

But rather than debating the legalities and/or ludicrousness of the report with the dispatcher, I merely said, "Officer Luz and Brigit responding."

I slid the mic back into the holder and hooked a tire-squealing U-turn that, for civilians, would have been an illegal maneuver. *Wheee!* It's fun when you can break the rules with impunity.

Two turns and twenty seconds later I pulled up behind an older green minivan parked at a curb in front of a classic Williamsburg-style home partially covered with the same ivy that filled the lush beds at its base. The van's hatch was open. A tiny elderly woman stood at the cargo bay, her waist-long silver ponytail hanging down the back of her paint-splattered denim overalls, her child-sized feet clad in classic red Keds. She wrangled a cockeyed and scratched wooden bookcase with a broken shelf into her van.

Movement at one of the house's front windows caught my eye. The resident, a middle-aged blond woman, had pulled back the curtains and was peering through the sheers. No doubt she'd been the one to call in the report. She might have too much time on her hands, but didn't she realize we cops had better things to do than harass harmless scavengers? She was as bad as Mr. Cuthbert.

I slid the gearshift into park, turned off the cruiser, and climbed out. I let Brigit out, too, to stretch her legs. "Good morning, Honeysuckle."

It wasn't a term of endearment. It was the woman's given name. I'd first met her a few months earlier when Derek and I had pulled her over for failing to put a red flag on a long rolled-up rug that stuck out of the back of her van. I'd had to fight a chuckle when I saw the name on her license. Honeysuckle Mae Sewell. What had her parents been thinking? Rose, Daisy, and Lily, sure. Iris, even. But *Honeysuckle*? The name belonged on a cat, not a human being.

The woman had been friendly and contrite, so I'd let her go with a warning, despite the Big Dick's suggestion I stick it to her with a citation. Heartless, that guy.

Honeysuckle lived on the East Side, outside of my beat but not far from my apartment complex. To supplement her meager Social Security checks, she ran a perpetual yard sale in front of her ancient wood-frame house. I'd bought my card table and chair from her. At seven bucks they were a steal.

Honeysuckle looked up and offered me a smile. Cops don't get many of those. Few people are happy to see us. Honeysuckle's smile was wrinkle ringed and gap-toothed but also wide and warm.

"Hello there!" she called. "Officer Megan, right?"

I nodded and returned the smile.

Her eyes went to my head. "Your hair looks especially shiny today."

"New shampoo." Thank goodness she didn't ask me for the brand. "Whatcha got here?" My words were a bit folksie, but I'd found that being congenial and casual could sometimes diffuse situations much better than being cold and formal.

"Bookcase," she said. "It's a little off-kilter and one of

the shelves is broke, but I can glue the wood and set it straight again. Think I could get twenty bucks for it?"

"Betcha could," I said. "I just might buy it from you myself." I took another step closer and lowered my voice. "Listen, Ms. Sewell, I'm here because a homeowner reported someone stealing trash."

"Stealing trash?" Honeysuckle's brows formed a perplexed V. "That makes no sense. How can a person steal something that someone else threw it away?"

"Beats the heck out of me." I gave her a wink to let her know I was on her side, then gestured to the woman behind the curtain to come outside.

The woman stepped out onto her porch but came no closer, as if afraid she might catch fleas from us. Then again, with Brigit along, she just might.

I shaded my eyes against the sun. "Are you the one who reported a person stealing your discards?" I'd chosen the word "discards" to make a point. The point being that her complaint was nonsensical.

The woman seemed hesitant to admit it at first but finally said, "Yes. I'm the one who called."

I gestured to Honeysuckle. "Is this the alleged thief?"

The woman nodded.

"Did she take anything that wasn't set out here for the g-garbagemen to haul off?"

The woman frowned. "Well, no, but we don't like people coming into our neighborhood and making a mess."

I failed to see how picking up a discarded bookcase was making a mess. If anything, Honeysuckle was helping to rid the neighborhood of clutter. I said as much.

Clearly, that's not what the woman wanted to hear. "She's trespassing."

She wasn't trespassing. She was just collecting castoffs she could repair and sell. She was just trying to make a living. Maybe this woman ought to give it a try sometime.

"This is a public street," I pointed out.

Honeysuckle looked up at me. "I'm always careful not to go into anyone's yard."

I tilted my head to indicate the shelves. "You want the bookcase back?" I asked the woman.

She looked from me, to Honeysuckle, then back to me. "Well . . . no."

Then why all the fuss, for God's sake? Of course I couldn't say that or I'd risk a complaint. I turned my attention to Honeysuckle. "All done here?"

She wasn't breaking the law, but the quickest way to resolve this matter would be for her to move along. She knew it, too. This wasn't the first time she'd been shooed.

"Sure am," Honeysuckle said. "I'll get on my way."

With that, Honeysuckle pulled a lightweight plastic stepstool from her cargo bay and stood on it to grab the inside handle of the open hatch. She pulled the door down, closed it, and picked up the stool, carrying it with her to the driver's door. She set the stool on the passenger seat and climbed in, settling on top of the pillow she'd put on the driver's seat to help her see over the dash.

"You have a good day now!" she called before shutting her door and motoring off.

With Honeysuckle on her way, the woman said, "Looks like this is taken care of." She offered me a nod, but no *thank you* before going back into her house. Hence I made no attempt to stop Brigit from tinkling in the woman's ivy. Hell, I was tempted to tinkle in her ivy myself.

It was straight up noon when my partner and I climbed back into the car. I aimed the cruiser for the Chisholm Trail mall, where Brigit and I could scrounge up some lunch in the food court.

Today would be an especially busy day at the mall.

Several years ago, the Texas legislature established a sales tax moratorium on a specified weekend in August preceding the opening day of public schools. With sales tax abated for three days, shoppers came out in droves. Although the law was purportedly enacted to help the less fortunate afford clothing and school supplies for their children, the statute was actually the result of lobbying by retailers hoping to pad their bottom lines. Rather than offer additional discounts on their merchandise, retailers were more than happy to let the government take the financial hit.

Given the sales tax holiday, shoppers had turned out in record numbers and a long line of cars waited at the signal light. Brigit and I had to sit through three light changes before we could turn into the shopping center. A lesser cop might have turned on his lights and siren to cut in line, but I patiently waited my turn with the civilians.

The parking lot was packed, every spot filled, would-be shoppers driving up and down the lanes in a futile attempt to find empty slots, eager to begin their tax-free shopping spree. Not that anyone shopping at these exclusive stores really needed the tax break. Most drove high-end cars and could surely afford to pay full price. Still, I understood the thrill of the bargain hunt.

As I headed to my reserved parking spot, I noticed many of the usual cars in the employee lot. A midnight-blue Infiniti. A green PT Cruiser. A powder-pink '86 Cadillac Coupe de Ville.

After allowing Brigit to sniff around in the grassy area flanking the lot, I headed into the mall with her black nylon leash in my hand, my partner trotting along beside me. Reaching down to my belt, I removed the walkie-talkie mall security had given me when I'd first been assigned the beat. The device allowed me to keep an ear on communications among the mall's security personnel and, in the event of an emergency, would enable us to get in quick contact without having to go through police dispatch. Not that there were many real emergencies in the mall. I'd recently been summoned to break up an argument between two women tangling over the last pair of size 7 Gucci loafers on a half-price rack, but when Brigit grabbed one of the shoes and sunk her teeth through the leather, the debate ended instantly.

My partner had the wisdom of Solomon.

Or Snoopy.

I flipped the switch to turn the walkie-talkie on. "Officer Luz on-site."

Three security guards responded with an acknowledgment.

I returned the radio to my belt.

Potted ornamental trees placed here and there along the main walkway provided only dappled shade, so Brigit and I stuck to the perimeter, walking in the shadows of the store awnings to avoid the relentless late-summer sun. How a real estate developer could think that an open-air mall in Texas was a good idea was beyond me. But mall management surely saved a fortune on their electric bills, since they didn't have to air-condition the common areas. What's more, the heat discouraged loitering and encouraged customers to go into the shops and spend their money. On second thought, maybe the idea of an open-air mall wasn't so ridiculous after all.

Clang! Clang! The mall's trackless choo-choo train inched its way down the path, the conductor having to repeatedly ring the bell to signal pedestrians to clear the way. *Clang! Clang!*

Brigit and I made our way slowly past the shops, weaving our way in and out among shoppers. Most were mothers with young children or groups of high school kids.

Judging from their expensive couture and coiffures, they likely lived in the nearby country club neighborhood.

The organ music from the Western-themed carousel in the middle of the mall grew louder, then softer as the glass doors to the courtyard opened and closed ahead of us, letting shoppers in and out. Rather than the traditional tunes, the organ music consisted of classic country and folk songs. "Happy Trails." "Ragtime Cowboy Joe." The themes from *Bonanza* and *Rawhide*. And, of course, "The Old Chisholm Trail," the classic song that had been recorded over the years by a number of musicians ranging from Woody Guthrie to Tex Ritter to the Charlie Daniels Band. I knew the lyrics by heart thanks to my second-grade music teacher.

> *Oh, come along, boys, and listen to my tale,*
> *I'll tell you all my troubles on the ol' Chisholm*
>   *Trail.*
> *Come a-ti yi youpy youpy yea youpy yea,*
> *Come a-ti yi youpy youpy yea. . . .*

The songs were on a ninety-minute loop, repeating each hour and a half. If I had to hear the same hokey songs five times a day, day after day, I'd shoot myself in the head. Of course, given that I'd ranked lowest in my training class in firearms skills, I'd probably use up the entire magazine trying to off myself.

While I sucked with my gun, I'd been the most adept with my baton. The stick felt natural in my hand, right, like an extension of my body. Who knew all those years of twirling with the high school band would come in handy in my police career?

I stopped in front of the bookstore, checking out the window display for the latest releases. I made a mental note to stop back when I was off duty and pick up a thriller that caught my eye. Window-shopping was one thing, but if I made any actual personal purchases while on the clock I could find myself facing a disciplinary action.

I'd just passed the wine shop, noting the Buy One Get One Free sign posted in their window, when the unmistakable grind of skate wheels on cement came from behind me. Two shaggy-haired skater boys wearing black skinny jeans and T-shirts came zipping toward us down the middle of the walkway, narrowly missing a toddler who'd stepped away from her mother.

I knew these punks. In fact, I'd warned them once before not to skate at the mall. At least I think it was them. All of these shaggy-haired kids looked alike. C'mon, boys. Try some originality!

I raised my whistle to my lips. *TWEET!* Letting the whistle fall back on its cord, I hollered, "Off the boards! Now!"

I moved to the middle of the walkway, spreading my legs and stretching out my arms. Brigit followed suit, standing sideways, the two of us forming a barrier.

When the boys ground to a stop in front of us, I lowered my arms. "No skating in the mall, boys. Parking lot's off-limits, too. I'm not g-going to tell you again. Next time I'll take your boards."

The boys didn't address me directly, just stepped off their boards, tucked them under their arms, and wandered on, muttering under their breath about police oppression. Such drama queens.

Brigit and I made our way slowly past the shops. I glanced into each one, raising a hand or offering a nod to the staff, most of whom I knew by either name or sight. I'd made a point of introducing myself to the store managers and employees when I'd first begun working the beat with Derek months ago.

As I walked, the song lyrics kept running unbidden through my head.

On a ten-dollar horse and a forty-dollar saddle,
I was a-ridin' and a-punchin' those Texas cattle.
Come a-ti yi youpy youpy yea youpy yea,
Come a-ti yi youpy youpy yea. . . .

One of the mall's maintenance team, an African-American guy in his early fifties, knelt down on the walkway next to the door of the Yankee Candle shop, a large red toolbox beside him. Dressed in blue coveralls and steel-toed work boots, he fingered through an assortment of screws and nails, trying several in the hole before finding one that fit.

I raised a hand in greeting. "Hey, Irving."

"Hey yourself, Officer Luz." He cupped a hand under Brigit's furry chin and made a smoochie face. "Hello to you, too, pretty girl."

My partner responded to his attentions by licking his cheek.

Irving released her and picked up a screwdriver to finish his work. Brigit and I continued on.

It's bacon and beans most every day,
I'd just as soon be eatin' prairie hay.
Come a-ti yi youpy youpy yea youpy yea,
Come a-ti yi youpy youpy yea. . . .

A couple stores down was Brackenburg Furriers. Given the heat, no one was shopping for fur coats this weekend. The store's owner, Ariana Brackenburg, leaned casually against the stone wall in her doorway, an expression of equal parts condescension and boredom on her face as she sucked iced coffee through Botoxed lips. The platinum-haired, painfully thin woman wore a lightweight bloodred suit and stood nearly six feet tall in her pointy-toed red pumps.

As we approached, the store owner glanced down at Brigit, her expression morphing to one of appreciation, as if she were imagining the beautiful coat my partner would make.

Brigit emitted a soft growl at the modern-day Cruella De Vil.

Ariana gave my partner a pointed look. "Reading my mind, were you?" She chuckled and turned her kohl-lined eyes my way. "I don't think she likes me."

That makes two of us. I shrugged.

I continued on to the center courtyard, opening the glass door for Brigit and following her through. Inside, the carousel music filled the space, providing a carnival-like atmosphere. The ride was in full swing, smiling children moving up and down and round and round on their colorful steeds. Those prone to motion sickness sat green faced on the stationary benches, trying not to throw up the Cinnabons they'd begged their mothers to buy them.

Randy, the carousel operator, sat on his cowhide barstool, wearing his usual gray ostrich cowboy boots, jeans, and a long-sleeved Western-style pearl-snap shirt. Completing the ridiculous getup were faux-suede fringed chaps with a matching vest. Tucked into the hatband of his straw Stetson today were a ticket stub from a 2012 One Direction concert, a business card from a plastic surgeon, and a coupon for Valtrex, the herpes medication.

The guy had thin lips and wide-set eyes, along with light-brown hair cut as short as the grass on the golf course greens. He wasn't ugly, exactly, but he hadn't made any effort to make himself attractive, either. Nonetheless, Randy had a few things going for him. Straight, white teeth for one. The aforementioned sense of humor, for two. And last, while he might not earn big bucks on his job, he always showed up for work on time, a testament to his reliability. His punctuality was also a testament to the reliability of his car, the pink Mary Kay Cadillac. He'd evidently snagged the car for next to nothing at a government auction. Perhaps I should add good money management skills to his list of positive attributes.

Randy unclipped his lasso from his waist. "Check out the new trick I've been working on."

He took a few steps back and began to rotate his right hand, the rope loop circling in front of him. Once he'd gained some momentum, he angled the rope downward to his right so that it spun parallel to the floor, a half foot from the tile. Randy hopped into the moving rope circle, then out, then back in again.

I clapped my hands. "Bravo, Buckaroo."

"Wait," he said, raising the index finger of his left hand. "There's more!"

Standing inside the circle, he slowly raised his rotating hand, the spiraling rope moving up his legs and torso and past his face until it went cockeyed and hit the brim of his cowboy hat, sending it flying off his head. He stopped spinning the rope and it went slack, hanging limply in his hands. "That wasn't supposed to happen."

I offered him an encouraging smile. "Keep working on it."

Brigit trotted over to Randy's errant Stetson, grabbed the brim in her teeth, and retrieved it. I took the hat from her and stuck a dollar tip in it before returning it to Randy. "Thanks for the show."

He held his hat out to his side and put his other hand on his stomach, bending over in an exaggerated bow. "Anytime, milady."

Brigit and I headed to the food court. On the way we

passed the mall manager, a stocky, white-haired sixtyish man whom everyone referred to as Mr. Castleberry. He looked happily frazzled today, the sales tax holiday no doubt creating both more work for the mall's management team and ecstatic tenants who were sure to earn record profits this weekend.

I raised a hand in greeting.

"Officer Luz!" he called, returning the gesture as he scurried along. "Good to see you, as always!"

Like everywhere else in the mall, the food court was packed to claustrophobic proportions. Brigit and I stood in line for ten minutes at the shish-kebab counter before finally reaching the front of the line.

Stick People served all kinds of shish kebabs, from beef, to chicken, to lamb, and even vegetarian varieties. Their basic black-on-white logo featured a stick person with arms extended out to the sides, both hands holding erect shish-kebab sticks stacked with cartoon meat and veggies. Frankly, I thought the logo looked like a person directing airplane traffic on a tarmac, but who was I to judge?

The man working the counter was the owner, a Turkish guy named Serhan Singh. He sported a Dallas Cowboys jersey and a thick beard even Chuck Norris would envy.

Singh raised both hands skyward. "Officer Luz!" he cried, as if greeting an old friend he hadn't seen in some time, as opposed to the same cop who bought lunch at his booth at least twice a week. "So good to see you."

"Same here," I said. "You sure are busy."

"We make money by fist over hand today," he said.

The guy hadn't quite gotten the expression right, but the mere fact that he was trying showed his attempts to assimilate. As I'd learned the first time I'd bought lunch at his stand, he had come to the United States ten years ago to attend college at the University of Texas branch campus in nearby Arlington, where he'd met his wife, Aruni, an Indian-American. After earning his business degree, Serhan had managed various restaurants before opening this stand, the first of what he hoped would become a regional chain. The American dream wasn't just for native-born Americans. Naturalized citizens shared the dream, as well.

"The usual?" he asked.

I nodded.

Serhan fixed Brigit a beef and chicken kebab, hold the pepper and onion. He served the meat in a red-and-white-checkered paper basket. I didn't indulge myself. In the hopes of not becoming a fat-cop cliché, I generally stuck with salads from the deli two booths down.

I handed Serhan some bills and took my change.

He gave me one last smile before I stepped away. "You have a good day!"

I returned the smile and the sentiment: "You, too."

Brigit and I stepped over to the deli and waited in line again. Five minutes later, the teenage boy working the pickup counter pulled the flexible microphone mounted on the countertop toward him and spoke into it. "Number two-four-three, your order is up. Two-four-three."

I stepped forward and grabbed the tray containing my salad and fresh-squeezed lemonade. "Thanks."

My partner and I snagged a small booth and ate our lunch, Brigit sitting on the seat as if she were a person and gulping down the pieces of meat I fed her one by one.

By the time we finished, the noise and crowd at the mall had begun to get to me. I tossed out my trash and led Brigit back down the row of shops. We took a shortcut through Macy's, where we spotted two of the security guards, a chubby white guy named Scott and a lanky Latino named Ricky. Sporting their required orange safety helmets, they stood on their goofy three-wheeled scooters in front of an enormous big-screen television, watching ESPN. Flagrant dereliction of duty. But how could I fault them when I took advantage of my beat to window-shop?

Just for kicks I pulled my walkie-talkie from my belt and pushed the talk button. "Officer Luz for Scott and Ricky. Come back."

From my vantage point in Kitchen Appliances, I saw Scott pull his device from his breast pocket. He squeezed the button. "Scott and Ricky here."

"You two quit working so hard. You might hurt yourselves."

Their heads swiveled until Ricky spotted me by a refrigerator. He tapped his coworker on the arm and pointed my way.

Scott put the walkie-talkie back to his mouth. "Good one, Luz. Any beer in that fridge?"

"Wishful thinking, buddy." With that, I slid the radio back onto my belt, lifted a hand in good-bye, and led Brigit out of the mall to patrol the rest of our beat.

TWENTY
HAPPY TRAILS TO YOU, UNTIL WE MEAT AGAIN

Brigit

Lunch had been delicious. Life didn't get much better than when she could indulge in both beef and chicken. Toss in some lamb and she would've achieved canine nirvana.

Still, the mall had made her nervous today. There were too many people walking about, too many chances her paws would be stepped on or rolled over by a stroller or a kid would pull her tail. She was glad Megan hadn't remained there long. Especially now that they were patrolling the zoo. Unlike that store at the mall where the empty animal skins hung, these animals were alive and well and still wearing their hides.

Of course that didn't stop Brigit from wishing she could hop into the enclosure and eat a gazelle. Unfortunately, her partner had her on a very short leash. Her partner could be a real party pooper sometimes.

TWENTY-ONE
PRACTICE MAKES PERFECT

The Rattler

Since the travel alarm clock hadn't worked, he decided he'd try a different tack today and use a kitchen timer.

He grabbed his backpack and set out into the trees again, returning to the location he'd chosen previously, determined that today would be a success. He repeated the steps, spreading the newspaper's business pages on the ground and assembling the bomb on top of the stock reports. This time, when he counted down behind a live oak tree, his efforts were rewarded.

Three.

Two.

One.

KAPOW!

The initial blast was followed by the sounds of shrapnel and leaves falling to the ground.

He shot a fist into the air and pulled it back to his waist in a celebratory gesture. "Yes!"

Sitting quietly for a few minutes, he listened intently

for sirens, voices, the sound of ATVs coming his way. He heard nothing. No one had come to investigate.

Good.

If anyone had stumbled upon him out here, he might've been forced to shoot him or her. How unoriginal and boring that would be.

He headed back toward the site where he'd left the bomb, making his way as quietly as possible. When he approached within fifty feet, he noted an increasing concentration of nails, screws, and fishhooks stuck in the trees and on the ground. The sharp metal pieces had spread quite a distance. Without trees in the way, they'd travel even farther next time. He couldn't wait to see just how far.

Something bright red lay among the dirt and leaves on the ground ahead. A cardinal. The Rattler bent down and used a twig to turn the bird over. The corpse contained no metal. The bird likely had been killed by the percussive effect of the bomb or, attempting a frantic escape, had inadvertently flown into a tree and broken its neck.

The Rattler plucked a red feather from the bird's wing, stood, and continued on.

Ten feet from ground zero, a squirrel in the final throes of death twitched on the ground, two screws and a roofing nail in his belly. When his body stilled, the Rattler nudged him with the toe of his boot. "Too bad, buddy. Wrong place, wrong time."

TWENTY-TWO
SHOP TILL YOU DROP

Megan

Unfortunately, police work wasn't exactly a nine-to-five, Monday through Friday kind of job. So here I was, dragging my tired butt out of bed at 7:00 on Saturday morning for another full-day shift. What's more, I had to climb over my furry partner, who continued to doze contentedly, snoring through her big, black snout.

Yes, the darn dog insisted on sleeping on the futon with me. What's more, she demanded the side of the futon that faced the room, leaving me cramped against the wall. The first night she'd climbed onto the bed I'd shoved her off at least a dozen times, but each time she jumped right back on. She'd even grabbed my shirt in her teeth and pulled me off the bed herself. It was almost as if she thought *she* were training *me,* instead of vice versa. Exhausted, I'd finally given in. I really didn't want a face full of dog fur on my pillow, but winter would be coming soon and with a warm dog curled up next to me I could turn the heat down and save on my electric bill.

What a sucker I am, no?

After a bowl of granola with soy milk, I opened a can of food for my roommate. I poured it into her bowl on the kitchen floor.

"Wake up, sleepyhead!" I called as I made my way to the shower.

An hour later my partner and I were out on our beat.

Our day started off bad and only got worse.

I hadn't even finished my travel mug of coffee before I was forced to issue a citation to Cuthbert for once again violating the water-rationing regulations. He'd been none too happy about the $1,000 fine he faced, but he'd been issued two warnings already and ignored them. Clearly it was time for bigger measures.

The red-faced man clutched the ticket in his fist as I drove away. "I'll have your badge!"

He could have my badge, all right. I'd happily cram it down his throat myself.

As I cruised down Rosedale, I spotted two adolescent boys tagging a bridge with bright-blue spray paint. They'd only managed to write *FU* when I pulled to a stop behind to them.

I grabbed the mic for my cruiser's public-address system. "Freeze, boys."

Despite my orders, one took off running without even looking back. The other turned around and shot his hands into the air. Unfortunately, his finger was still on the trigger of the paint can. *Kssssssh.* He coated my door, window, and part of my light bar with paint before dropping the can on his toe and hopping around on one foot, cursing. "Ouch! Damn! Ouch!"

I leaped from my car. "Stay here!" I ordered the tagger with the bruised toe.

I took off after the one who'd run away. Brigit would have been faster than me, but no sense sending her across

four lanes of traffic and risking her life for a minor graf-
fiti offense. I was only three steps behind the brat when
he tripped over the curb on the other side of the street and
fell, throwing out his hand to stop his fall.

CRUNCH!

"*Aaaaaaaah!*" the boy screamed in agony, and rolled
onto his back, cradling his mangled arm in the other.
From the odd angle of his forearm, my guess was he'd
severely fractured his radius.

HOOOOONK!

A city bus passed mere inches behind me, sending up
a warm cloud of dust, grit, and cigarette butts from the
gutter. *Lovely.*

I waved the cloud out of my face, blinked the grit from
my eyes, and activated my shoulder-mounted radio. "I
need an ambulance and backup."

Fortunately, the children's hospital was only a mile up
the road. Unfortunately, the closest cop in the district was
Derek.

The Big Dick pulled up to the curb a minute later, his
siren wailing and lights flashing. He cut his siren but left
the lights on and climbed out of his car. As he approached,
he tugged his pants up in a gesture that seemed less intended to hike up the waistline and more intended to jug-
gle his balls. "'Smatter, Luz? Two little boys too much for
you to handle?"

I ignored his attempts to rile me and jerked my head to
indicate the boy waiting across the street, his hands still
in the air. "I need you to take that kid in. Caught him
t-tagging."

Because the dogs rode in the backs of the cruisers, K-9
teams did not haul in the suspects they apprehended.
Rather, another officer would transport the suspects to
the station for booking. This procedure was fine with me.
It had always given me the willies to have bad guys sitting

behind me in the car, even with a protective barrier of metal bars between us. Having the creeps breathing down my neck, cursing, and glaring at me in the rearview mirror with murderous intent in their eyes made me feel anxious and vulnerable.

Derek looked over at the kid, then checked the street for cross traffic. The road was clear. Derek put two fingers in his mouth and whistled: *Fweet!* "Get your sorry butt over here, boy! You're going for a ride downtown."

The kid walked across the street toward us. When he was within reach, Derek grabbed him much more roughly than necessary and slammed him up against the cruiser.

"You ever been in trouble before, boy?" Derek asked the kid.

"No."

"You got any needles in your pockets? Any weapons or anything sharp?"

Again the kid said, "No."

Derek grabbed the kid's right arm and checked for needle tracks. Finding none, Derek checked the left. Also clean. He patted the kid down, pulling a cell phone and wallet out of his pockets. The Big Dick opened the wallet and thumbed through it. Finding nothing of interest, he punched the button to activate the camera on the kid's cell phone, held the camera up, and ordered the kid to turn around. "Say cheese."

Derek snapped a photo of the scowling kid and chuckled. "Now you've got a souvenir."

The Big Dick shoved the kid into the back of his cruiser, then kept an eye on the injured boy while I returned to the bridge and retrieved the can of spray paint, picking it up with a pair of metal tongs and sliding it into an evidence bag.

When I came back across the road, Derek yanked the bag out of my hands. He looked from me to Brigit, who had her nose pressed against the back window of my patrol car, watching the activity. "Carry on, bitches."

I fought the urge to whip out my baton and knock out Derek's teeth.

The ambulance pulled up now to collect the kid with the injured wrist. As the techs helped him onto a gurney, he cringed and moaned in pain. Even though the situation was entirely his fault, part of me felt sorry for him.

Holding up my cell phone, I asked, "What's your mother's number?"

He rattled off the number and I placed the call, getting only a voice mail. I left a message telling her where she could find her son. I contacted Dispatch for a second officer to meet the ambulance at the hospital. Once the kid was treated and released, the officer could take him to the station for booking.

The tagging crisis now resolved, my partner and I continued on to the Chisholm Trail mall, which had opened early for the tax-free weekend. A group of people paraded back and forth on the grassy strip at the perimeter of the parking lot. Their signs, which featured enlarged photographs of minks, chinchillas, rabbits, and foxes, read:

GIVE FUR THE COLD SHOULDER!
COMPASSION IS IN FASHION!
GIVE FLEECE A CHANCE!
BRACKENBURG FURRIERS——END YOUR BLOODY BUSINESS!

A middle-aged curly-haired blonde wearing bright-orange tennis shoes and a faded red bikini held a sign that read: We'd Rather Go Naked Than Wear Fur! Next to her, a man with a bushy gray beard and hair pranced around wearing only black hiking boots and a pair of much-too-small, much-too-tight bicycle shorts. The shorts brought to mind the *Live Strong* motto of the foundation started by Lance Armstrong, the seven-time Tour de France winner from Austin now shamed by a doping scandal. Glancing at the sizable bulge in the protestor's spandex shorts, I thought perhaps a more appropriate sentiment would be *Live Schlong*.

While the couple's aims were admirable, their sagging pasty butt cheeks might do more to hurt their cause than help it. But at least they were getting people's attention. No fewer than four cars had honked at them while I'd been observing. A guy in a pickup had even rolled down his window and hollered, "How much for a hand job?" Of course it was unclear whether he'd been propositioning the woman in the bikini or the man in the bike shorts.

I pulled up next to the group and rolled down my paint-splattered passenger window. The curly-haired blonde looked my way. When I waved her over, she stepped up to my window, followed by the others. She leaned in to listen, hooking the fingers of her left hand over the open window of my cruiser. Her short fingernails bore no polish and her fingertips appeared calloused, the hands of a woman with little vanity and lots of hard work to do. A plain silver wedding band encircled her ring finger.

I looked from her to the others gathered behind her and reminded them to remain on the public right-of-way or the mall management would have the right to order their removal. "As long as you stay on the grass they can't make you leave or have you arrested for trespassing." I handed her my card. "If anyone gives you trouble, call me."

"Thanks, Officer," she said.

I gave the group a nod. "Good luck with your protest." Brigit barked as if in agreement: *Arf!*

We drove to our reserved spot and parked. I pulled my

walkie-talkie from the car's visor and checked in with mall security: "Officer Luz on-site."

No sooner had I climbed from the car than I heard an unmistakable *pop-pop-pop* from across the parking lot.

Oh, my God!

Was it gunfire?

My body went limp with fear until I saw the two skater boys from the day before sailing through the lot on their boards, tossing fireworks into the air. *Pop-pop!*

I stood up straight, grabbed my whistle, and blew until I thought my lungs would burst: *TWEEEEEEEET!*

The boy in back glanced my way. "Cop!" he shouted to his friend. Evidently they'd heard that possession of fireworks within the city limits was illegal and subject to a fine of up to two grand. They'd have to mow an awful lot of lawns to make that much money.

Before I could even make a move in their direction, the two sped up and out of sight. It was probably just as well. I couldn't run fast enough to catch them and I wasn't about to send my K-9 partner on a chase that could lead her into traffic.

"Officer Luz!" came Ricky's voice across the radio. "You're needed at the main doors of Macy's. There's a fight about to break out."

Visions of gang warfare in my head, I opened the back door, grabbed Brigit's leash, and pulled her out, taking off at a full run with my partner galloping alongside me. We didn't get far before the tight crowd slowed us down.

"'Scuse us!" I called, weaving as fast as I could through the crowd. "Police! Out of the way, please!" When my polite pleas fell on deaf ears, I escalated to the less amenable, "Move aside! Now!"

We rushed down the walkway, barreling past the choo-choo train, the passengers' heads swiveling to watch the cop and her K-9 partner. *Clang! Clang!*

When we finally reached Macy's, I found no gang-bangers, just two girls engaged in an all-out catfight, clawing and scratching and kicking at each other.

"You slut!" screamed the blonde as she dug her pink-tipped fingernails into the redhead's face.

The redhead countered with a kick to the shins and a cry of, "Bitch!"

A group of teens had gathered around to watch and cheer for one of the girls or the other. There were even a few grown men in the crowd. I supposed the catfight was a titillating alternative to mud wrestling. Scott and Ricky had joined the crowd, too. Though they'd stepped off their scooters, they'd made no move to intervene in the conflict. It wasn't clear if the security guards were just being lazy or if they were afraid to involve themselves in a physical confrontation with young girls. With everyone being sue happy these days, I couldn't much blame the guards for not wanting to use force on female teens.

"Break it up! Now!" I hollered, attempting to step between the girls and force them apart. My efforts earned me a slap from the redhead and a scratch from the blonde. I debated siccing Brigit on them, but both wore light-weight halter-style tops and I was afraid she'd pull their shirts off or down and expose the girls' boobs. I could only imagine the crap I'd get for that.

I whipped my baton from my belt and flicked my wrist to open it. *SNAP!* I brandished the baton. "I said break it up!"

I almost hoped they'd ignore me again. After the threats from Cuthbert and my encounter with the Big Dick, I really felt like hitting someone.

The redhead got in one last kick before backing away. The blonde stopped the physical attack but not the verbal: "Whore!"

I raised the palm of my free hand. "Enough!"

After ordering the girls to step up to the wall and turn to face it, I determined who in the crowd had witnessed the entire series of events and ordered the others to move on.

I pointed my baton at the grown men as they wandered off. "You should be ashamed of yourselves."

Should be.

Weren't.

I pulled the witnesses aside, then gestured for one of them, a cute teen girl with dark curls, to follow me a few feet away from the crowd where the others couldn't hear our conversation. "Did you see what happened?"

The girl bit her lip and nodded.

"And?" I prodded.

She cut her eyes to the blonde at the wall and whispered, "Kirstie's boyfriend Taylor told her that he couldn't go out last night because his aunt and uncle had come for a surprise visit. But then Lauren called Kirstie and told her she'd seen Taylor making out with Amanda at the movies."

Teen drama.

Blurgh.

I tilted my head to indicate the two girls at the wall. "Amanda's the redhead?"

Curls nodded, her eyes narrowing. "Amanda knew Taylor and Kirstie were seeing each other. She's trying to break them up so she can have Taylor."

My lip quirked. Taylor sounded like a jerk. Why the heck would any girl want to be with the guy? "How did the fight start?"

"Kirstie saw Amanda and called her a slut. Then Amanda shoved her."

"Got it." I dismissed the witness and pulled another from the group.

This one was a petite girl with honey-colored hair and

light freckles. She corroborated the story the curly-haired girl had told me, though she did so reluctantly and pointed out that Taylor had told Amanda he'd broken up with Kirstie. "So technically Amanda isn't a slut."

Technically. As if there were some type of penal statute defining the term.

"You're a friend of Amanda's?" I guessed.

Honey-hair nodded. "You're not going to tell her what I told you, are you?"

"No." I dismissed her, too, and stepped over to the wall.

"No boy is worth fighting over," I told the girls, "especially one who lies."

Frankly, it seemed to me the two should've joined forces against the boy and toilet-papered his house or egged his car. Not that I condoned lawbreaking. I just hated to see the little cheat get away with his crimes of passion.

These girls had not only assaulted each other; they'd assaulted me as well. Still, I'm not sure the slap and scratch I'd received had truly been intended for me, and if I called for backup to haul these girls in I risked another encounter with Mackey. Besides, the girls looked embarrassed now, their cheeks pink, their heads down. I'd let them go.

"Go home," I told the girls as I collapsed my baton and returned it to my belt. "Don't come back here this weekend." That ought to give them time to cool down.

Once the girls left, I glanced at my watch. Three minutes till noon. Time for me and Brigit to take our lunch break. *Thank God.* One more idiot and I would lose it.

We made our way down the walkway toward the mall's food court, the smells of pizza and burgers, garlic and onions, grease and more grease growing stronger as we drew near.

The courtyard teemed with people and movement, like an ant pile that had been poked with a stick. The carousel music blared "Whoopie Ti Yi Yo, Get Along, Little Dogies" over the roar of chatter. Today Randy's hatband sported a losing lottery ticket, a dark-haired paper doll in Victorian dress, and his third-grade report card—As in every class and a complimentary comment from a pleased teacher that read: *Randy is an exemplary student.*

The comments on my third-grade report card were more along the lines of *Megan needs to work on her social skills* and *Megan refuses to participate in class discussions.* I supposed my parents might have worried more about these issues if they'd been aware of them. But my parents were too busy taking care of five children to notice when the six weeks' reporting period was up. I'd forged my father's signature on the report, along with a reply that read: *She's smarter than you think.*

All around the food court, huge clusters of colorful helium balloons floated in the air, anchored to railings by shiny silver curling ribbon. An enormous banner hung over the food stands: Enjoy Your Tax-Free Shopping Weekend!

Brigit tugged on her leash, pulling me over to the shish-kebab stand again. She was like an addict with a habit.

When we heard the clerk call, "Next please!" Brigit and I stepped up to the counter and placed our order with the young man who was working the register today. Brigit would get her usual beef and chicken, while I'd have the veggie kebab.

Serhan waved to me through the window that looked out from the kitchen, his smile all the more bright in contrast to his brown-skinned face. A moment later, the swinging door opened and a woman, a young girl, and Serhan emerged.

Serhan ushered the woman and child our way. "Officer Luz, so good to see you." He gestured to the delicate woman standing next to him, dressed in a bright-yellow sari. "This is my wife, Aruni."

I stretched my hand out to her. "Nice to meet you, Aruni."

The woman shook my hand and smiled. When Aruni released my hand, she put her palms on the girl's shoulders. "This is our daughter, Kara."

Kara smiled up at me. She was a beautiful girl, with enormous brown eyes and dark ringlets crowning her head. She was missing several teeth, like an adorable human jack-o'-lantern.

She looked from me, to Brigit, and back to me again. "Can I pet your dog?"

Most K-9 officers discouraged interaction with their dogs and perhaps I should, too. But despite our power plays, I trusted her with civilians. For as hard as she worked she deserved some attention. "She'd like that."

Kara ran her hand down Brigit's back.

Serhan gave Brigit a pat on the head, too. "We are shopping for school clothes today."

Kara held up two tiny fingers. "I start kindergarten in two weeks!"

Her excitement got me thinking back to my kindergarten days. I'd been excited and hopeful, too . . . in the beginning. Those hopes were soon dashed when every time I opened my mouth to speak the other children stared at me and giggled. It wasn't long before I first heard the word. That awful word, that cruel word, the word that seemed to wrap itself around me and refuse to let go.

"Stupid."

I felt my fingernails digging into my palms, a manifestation of long-repressed, festering frustration that had yet to find its release. I forced my memories aside and smiled at Kara. "You'll have a great time."

Farther down the row at the deli, a clerk pushed the button on the flexible microphone. "Order three-six-four is ready for pickup. Three-six-four."

After bidding Serhan and his family good-bye, I grabbed our lunch from the counter and looked around the crowded area for a free table. Brigit and I got lucky. Two teenage girls were vacating one of the booths along the perimeter of the food court. My partner and I hurried over and, as soon as the girls slipped out, we slipped in, one on each side.

Across the table, Brigit salivated and licked her lips while I used a fork to push her meat off the stick. I slid the basket her way. "Here you go, girl."

The carousel music fell silent, signifying the operator's half-hour lunch break. I can't say I was sorry. The repetitive, hokey songs were getting on my nerves and the overcrowded food court was noisy enough today even without the organ. As I took a sip of my fresh-squeezed lemonade, I glanced over to see Randy stashing his lasso under the ticket booth and locking the ride's control box. Good thing. After the morning I'd had I wasn't up for chasing horse rustlers, even if it was only in a circle.

Famished, I'd just bitten into a chunk of red pepper when Irving and another maintenance worker walked into the food court, both dressed in their usual coveralls and work boots. Irving carried his toolbox in one hand and a cardboard box in the other, while his assistant carried a folding metal stepladder. The assistant opened the ladder and positioned it in front of one of the broad support beams nearby. Irving set his toolbox on the floor and placed the cardboard box on the platform near the top of the ladder that was often used for paint cans. After ascending the ladder, Irving proceeded to replace several burned-out bulbs in a light fixture mounted over a decorative bronze clock on the beam.

Turning his head to avoid the harsh light of the bulbs, Irving noticed me and Brigit and gave us a friendly wave. "Can you believe how busy this mall is today?" he called.

"It's crazy!" I agreed.

I finished my meal in record time, wolfing it down almost as fast as Brigit devoured hers.

When I'd finished eating, I pulled out my cell phone, laid it on the table, and accessed the Internet. I pulled up the Web site for the Perot Museum of Nature and Science, a relatively new museum in the neighboring city of Dallas. I had yet to visit the place, though it had received rave reviews. According to the site, the museum was open noon to five on Sundays. I could attend the 9:30 AM mass at Saint Patrick's with my family tomorrow morning and still get to the museum by opening time.

I pulled up my e-mail account next. The only new messages were a couple of funny forwards from my sister, a spam ad asking if I wanted to meet hot Asian women, and a reminder from my auto insurance company that my monthly payment was due. Already? It seemed like I'd just paid that bill.

Arrur?

Across the booth, Brigit had pricked her ears and seemed to be listening to something, a distinct sound. She stuck her nose in the air, her nostrils twitching.

"What is it, girl?"

The carousel music started back up as Randy returned to duty, and Brigit seemed to lose interest in whatever she'd heard or smelled a moment ago.

I figured the rest of my lunch hour could best be spent taking advantage of the weekends' special bargains. Short as Texas winters were, I could still use a new sweater or two for the upcoming winter. I gathered up our trash and Brigit's leash and led her to the closest trash can. The plastic receptacle was filled to the brim, the door flap pushed back and up inside the bin, bags and napkins crammed into the hole. As busy as the mall was today, the custodians were evidently having trouble keeping up with garbage removal.

Before I could shove our trash in, Brigit reared up, propped her two front paws on the can, and sniffed the garbage, her nostrils twitching with the effort. *Sniff-sniff. Sniff-sniff.* She stuck her snout through the flap and grabbed dirty napkins and wrappers and food scraps in her teeth, dropping the refuse to the ground at my feet, creating a royal mess.

"Stop!" I ordered, yanking back on her leash.

When she sat down in front of the can, looking from it to me, giving her passive alert, I realized she wasn't merely scrounging for discarded bites of meat. *She smelled something in the can.* Given that she was only trained to detect drugs, it had to be marijuana, meth, crack, or another illicit substance.

Blurgh.

Duty required me to continue the search, no matter how messy or disgusting it might be.

The custodian stepped up then, rolling a large bin he used to collect trash from the smaller receptacles.

I begged a pair of latex gloves off him. "My dog alerted on this can. I need to search the trash."

The man held a plastic garbage bag open for me while I pulled off the can's dome-like cover and removed the pieces of trash handful by handful, holding them in front of Brigit's nose. She stood on all fours now, her ears still pricked, sniffing each fistful I placed in front of her. When she failed to alert, I dropped the trash into the janitor's bag and grabbed the next handful.

I'd dug down about a foot when I pulled out a large, surprisingly heavy white bag bearing the Stick People logo. Brigit took one sniff and sat, giving me the alert.

I pulled the bag open and peered inside.

What I saw made no sense to me a first. A bunch of metal utensils surrounding three metal tubes. The tubes were connected by wires to a digital kitchen timer giving off a *tick-tick-tick*. Two minutes and thirty-six seconds remained on the timer.

What the . . .

Holy shit!

A bomb!

My head instantly went light, as if all the oxygen had left my brain. I turned to the custodian, stunned and dazed. "It's a b-b-b-b-b—" *Shit!* I couldn't get the word out!

"A what?" he asked, looking down into the bag I held open.

My mouth finally cooperated with my brain: "A bomb!"

His eyes snapped wide. He turned and took off running.

Holycrap-holycrap-holycrap! I had to do something— *RIGHT NOW!*—or the families gathered in the food court would be injured or killed. I gingerly placed the bag on top of the trash in the garbage can and cupped my hands around my mouth. "Evacuate!" I hollered as loud as I could. "Everyone out now!"

A few people at the tables near me glanced over and tentatively stood, but anyone more than ten feet away couldn't hear me over the din of the carousel music and conversation.

I blew my whistle.

TWEEEEET!

"Everyone out of the courtyard!" I yelled at the top of my lungs. "Emergency!"

I was afraid to say the word "bomb" for fear of inciting a stampede. Someone might get trampled. Still, these people were slow to react, some still sitting, looking from me to their tablemates, trying to figure out what was going on, not wanting to be the first to react.

"For God's sake, move, people!"

I ran to the deli counter and grabbed the flexible mic from the hand of the kid announcing orders. "Everyone out now!" I shrieked into the mic, my voice coming loud through the overhead speaker. "There's a bomb in a trash can!"

Finally, people seemed to get the message and began to scramble for the doorways.

I ran up and down the food stands, shouting, "Get out! There's a bomb!"

An older man started to gather up his food.

"Leave it!" I screamed.

"But I paid seven dollars for this barbecue!"

"Is your life worth more than seven bucks?"

He looked up in thought and seemed to mull the question over.

Out of patience and running out of time, I swept his food off the table and onto the floor, where Brigit promptly helped herself to it. "Get the hell out of here!"

The carousel music continued behind me.

Oh, God! The children!

I turned and sprinted as fast I could toward the carousel, barking my shins on several chairs that had been pushed aside or turned over by people in their haste to evacuate. Oblivious, Randy sat on his stool, looking down at the screen of his cell phone.

"Randy!" I cried. "Stop the ride! There's a bomb in the food court!"

He looked up. "Did you say 'a bomb'?"

"Yes!"

"Holy shit!" He shoved his cell phone into the back pocket of his jeans, grabbed the key from his wrist bracelet, and jammed it into the control box, turning off the ride and the music. As the organ wound down and the carousel glided to a stop, the children on the ride turned their heads right and left, trying to figure out what was going on. The parents gathered around the ride glanced our way.

"Get your kids and go!" I screamed, waving both hands above my head in a go-away motion. "There's a bomb!"

With cries of alarm, parents leaped onto the carousel to retrieve their children from the horses and benches. Randy jumped onto the round platform to help a woman whose small son had become tangled in the safety belt.

Once everyone in the courtyard seemed to be exiting, I jumped on my walkie-talkie: "Security! There's a bomb in the courtyard! Get people as far away as possible!"

Mall management monitored our radio communications and in seconds Mr. Castleberry and two of his administrative staff came running out of the executive wing and dashed out the nearest doors.

In my terror and haste, I'd totally forgotten about Brigit. Luckily, she'd followed me even though I'd dropped her leash.

"Brigit!" I cried. "Come on, girl!" I ran to the doors, my arms pumping like pistons, my partner racing along next to me.

I had no idea how much time had elapsed.

Had it been two minutes and thirty-six seconds?

It felt like both an eternity and an instant.

I was ten feet from the door when the timer went off.

KABOOM-BOOM-BOOM!

TWENTY-THREE
HAZARDOUS DUTY

Brigit

Three loud *boom*s echoed through the courtyard, nearly bursting the poor dog's eardrums. Small, hard objects fell from the sky, landing all around her and painfully pelting her body. It was almost as bad as the time her first owner, the dipshit stoner, had left her outside in a hailstorm.

What the hell is going on?

TWENTY-FOUR
HAVING A BLAST

The Rattler

He ran down the mall walkway with dozens of other people as if competing in the fifty-yard dash in hell's field day. When the explosions sounded behind them, many screamed and cried out, terrified, as they streamed into the parking lot and rushed desperately to their cars. Lest he arouse suspicion, he ran along with them. He secretly savored each bomb blast, each shriek that met his ears, yet he knew today was only an appetizer, a simple hors d'oeuvre before the more complex, more filling meal to come.

Oh, how I love giving these people their just desserts.

TWENTY-FIVE
THIS JOB BLOWS

Megan

The explosions thundered though the glass dome, echoing off the walls and ceiling. Instinctively I dove to the ground, sliding forward and banging my head on the exit door. Following the initial blast was a cacophony of competing sounds.

CRASH! CLANK! POP! CLINK! TINKLE! WHOP! CRINKLE! SPLUCK!

All around me, metal projectiles, food wrappers, and leftover lunch scraps hit the doors, floor, and ceiling. It was as if I were inside some sort of nightmarish garbage disposal. Pieces hit my shoes, buttocks, back, and head. I wailed in terror.

A moment later, the cavernous empty space fell dead still and filled with an eerie silence broken only by my wheezing as I gasped for air with panicked lungs. I lay there for a moment, numb with shock, before mustering up the courage to push myself to my knees and take a look around.

The glass doors bore numerous web-like cracks and pockmarks. Nails, screws, and some type of hooks had lodged themselves in the door trim, walls, and ceiling. Those that had not sunk into the structure had fallen to the floor, littering it with shiny metal. A gooey piece of cheese pizza had struck the glass door and now slowly slid down it, leaving a greasy trail in its wake.

My vest had protected my back, but the rest of my body had been exposed. I reached around to the back of my head and pulled a pointy shish-kebab stick out of my thick hair bun. If not for the extra three inches of resistance the bun provided, the stick would've lodged in my skull. What an ungraceful death that would have been, hmm? One of my arms bore a smear of what appeared to be Thousand Island dressing, my leg a smudge of ketchup.

A soft whine to my left snapped me back to reality.
Brigit!

She lay flat on the floor, her ears back, her tail between her legs. I hadn't thought this dog was capable of fear, but she was definitely scared now. He entire body trembled.

"Brigit! Are you o-o-o—" Again, I couldn't get the word out, but it didn't matter. It's not like the dog was going to answer me, right?

I stood, slowly and gingerly, to the sound of more clinking and tinkling as shrapnel fell from my body to the floor. My partner stood, too. Using my hands, I brushed fish-hooks and screws and nails from her fur, picking out the more stubbornly tangled ones with my fingers. Thank God for her thick hair. Clearly it had provided her some protection from the projectiles.

I picked up her leash, shoved the damaged door open, and led her out onto the walkway. The fact that she could walk was a good sign, though she seemed to have a slight limp.

Outside, a hot breeze carried the far-off sound of sirens

approaching and the squeal of car tires as shoppers tried to put as much distance as possible between themselves and the mall. The empty choo-choo train sat at the far end of the row of stores where the conductor and passengers had abandoned it.

The Big Dick stalked around the end of the building and headed toward me, a bullhorn in his hand. He pushed the button and put the bullhorn to his lips as he stomped down the walkway. "Attention! Exit the mall immediately. This is a mandatory evacuation."

A few shoppers who'd cowered in the stores after the explosion dashed out the doors and headed down the sidewalk at a run.

Serhan and Aruni emerged from a shoe store, a crying Kara clutched between them, her pretty brown eyes wet with tears. The couple ran awkwardly down the walkway, using their bodies to shield their child in the event another explosion occurred. My heart went out to them.

Down the row, Ariana Brackenburg stepped out of her store and turned to lock up, her Chanel bag hanging from her shoulder. She tucked her keys into her purse and made her way down the sidewalk. Though her pace was brisk, she didn't run. Of course running might be impossible in those pointy-toed spike heels of hers.

Without a word to me, Derek turned and headed back down the row, repeating his order to evacuate the mall.

The initial shock now over, Brigit and I scurried down the pavement, hurrying shoppers along. I motioned in the direction of the parking lot. "Move, people! Go!"

A woman emerged from the Gymboree store with a look of absolute horror on her face and a child's hand in each of hers. The kids were too small to run fast. I scooped up one of the kids, she picked up the other, and we ran to the parking lot.

The demonstrators fled to the other side of the street, the man in the hiking boots and bike shorts leading the way. The woman in the bikini now bore sunburned butt cheeks. Must've forgotten the sunscreen. The group stopped in the parking lot of a gas station, reassembling to watch the activity at the mall.

Lines of vehicles streamed from the exits, among them Irving's PT Cruiser, Randy's pink Cadillac, Ariana's Infiniti, and an orange-and-white U-Haul truck. The mall's security team and my fellow officers made no attempt to stop them. Another bomb could explode any second. There was no way of knowing if the person responsible had planted more than the one device. Of course one of the cars might be carrying the bomber to his escape, but what could we do? We couldn't put innocent lives at risk. We'd have to wait until later to determine who planted the bomb, to bring the evildoer to justice.

Once I'd carried the child to the woman's car and assured myself the mall walkway was clear, I knelt down and gently ran my hands over Brigit again, performing a more thorough search for shrapnel among her fur. "It's all right, girl," I said, as much to soothe myself as her. "It's going to be all right."

Too bad I didn't believe my own words.

Until the bomber was captured nothing would be right.

My fingers hit something hard on Brigit's hindquarters and she emitted another whine. I separated her fur to find a short, thick nail lodged in her hip.

An ambulance pulled into the parking lot and stopped at the far edge. A fire truck from the neighborhood station followed, also stopping at the edge of the lot. Fortunately, while the pipe bomb had wreaked untold destruction inside the courtyard, it hadn't caused a fire.

The Big Dick radioed the other officers on-site to check

on casualties. There were a number of scraped knees from people falling in their rush to their cars but no one who needed medical attention.

As I led Brigit across the asphalt to the ambulance, a blue muscle car with orange flames painted down the sides pulled up to the officer at the entrance to the lot. The driver unrolled his window to speak to the cop.

Seth.

I'd wanted to see the guy again, but not like this. Not when I was covered in barbecue sauce and ranch dressing and totally freaked out.

I stepped up to the back bay of the ambulance where a male paramedic with a handheld radio waited for further instructions from someone in charge.

"My dog has a n-nail in her hip," I said. "C-can you help her?"

The paramedic glanced down at Brigit. "Does she bite?"

"Only on command," I assured him. "I'll hold her still."

In my peripheral vision, I saw Seth pull his ancient Chevy Nova into a spot thirty feet away. His license plate read: "KABOOM." If not for the circumstances, I might've found it amusing.

I wrapped my arms around Brigit's neck while the paramedic shaved a small square of her fur, applied a topical anesthetic to her skin, and eased the nail out of her muscle. She whined softly and squirmed a little, but once the nail had been extracted she licked the man's hand and wagged her tail in appreciation.

"Good girl." My brown eyes met hers and, for the first time since I'd been partnered with the beast, it felt as if we'd reached some kind of understanding. For better or worse, the two of us were in this together. It was time we stopped trying to get one up on each other and started looking out for each other instead.

After Seth climbed out of his car, his yellow Lab jumped

out, too, and trotted over. Blast and Brigit reacquainted themselves with a fresh round of sniffing, this time going for butts rather than snouts. So romantic.

Seth walked up and tilted his head, conspicuously eyeing my butt. He was as bad as his dog.

I shot him a pointed look. "Didn't your mother tell you not to ogle women?"

He made no apologies, just offered a cocky smile. "You've been screwed in the ass."

A glance over my shoulder confirmed a gold screw lodged in my right butt cheek. With all of the adrenaline flowing through me, the injury hadn't yet registered with my brain. I offered Seth a coy shrug in return. "There's a first time for everything."

The paramedic quickly tended to me, using a sharp pair of scissors to cut a small circular hole through my uniform pants and undies, applying the same topical numbing agent he'd used on Brigit and easing the screw out of my gluteus maximus. The experience gave new meaning to the term "buns of steel."

"Keep an eye on the wound," the EMT advised. "Any oozing or signs of redness and get to your doctor for an antibiotic."

"Thanks." I stepped away from the back of the ambulance.

"You need any help," Seth said, a mischievous glint in his green eyes, "I'd be happy to keep an eye on things back there."

Outwardly, I rolled my eyes. Inwardly, I was flattered.

"Um . . . that ain't right." The tech gestured to the dogs behind us.

We turned to find Brigit on Blast's back, holding him in a vise-like grip between her front legs as she humped his hindquarters. Seth's poor dog's face bore a humiliated expression.

Seth raised a brow. "Your dog's a slut."

"And yours is a candy ass."

"Touché."

I grabbed Brigit's collar and pulled her off Blast. He tossed me a grateful look and planted his ass firmly on the ground, where it would be unhumpable.

"So." Seth stood up straighter, all business now. "The screw in your ass tells me you were near the explosion. What can you tell me about the bomb?"

"It was a pipe bomb. Three sections of metal pipe attached to a kitchen timer. The bomb was inside a take-out bag from the Stick People stand. The bag had been placed in a garbage can in the food court. There were other metal things in the bag, too."

He raised a brow. "You saw the bomb before it went off?"

"My dog alerted on it."

"You're lucky it didn't go off in your face." Seth glanced down at Brigit. "Is she trained to detect explosives?"

"No. I figured she'd alerted on drugs, but I didn't see any in the bag."

"Anything else you can tell me?"

I shook my head.

Not far from where we stood, three news vans pulled up to the curb. Bad news travels fast, doesn't it? The stations probably had an intern monitoring the police scanners for potential breaking news stories.

The crews pulled their vans onto the grassy right-of-way to avoid blocking the street traffic and descended from their vehicles.

Mackey kept the reporters at bay: "The chief is on his way. He'll have a statement for you as soon as possible."

So Mackey had been in touch with the chief, hmm? I supposed that shouldn't surprise me.

A white SUV bearing the fire department logo was allowed through the entrance. The driver zipped the vehicle into the spot next to Seth's Nova, taking his attention from me. Two men climbed out of the car, leaving the windows down for a black Lab who stuck his head out and barked in greeting to Blast: *Bow-wow!*

The men might have been the other bomb techs who'd been in the police chief's office the first time I saw Seth, but I couldn't say for sure. I'd been too distracted by Seth and my looming ass chewing to pay much attention.

Seth stepped over to his coworkers and filled them in. While the other two men were taller than Seth and therefore looked down at him, it was clear that, metaphorically speaking, they looked up to him. Both listened intently to his instructions, asking questions in hushed tones, acknowledging the plan with a nod.

When Seth finished, he gave the others a congenial fist bump. "Time to suit up, boys."

Seth returned to his car and opened the driver's side door. He sat down for a moment, leaving the door open. He slid a CD into the car's stereo and cranked up the volume. Seconds later, the strains of AC/DC's classic "Big Balls" filled the air around us.

The three men sang along to the suggestive lyrics, expounding musically in obvious double entendres about the size and bounciness of their balls as they pulled their special explosion-resistant suits from their cars and slid into them. Made of thick and heavy padded material, the suits were not entirely unlike the K-9 bite suits. However, the bomb tech suit contained a reinforced panel along the front and back of the torso, as well as a clear helmet to protect their faces.

As I watched the men suit up, I wondered what compelled them to take on such a dangerous job.

Were they thrill seekers?

Wannabe heroes?

Just plain crazy?

I suppose it was hypocritical of me to have such thoughts. After all, people could wonder the same thing of police officers. Our reasons for wearing the badge were as different and unique as each of us.

When all three men were fully dressed they looked like astronauts about to step out onto the moon.

As they walked past with their dogs, Seth turned his head my way, his voice muffled through the helmet. He pointed a gloved finger at me. "If I'm still alive after we check the building," he joked, "I'm taking you out for a margarita."

"And if you're not alive?" I asked, unsure whether or not I was joking.

He offered me a soft smile. "Then you'll always wonder what might have been."

There was nothing I could do at the moment but sit on the open hatch of the ambulance to wait for instructions, information, and the aforementioned margarita or lifetime of wondering. I was hoping for the margarita. I twirled my baton in an attempt to combat my worries, using a basic thumb toss to send it into the air before catching it again.

"You're pretty good with that thing." The EMT who'd treated me and Brigit sat down next to me and pulled up a movie on his tablet, some raunchy made-for-men comedy starring Seth Rogen. The other EMT lay down on the collapsed gurney behind us and took a nap.

A half hour and approximately five thousand baton twirls later, Chief Garelik arrived on the scene. He was dressed in pressed cotton shorts, a polo shirt, and brown leather boat shoes, no socks. The civilian clothes were a sure sign he'd come to the mall straight from an outing and hadn't run home to change into his uniform. Given the urgency, who could blame him?

The chief held up a back-off palm to the gaggle of reporters and made his way over to Mackey, who stood with a cluster of male officers in the shade of a tree near the makeshift command center. Mr. Castleberry stood a few feet away with Scott, Ricky, and a third member of the security team.

The Big Dick had assumed command of the situation the instant he'd stepped foot on the mall property. I supposed I could be offended by that. I mean, I was the one who'd been on-site, who'd seen the bomb before it exploded, who'd ordered the initial evacuation of the courtyard and been bombarded with metal and garbage. Still, I was in no condition to take charge. I was barely keeping myself together. Besides, Derek did outrank me.

After they'd spoken for a few minutes, Derek pointed my way. The chief glanced over at me, gave the Big Dick a pat on the shoulder, and headed my way.

I stood as the chief approached. Returning my baton to my belt, I did my best to look fearless. Not easy when all I really wanted to do was curl up in a fetal position and suck my thumb.

"This is a fine mess, Officer Luz," he barked, as if the bombing were my fault.

What was I supposed to say in response? I wasn't sure, so I said nothing.

He put a hand on the back of his neck. "Mackey says you were here when the bomb went off."

I nodded.

"Her dog got hit with a nail," the EMT added from his spot next to me, his words punctuated by the movie's laugh track coming from the tablet's speakers. He lifted his chin to indicate me. "She got a screw in her ass." He reached over, plucked the screw and nail from a small plastic bowl, and held them out.

Chief Garelik's upper lip curled back in disgust. "No, thanks."

I took the screw and nail from the EMT's fingers and slipped them into my pocket. Might as well keep them as a memento, right? Maybe one day I'd visit an elementary school with Brigit, present the nail and screw at show-and-tell.

The chief asked me some questions and I told him everything I knew. When I finished, he looked past me and waved someone over. A moment later, a fortyish black woman with short, perky braids walked up, her strides wide and confident. Like the chief, she was dressed in civilian clothes, though she had a police-issue gun holstered at the waist of her khakis.

"Detective Jackson," Chief Garelik said, addressing the woman, "this is Megan Luz. She was here at the mall when the bomb exploded."

I shook the woman's hand.

"It's hotter'n hell out here," she said. "Let's talk in my car."

She gestured for me to follow her to her vehicle, which was a plain white unmarked police cruiser. I led Brigit over and we climbed inside, the detective and me in the front, Brigit in the back. Detective Jackson turned on the engine and cranked up the AC.

She pulled a pen and small notepad out of her breast pocket and turned to me. "Got some questions for you." She asked first about the bomb itself: "Describe it for me."

I repeated the information I'd told Seth. "Three metal pipes attached to a kitchen timer. It was inside a bag from Stick People."

"Stick People? What's that?"

"The shish-kebab stand in the food court."

She made notes on her pad. "You know the staff there?"

"Some of them," I said. "Most are high school or college kids. The owner's name is Serhan Singh. He's at the stand most days during lunch, but today he and his wife were in the shoe store shopping for their daughter. She starts kindergarten soon."

"Serhan Singh," she repeated. "He's foreign?"

"Yes. He's from Turkey. He came here to attend school at UT Arlington years ago. He met his wife in c-college and decided to stay."

"She Turkish, too?"

"Indian," I said. "I'm not sure if she was born in the U.S., but she was raised here."

"Anything unusual about them?"

I shook my head.

Jackson eyed me intently. "Given that the bomb was in a bag bearing Singh's logo, he might be the one who planted it."

As much as I didn't want to believe it, she could be right. Nobody would think twice if they saw him carrying a bag from his own food stand. Still, it felt as if we were barking up the wrong tree.

"He just doesn't seem like the type," I said. "He's assimilated well. He's a huge Cowboys fan." The Dallas Cowboys were *America's Team*, after all. It just didn't seem like an ardent fan could do something so awful to his fellow Americans. "He's always been very friendly to me."

"Maybe *too* friendly?" she asked, her lip quirking in question.

I couldn't deny it. "Maybe."

Were my warm feelings toward Serhan misguided? After all, the fellow members of Dzhokhar Tsarnaev's high school wrestling team had thought he was a good guy until he was arrested for his part in the Boston Marathon bombings. People were routinely shocked to learn that their nice-guy neighbors were murders, rapists, or pedophiles. Appearances and behavior could be deceptive and misleading.

She tapped her pen on the pad. "How deep was the bag in the can?"

"Only a foot or so," I said.

"So whoever put the bag in the can must have done so fairly soon before the bomb exploded."

I nodded. "The food court was very busy today. The cans filled up fast."

Detective Jackson proceeded to lead me back through the events preceding the explosion. Had there been any unusual activity in the food court today or in the recent past? Had I seen anyone suspicious? Did I know of anyone who might have a reason to target the mall?

"Maybe a former employee who'd been fired?" she suggested. "A pissed-off customer? A tenant who has a beef with management?"

I racked my brain, but the only people who came to mind immediately were the skateboarders and the women who owned the wine store. Other than that, things had been business as usual at the mall. "There were a couple adolescent boys skateboarding here yesterday," I told her. "I made them get off their boards."

"They seem dangerous?"

"Not especially," I said, but what did I know? A sadistic criminal had slipped a bag of explosives into a garbage can not fifteen feet from me and I didn't even notice. Not exactly the kind of attention to detail a wannabe detective should possess. Then again, I had been on my lunch break. Nobody can be on 24/7, right? "They were back here this morning. They set off some fireworks in the parking lot."

The detective arched an interested brow. "Sometimes fireworks are used in bombs. They're a cheap and easy-to-obtain source of gunpowder."

Maybe I'd underestimated the risk the boys posed.

She cocked her head. "Did you see any fireworks in the bag with the bomb?"

"No. Just the pipes and the timer and what looked like utensils or scrap metal."

"Any idea who the boys are?"

I shook my head.

"Anyone else who might have a motive?"

"The two women who own the wine shop have been struggling financially," I continued, noting the conversation I'd overhead between them and the mall manager a while back. "They asked to be let out of their lease, but he refused."

The detective jotted another note.

I glanced across the street. The demonstrators had left the gas station and were nowhere to be seen.

"There were antifur protestors here earlier," I added, though it was doubtful a group advocating compassion and the sanctity of life would do something so violent and potentially deadly. Despite the revealing bikini, the too-short bike shorts, and the saggy sunburned butt cheeks, the group hadn't seemed extreme. Besides, I hadn't noticed any of the protestors in the food court. Still, the group might have a rogue member who'd taken things too far. At this point, we couldn't rule out any possibilities.

"You know who the protestors were?" Jackson asked.

"No." Since their group was small, no city permit would have been required for the gathering, so there would be no official documentation of the participants, either.

"What did they look like?"

The only ones I could remember in any detail were the curly-haired blonde wearing the red bikini and bright-orange sneakers and the gray-haired, bearded guy in the tiny bike shorts and hiking boots. I described them to Jackson.

She made some notes on her pad. "Sounds like a freak show."

"It drew attention to their cause." I shrugged. "Honestly, they seemed harmless. I spoke with them briefly and they were polite and nonconfrontational."

"Old hippies?"

"Exactly."

She seemed to weigh my assessment for a moment before moving on. "What about after the explosion? Anything unusual happen during the evacuation?"

"I saw a U-Haul pull out of the lot. I know rental trucks have been used in bombings before, so it caught my attention."

"Did you get the license plate?"

"No. It was too far away."

She made a note on her pad. "I'll check the outside security cameras, see if the feeds picked it up."

I told her that Ariana Brackenburg had seemed relatively nonplussed and nonchalant. Then again, the woman dealt in death. Maybe a bomb was nothing to someone who sold electrocuted and skinned rabbits for a living.

Jackson made another note. "Any heroes?"

"What do you mean?"

She circled her pen in the air. "Anyone acting unusually brave? Helping out?"

I thought back. "The guy who runs the carousel pulled a kid or two from the horses, but he didn't stick around long." The only ones who hadn't hightailed it out of the courtyard as quickly as possible were me and Brigit.

The detective glanced out the window at Seth's Nova, her eyes taking in the flames painted on the sides, the "KABOOM" license plate. "How quickly did the first responders arrive?"

I thought back. "Ten minutes or so for most of them, but Officer Mackey was here just a m-minute or two after the bomb went off. I ran into him on the mall's southwest walkway when I left the courtyard."

"Is he assigned to this division?"

"Yes." *Unfortunately.*

"So he wouldn't have been too far away, presumably." She glanced over at him, her eyes raking him up and down as if trying to scratch below the surface and see what lay underneath. "How much time would you say elapsed between when you first began evacuating the food court and when you saw Mackey on the walk?"

I mentally calculated. "Four minutes," I said. "Maybe five."

She looked up in thought. "I suppose he could've made it here that quickly. Calls came in to Dispatch before the bomb even went off."

Shoppers must have dialed 911 from their cell phones as they fled the food court.

She turned her focus back to me. "What about the other first responders?"

"The first bomb tech to arrive was the guy who drives the N-Nova. His name's Seth Rutledge. He got here right after the ambulance and fire truck."

"He came in his own car?"

I nodded.

She tapped her pen against her lips before speaking again. "He must have been close by, too. Did he mention where he'd been before the bombing?"

When I shook my head she made another note.

After I'd told her all I could, she turned off the AC and

cut the engine. "Let's have a chat with the mall manager and the security team."

As we climbed out of the car, she glanced into the backseat. The upholstery and floor mats were coated in Brigit's long black fur. "Lord," the detective said. "I'll have to get this thing vacuumed."

We went over to Mr. Castleberry and the security guards. Detective Jackson asked them many of the same questions she'd asked me. Unfortunately, they had even less information to offer than I had. None of them were aware of any disgruntled employees, angry shoppers with an axe to grind, or unhappy tenants other than the owners of the wine shop. None had noticed anything unusual at the mall this morning. Not surprising, really. Ricky and Scott had probably spent the morning in front of the televisions at Macy's again.

"As soon as the bomb techs are done," Jackson directed the manager, "pull the security tapes. I want to see all of them." She looked over the notes she'd made, slid the notepad back into her pocket, and handed business cards to the men. "If you think of anything else, give me a call."

As we waited outside the mall, my cell phone vibrated with an incoming text. I checked the screen. It was from my little sister, Gabrielle.

Heard about bomb at mall. U ok?

I texted her back: *I'm fine.* A blatant lie if ever there was one. But I had to keep myself together. No way would I let the Big Dick or the chief see me cry.

Two long hours later, Seth and the other bomb techs emerged from the mall. No more bombs had exploded, and from the fact that the men had removed their helmets it appeared the bomb detection dogs had uncovered no further explosives.

The men made their way back to their vehicles. After removing and stowing their protective gear, they pulled out white gym towels to freshen up. Judging from the sweat stains on their T-shirts, their suits must've been extremely hot.

When Seth pulled his T-shirt off over his head my lungs released an instinctive, primal rush of air in response: *Huhhhhh.*

Seth's back was broad and muscular, with a tattoo of an eagle spread across it, the wings spreading over his shoulder blades. The eagle clutched the traditional olive branch in one talon, a bunch of arrows in the other, symbolizing the eternal irony that to have peace you sometimes had to fight for it. Maybe one day humans would learn to get along, to coexist, and the eagle could trade in the olive branch and arrows for a TV remote and a caramel macchiato. One must retain hope, right?

My eyes moved down to Seth's lower back. My God, it looked as if someone had used the guy as a piñata. A number of haphazard scars crisscrossed his skin. Some of the scars were thin, short, and faint, while others were wider, longer, darker, and deeper.

What had caused his scars? Could it have been a bomb?

I watched, but pretended not to, as Seth ran the towel over his shoulders and chest. I was tempted to offer to help with those hard-to-reach places on his back, but as hot as he'd made me already, I feared touching him would cause me to self-combust. At least there was a fire truck on-site for that eventuality. They could hose me down.

Dressed in fresh tees now, the bomb squad made its way over to Chief Garelik, Detective Jackson, and the Big Dick for a quick powwow.

When the group broke, Derek came over and informed the waiting firemen and EMTs they were free to leave.

I bade good-bye to the tech who'd tended to me and Brigit. "Thanks."

Detective Jackson waved me over. "The lead bomb tech and I are going inside with the crime scene techs to take a look around. We want you to come with us."

TWENTY-SIX
DOGGIE BAGGIN'

Brigit

Megan and Seth led their K-9 partners into the enclosed courtyard, found an out-of-the-way spot, and ordered the dogs to stay. Given the abundance of food scraps within belly-crawling distance, Brigit was more than happy to comply.

Blast stayed put as ordered, but the second Megan turned her back Brigit slunk forward and snatched the remains of a chopped-beef sandwich from the floor. She returned to her designated spot and wolfed down all but the last bite. She dropped the final piece to the floor and nudged it toward Blast. No need to be stingy. Besides, the yellow Lab was kind of cute. She'd always had a thing for beta males.

TWENTY-SEVEN
IF AT FIRST YOU DON'T SUCCEED . . .

The Rattler

Through a window of a pizza place across the street he watched the first responders mill about the mall parking lot. The beer he nursed did nothing to tamp down the rage roiling inside him.

Things had not gone according to plan.

The only ones hurt had been that stupid female cop and her dumb hairy dog, and from what he could tell their injuries had been minor. The EMT had slapped Band-Aids on them and sent them on their way.

But as they say, the second time's the charm. . . .

TWENTY-EIGHT

SOMETHING FISHY
IS GOING ON

Megan

Once Seth and I got our dogs settled in a quiet place in the courtyard, Jackson handed us blue paper booties to put over our shoes. "Stick close to me," she advised. "Don't touch anything without talking to me or one of the crime scene technicians first. We don't want to contaminate the evidence."

A half-dozen crime scene techs milled about. Three made their way around the space taking photographs, while the others trailed after them, picking up the shrapnel with tongs and placing it in large plastic evidence bags.

I followed the detective and Seth around the courtyard as they examined the evidence. As we neared the epicenter, I pointed to the trash can, which now lay on its side. The thick plastic remained surprisingly intact.

Jackson motioned to the lid, which rested on the floor nearby. "Looks like the blast blew the lid off."

"No," I said. "When Brigit alerted on the can, I took the lid off to search it."

It dawned on me that if I'd put the lid back on the can it might have suppressed the blast and prevented it from wreaking such widespread damage. I'd unintentionally assisted the bomber in his evil deeds. *Dammit!* I was tempted to whip out my baton and hit myself in the head. It was my own fault I'd been screwed in the ass, my fault Brigit got a nail in her hip. She would definitely get some extra treats later.

Seth knelt down to examine a section of floor littered with metal and small shards of thin glass.

Detective Jackson knelt down next to him. "What do you think?"

"There's the usual nails and BBs and screws," Seth said, pointing, "but there's quite a bit of glass, too."

Jackson leaned in for a closer look, then looked up and around, her eyes taking in the sconces on the nearby pole. All of the oversized bulbs inside had been busted, a few pointy shards remaining attached to the base and sticking out of the sockets. "Looks like this glass is from broken lightbulbs."

Irving.

"One of the maintenance guys replaced those bulbs just before the bomb went off," I said, remembering back to yesterday when he'd been fixing the door outside. His toolbox had been filled with assorted screws and nails. But that was to be expected, wasn't it?

Still crouching, the detective pulled her pad and pen back out of her pocket. "What's the guy's name?"

"His first name's Irving," I said. "I d-don't know his last name."

"I'll get it from the mall manager," Jackson said, scribbling a note.

Seth pointed at some metal pieces a little farther away, "Are those fishhooks?"

Jackson took a look. "Yup."

Did the hooks mean something? I bent down now, too. "Think the fishhooks could be a signature of sorts? Or maybe intended to send a message?"

The detective lifted a shoulder noncommittally. "Could be. Course it could just mean the bomber was being creative. Or that fishhooks were easily accessible to him. Or that they're cheap."

I noticed the detective had used the word "him." True, most violent criminals were men, but a female suspect couldn't be ruled out, right? Then again, if a woman had planted this bomb, it would've been filled with tweezers and nail scissors and safety pins. Way for me to engage in sexual stereotypes, eh?

The detective cut an intent look at me and Seth. "These fishhooks," she said. "Keep that information to yourselves, okay? Along with anything else we might find."

We both indicated our agreement to keep mum.

"There's a pet store in the mall," I told Jackson. "They sell fish. They've got a big aquarium in the front window."

She said nothing, though her lips pursed and she made a note on her pad. She lifted a chin to indicate the food court. "There's a sushi stand over there, too. They serve fish."

Another possible connection, though I considered it unlikely. No pun intended, but nobody at the sushi stand had struck me as fishy.

When the detective stood and continued on, Seth and I followed her, side by side, carefully looking over the assorted shrapnel littering the floor. Thumbtacks. Straight pins. Sewing needles.

Jackson stopped and knelt again, examining the mess more closely. "Is there a sewing shop in the mall? Some kind of craft store?"

"No," I said, "but the bridal shop employs a full-time tailor. He's an older guy named Vu."

"Vietnamese?"

"I think so."

Jackson stood, jotted another note on her pad, and stepped forward again.

"You wouldn't believe the weird stuff people put in bombs," Seth said. "When I was in Afghanistan we dismantled one that was filled with old car parts. Spark plugs, engine bolts, even rusty wiper blades. They'll use whatever they can get their hands on."

"You served in Afghanistan?" I asked.

"Spent eight years in the Army as an explosive ordnance disposal specialist."

Most people try to avoid bombs. I couldn't even imagine what it must have been like to go out looking for them, to know each mission could be the last. His job had been one of the riskiest in the Army. The news was filled with reports of troops maimed or killed by improvised explosive devices. Had Seth lost others from his platoon? Friends?

Seth's eyes grew dark as he glanced my way. "Operation Enduring Freedom. What a name for a war, huh?" He chuckled without mirth. "How the hell can freedom 'endure' in a place where there was no freedom to begin with? Someone want to explain that to me?"

Our eyes locked and I found myself wishing I had answers to give him. He looked like he could use some. Clearly those scars on his back weren't the only scars he suffered.

As if realizing he'd said too much, Seth shifted his focus back to the floor in front of us. Detective Jackson eyed him with an assessing glance before turning her attention to a trio of nails lodged in a table.

I tried to think of something appropriate to say in response to Seth but could only come up with, "Thanks for your service."

"It's not over yet," he said. "I'm still in the reserves."

That explained the short haircut.

When he walked on, I went with him, feeling much too aware of him, of his proximity, of the conflicted soul trapped inside that undeniably delectable body. No doubt this bomb brought back bad memories for Seth. But this was not the time or place to analyze him. I needed to focus on the task at hand—looking for clues that might tell us who the bomber was.

My eyes scanned the room, searching for something that might trip a latent recollection. I wished I could replay the morning in my mind, check my mental footage for an important detail I might have missed. Maybe I could go under hypnosis and see if that helped. I'd heard the process could release repressed memories.

As we traversed the room, we found four mangled fondue forks on the floor, a unicorn-shaped corkscrew impaled in the front flank of a blue carousel horse, a barbecue spatula with a serrated edge on one side, and a pointy meat thermometer lodged in the dirt of a potted plant, the clear plastic cover over its face shattered.

An hour later I followed Seth and the detective out of the mall, more disturbed, more anxious, and more in awe of Seth, but none the wiser.

When we reached the detective's car, she handed both of us a business card. "Call me if you come up with something." With that, she climbed in and drove off.

Seth and I continued over to where the chief was speaking to members of the media, giving them select details about the day's events.

In front of the pack stood Trish LeGrande, a pushy, big-busted reporter from one of the Dallas stations. Trish had a unique shade of blond hair akin to butterscotch pudding and owned a predominately pink wardrobe. Today she wore a sleeveless pink ruffled dress that would be more appropriate for a cotillion dance than a field report. She used to do the upbeat feel-good filler segments on slow news days, reporting on a neighborhood beautification project, a boat show at the convention center, or the latest fried-food craze at the state fair: *You gotta try these delicious fried cactus bites! Yummy!* She'd recently been promoted to a field reporter position. I wondered who she'd slept with to land the promotion.

The chief looked into the closest camera. "I'm very proud of the way my officers handled this crisis." He put a hand on the Big Dick's shoulder. "Officer Derek Mackey here was one of the first responders. He risked his life to evacuate the building. That's the kind of exemplary behavior the citizens of Fort Worth can expect from their police force."

Uh . . . *hello*?!?

All Mackey had done was holler through a bullhorn. Brigit had found the bomb; then she and I had raced a ticking clock to make sure everyone got out of the courtyard. She'd suffered a nail in the hip and I'd taken a screw in the ass for the city's citizens. Where were our accolades? Reflexively my hand went to my baton and ripped it from my belt. A flick of my wrist and the baton extended. *SNAP!*

At the sound, everyone's heads turned toward me.

Uh-oh.

I looked down and used my baton to knock nonexistent dirt off my shoe.

Next to me, Seth chuckled, this time *with* mirth. Under his breath he said, "I saw that."

"Hush," I whispered, cutting my eyes to indicate my stick, "or you'll be next."

"That's okay," he replied with a grin. "I think I'd like it."

Trish called out to me. "Were you one of the first responders, too?"

Normally, the police department designated one of the public-relations experts to handle press conferences lest an officer inadvertently let a secret detail slip. I had to be careful with my words. As the cameraman stepped into place to film me, I glanced over at the chief.

He answered for me: "Officer Luz was having lunch in the courtyard when the bomb exploded. Due to the serious nature of this crime and the ongoing investigation, she will not be able to engage the press."

Undaunted, Trish turned back to me and leaned to her left, eyeing the right side of my head. "Surely you can at least tell me what's in your hair?"

My hair?

I put my hand up to my temple to discover a squishy, greasy glob stuck to my locks. I pulled the goo from my head and held it up in front of my face. The smell was unmistakable. "It's tuna salad."

Blurgh.

Brigit leaped up and licked the remaining fishy, mayonnaise-drenched blob from the side of my head. Derek and the reporters broke out in laughs.

"Hahaha!"

"Did you see that?"

"What a riot!"

Boy, did this day suck.

I turned to Seth for support only to find him fighting a laugh, too. The man must have a death wish.

I shot him a glare. "You promised me a margarita. Time to pay the piper."

TWENTY-NINE
AN UNEXPECTED TREAT

Brigit

Fish! Yum!

THIRTY
BREAKING NEWS

The Rattler

His pizza and beer now processing through his intestines, the Rattler decided it was time to go. No sense hanging around the restaurant too long and raising suspicions. Besides, it was nearly five o'clock and he was eager to see Trish LeGrande's early news report on the bombing. For the first time ever, he'd actually listen to what the woman had to say rather than just staring at her tits.

THIRTY-ONE
FROZEN, WITH SALT

Megan

Seth typed my address into his phone's GPS.

"When you see a crappy blue apartment complex," I told him, "you'll know you've arrived."

He slid his phone back into his pocket. "Is six o'clock good?"

I glanced at my watch. "Sure." I had just over an hour to freshen up before our . . . *date*?

It was a date, wasn't it? Or was it merely a friendly invitation for a drink from one public servant to another? Time would tell, I suppose.

When I left my cruiser in the parking lot at the W1 station, fifteen minutes remained on my shift. Cutting out early constituted dereliction of duty, but screw it. The chief and the citizens of Fort Worth would just have to deal. I'd more than earned my pay today already. I did, however, take advantage of the extra time to deliver a solid *whack* with my baton to Derek's rubber testicles.

On my way home, I pulled into the drive-thru at the

dry cleaner's and wriggled out of my uniform. A moment later, the owner's adolescent son came to the window. Just my luck. Thank goodness my Kevlar vest covered my chest.

I slunk down in my seat as the skinny Asian kid looked down into my car. He eyed my Kevlar vest before his gaze moved down to my panties. The pair read: "PINK" across my pubic bone as if describing their intimate contents.

I shoved my pants and shirt at him. "Here."

The boy took them from me and looked them over. "What's all this?" he asked, gesturing to the stains.

"Ketchup," I told him. "Mustard. Barbecue sauce. Tuna." My clothes bore a few greasy French fry stains, too, though God only knew what the green goop was. Guacamole from the taco stand, wasabi from the sushi counter, or green goddess salad dressing from the deli. Take your pick.

The kid handed me a claim ticket and gave me their standard not-all-stains-can-be-removed spiel. "We'll do our best. No guarantees."

That's really all anyone can ask for, right?

"Can you patch the hole in the pants, too?" I asked.

He separated the pants from the shirt and took a quick look. "Mom!" he called back over his shoulder. A woman appeared at the window a moment later. The boy said something to her in Cantonese and stuck his finger through the hole the EMT had cut in my pants.

The woman replied in her native tongue to the boy, then turned to me. "We can do. Ten dollar more. Okay?"

"Great. Thanks."

When I pulled into my apartment complex a few minutes later, Rhino was sitting in his usual spot on the side of the pool. Ditto for my elderly neighbor on the stairs. Neither batted an eye as I made my way up the stairs in my black socks, loafers, hole-in-the-back panties, and Kevlar vest. I should probably consider moving.

Once inside my apartment, I poured a full cup of lavender-scented bubble bath into my tub and turned on the hot water. A warm bath would relax me. Of course the water that came out of the hot tap in this place was barely tepid and would cool off in seconds. To supplement the meager hot-water supply, I pulled my only two pots out of the cabinet, filled them with water, and set them on the stove to boil.

I turned on the news as I eased myself out of my ballistic vest. There was Trish in her pink ruffled dress and butterscotch hair, expounding on what few details the chief had revealed about the bomb. It's not like we knew much at this point, but she managed to take up two full minutes providing virtually no hard facts. The woman sure could hog the airtime.

Near the end of the segment, my face popped up on the screen. The voice-over noted that the explosion had caused no serious injuries and had merely spewed garbage throughout the mall courtyard. One unnamed officer—*me*—had been bombarded. Trish could be heard asking what was in my hair.

On the TV screen, my hand went to my head and removed the glop. "It's tuna salad."

Laughter erupted in the background as Brigit jumped up and licked the side of my head.

Oh, God.

I clicked the television off, logged on to my laptop, and pulled up YouTube, searching with the key words "cop," "dog," and "tuna."

Sure enough, the site featured a teaser snippet of me and Brigit that had been played on television an hour ago. The video, which was captioned "Tunabomber," had already gone viral: 89,347 hits, with only three thumbs-down.

I glanced down at Brigit. "We're Internet stars."

She cocked her head and gave a tentative wag of her tail as if to say, *That's all well and good, but where are my treats?*

As I logged off my computer, fresh fury welled up in me. I'd been scared to death this afternoon, afraid for my life, afraid for the lives of the people I'd sworn to protect, yet the news agencies and Internet surfers saw the incident as nothing more than a petty crime, a harmless prank, a joke.

I wasn't a hero.

I was a *clown*.

I just might need a whole pitcher of margaritas.

I stripped off what few articles of clothing remained on my body, retrieved the pots of boiling water, and dumped them into my tub. The tears I'd fought back all afternoon welled in my eyes as I lowered myself into the bubbles. When I'd settled in, my body began to shake, causing the water to quiver and slosh.

Brigit stepped into the doorway and looked at me, emitting a soft whine. When a tear broke free and rolled down my face, she came over and licked it off my cheek with her warm, wet tongue. The gesture was surprisingly sweet and tender, and her concern pushed me over the emotional edge into an all-out sob.

Hank was right. This damn dog has become my best friend.

When Brigit put a paw over the side of the tub I pushed it back. "I'll b-b-be okay, Brig," I spluttered between sobs. BFFs or not, the last thing I needed was a hundred-pound dog in the tub with me. Unfortunately, Brigit thought a dog in my bath was the *first* thing I needed. She leaped in on top of me, sending up a splash that showered the floor and walls with water and suds.

"No!" I tried to push her out, but it was no use. She

crouched down in the suds and became deadweight, impossible to lift. She continued to lick my face as I cried. A moment later I was no longer trying to force her out of the tub but clinging to her for dear life, sobbing into her fur.

When I was all cried out, I sat up, catching a glimpse of my reflection in the full-length mirror hanging on my bathroom door. *Whoa!* My face was coated in fur. I looked like Chewbacca.

Lovely.

When I stood, Brigit hopped out of the tub, dripping water all over the floor before shaking herself. While I pulled the drain plug, she trotted out the door, leaving a wet trail behind her. I heard the unmistakable *thud* of her still-damp body landing on my futon. Great. My bed would be soaked tonight.

I turned on the shower, washing my hair and rinsing it with the lukewarm water, kicking my feet in the standing water to remove Brigit's fur from my ankles. I wondered if there was any chance of convincing Grigsby to buy larger or more efficient water heaters for the complex. Given that he'd spent thousands on the AC unit only a few weeks earlier, the chances were slim to none.

Finished now, I stepped out of the tub and toweled off. The water drained rhythmically for a moment; then the drain began to gasp with a *glug-glug-glug* as Brigit's hair clogged the pipes. Two inches of water remained in the tub when it stopped draining altogether.

Walking into my living room, I pointed an accusatory finger at my partner. "You clogged the drain, you hairy beast."

She simply batted her big brown eyes in reply.

I picked up my phone and called Grigsby. "My bathtub drain is clogged."

"Plumbing stoppages are the tenant's responsibility," he snapped. "Read your lease."

After the day I'd had, there was no fight left in me. "Have I told you how much I hate living here?"

"You and everybody else," he replied, unconcerned. "You don't like it? Move."

I hung up without saying good-bye.

I found a metal coat hanger in my closet, manipulated it into a hook shape, and fished what looked like a wet kitten out of my drain. Had I been the crafty type, I could've glued googly eyes to it and sold it on Etsy.

The plumbing crisis now resolved, I blow-dried my hair and slid into a pair of jeans, sandals, and a black crossover top that tied on the side. Cute, but not overtly sexy. I'd just finished putting a little curl in the ends of my long hair and applying my makeup when a knock sounded at the door. It felt as if my heart were returning the gesture, knocking against my ribs.

I opened my door to find Seth standing on the walkway in jeans, loafers, and an old-fashioned gray vest over a black T-shirt. A pewter pocket watch was tucked into the vest, the chain draping down over his hip, the end clipped onto a belt loop. The effect was old-fashioned, quaint, and a little peculiar.

Seth glanced inside my place. "You're right. This is a crappy apartment."

"That's rude," I said.

"No," he replied, "it was honest."

"Sometimes honest *is* rude. Didn't your mother teach you about white lies?"

"I was only agreeing with what you said earlier." His eyes ran over my face and offered me a soft smile. "Would it help if I said you look pretty?"

Despite myself, I found my lips returning the smile. "It might."

"You smell good, too. Like lavender." His nose wrinkled as he got a better whiff. "With undertones of wet dog."

"Brigit climbed into the tub with me." Next time I'd lock the bathroom door.

"Wow." Seth walked past me into my apartment. "You've got an awful lot of books."

I glanced at the teetering stacks shoved against the wall. "I like to read. You?"

He didn't answer for a moment but rather picked a few books off the stack and looked them over. *Criminal Psychology.* Maya Angelou's *I Know Why the Caged Bird Sings.* A treatise on Buddhism. Nora Roberts' latest romance novel.

He returned the tomes to the stacks and looked up. "The last book I read was *To Kill a Mockingbird.* It was required reading sophomore year of high school."

"You didn't read the assigned books your junior and senior years?"

He said nothing, simply eyeing me and offering a shrug. He must've cheated and read the *Cliffs Notes.*

"So you haven't read a book in . . . what? Ten years?" I couldn't even imagine going that long without books. They'd been my escape all those years ago, and now they provided not only a refuge from the real world but also information and entertainment.

He lifted a shoulder. "I've been busy."

"Defusing bombs in Afghanistan?"

"Among other things." His eyes traveled around the rest of my space. "Rifles?" he asked, gesturing at the three long metal cases in the corner.

"No." I retrieved one of them. "F-flaming batons."

I opened the end of the case and slid the baton out to show him. "You just light the ends," I said, stepping back and beginning to twirl it, "and the crowd goes wild." With a simple thumb toss, I sent the baton spinning a couple of feet into the air. Would've been more impressive if I'd had higher ceilings.

Seth's head bobbed in appreciation of my skills. "And you can do all three at a time?"

"Yes," I said. Twirl *à trois*.

A sexy smile played about his lips. Amazing how turned on men get by such things. Shake a pair of pom-poms or twirl a baton in their faces and they turn to lust-crazed mush.

After returning my fire baton to its case, I dropped a handful of liver treats into Brigit's bowl, gave her both a scratch behind the ears and a kiss on the nose, and told her I'd be back in a couple of hours. "Be a good girl, 'kay?"

The look she gave me in response said, *I'll think about it. No guarantees.* She was as noncommittal as the kid at the dry cleaner's.

Seth followed me down the steps to his Nova, where he opened my flame-covered door for me.

Rhino stepped up to the fence around the pool and let out a wolf whistle. "That's one bad-ass car."

Seth lifted a chin in reply. "Thanks, man."

I climbed onto the blue vinyl bench seat, which was cracked in places and repaired with duct tape. The dash, too, bore several strips to cover the cracks the Texas sun had meted out. Rhino was right, though. Despite the signs of age and the ridiculous paint job, the car did have a certain bad-ass charm.

While the car was ancient, the stereo was state-of-the-art, with six speakers installed throughout the car. Seth climbed in the driver's side and punched a button to turn on the radio, which was tuned to a classic-rock channel. "What station do you like?"

"Ninety-point-one."

His brow furrowed as he attempted to place it but evidently could not. He twisted the button to tune it in, his lip quirking when he realized the station was the local NPR affiliate. "You like this brainy stuff?"

"Sure," I replied. "It's interesting. I always learn s-something new."

He narrowed his eyes at me. "You're smart, aren't you?"

"Very."

He sighed. "Damn. I don't normally go for smart girls."

"And why is that?"

"Harder to impress. With dumb girls I just have to flex my guns and they're putty in my hands."

To illustrate, he raised an arm and flexed his biceps. I wasn't dumb, but at the sight of his bulging muscle I was reduced to near putty myself. I blamed the primal instincts coded into my female DNA, telling me to hook up with a man who'd be a good protector, who could take down a woolly mammoth for dinner and fight off a saber-toothed tiger intent on eating our baby.

He cut me a sly grin. "Admit it. You're kind of impressed, too."

I rolled my eyes. "You're going to have to work harder."

"What do I have to do? Quote Shakespeare? Perform calculus computations?"

It never hurt to keep a guy on his toes. "We'll see."

With one last, assessing look my way, he started the car and pulled out of the lot.

On the drive over, in response to my request, Seth gave me a primer on bombs. Pipe bombs were some of the easiest to make and transport, he said, hence their popularity.

"Sometimes people put chlorine tablets in them," he said. "Other times it's sparklers. Any kind of combustible substance will do."

I found myself wondering again whether the skater boys had planted the bomb.

"What about the bomb at the mall?" I asked. "Can you tell what was used in that one?"

"Judging from the damage, my guess would be gunpowder and a very powerful model rocket engine."

Both items could be purchased easily in stores or on-line with no identification required. It was chilling to realize how much the safety and security of the American public depended on people's innate sense of right and wrong and general tendency to refrain from violence. Even more chilling to realize how easily a person intent on evil could exploit the situation.

Twenty minutes later, the Latina hostess at Joe T. Garcia's seated us at an umbrella-shaded table on the restaurant's extensive patio. The place had been a Fort Worth landmark for years. They served their Mexican food family-style and their margaritas strong.

The group of middle-aged couples at the next table was discussing the explosion.

"They're calling him the Tunabomber," one of the women said as she read over the menu.

"Why's that?" asked one of the men.

"Because he planted dynamite inside a fish," replied another.

Seth and I exchanged glances but made no effort to correct the man. No sense getting dragged into a conversation when we'd been warned by the detective not to give out any details.

"I've made my decision." The first woman set her menu down. "I'm getting the fish tacos."

Seth fought a grin, held up his menu to give us privacy, and whispered, "I'm guessing you will *not* be having the fish tacos."

"You've guessed correctly."

The waiter came by with a basket of chips and bowls of salsa and took our drink orders.

"So," Seth asked when the waiter departed, "how long you been a cop?"

I snatched a chip out of the basket and used it to scoop up some salsa. "Since January. I got a degree in criminal j-justice from Sam Houston State last May and attended the police academy in the fall."

With four remaining kids to support, my parents hadn't been able to help me out financially once I left for college. I'd paid for my own education and hadn't wanted to come out with too much debt hanging over me, so I'd worked part-time during the school years and full-time during the summers. It had taken me six years to complete college and another four months to finish the academy. I still owed fifty thousand on my loans, but at least the monthly payments were relatively manageable so long as I watched my expenses.

Seth broke a chip in two. "You like your job?"

Not exactly. I saw it as a means to an end. But I hardly knew this guy and, what's more, I didn't know whom he was acquainted with. I couldn't very well tell him I was only biding my time as an officer until I made detective. The information might get back to my superiors, make them question my commitment to the department. I gave him an ambiguous answer. "For the most part. What about you?"

He dipped one piece of his chip in salsa, too. "I *love* my job."

"You enjoy risking your life defusing bombs? Are you crazy?"

"Certifiable."

"What makes you do it?"

His eyes gleamed. "You never feel more alive than when you look death in the face and tell it to go to hell."

Whoa. What I wouldn't give for just an ounce of his courage. When I'd looked death in the face today it had laughed back in mine. *Mwahahaha!*

"So that's why you do it?" I asked. "For some kind of thrill? To ch-cheat death?"

I wasn't quite sure how I felt about that. Why take such

big risks for a fleeting buzz? What did it say about Seth that he was willing to do such a thing?

He shrugged. "Somebody's gotta do it, right?"

"I suppose so."

The waiter arrived with our drinks, setting Seth's beer in front of him and my jumbo frozen margarita with salt on the rim in front of me. After taking our food order, the waiter left again.

I took a slow sip of my frozen drink to avoid a headache. When I looked up, I caught Seth eyeing me intently.

"You okay?" he asked softly.

I was tempted to lie, to pretend to be unfazed by the day's events, to tell him that everything was fine. After all, guys didn't want to hear women complain or whine, right? But when I looked into his green eyes, eyes dark with knowledge and experience, I realized he'd see past any lie I offered.

Still, no sense getting too emotional. "Someone p-planted a bomb right under my nose and I didn't even notice. I feel really . . ."

Stupid. That's how I felt. But I wasn't about to say that ugly word. If not for Brigit alerting on the bag, though, there was no telling how many people would have been maimed, or blinded, or worse. Hell, I'd been sitting only a few feet away from the bomb. I could've been among the dead or injured, my corpse zipped inside a plastic body bag, my bloodstained uniform accessorized with a toe tag. At least I had a fresh pedicure.

"Don't blame yourself," Seth said. "Surely the bomber took pains to avoid being noticed. You had no way of knowing."

What he said was undeniably true, yet it made me feel only marginally better.

"Besides," he added, "you got everyone out of the mall

safely. That took some quick thinking. You can be proud of that."

I might've felt more proud if Chief Garelik had acknowledged my actions rather than seeming to place blame on me. The man could be a real ass sometimes.

I fished another chip out of the basket and dipped it in the salsa bowl. "Who would plant a bomb in a shopping mall? What would they hope to gain?" I held the chip aloft, waiting to see what insights Seth could offer.

He lifted a shoulder. "There's no point trying to make sense of random violence. Whoever planted the bomb is some sick bastard who likes to hurt people. The world is full of them."

I ate the chip while I pondered his words. Was he right? Was the bomber some type of insane psychopath who simply enjoyed hurting others? Or had there been more to it, some message the bomber intended to send? Thinking back on my conversation with Detective Jackson, how she'd noted Seth's fast arrival at the mall, I forced my voice to sound nonchalant. "You arrived quickly today."

"Got there as fast as I could." Seth took a long drag on his bottle of Dos Equis but said nothing more.

"Were you in the area?"

A simple "yes" was his only reply. He wasn't making this easy.

"Where were you?" I asked.

"You interrogating me?" His green eyes sought mine and hardened, as if challenging me to cut the crap and shoot straight.

Okay, then. I would. "I guess so."

He gave me a well-deserved grunt. "I take you out for dinner and margaritas and you accuse me of attempted murder. Now who's being rude?"

Me, evidently. So why stop now? "Where did you come from?"

"The pool in Forest Park," he said. "I was swimming laps. You can verify my whereabouts with the lifeguard if you'd like."

Seth was a swimmer, hmm? That explained the well-developed shoulders.

He cocked his head. "Why would a guy on a bomb squad *plant* a bomb? That doesn't make sense."

"Job security," I pointed out. "The city's announced across-the-board layoffs. They won't reduce the bomb squad if there's a bomb problem going on."

Seth stared at his beer bottle for a moment, turning it in his hands as he thought over my words. "Couldn't the same be said for the police force? In fact, maybe *you* planted the bomb. After all, the bomb squad works the entire city while you have a specific beat, right? Like you said, the bomb was planted *right under your nose*."

His face was smug. I supposed he'd earned the right to smirk, though.

"All right. You made your point." I wiped some condensation from my margarita glass and flicked it at him.

He chuckled as he used a napkin to dab the droplets from his cheek. "You've sure got a short fuse."

I could have argued but decided against it. Putting up a fight would only prove him right. Besides, it was true. "Irish temper. I get it from my mother."

My father, on the other hand, had given me both the dark hair and the last name Luz. The word meant "light" in Spanish. Ironic that with a name like that people still didn't realize how bright I was.

I took a sip of my drink. "I hope we can bring the bomber in before he does it again."

"I'm sure the detectives will do their best," Seth said. "It's really not your problem."

"Of course it is!"

He raised a conciliatory palm. "You know what I mean.

It's your job to deal with immediate situations and it's the detectives' job to solve the crimes, right?"

What he said was true. Still, it didn't mean I shouldn't try to assist in the investigation.

Seth tossed back the last of his beer and signaled the waiter for another before leaning across the table. "The best you can do at this point is keep an eye out for males carrying duffel bags, backpacks, boxes, anything they could hide a bomb in. Also be aware of anyone who seems to be taking an unusual interest in the area of the explosion. In my experience, bombers sometimes return to the scene of their crimes to see how much damage they've done. Their curiosity gets the best of them. We caught several insurgents in Afghanistan that way."

My thoughts slipped out of my mouth before I could stop them. I blamed the tequila in the margarita. "Did you get those scars on your back when you were in the Army?"

Seth's upper lip quirked. "Were you checking me out when I changed into my bomb suit?"

He and his buddies had stripped down in broad daylight while belting out the lyrics to "Big Balls." I wasn't about to apologize for watching him under those circumstances. "You were hardly being modest." Of course, with a body like his, who could blame him?

He lifted his chin in agreement, but his smile faded. "Yeah, the scars are a souvenir from Afghanistan. I gave a ten-year-old a pack of gum and he threw a grenade at me."

What?!?

My mouth fell open. I couldn't even imagine how frightening that must have been. Well, actually, after the explosion in the mall this afternoon maybe I could. I had no idea what to say in response, though. The words that came out were infinitely inadequate: "What an ungrateful brat."

Seth chuckled. "I can't fault the kid too much. The insurgents put a lot of pressure on their sons to follow in their footsteps. At least the boy warned me first. He made a running motion with his fingers before pulling the pin."

"Oh, Seth, I—"

He raised a palm again to stop me. "It is what it is. I'm fine." Smiling now, he wagged his brows suggestively. "Besides, the scars get me lots of sympathy from the ladies."

I narrowed my eyes at him. If Seth was some kind of man-whore, I wasn't interested. Still, something told me he wasn't. Most man-whore types were overly familiar and handsy and tended to invade a woman's personal space. Seth had done none of these things. He hadn't touched me at all, in fact, and after I'd sat at the table he'd chosen the seat across from me rather than the closer one next to me.

The waiter arrived with our food, putting an end to our discussion. Over the meal, our conversation turned to lighter, less personal matters: The upcoming end of summer and its brutal temperatures. The delicious flavor of the guacamole. Our dogs.

"How long have you and Blast been p-partners?" I slurped up the remnants of my first margarita and started in on the second.

Seth swallowed a bite of his enchiladas. "Two years, give or take. He was only eight months old when we began training, but that dog was born for bomb detection. Best nose in the business."

Seth's words got me wondering again why Brigit had alerted on the bag with the bomb. Had she heard the ticking and realized it was out of place? Surely that was too much to expect of a dog not trained to listen for that particular sound, especially in such a noisy, crowded area. Had the bag contained drugs or been handled by someone with drug residue on his or her hands? I found myself wishing Brigit could speak and tell me what she'd been thinking. I asked Seth his thoughts on the subject.

"Who knows?" he said. "But I think you should take her a doggie bag of chicken fajitas, let her know she's appreciated."

"Good idea."

I asked Seth more about his job then, and he explained that he primarily served as a firefighter, pulling bomb squad duty on the rare occasions such skills were needed. He was assigned to Station #10 on Hemphill Street. His jurisdiction largely overlapped with mine. Chances were we'd run into each other on occasion even without trying. Fire department and police personnel worked together on alarm calls and fires, the cops performing crowd control and directing traffic around fire sites.

When dinner was over, Seth drove me and my doggie bag home. He'd ordered a round of fajitas for Blast, too, asking the waiter to hold the onion. The two of us said little on the drive. The margaritas had freed my thoughts and now there were too many of them bouncing around in my head—and too much tequila in my bloodstream—to make coherent conversation:

Who was the bomber?
Was he some random stranger, or could he be someone I'd met before?
Why had he chosen to detonate the bomb in the mall?
Was Seth crazy for taking a job on the bomb squad?
Did I want to get involved with someone who might be crazy?
Would Seth kiss me when we got back to my place?

God, I hoped he would. After the day I'd had I could really use the distraction.

When we arrived at my complex, the sun had begun to set, just a pinkish-orange tint remaining on the horizon. The only lights at the complex came from the apartment windows and the streetlight situated near the entrance. Not exactly a warm and inviting place. Nonetheless, Seth opened the car door for me and followed me up the stairs to my unit.

I stopped at my door and turned to face him, my heart throbbing in anticipation. "Thanks for dinner."

"No problem."

Warmth pooled south of my belly button as his smoky gaze flickered to my lips, a signal that he was about to lean in and kiss me. I stood there a moment, warm and wanting, waiting for him to make his move.

But he didn't.

When Seth began to back towards the stairs, my hopes imploded like an outdated Vegas casino.

He put a hand on the rail. "Remember what I said. Keep an eye out for men with bags and backpacks."

I nodded, hoping my disappointment wasn't written on my face. In case it was, I said a quick, "Bye," unlocked my door, and slipped inside with my doggie bag. I leaned back against my door and closed my eyes.

Why hadn't Seth kissed me? Had this dinner been only a friendly gesture and not a date, after all? Did my breath smell like onion and garlic? Was it because of my stutter?

How I wish I knew.

Being left at the door without a kiss had been upsetting enough, but when my eyes opened and took in the half-chewed shoes strewn about my floor my anger erupted like Mount Vesuvius. I dropped my purse, tossed the bag of fajita meat onto the kitchen counter, and snatched the stiletto Brigit was currently mouthing out of her teeth. "Bad dog!"

Some BFF she'd turned out to be.

The closet door gaped open. No doubt the lever-style handle had made it a cinch for Brigit to open it. Just a little pressure from her nose or a paw and the latch would release. Looked like I'd have to make a trip to the hardware store for a hook and eye latch to keep the door closed.

I picked up my ruined shoes and hurled them into my trash can one at a time, taking out my fears and frustrations on my footwear.

Thunk!

Thunk!

Thunk!

Thunk!

I double-fisted the next two.

Thunk-thunk!

When Brigit dared to growl, I whirled on her. "Stupid dog!"

THIRTY-TWO
SHUT UP OR YOUR PURSE GETS IT, TOO

Brigit

Her partner was angry. *Well, good.* That had been the plan, after all.

How dare Megan leave Brigit at home after the day they'd had! Megan wasn't the only one who'd needed emotional support. Brigit did, too. And if her partner wasn't going to give it to her, the dog had no choice but to calm herself by chewing on something. If Megan didn't like Brigit chewing up her shoes she should've bought the dog a chew toy. Maybe now Megan would learn not to leave her partner at home when she went out.

THIRTY-THREE
TUNABOMBER

The Rattler

The Tunabomber?

He slammed his laptop closed, dropped it to the floor, and stomped it hard with his boot. Still not satisfied, he gave it a kick, sending it crashing into the wall.

Who the fuck did these Internet idiots think they were, hanging such a ridiculous label on him? They treated him as nothing more than a practical joker. Hell, he could've injured dozens of people today, maybe even killed someone. It wasn't like he hadn't tried. If not for that damn dog he would've accomplished his aims. She must've scented the leftover marijuana residue. That's what he got for storing the pipes in the same backpack he'd stashed his weed in.

Man's best friend. What a bunch of bullshit.

THIRTY-FOUR
FORSAKEN

Megan

The instant the words left my mouth I realized I was being a mean, nasty bitch. Brigit was anything but stupid. She had saved not only my life but also the lives of countless others, yet here I was yelling at her. Some pack leader I was.

I pulled a loafer out of the trash and dropped to the floor, placing the shoe in front of Brigit as a peace offering. Probably not what a trainer would recommend, but I'd rather sacrifice a shoe than have Brigit hate me.

My eyes filled with fresh tears as I put my nose to hers and scratched her behind each ear. "I'm sorry, Brigit. I shouldn't have y-yelled at you. I'm so sorry."

Initially she stiffened at my touch, but a moment later she relaxed. Her tongue slid out of her mouth and licked my chin once, giving me a doggie kiss, letting me know all was forgiven.

I returned the gesture, giving her a smooch on the snout. "I really don't deserve you, do I?"

* * *

Despite the two margaritas, I tossed and turned until the wee hours Saturday night, unable to quiet my mind enough to rest. Around 3:00 AM, Brigit finally had enough and climbed down onto the floor where she could sleep in peace.

Sunday morning, bleary-eyed and more bushed than bushy-tailed, I dragged my butt out of bed, showered, and threw on a pair of jeans, sandals, and a green blouse. I fed Brigit, loaded her in the car, and, twenty minutes later pulled up to the curb in front of my childhood home.

The house was a three-bedroom, two-bath, one-story wood frame model in the Arlington Heights neighborhood of Fort Worth. The yellow paint had faded unevenly and most of the trim was peeling, but the lackadaisical upkeep served to give the small house a comfortable and unpretentious feel. It also served to give the homeowners association a reason to send an occasional letter to my parents, suggesting some sprucing up was in order. Those letters, in turn, served to ignite my mother's Irish temper. How many times had I heard her say, *I'll be damned if I'll have some busybody tell me when it's time to paint my house!* My father, who would be tasked with the unenviable job of painting the house, gave my mother his full support and wholeheartedly agreed they should stand their ground and leave the house as is.

I climbed out of my car and Brigit hopped out behind me. I'd dressed my partner in her police vest so she could attend church with us this morning. After that stunt she'd pulled last night chewing up my shoes, I didn't trust Brigit enough to leave her home alone. If I didn't know better I'd think this had been her plan all along.

Taking a breath to prepare myself for the noise and chaos that characterized my childhood home, I put my shoulder to the cockeyed front door and forced it open. Brigit trotted in ahead of me, generating a protest from

my mother's trio of indistinguishable orange tabby tom-
cats. They stood from their perches on the back of the
sofa and arched their backs.

Yooowwwl!

Hisssss!

Rurrrrrrr!

"Get over yourselves," I admonished them. *Snobs.*

Brigit ignored their insults, exacting payback by trotting into the kitchen and promptly wolfing down their
kitty kibble. *Crunch-crunch-crunch.*

As always, my auburn-haired mother flitted around the
kitchen like a hummingbird on speed, gathering up the
breakfast dishes, trying unsuccessfully to find her mis-
placed house keys among the clutter on the countertop,
and calling out to my father, "Hurry up, Martin, or we'll
be late!"

We were late every week. It was our family tradition.

She waved a dish towel at me in greeting while she
downed the last of her coffee. After adding her mug to the
stack of dirty dishes in the sink, she fluttered her hand
about. "See if you can find my keys."

She'd been misplacing her keys for years. When would
this woman learn to get a routine?

While I began to poke around on the counter, my
mother hustled off to check my dad's status, stopping in
the hallway to holler, "Gabby! Joey! Get a move on!"

The errant keys were lodged behind the toaster. I'd
just retrieved them when my fifteen-year-old sister, Gabrielle, slipped into the kitchen. Like me and our other
siblings, she had my father's dark hair and my mother's
freckled face. Though Gabby had swiped a coat of mascara onto her lashes and slipped into a cute sundress, it
was clear from the lack of accessories and her haphazard ponytail that she'd rolled out of bed only minutes
before.

"Hey, Megan," Gabby said, her voice still croaky from sleep.

As the only two female offspring, Gabs and I had shared a room until I left for college seven years ago. With ten years' age difference between us, the arrangement had been far from ideal. I'd wanted peacock-blue spreads for our twin beds, but she'd pouted and whimpered and argued until she'd gotten her way and our beds were adorned in a childish princess pink. I constantly tripped over her menagerie of stuffed animals, while she routinely played in my makeup. She'd set our curtains on fire once when she'd played with my flaming batons without permission. Fortunately, with Gabby approaching adulthood now we had much more in common and were growing closer.

I gave my sister a hug, then stepped back. "You look extra-tired today." It wasn't intended as an insult, merely an observation.

She yawned and smiled at the same time. "I had a date last night. I was too excited to sleep."

I'd possibly had a date last night and been unable to sleep, too, though I couldn't claim my insomnia was due to excitement.

"Deets," I demanded, taking Gabby by the shoulders. "Now."

She glanced behind her to make sure our mother wasn't around. "His name is T.J.," she said in a stage whisper. "He's totally adorbs! I met him at a party and he goes to Paschal and he's, like, the best kisser ever!"

Adorbs? Really, when did people get too lazy to finish their words?

I forced enthusiasm into my voice: "Yay!"

My little sister was getting more action than me. How sad was that? Still, I was happy for her even if I was feeling a little sorry for myself now.

My dad slunk into the kitchen, putting an end to our girl talk. Dad was tall and black haired, with a lean but strong physique thanks to his job on the line at the General Motors assembly plant in nearby Arlington. While my mother tended to be hyperactive, highly energetic, and high-strung, my father was just the opposite. Slow moving, serene, sedate. There were times I was tempted to check him for a pulse.

He gave me a kiss on the forehead and ruffled the fur on Brigit's butt. "Your dog's getting fat."

"She's not fat," I insisted. "She's just big boned." Actually, Brigit had gained four pounds since becoming my partner, but that wouldn't stop me from coming to her defense.

Joey, who moved like a stealthy spy, appeared next to my dad. "Hey, tuna head."

I pointed a finger at him. "Don't make me hurt you," I said, "'cause you know I will."

Mom stepped back into the kitchen and I tossed her the keys. "What's this about tuna?"

My parents tended to be a little out of touch. Raising five children, they'd had no time to watch television while we were growing up. With me out on my own and my other two brothers in college, only two of their children remained at home now. But these days they DVRed their favorite shows and skipped the commercials and news blasts.

Joey snorted. "Get a clue, Mom. A bomb went off in the Chisholm Trail mall yesterday and Megan got splattered with all kinds of gross stuff."

"A bomb?" My mother's eyes went wide and she looked from my brother to me. "Oh, my God!" she shrieked. "Why didn't you tell us?"

The better question was why hadn't my sister or brother thought to tell my parents? Both of them had been aware of it. Come on, people. Communicate!

"It was a crazy day," I said. "Super b-busy."

The truth of the matter was that, early on, I'd stopped trying to share my feelings with my parents. They'd been too busy producing one child after another, and each new baby's needs had taken priority. Stuttering made conversation difficult enough for me, but trying to share my intimate feelings with an exhausted mother and father over the wails of a crying sibling just seemed futile. I'd withdrawn and learned to work through my emotions on my own, mostly by escaping into books or, if I was particularly angry, using Dad's hammer to break small rocks on the patio out back. The baton twirling had later replaced the hammer, allowing me to hurl my problems into the air and forget about them momentarily.

Of course what goes up must come down. . . .

I knew my parents wanted to be there for me now, to provide what support they could, but old habits are hard to break.

"Did anyone get hurt?" my mother asked, her face drawn in concern.

No sense telling them about the screw in my ass. It would only worry them. "Brigit got a nail in her hip, but that's it."

My dad looked down at her. "Is that why she has the bald patch?"

I nodded. "The EMT had to shave her to apply the anesthetic." I glanced up at the clock, as much to end the conversation as to remind everyone we had no time to dawdle. "We better get going."

I loaded Brigit back in my car and followed my parents' Suburban to the church. We arrived just in time to sneak into the back row while the priest and acolytes were making their way up the steps to the altar. A few of our fellow congregants glanced back on hearing Brigit's tags jingle but soon turned their attention back to the front of the church.

We sat down, Brigit taking a spot on the pew next to me and resting her head in my lap. The hard pew was bad enough on a good day, but with the tender puncture wound on my butt sitting on the hard surface today felt like a penance. Perhaps God was punishing me for lusting after Seth yesterday.

The priest began his usual machinations and recitations. I'd like to say I paid attention to the mass, but my thoughts were elsewhere. Mumbling, "Thanks be to God," at the requisite intervals, I looked up at the cross that hung on the wall over the altar, at the bloody half-human, half-divine being affixed to it. Maybe I shouldn't feel so bad that people were making fun of me on YouTube. After all, I might be a cop who risked my life for the people of Fort Worth, but Jesus had actually given his life to save all of mankind and look what people had done to him. Stuck a crown of thorns on his head and nailed him to a cross. A crappy way to treat the purported messiah, wouldn't you say? I supposed I couldn't expect more for myself than the Son of God had received.

When it was time for communion, I picked up Brigit's leash and led her down the aisle with me. Call me crazy, but the concept of communion had always creeped me out a little. If transubstantiation truly occurred, turning the wafers into Christ's body and the wine into his blood, wouldn't participating in the sacrament make us some type of vampire cannibals? I might raise the issue with one of the deacons if I didn't think I'd be referred for an exorcism.

When the priest put the communion wafer in my hands, Brigit glanced up, looking pissed that the priest had given me a treat and not her. She didn't know it, but she wasn't

missing anything. I mean, I know communion was supposed to be a blessed sacrament, but the wafers tasted like
cardboard and stuck to the roof of your mouth. You'd think
the messiah's body would be a little more appetizing. At
least his flesh was gluten-free and low calorie. If the pope
really wanted to grow the church, he'd think about replac-
ing the dry, tasteless wafers with Thin Mint Girl Scout
cookies.

But perhaps I think too much. . . .

It might have been a sin, but I bit off only half of the
wafer. Once we'd returned to the pew, I discreetly fed
the rest to Brigit. God wouldn't mind, right? After all, she
was one of his creatures. But did he really have to give
her so much fur?

Uh-oh . . .

Brigit opened her mouth and extended her neck, making a hacking noise that reverberated throughout the quiet
cathedral.

Hack!

Haack!

Haaaack!

Crap! The darn dog was gagging on the communion
wafer. Heads turned to gawk at us.

Haaack!

The wafer ejected from Brigit's mouth covered in sa-
liva and landed on the floor. I kicked the gooey blob under the kneeler, hoping nobody would realize what she'd
coughed up. Grabbing Brigit's leash, I hustled her out the
back doors and into the foyer. Before I could stop her,
she'd dragged me over to the font, propped her front legs
on it, and lapped up a mouthful of holy water. *Slurp-
slurp-slurp.*

I covered my eyes with my hand. I hoped the Big Man
had a sense of humor or my soul would be sent straight to
hell. Thank God we were the only ones in the foyer and

none of the other parishioners had seen Brigit drink from the font. The church would've excommunicated me.

When mass was over, my family reassembled at my parents' house for lunch. My mother made sandwiches for all of us, fixing one for Brigit as well. My partner made short work of her lunch, wolfing it down in four bites. So much for manners.

When lunch was over, I gave each of my parents a kiss on the cheek and chucked Joey under the chin. "See y'all later."

Gabrielle walked me out to my car. Her face looked pensive. "Do you think the bomber will strike again?"

I shrugged, though honestly I thought the chances were close to 100 percent certainty the sicko had plans to detonate another bomb. Whatever aims the bomber had hoped to achieve by planting explosives in the mall had likely gone unfulfilled. But when and where the next explosion would take place was anyone's guess. "Don't worry, Gabs. I'll be careful."

Tears welled in her eyes. "Promise?"

"Promise." I gave her a hug. It was sweet of her to worry, though I hated to see her emotionally burdened. The teen years were hard enough without a bomber piling on more angst. "Let me know how things go with T.J."

Her face brightened. "I will!"

Brigit and I settled into the car and, with a final wave and good-bye bark, headed off for the mall.

THIRTY-FIVE
THANKS, BUT NO THANKS

Brigit

Brigit made a mental note not to beg for a treat if they ever went back to the big building that smelled like incense and candles. That dry, tasteless tidbit the man in the dress had given to Megan hadn't been worth the trouble. Nice of them to keep a big bowl of water handy, though.

THIRTY-SIX
A MATERIAL WORLD

The Rattler

He couldn't help himself. He had to go back to see how much damage his bomb had caused, to see whether those greedy, self-indulgent shoppers and store owners had received the message his bomb had been intended to send.

As he made his way down the nearly empty southwest wing to the courtyard, Madonna's classic "Material Girl" burbled from speakers mounted on the light poles. He chuckled inwardly at the irony.

When he reached the courtyard, a velvet rope stopped him from entering. Fortunately, a handful of other people had gathered at the rope to gawk, making his presence less noticeable.

A man from a door company had removed one of the cracked and pocked panels of glass, giving the Rattler an unobstructed view into the courtyard. The janitors and custodians milled about inside, cleaning up the mess and repairing the damage. He felt a small tinge of regret that these powerless, lower-paid workers—whom Karl Marx had referred to as the proletariat—had been tasked with restoring the place, but he knew his actions would impact his intended targets even more. Though his bomb had failed to effect significant casualties, he'd nonetheless accomplished some of his aims. He'd hit the money-hungry bourgeois retailers where it hurt them most—*in the wallet*.

He would not be satisfied yet, though. Despite his father's constant mumblings about his purported laziness and lack of ambition, the Rattler would work hard to ensure his next bomb packed a wallop.

Perhaps he'd even deploy several bombs just to keep things interesting. . . .

THIRTY-SEVEN
UNPAID OVERTIME

Megan

While the Chisholm Trail mall had been a buzzing hive of activity before yesterday's explosion, today the place was a ghost town. I wouldn't have been surprised to see a tumbleweed blow by.

Only a handful of cars were in the lot, and I was able to snag a spot on the front row. A Fort Worth PD cruiser sat in the reserved law enforcement spot. Car 935. The Big Dick's cruiser. Parked next to it was Detective Jackson's unmarked car. Parked next to her car were three more FWPD cruisers and a brown-and-tan patrol car from the Tarrant County Sheriff's Department. Evidently the county authorities didn't want to be left out. But who could blame them for horning in on the action? A crime like this didn't come along every day.

As we made our way into the mall, Brigit stopped to tinkle in the grass flanking the bronze cattle statues. If I didn't know better, I'd say the cattle had shifted positions, as if trying in vain to flee the mall but held in place by the granite foundation.

But perhaps my imagination was getting the best of me. . . .

As Brigit and I walked down the row, I noted that at least half of the stores were closed, their doors locked and their windows dark. Madonna's classic "Material Girl" played over the mall's speakers, the lively, upbeat tune totally at odds with the somber faces on the few employees and shoppers who had dared to venture to the mall today.

Ricky and Scott cruised up the pathway on their three-wheeled scooters, their expressions equal parts weary and wary. I stopped them with a raised hand.

"Any news?" I asked.

Scott shook his head.

"A bunch of people called in sick," Ricky said.

No doubt they were afraid to come to work. Ironic, really. With a small army of law enforcement on-site and everyone on high alert, today was probably the safest day ever to be at the mall.

Ricky went on to tell me that some of the other shops had closed when they saw how few people were shopping here today. The bomb would not be good for their bottom lines.

"Have you seen Detective Jackson?" I asked.

Ricky hiked a thumb over his shoulder. "Castleberry's office."

"Thanks."

I continued on, noting that Brackenburg Furriers was open for business. Ariana stood at the window, a frown on her face as she gazed out at the empty sidewalks.

As we passed the store, Brigit's growl was louder and more guttural than usual. Did she know something about Ariana that I didn't? Once again I found myself wishing my partner could tell me what had led her to the garbage can yesterday.

I continued on to the courtyard. The yellow crime scene tape that had surrounded the site the day before had been removed and replaced with velvet ropes hanging between portable metal stands. Paper signs on the doors read: Closed. Do Not Enter.

I ducked under a rope, ignored the signs, and went inside. I might be officially off duty, but a cop is a cop, 24/7.

The courtyard was still in relative shambles, though it was clear progress has been made. Mr. Castleberry scurried about, dressed in a T-shirt and a wrinkled pair of jeans today rather than his usual suit and tie. He spoke with the managers of several food booths, who'd come by to assess the damage and clear the money from the unlocked cash registers their staff had been forced to abandon yesterday. Two of my fellow officers from the W1 district stood like sentries at either end of the courtyard, their presence intended to restore a sense of order to the place and to prevent the looting of funds, hairnets, and gallon-sized jars of pickle relish.

While much of the nails, screws, and thumbtacks remained, the crime scene techs had been careful to remove all of the telltale shrapnel yesterday so that those cleaning up today wouldn't be aware of the bomb's unusual contents. The fishhooks, sewing needles, corkscrew, meat thermometer, and fondue forks would remain secret details, known only to the forensic team, me, the members of the bomb squad, Detective Jackson, and, of course, the bomber him- or herself.

The janitorial and maintenance staff were working hard to clean up the remaining mess and repair the damage. Two of the custodians swept up glass and garbage, while a third followed behind with a mop and bucket. One of the maintenance staff stood on a tall stepstool in the food court, re-replacing the lightbulbs that Irving had just installed yesterday. Irving himself worked a few feet away, his steel-toed work boot propped on the crossbeam of a wooden chair for leverage as he used pliers to wrench nails and screws out of the seat. As he extracted each piece of metal, he tossed it into a one of the mall's shopping bags, which sat open on the floor.

I eyed him for a moment, assessing his demeanor but noting nothing suspicious, before stepping over to him. "Hi, Irving."

"Hey there, Officer Luz." He offered a smile as he stood. "I hardly recognized you without your uniform on."

With my hair down and no weapons strapped to my hips, I didn't look at all like a cop. Was that a good thing or a bad thing? Hmm. Jury's still out on that one.

My eyes scanned the area. "What a mess."

"You're telling me." He exhaled a sharp breath. "I've been at this for two hours and I'm not even halfway done."

I peeked into the shopping bag. At first glance it appeared to contain the same assortment of nails and screws I'd seen strewn about yesterday. When I looked closer, though, one particular odd-shaped nail caught my eye.

I scurried over and retrieved a napkin from the barbecue stand. Covering my hand with the napkin, I plucked the nail from the bag, careful not to make direct contact with it in case the crime scene techs might be able to lift a print from it.

I held the nail up. Unlike the other nails, which had the standard flat, round heads, this nail had a thicker, square head. The tip of the nail was far sharper than a standard nail, too.

I looked up to discover Irving's eyes on me. I laid the nail flat on the napkin and held it out in my palm to show him. "What kind of nail is this?"

He craned his neck for a closer look. "No idea. Doesn't look like a standard type."

"Have there been many like this?"

He shrugged. "Can't say for sure. I haven't been paying close attention. Just been working as fast I can to get the metal out of the furniture. Mr. Castleberry wants this place back in full operation ASAP."

I wrapped the napkin around the nail and slid it into my pocket. "See you later, Irving."

He replied with a two-fingered salute.

I turned and headed for the management office. The door to the manager's reception area contained a glass window. I peeked through to see Aruni sitting in one of the chairs, her daughter on her lap. Both wore apprehensive expressions. The Big Dick stood inside the small space, looming over them.

The door was unlocked, so I stepped inside. I greeted Aruni and her daughter with a smile and a "hello." Aruni responded with only a nervous nod of her head, as if she was too frightened to speak in front of Derek.

Mackey cut his eyes my way. "You're not on the work schedule today."

"Neither are you."

He rocked back on his heels, a self-satisfied smile on his face. "The chief asked his best men to put in some overtime."

Grrr. Everyone else would take a financial hit thanks to the bomb, but the chief's golden boy would profit from it. Where was the fairness in that? If anyone deserved some paid overtime it was me and Brigit. After all, we were the ones who'd been injured in the explosion. I felt a twinge in my ass just thinking about it.

Mackey hiked up his pants in another ball-juggling yank. "What are you doing here, Smegan?"

I ignored his disgusting reference. "Just stopping by to see if I can help."

"I've got things under control." He made a shooing motion at me, as if I were a pesky fly. "Go back home and paint your toenails."

Jerk. "I'm not leaving until I speak with Detective Jackson."

"What about?"

"Nothing that concerns you."

Derek crossed his arms over his chest. "If it concerns the bombing it concerns me. This incident happened on *my* beat."

"It's my beat, too," I pointed out. "Besides, it's not about the b-bombing. It's about what color polish I should use on my toes." *Ha!*

Derek glared at me and I glared right back.

A couple minutes later, the door opened and Serhan emerged looking shaken and fearful. Like his wife, he, too, responded to my greeting with only a nod. Aruni stood with Kara in her arms and the two exited the room.

"Officer Luz," Detective Jackson said from the doorway. "I didn't realize you were on the schedule today."

"I'm not," I said. "But there's something I'd like to discuss with you." I cut a sideways glance at Derek. *"Privately."*

Jackson looked from me to the Big Dick, then back to me. She jerked her head in invitation and closed the door behind me and Brigit.

The detective reclaimed her seat behind Mr. Castleberry's cluttered desk and looked at me with eyes underscored by fresh bags. "I hear you used to be partners with Mackey."

"That's correct."

Her lip curled up in disgust. "For God's sake, woman.

Why didn't you shoot the asshole and feed his sorry car cass to the tigers at the zoo while you had the chance?"

"I Tasered him in the testicles once."

The detective chuckled, probably assuming I'd been joking.

"You look exhausted." I hoped she'd realize I meant to express concern, not insult.

"I was up all night going over the security tapes," she said. "I only got three hours' sleep and that was on the couch in the employee lounge next door. I'm running on Mountain Dew and adrenaline."

Such sacrifices must be common for detectives investigating time-sensitive cases such as this one. The more time that passed without the bomber being apprehended, the greater the chance he'd get away or strike again.

"Whatcha got for me?" Jackson asked, stifling a yawn.

I pulled the napkin from my pocket, set it on the desk, and unwrapped it, exposing the oddly shaped nail. "This was pulled from one of the chairs in the food court."

The detective leaned in for a closer look. "It doesn't look like any of the other nails. What kind is it?"

"I have no idea. I asked Irving, but he didn't know, either."

She folded the napkin back over it and slid it into an evidence bag. "I'll have one of the techs look into it." She stared up at me as if waiting for me to say more. When I didn't, she asked, "Is that all?"

"I . . . I g-guess so," I stammered. But it was a lie. I wanted to be involved, to help with the investigation. I wanted to help nail the bomber, to see justice done.

When I still made no move to go, Jackson exhaled loudly. "Look, Officer Luz. Nobody blames you for what happened if that's what you're worried about."

I shook my head. "That's not it. It's . . . w-well . . . it's . . ."

Jackson tossed a hand in the air. "Spit it out, Officer Luz. I don't have all day."

How many times had I heard similar words from similarly impatient people? *Too many* times, that's how many. "I want to help in the investigation."

There. I'd said it.

She gave me a slightly patronizing smile. "That's awfully nice of you, but it's not your job."

Might as well go for broke, right? "I want it to be."

Her brows rose. "Excuse me?"

"I want to be a detective someday."

She cocked her head and stared at me for a long moment. "You know you can't even apply until you've been a street cop for four full years, right?"

I nodded.

"And you know the burnout rate for cops is extremely high? Many don't even make it four years."

Another nod.

"The written test is a bitch."

"So I hear." I'd study hard and ace it.

She raised a brow. "You think you have what it takes?"

I met her gaze. "I *know* I have what it takes."

She chuckled. "Well, one thing it takes is balls and it seems you've got a pair, undeveloped as they might be as yet. If you're willing to put in some unpaid overtime and help me out I'd be an idiot to refuse, wouldn't I?"

"Yes."

Her brows angled inward as she seemed to consider whether my response implied that she was an idiot. Heck, I wondered the same thing. She might want to work on her phrasing next time.

She narrowed her eyes. "You're not going to file some type of complaint with the Workforce Commission claiming we owe you extra pay for this, are ya?"

"Wouldn't dream of it."

"All right, then. Take a seat."

I dropped into a chair and Brigit sat at my feet, looking up at me. I scratched her ears with one hand while I used the other to gesture at the laptop and papers spread about the desk. "Any luck yet?"

"Nothing definitive," she said, taking a sip from a can of Mountain Dew. "The crime scene techs found no fingerprints on the bomb materials. The bomber was smart enough to wear gloves, apparently. I've talked to a few people, so I suppose that's progress. That Serhan sure seemed nervous."

His anxiety was understandable. The fact that the bomb had been placed in a bag from his food stand didn't look good. Still, my gut told me the guy was innocent. Of course my gut had once told me the Greek yogurt in my fridge hadn't yet gone bad. Boy, had my gut been wrong that time.

"If Serhan had planted the bomb," I suggested, "wouldn't he have avoided using a bag from his own shop?" Surely he'd realize the bag would raise suspicions.

Jackson tilted her head first one way, then the other, indicating *maybe, maybe not.* "I doubt whoever planted the bomb expected it to be found before the explosion. When the bomb went off the bag was blown into unidentifiable confetti. If you hadn't seen the device inside the Stick People bag we never would have known."

Hmm. . . .

She set her soda can down, maneuvered the wireless mouse next to her laptop, and motioned for me to come around the desk. "Take a look at this."

I leaned in next to her. On her computer screen was a feed from a security camera in the food court. As was typical, the mall utilized a combination of visible and hidden cameras—visible cameras to deter crime and hidden cameras to catch it on film. As we'd made our way around the food court yesterday, I'd noticed Jackson mentally cataloging all of the visible cameras. Given the angle on the screen, this feed must have come from a hidden camera inside the decorative bronze wall clock. A timer in the bottom right corner read out yesterday's date and the time: 12:04 PM.

The camera's scope was broad, taking in an area measuring approximately fifty feet by fifty feet. Though the garbage can was visible at the back of the space, its opening faced away from the camera. The constant movement of the busy crowd in the foreground sometimes obscured the can from view for several seconds at a time, as did a cluster of balloons that floated back and forth in the air currents.

"I've been over this footage a dozen times," Jackson said, "but maybe you'll catch something I didn't."

As I watched, scores of unidentifiable people came and went, shoving trash through the unseen door flap. Two of them threw out large white bags, though from this distance it was impossible to tell whether the bags were from Stick People. The first was a woman with three adolescent boys in tow. The second was a paunchy man wearing mirrored sunglasses and a purple TCU baseball cap that hid the top half of his face in shadow. He glanced first left, then right before shoving his bag into the can. *Odd*.

I gestured to the screen. "You think he's the bomber?"

"Possibly," Detective Jackson said. "He bought lunch at the shish-kebab place twenty minutes earlier. I've tracked his movements the best I could from the different camera feeds. As far as I can tell he didn't visit any stores before going to the food court. Of course he might have been planning to eat first, then shop. I've watched the exterior camera feeds, too. He was the one driving the U-Haul."

"Any idea who he is?"

"Not yet. Neither the mall manager nor any of the security team recognized him, but I was able to snag the license plate of the rental truck from the camera footage. U-Haul should be able to give us his contact information."

Of course that assumed he hadn't provided false identification to U-Haul. But I was getting way ahead of myself here. We weren't even sure the rental truck had anything to do with the bomb.

Brigit and I appeared on the screen, first as tiny figures in the background ordering our food at Stick People, then becoming larger as we made our way to the booth.

Irving's face suddenly appeared on the screen, filling the entire field as if he were a giant.

"Whoa!" I jerked my head back reflexively.

On-screen, Irving reached up to unscrew a lightbulb, his mouth falling open and giving us a close-up view of his tonsils. *Lovely.* Now I knew how dentists felt. Irving turned his head to the side and his lips moved. Though there was no audio feed, I realized what I'd just witnessed was him greeting me yesterday. He looked down as he passed the old bulb to his assistant, who handed him a new one. The two repeated the process three more times over the course of nearly four minutes according to the clock. At one point my eyes spotted a flash of something bright orange in the background near the trash can, but then Irving moved and blocked the lens again.

Jackson clicked her mouse to pause the screen and eyed me. "Thoughts?"

My first thought was that Irving had a cracked molar, but that wasn't exactly what the detective was looking for. My mind raced with possibilities. "Assuming Irving knew there was a hidden camera in the clock, he might have intentionally blocked the lens to allow someone else to plant the bomb." Wow, I'd gotten through that entire complicated sentence without a single stutter. Good for me. "But wouldn't one of the visible cameras have recorded the same area, too?"

"Normally that would be the case," Jackson said, shooting me a pointed look before maneuvering her mouse again. "But not yesterday."

She pulled up a feed from another camera. All it showed was the tile floor and the tops of people's heads, including a bleached blonde who was two inches overdue for a root touchup.

When I offered a questioning look, the detective said, "Remember that banner hanging in the food court? Irving hung it from the camera's support bracket on Friday morning. When I asked about it he said he must've bumped the camera out of place without realizing it."

A plausible story. But was it a *true* story?

I gestured to the screen. "Don't the security guards keep a real-time eye on these feeds? It seems like they would've noticed the problem with the camera."

Jackson raised a brow again, as if challenging me to think things through.

I racked my brain. "Maybe the security team was so busy dealing with the crowds that they didn't constantly monitor the feeds. Or maybe someone from Security noticed but decided they could take advantage of the situation. Maybe the bomb was planted by a member of the security team."

She took another sip of her Mountain Dew. "Now you're thinking like a detective."

Using the mouse, I took the feed back a few seconds earlier. "See that?" I pointed to the orange flash. "That could be one of the security guards' helmets."

"Good eye, Luz."

"Have you questioned them?"

"Of course. Your guess was spot on. They've usually

got one person pulling desk duty, watching the cameras. But increased traffic means an increase in shoplifters. Thieves think the store personnel will be too busy to notice them sticking things in their pockets, or that they can easily escape into the hordes. The security team was running like crazy all day Friday and Saturday morning dealing with shoplifters and never got around to fixing the camera. The food court isn't a high-priority area since there's no pricey merchandise for thieves to snag."

"That doesn't rule them out as s-suspects, though, right?"

"Nope."

As I continued to watch the screen, the protestor with the saggy, sunburned butt cheeks appeared near the front of the screen wearing a gauzy cover-up over her bathing suit. I recognized her blond curls and Day-Glo tennis shoes. The gray-haired man in the bike shorts walked next to her, though thankfully he'd put on a T-shirt that hung down over his nards. He held a large white bag in front of him as he walked. Unfortunately, the bag faced inward, toward his abdomen. Given that the Stick People bags bore the printed logo on only one side, it was impossible to tell if the bag was from that particular food stand. He walked over to the trash can and deposited the bag inside.

Extremist animal rights advocates had been known to destroy labs and free caged animals. But would this couple plant a bomb to deter people from buying fur coats? Seemed overkill to me. The hot Texas summer was deterrent enough, at least for the time being. "Think he's the bomber?" I asked.

"Possibly," Detective Jackson said again. "The woman bought their lunch at Stick People earlier. She may be an accomplice."

Randy headed toward the can next, a plastic grocery store bag in his hand. The guy always brought his own homemade lunch and often ate alone outside, a habit he'd likely developed years ago in school. Given his quirkiness, I'd hazard a guess that making close friends had been about as easy for him as it had been for me. The balloons drifted in front of the camera, obscuring Randy from view, but when he walked off to the left of the screen it was clear from his now empty hands that he'd discarded the plastic bag in the can.

Jackson paused the feed and lifted her chin to indicate the screen. "This guy who runs the carousel. What can you tell me about him?"

"Randy?" I shrugged. "He's an odd guy, but he seems harmless." I reminded her that he'd helped to remove a couple of children from the horses before fleeing out the door himself.

"So he was back at work when you discovered the bomb?"

I nodded.

"That rules him out," Jackson said. "The fact that the bomber set a timer means he wanted to be out of the vicinity when the bomb went off." She scratched his name off her list and resumed the camera feed.

On-screen, two customers walked up to the can. One threw out what appeared to be a paper plate containing pizza crust, while the other tossed out an empty French fry basket.

On-screen, the two boys I'd repeatedly caught skateboarding on the property walked up behind me, their skateboards in their hands. One saw me and elbowed the other, pointing my way. The two began making faces behind my back, sticking out their tongues, waving their hands in the air. One even raised his middle finger and danced a little jig. Of course I'd been on my lunch break and too absorbed in my Internet surfing to pay much attention to the activity around me. It was embarrassing to see myself sitting there, ignorant and oblivious.

Jackson shot me a look. "You want to make detective? Work on your observational skills."

"Point taken." I watched the boys move about the screen. They, too, put something in the can, though the camera angle and constantly moving foot traffic made it impossible to see what it was.

Jackson paused the feed again. "We need to find out who those boys are. If you see them again, hold them for questioning."

A moment later, Ariana shoved an empty cardboard coffee cup into the can. The woman seemed to live on lattes alone. The cup was much too small to accommodate a bomb and, besides, it was not inside a Stick People bag. *Darn.* I'd kinda hoped she'd be sentenced to death in the electric chair, get a feel of what the rabbits and minks experienced. I'm just sayin' . . .

There was a knock at the door, but before Jackson could respond Mackey opened it and stuck his head in. *Nosey ass.*

He looked from me to Jackson. "Everything okay in here?"

The detective skewered Mackey with her gaze. "Don't you *ever* open a door on a private conversation without permission from your superior officer. Do you hear me?"

Mackey muttered something about "women on the rag" before closing the door.

Jackson exhaled a sharp breath. "I'll never understand how that prick became the chief's golden boy."

The interruption over, we resumed watching the video footage. Next on the screen was Serhan. He held a large white bag from his stand in each hand. He pushed first one, then the other into the can.

Uh-oh. . . .

Detective Jackson paused the feed. "Not looking good for our Turk, is it?"

Given the frozen image on the screen and the time

shown in the bottom corner, I had no choice but to agree. But was Serhan really the bomber? Would he sacrifice a happy life with his wife and young daughter and risk going to jail? If so, to what end? He served beef at his stand, but I didn't know him to *have* a beef with anyone.

I chewed my lip, half in thought, half in concern. I didn't want Serhan to be a suspect. I liked the guy. But I couldn't let my personal feelings get in the way of my judgment. The facts had to be examined as objectively as possible. Yet . . .

"He didn't seem to be very careful when he put the bags in the trash," I pointed out. "If there had been a bomb in one of them, wouldn't he have been more gentle?"

"Depends," Detective Jackson said. "If he's used to handling explosives, he might be less worried about accidentally setting them off."

"Did you question him about it?" I asked. "Show him the video?"

She nodded. "He claimed the bags were from his family's lunch."

Again, a plausible explanation. But was it a *true* explanation?

"You didn't arrest him," I noted.

"The video alone doesn't provide enough evidence for an arrest," she said. "It may not even be sufficient to support a search warrant for his home, but we've got people working on that."

"So where do we go from here?"

She exhaled a long breath. "We look into anyone and everyone and start eliminating suspects."

THIRTY-EIGHT
I'VE GOT A BONE TO PICK WITH YOU

Brigit

When Megan had pulled her car into the mall parking lot, Brigit first felt apprehensive. Yesterday had been scary. But then her stomach superseded her brain and her mouth watered in anticipation of more meat from the shish-kebab stand. But when they'd arrived in the mall courtyard it had contained only residual smells of food. Nobody seemed to be cooking today. *Rats.* Heck, Brigit would eat a rat if she could find one. It would be a nice way to top off the sandwich Megan's mother had made for her.

If she couldn't have more food, she could at least have a nap. With all her tossing and turning, Megan had made it impossible for the dog to sleep well last night. Brigit settled on the floor, closed her eyes, and in minutes was dozing peacefully at her partner's feet.

THIRTY-NINE
A CLOSE SHAVE

The Rattler

While the fishhooks had been a creative purchase on his part, he wanted his next bombs to have their own unique flair. Razor blades and throwing stars should do the trick nicely.

Though Texas law gave lots of leeway to gun owners, it prohibited the possession of throwing stars. If you wanted to kill someone in the Lone Star State, the legislature preferred it be with a good old-fashioned bullet rather than some type of ninja blade. Texans were nothing if not traditional, and gunfights had been a way of life here since back in the days of the Wild West. But throwing stars? That was something relatively new and unknown and therefore to be feared. It was a ridiculous distinction, really. After all, dead is dead.

Despite the fact that throwing stars were illegal, they were easy to find and buy. All it took was one trip to a flea market, a few subtle hints dropped to a knife dealer, and the Rattler left with a half-dozen eight-point stars, three five points, and even one shaped like a butterfly. He liked the irony of that particular model. The entire purchase had cost him less than two hundred dollars.

Though he'd disguised himself with the mirrored sunglasses and baseball hat at the flea market, the Rattler didn't fear that the dealer would come forward even if word got out about the stars being in the Rattler's next bomb. No way would the dealer willingly implicate himself in a violent felony. Hell, the jury might decide to convict him for the crime and he could find himself facing lethal injection.

Rather than return to Home Depot, the Rattler purchased the razor blades along with more screws and nails at a small Ace Hardware location. Fortunately, he had enough pipe left at home to make several bombs. The only question now was where he should plant his next bombs.

Decisions, decisions.
Eenie-meenie-meinie-BLOW!

FORTY
DIGGING DEEP

Megan

I felt a little odd sharing the next tidbit of information with the detective, but Jackson would need every fact she could get her hands on as quickly as possible in order to rule out suspects and move this case along. Besides, Jackson was the one who'd raised the issue of first responders yesterday.

"I spoke with the bomb tech who arrived first yesterday. He told me he'd just finished swimming at the Forest Park Pool when he got the call."

The pool was only a mile or so from the shopping center and he could have driven the distance in less than two minutes.

Jackson's eyes narrowed. "You questioned a potential suspect?"

A blush warmed my cheeks. "He invited me out for drinks and it came up in conversation."

She stared at me a moment. "Look, Officer Luz. I know you want to help out here, but you've gotta be careful not to overstep or you could jeopardize the investigation. Before you ask anyone questions, check with me first, okay?"

She made a valid point, but it still rankled. I'd taken shrapnel in the butt. Shouldn't that entitle me to do some snooping? No sense arguing with her, though. Sometimes it was easier to ask forgiveness afterward than to get permission beforehand. "Okay."

"That said, I'm glad for the assistance. You can do some of the grunt work."

Grunt work? How flattering. Still, grunt work or not, I was thrilled to be included in the investigation.

Stifling another yawn, she handed me a slip of paper with the letters *MN* and *TX* written on it, each followed by a sequence of numbers. "I was able to snag the U-Haul's license plate number from an outside camera feed. It's the Minnesota plate. Call U-Haul, find out who rented the truck, and run a criminal background check. The Texas plate belongs to the protestor in the bikini. Get her name and address for me, and run a check on her, too."

Next, she handed me a stapled document approximately twenty pages thick. "That's a list of everyone who's worked in the mall in the last six months. Run checks on all of them. Start with the names I've underlined."

I thumbed through the list of workers. The document included each worker's name, birth date, Social Security number, and date of hire. When applicable, the list also included the date of the worker's termination or resignation. There had to be at least three hundred names on the list, but only seven were underlined: Irving Boles. Richard Espinosa. Serhan Singh. Scott Rylander. Stacy Vandercook and her partner, Karla Kuykendall. And, last, Vu Tran.

Jackson gestured to a metal file cabinet in the corner. "Take a look in their personnel files, too. See if you find anything unusual."

Electronic files would have been more convenient and secure and taken up less space, but given that the mall manager was in his early sixties, I supposed he liked to do things the old-fashioned way and maintain paper copies.

"I'll need a computer to run the background checks," I told the detective. "I don't have mine with me."

She stepped to the door and opened it a couple of inches. "Mackey! Bring me your laptop. Officer Luz needs to use it."

He began to voice a protest, but Jackson cut him off with a chop of her hand. "Just do it."

As we waited for Mackey to return with the computer, Detective Jackson continued to review the video feeds, going back in time minute by minute to see if she could spot anyone acting suspicious in the food court area earlier yesterday morning. Meanwhile I searched the Internet on my phone and found a number for a U-Haul rental location not far from the mall. When I called and explained that I needed information on the party who had rented a particular truck, the clerk transferred me to a manager. The manager, in turn, refused to provide the information unless an officer came to the location in person.

The detective sighed when I gave her the news. "What's the address? I'll run by there right quick while you dig around on the computer."

I jotted the address down and handed her the slip of paper. Just after she walked out, Mackey walked in with his laptop.

He scowled as he held it out to me. "You better be careful with it, Luz. It's brand-new."

I took the computer from him, noting it was much lighter weight and had a faster processor than the one in my cruiser. *Lucky jerk.*

I logged into the DMV system and ran the license plate number associated with the protestor in the bikini. According to the Texas Department of Motor Vehicles, the plates had been issued for use on a Nissan Leaf. No surprise that a socially conscious activist would drive an environmentally friendly electric car. The owner's name was Sherry Ketchell Lipscomb. The registered address was in the town of Benbrook, which sat directly to the southwest of Fort Worth. I double-checked the driver's license records to make sure the address on Sherry's license matched that on the registration. It did. I wrote the information down on a fresh sticky note.

Now that I knew the identity of the woman in the bikini, I typed her name into the criminal background check program. The system whirred for a moment before spitting out the data.

Whoa.

Sherry Lipscomb had a rap sheet that started two decades earlier and included a variety of charges. Her first brush with the law was a theft charge at the age of twenty-three. Over the years she'd gone on to commit several acts of vandalism, criminal trespass, and burglary, at shorter and shorter intervals. Most recently, she'd pled guilty to felony destruction of property. For this particular offense she'd paid a fine and restitution, served a month in jail, and been sentenced to two years probation.

Though Sherry's criminal record would prevent her from being nominated for a citizen-of-the-year award, it contained no violent crimes. But there's a first time for everything, isn't there? And her crimes had been escalating, in both frequency and egregiousness.

Hmm. . . .

When she'd stepped up to my cruiser I'd noticed she wore a wedding band. Now that I knew the woman's name, it took little time to check the marriage records.

Per the vital statistics data, she'd married a Michael Lipscomb fifteen years prior. I ran a criminal background check on him and found that he, too, had a well-developed rap sheet, many of his convictions coinciding with Sherry's. Evidently the two had been partners in crime on several occasions. While Sherry's record contained no violent crimes, Michael's contained an assault charge. Unfortunately, the system gave only dates, the degree and type of offense, and the disposition. The particular details of the crimes were not included.

Fortunately, where the government system left off the Internet news reports often took over. A quick Google search brought up an image of Michael Lipscomb from a newspaper report on the assault. The guy in the photo had bushy gray hair and a beard. Sure enough, he was the guy in the bike shorts. The short article stated that Lipscomb had been convicted of assaulting two men at a truck stop in the South Texas town of McAllen. The men had been hauling horses to Mexico for slaughter. The article noted that there had been an argument prior to the assault but failed to detail the victims' injuries.

Finished with my first task, I minimized the window and moved on to the next assignment—background searches on Irving, Serhan, Ricky, and Scott.

Irving had no criminal record. Same for Serhan and Ricky. Scott was another matter. My research indicated that he'd once been arrested for criminal mischief, but the charges had been dismissed.

Hmm. . . .

The Texas criminal mischief statute was a broad one, providing a wide range of punishments for property damage based on the value of the property. Depending on the extent of the damage, a violation could constitute anything from a Class C misdemeanor to a felony of the first degree. I wondered what Scott had done to raise the arresting officer's suspicions. I also knew that the failure of the district attorney to prosecute didn't necessarily mean a person was innocent. It usually meant the DA thought there was insufficient evidence to win the case.

I stood and stepped over to the file cabinet. Inside were the personnel files of those employed directly by the mall itself, including the mall administrative team, the security staff, maintenance and custodial workers, and the carousel and train operators.

Irving's file contained nothing suspicious. Nothing even remotely interesting, for that matter. Irving had been employed for the last decade by the development company that owned the Shoppes at Chisholm Trail. He'd begun his career as a lowly staff member in one of the smaller malls in the outer suburbs, working his way up the chain to larger malls and a shift supervisor position before becoming the foreman here. Before working for the developer, Irving had operated his own handyman service. Under "Reason for Leaving" his handyman job, he'd written: *Want steady work.* I set his file on the desk for easy reference later when Detective Jackson returned.

As I resumed thumbing through the file folders, Randy's file caught my eye. Curious, I pulled his folder from the cabinet. According to his application, his full name was Timothy Randall William Dunham III. A pretty fancy name for a not-fancy-at-all guy. In the education section he'd noted that he'd spent a little over two years as a philosophy major at Southern Methodist University in the neighboring city of Dallas and achieved a 4.0 grade point average. Impressive. Judging from the dates listed, though, he'd dropped out midterm during the fall of his junior year ten months ago. I found myself wondering why. Had he lost interest? Run out of money? Realized that the job market for existentialists was nonexistent?

The résumé Randy had submitted with his application

noted he'd been involved in various theater groups in the area, having once played the leading male role in a production of *The Best Little Whorehouse in Texas*. Could his dramatic ambitions have derailed his college career? Did he see his position as the cowboy carousel operator as some type of role, a small stepping-stone on the way to bigger things, maybe a bit part in the popular *Nashville* TV show?

Oh, well. No point in wasting my time on an idle curiosity. People dropped out of college all the time for all kinds of reasons. It wasn't for everyone.

I returned Randy's file to the cabinet and pulled out Ricky's paperwork. His full name was Richard Alexander Espinosa. When he'd applied for the security position nine months ago, he'd provided only a local post office box number on the application even though the form specifically asked for a physical home address. On his I-9 Employment Eligibility Verification form he listed a residential address in El Paso. This same address appeared on the copy of his driver's license included in his file.

Mr. Castleberry really needed to pay more attention to detail. No way was Ricky commuting from a town six hundred miles to the west. But where was he living now?

Curious, I stepped over my sleeping, snoring partner and returned to Mackey's laptop to check the driver's license records. The El Paso address was the address currently on record with the state. Ricky hadn't yet updated his information with the DMV, despite the fact that Texas law required updates to be made within thirty days of a change in residence. But did this discrepancy mean anything? Perhaps not. After all, who hadn't gotten so busy with everyday life that they'd forgotten to take care of a bill or missed a dental appointment? Failure to update a driver's license could be a similar innocent oversight.

I set Ricky's file on the desk for the detective to look at

when she returned and riffled through the remaining files until I found Scott's documentation. The home address on all of his documents was the same, and the address matched the one listed in the DMV's driver's license and motor vehicle registration database. The only question now was whether he actually lived at the address, which was in the northwestern part of town, not far from Greenwood Cemetery.

Per Scott's employment application, he'd attended the University of North Texas in Denton for four years but hadn't graduated, earning a total of only sixty-six credit hours and a cumulative GPA of 2.1 during that time. While his academic record had been undeniably substandard, he had held a variety of leadership positions in his fraternity. Recruitment Event Organizer. Chair of the Party Planning Committee. Sorority Liaison, which he spelled as *Leazon*. If I had to hazard a guess about the end of his academic career, I'd say his parents had tired of his hit-or-miss approach to his studies and cut him off after his arrest.

Though Scott had not disclosed the criminal mischief arrest on his application, I couldn't blame him. The question on the form asked only about convictions, not arrests, so technically he hadn't lied.

Though there was no personnel file on Serhan, Stacy, Karla, or Vu, Mr. Castleberry did maintain files for each of his tenants. I took a peek at each in turn.

Serhan's file included his lease application, a copy of the booth rental agreement, and a copy of the credit report Castleberry had run to ensure Serhan wasn't a deadbeat. Serhan had a good payment history, though his credit score suffered under mounting debt. It appeared he'd taken out a second mortgage on his house to finance the launch of his shish-kebab stand.

I added Serhan's file to the stack on the desk and pulled

Stacy and Karla's wine shop file from the stack. Their file also contained copies of their credit reports and booth rental agreements, none of which raised any red flags. The lease application indicated that both women had held only part-time jobs prior to opening their wine shop. My guess was they'd sacrificed their careers in order to be home with their children until the kiddos had left the nest, then had decided to open the wine store. While Karla had served as a substitute teacher prior to opening the shop, Stacy had done stints as a reservations agent for Southwest Airlines, a hotel desk clerk, and a bank teller. Neither had retail experience, which probably explained why their wine store was in trouble. A quick criminal background check indicated that both had clean records.

Vu's background check was significantly more interesting. The man had a felony conviction for possession of a controlled substance, as well as a misdemeanor conviction for discharging fireworks within the Fort Worth city limits. He'd pled guilty to both charges. Somewhat shocking. I'd had only brief interactions with the man, but he seemed like a hardworking, gentlemanly, grandfatherly type. Again, the report was short on details, though it provided dates for the offenses and convictions. Vu had been arrested for both violations on January 23, 2012. He'd been convicted of both offenses three months later and ordered to pay a $2,000 fine and serve six months probation.

Detective Jackson returned to the office, holding up a copy of the U-Haul rental form. "Got a name, number, and address here." She dropped back into the rolling chair and pulled the file folders over in front of her. "Find anything interesting?"

"Mr. Tran has two convictions. A fireworks violation and drug conviction."

"No kidding?"

"No kidding."

"Well, then. I'll need to pay him a little visit, won't I?"

I told Detective Jackson that Ricky's documentation was questionable, though Scott's checked out on its face.

"I'll talk to Ricky." She glanced at the schedule the mall manager had provided to her. "Looks like he'll be in tomorrow. What about Irving and Serhan?"

"Nothing on Irving," I said. "Serhan checks out, too. I feel bad for the guy, though. It looks like he took out a second mortgage to finance the launch of his booth."

It was unclear when the courtyard would be reopened. The loss of several days' income could be devastating to a small business like his. If the bomb caused a long-term reduction in traffic at the mall, Serhan's dream of expanding his food booth into a chain could go down the toilet.

Jackson's eyes roamed over the rental application, the booth lease, and the credit report. "Good eye, Luz. We may have found a motive."

"Excuse me?"

"If Serhan was having financial problems, he might have planted the bomb as an excuse for breaking his lease."

What Jackson said made sense logically, but it just didn't sit right with me. Serhan seemed proud of his booth, small as it might be, and he had big plans for the future. Even if the venture had yet to produce significant profits, I simply couldn't see him jeopardizing the business he'd built. Unlike Stacy and her partner, who seemed to have opened their wine store on a whim and without proper experience or a solid business plan, Serhan had paid his dues working at other eateries, learned the trade before venturing out on his own. He'd also started relatively small, which posed less risk.

Jackson whipped out her cell phone and dialed a number. "Hi, Mr. Castleberry. Could you come to your office, please?" A short pause followed. "Thanks." She ended the call and tossed her phone back onto the desk.

A rap sounded on the door a moment later.

"Come in!" Jackson called.

Castleberry stepped into his office, shutting the door behind him.

"Where do you keep the mall's rental income records?" Jackson asked.

Castleberry gestured to his desktop computer.

Jackson stood and gave the man her seat, which was, in actuality, *his* seat. "Pull up the records for the Stick People stand."

Castleberry logged on to his computer and into the bookkeeping program. Given that his assistant normally took care of the finances, it took Castleberry a minute or two to remember how to generate a report. "Here we go," he said, lifting his fingers from the keyboard.

Jackson stepped up behind him to peer over his shoulder. I, in turn, stepped up behind her and peered over hers.

The report indicated that Serhan had been late on his rent twice in the last nine months but both times had made good on the rent plus late fees and interest within a week of the due date.

"That doesn't look so bad," I said.

Jackson grunted. "It doesn't look so good, either."

The detective asked Mr. Castleberry to print out the report and slid it into a folder. Her "thanks" was clearly as dismissive as it was grateful, and the mall manager took her word as his cue to leave the room.

Once the door had closed again, Jackson turned her eyes on me. "Got a name and address for the protestor?"

I pulled up the window on my laptop. "Check this out."

Jackson looked over Sherry Lipscomb's arrest record and offered a condemnatory "tsk-tsk" to the screen.

"Sherry, Sherry, Sherry. You haven't behaved yourself, have you?"

"Her husband has a record, too." I pulled up Michael's report next, then showed her the online newspaper report regarding his assault.

"Looks like we may have ourselves a modern-day Bonnie and Clyde here."

Jackson noted the Lipscombs' address on her pad and slid it back into the breast pocket of her shirt. "Time to make some house calls. As long as you'll keep your mouth shut, you're welcome to come with me."

I nearly leaped out of my skin in excitement. "Really?"

"Really. Just remember, you're only there to observe and learn."

"Got it." My nerves tingled with giddiness. I was going to be involved in an interrogation! Me, the rookie! How cool was that?

As the detective, Brigit, and I left the manager's office together, I returned Mackey's laptop to him. "Thanks." Just because I despised every cell of his being didn't mean I couldn't be civil.

He narrowed his eyes at me. "Where are you going?"

Jackson answered for me: "Out."

In the lot, Jackson motioned for me and Brigit to climb into her car. "Might as well. I haven't had time to vacuum the fur out yet."

FORTY-ONE
FROM SERGEANT TO PRINCESS

Brigit

The backseat of the detective's car was warm and stuffy, but at least the woman agreed to drive through Burger King so Megan could buy Brigit some dinner. Two all-beef patties, hold the special sauce, lettuce, cheese, pickles, onion, and sesame-seed bun.

As the detective pulled out of the parking lot, Megan slid tab A into slot B to assemble the golden cardboard crown and slid it onto Brigit's fluffy head. The dog was tempted to use her paw to push the thing off but decided against it when Megan showed her teeth and laughed. As Brigit had quickly learned after the two had been teamed up, when her partner was happy she tended to be more generous with the treats and more forgiving of Brigit's misdeeds. Brigit had no immediate plans to chew up another pair of shoes, but why not keep her options open?

FORTY-TWO
YESTERDAY'S NEWS

The Rattler

He turned on the evening news, eager to hear the latest developments about the bombing investigation and aftermath. He knew his actions had scared shoppers away, but did the cops have any suspects? Had Fort Worth PD assigned a profiler to determine his motives? Had they found the clue he'd left for them?

To his shock and dismay, the evening news made no reference whatsoever to the event.

Only one day later and it's as if it never happened.

He grew hot with rage. He wouldn't let them get away with this next time. He needed the newscasters to help him spread his message. Of course the only way to stay in the headlines was to escalate his efforts. Mere property damage was not enough to get the public's attention.

Next time, there would have to be injuries. Serious ones.

At least watching the news hadn't been a total loss. Trish LeGrande had worn a low-cut blouse for her report tonight, giving viewers a generous view of her chest. He ogled her foot-wide breasts on the 60-inch high-def television, putting his face to the screen and pretending to motorboat them. *Buh-buh-buh-buh-buh.*

His father walked into the den. "My God, Son! What the hell are you doing?"

FORTY-THREE
TAKE A HIKE

Megan

Using my phone's GPS, I navigated while Jackson drove. Our first stop was the home of Vance Ulster, the man who'd rented the U-Haul.

Ulster lived in a ranch home in the Wedgwood area, not far from Wedgwood Baptist Church, the site of a 1999 mass shooting by a deranged man who killed four teens and three adult members of the church ministerial team before turning the gun on himself. I'd been only ten years old at the time and desperate to make sense of the senseless violence. I couldn't, of course. No one could. For months afterward, I'd been terrified to attend mass, scrunching down in the pew to make myself as small a target as possible, wondering how my parents would shelter their five children should someone with a gun target our congregation. I feared they wouldn't be able to protect us all. I also feared they'd save our lives but die in the effort.

No child should have to live with such terror.

Of course, even then Texans were familiar with mass gun violence. Hell, we practically invented it. In 1966, a shooter ascended the tower at the University of Texas in Austin with multiple rifles and a sawed-off shotgun, proceeding to shoot seventeen people to death. While that particular incident occurred before my birth, many others had taken place during my lifetime. A 1991 mass shooting at a Luby's cafeteria in Killeen left twenty-three dead. The massacre held the record of deaths incurred in a shooting rampage until the incident at Virginia Tech in 2007. In 1993, an ATF raid at the Branch Davidian compound near Waco resulted in the shooting deaths of four federal agents and six members of the weapon-stockpiling sect, with eighty more of the group's members dying when the compound caught fire later after a prolonged standoff. In 2009, violence returned to Killeen when a member of the Army turned on his fellow soldiers at Fort Hood, killing thirteen.

Crazy and weapons are a bad combination, and we had plenty of both in Texas.

Of course I had no delusions that law enforcement could prevent every act of violence. Unbalanced people intent on hurting others often withdrew from family and friends, thus leaving no one to unearth their evil intentions. Still, if there was anything I could do to prevent such violence, to save a person from death or injury, to save another child from fear, to stop the bad guys, I'd do it. Somewhere along the way, my fears and frustrations had evolved into a calling.

As the cruiser made its way slowly up the street, I pointed to a white-brick house with Indian hawthorn bushes and a pecan tree in front. "That's it."

Jackson pulled to a stop in a shady spot at the curb and rolled the windows down far enough to allow Brigit to receive air but not far enough that she could jump out.

"Stay, girl," I told my partner.

She flopped down on the seat, looking irritated.

As Jackson and I walked up the driveway, we heard a *yip-yip-yip* from inside the house. The yipping got louder after we rang the bell, then suddenly stopped.

A moment later, a dark-haired, fortyish woman opened the door, a black teacup Chihuahua cradled in her hands. The bug-eyed dog yipped at us again: *Yip-yip-yip!*

Brigit returned the sentiment through the cruiser's window: *Woof! Woof-woof!* Translation: *You'd make a nice little snack. I've always loved Mexican food.*

Detective Jackson flashed her badge. "I'm Detective Audrey Jackson, Fort Worth Police Department." She wagged a finger my way. "My assistant, Officer Luz."

"Assistant detective." I liked the sound of that, even if it was an unofficial title.

The woman ran her gaze over my sandals, jeans, and casual blouse, her eyes squinty with skepticism. "You're a cop?"

"Yes, I am." I pulled a business card from my purse and handed it to her.

Jackson rocked forward on her toes, her movements indicating her impatience. "We'd like to speak to Vance Ulster, please."

The woman stepped back to allow us inside the foyer. "What is this about?" Her brows angled in concern. "Is something wrong? Is someone hurt? Are our kids okay?"

Jackson raised a palm. "No one is in any immediate danger." She closed the door behind us. "As far as why we're here, we'll take that up with Mr. Ulster."

"Oh . . . okay." Confused and clearly annoyed she couldn't get more information out of us, the woman frowned and gestured with the Chihuahua for us to follow her. She led us through a kitchen decorated in a red-and-black rooster motif and opened the sliding glass door at the back of the room. "Vance?" she called out the door. "There's a couple of policewomen here who want to talk to you."

The man from the video feed stood in front of an enormous gas-powered grill at the back of a covered patio. He held a bottle of light beer in one hand, a large metal spatula in the other. Two skinless chicken breasts roughly the size and thickness of a Ritz cracker sizzled and steamed on the grill. Hardly seemed worth the effort. He could've cooked the meat quickly and easily in a small frying pan.

The man looked our way, surprise registering on his face. "Oh . . . hello. Do you two mind coming out here so I can keep an eye on this meat?"

Immediately my mind went to the barbecue spatula and meat thermometer we'd found at the bomb site. In addition to the metal spatula in his hand, a long-handled two-pronged meat fork hung from the grill, within easy reach of Ulster. Detective Jackson and I exchanged glances. Evidently she'd noticed the potential weapons, too. Her left eye twitched slightly in what I took as a signal that we should proceed with caution.

I put a hand in my purse and felt around for my baton. *Ah. There it is.* If Ulster made any wrong moves, he'd receive a prompt and thorough whacking.

Jackson led the way. Without being invited, Mrs. Ulster followed the detective outside. I took up the rear.

While the woman walked over to stand by her husband, Jackson and I stayed a good ten feet away. A cop's reaction time was normally three-quarters of a second to one and a half seconds after a bad guy's move. Putting some space between us and Ulster gave us time to react should he lunge at us with the meat fork.

"We have some questions about the U-Haul you rented," Jackson told him.

"Was there a problem with the truck?" he asked. "It was in good condition when I turned it in."

Mrs. Ulster chimed in: "We've got the paperwork if you need to see it."

Ignoring Mrs. Ulster, Jackson kept her focus on Vance. "What did you use the truck for?"

The man turned off the gas feed to the grill. "We bought a new living-room set. The store—"

"—wanted to charge us a one-hundred-and-fifty-dollar delivery fee," Mrs. Ulster said, finishing her husband's sentence. "That's highway robbery, if you ask me. Vance rented the truck so he could pick up the furniture himself."

"Where did you buy the furniture?" Jackson asked Vance.

The man began, "The Sofa Spot in—"

"—the Chisholm Trail mall," Mrs. Ulster said.

I'd heard of people being married so long they could finish each other's sentences, but in this case Mrs. Ulster's words didn't seem so much an act of love as a form of control.

"Want to see the furniture?" she asked. Without waiting for an answer, she said, "Show 'em, Vance."

The man pushed the skinless meat to the back of the grill, turned off the gas, and hung the spatula from a hook on the side. He gestured for us to follow him back into the house. Inside, he led us to a family room, his wife on his heels. Sure enough, a new sofa and matching love seat sat in the room, still wrapped in the shipping plastic.

"When did you pick the furniture up?" Jackson asked.

"Around noontime yesterday," Vance said. "They'd just finished loading it on the truck when—"

"—that bomb went off in the food court," Mrs. Ulster said. "Vance got out of there as fast as he could."

"Can't say as I blame him," Jackson replied. She pulled

her notepad out of her pocket and turned her gaze on Vance. "When you were at the mall, did you go anywhere other than the sofa place?"

Of course the detective and I already knew the answer to that question.

Ulster's eyes cut to his wife. "No. The only place I went—"

Again his wife completed his sentence. "—was the sofa store."

Wrong answer.

I glanced over at Jackson but noticed she maintained a poker face, remaining cool and loose. If I wanted to make detective, I'd have to learn how to do that.

"So you didn't visit any other shops?" Jackson asked. "Maybe stop for a drink somewhere or have lunch?"

Vance's gaze again cut to his wife. "No."

Liar!

The word roared so loud in my head I feared the others would hear it. I felt myself go rigid and hoped Ulster wouldn't notice. My grip instinctively tightened on my baton.

"Did you happen to notice anything unusual at the mall?" Jackson asked. "Anyone suspicious?"

"Nothing," he replied. "Everything seemed normal until—"

"—the big *boom*!" Mrs. Ulster supplied, raising the Chihuahua in the air as if punctuating her words with the pup. The poor dog wriggled in her grip, tired of being used as a prop.

Jackson whirled on Mrs. Ulster. "Were you even there?"

"Well, no," said the woman, taken aback. "But Vance told me all about it."

"I'd appreciate it if you'd let *him* tell *us,* too."

The woman's eyes flashed and her lips pursed into a tiny pink raisin.

Jackson pulled a business card from her breast pocket and handed it to Vance. "If anything new comes to mind, give me a call. Thanks for your time."

Wait a minute. Wasn't she going to arrest this guy? He was clearly lying.

Mr. Ulster went back outside to tend to the chicken while Mrs. Ulster walked us back to the front door, closing and locking it behind us without saying good-bye. *Click.*

Jackson headed down the walkway to her car.

I followed. "Ulster was clearly lying. Why didn't you arrest him?"

She turned. "And waste my time? That chickenshit in there isn't the bomber. He's just some pussy-whipped—"

A loud *PSSST* interrupted her.

Psst! Psst! Vance's voice followed: "Over here!"

We turned to see his head peeking around the corner of the house. His eyes were wide. "I went to the food court!" Vance said in a loud, frantic whisper. "I got lunch at that meat-on-a-stick place. I didn't want my wife to know. She's got me on a strict diet. I mean, look at me!" He held up his bottle. "She's got me drinking *light* beer and eating skinless chicken. Those tiny pieces of meat aren't even big enough for the dog!"

Jackson's jaw clenched and she pointed a finger at him. "I have half a mind to drag you in for obstructing justice. I don't care how afraid you are of your wife, you don't *ever* lie to a police officer. You hear me?"

"I'm sorry!" he hissed. "But last time my wife caught me cheating on my diet she fed me nothing but kale and cauliflower for an entire week!"

Jackson exhaled loudly. "Tell me the truth, now. Did you see anything suspicious in the food court? Anyone that looked out of place?"

He shook his head. "I was too busy keeping an eye out

for my wife. She follows me sometimes to make sure I don't cheat on my diet."

"Maybe you two should go to couples therapy," I suggested. Or maybe this guy could just grow a pair. Then again, he could stand to lose a pound or two. Maybe his wife was just looking out for him. I'd dated only sparingly. What did I know about the dynamics of love?

Jackson shot me a glare. "What part of 'keep your mouth shut' did you not understand?"

I offered a contrite cringe in response.

The detective waved a dismissive hand at Ulster and we returned to her car.

Once we were seated with the windows up, Jackson said, "Which way now?"

I typed the address for the Lipscombs' house into my GPS. "West on I-Twenty. Take the Winscott Road exit."

Fifteen minutes later we pulled up to a modest house in an older neighborhood. The house was covered in light-blue aluminum siding and had a small covered porch but no garage. There were no cars in the driveway.

Brigit waited in the car again while Detective Jackson and I went to the door. She rapped loudly three times and we waited to see if someone would come to the door. I felt exposed on the porch without my ballistic vest. What if the Lipscombs had been the bombers and, after they invited us in, they attacked? What if they decided to shoot us through the door? What if I was becoming paranoid?

When nobody had come to the door within a reasonable time, Jackson jabbed the doorbell three times in quick succession, like a sugar-crazed kid on Halloween. *Ding-dong-ding-dong-ding-dong!*

Still no response.

She stepped to the front window and cupped her hands

around her face to peer inside. Though the curtains were drawn, there was a half-inch gap between them.

"See anything?" I asked.

"The world's ugliest easy chair and a bunch of stained carpet."

She stepped aside so I could take a look. She was right. The recliner was shaped like Buddha and covered in an earwax-gold fabric. The light-tan carpet bore a number of dark stains. Along the back wall was a huge aquarium with a light shining into one part of it. There were no fish inside. Rather, the glass box was filled with dirt, a shallow ceramic water dish, and a snake that looked to be about six feet long. Hard to tell for sure, given that he was curled up.

Jackson consulted her notepad and dialed the Lipscombs' home phone number. We could hear the phone ringing inside.

Rrring . . . rrring . . . rrring.

Eventually a machine picked up. "You have reached Sherry and Michael—"

The machine clicked off when Jackson hung up.

The roar of a lawn mower starting up across the street drew our attention. A sturdy barefoot woman pushed a three-wheeled mower over her small lawn, kicking up a cloud of dirt and grass clippings. If she wasn't careful, she might soon be kicking up a toe.

Jackson gestured for me to follow her. "Maybe she knows something."

Brigit stood on the backseat of the unmarked cruiser, her head turning to watch us as we crossed the street. When we reached the curb on the other side, Jackson flashed her badge and motioned for the woman to turn off the mower.

"Sorry to interrupt," the detective said, introducing

herself. "We're looking for Sherry and Michael Lip-scomb. Any idea where they might be?"

"They headed out yesterday evening for a camping trip," the woman said.

Jackson waved a fly out of her face. "Do you know where they were going?"

The woman lifted her shoulders. "*They* didn't even know where they were headed. They said they'd go wherever the winds blow them."

Interesting choice of words.

Jackson continued to fish for information: "Any idea when they're coming back?"

Up went the shoulders again. "Who knows. Last fall they spent five weeks out in Big Bend and another three at some state park in Oklahoma. They go to Arkansas on occasion, too. Anywhere there's good hiking trails. They're into all that nature stuff."

"They camp in tents?"

"Sometimes," the woman said. "Sometimes they'll get a cabin if business has been good."

"What kind of business are they in?"

"Batik. Sherry makes dresses and scarves and stuff, and Michael sells them at craft shows and online."

"You know them well?" Jackson asked.

"Well enough," the woman said.

What the heck did that mean? Well enough for *what*, exactly?

Jackson scratched at a spot on her cheek. "You know if they've got anyone checking their mail? Feeding the snake?"

The woman shrugged. "If they do, it's not me."

"I'd love to reach them," Jackson said. "Any chance you've got their cell numbers?"

"They're in my contacts list," the woman said. "I'll get my phone and be right back."

The woman disappeared into her house for a couple of minutes.

"Think she's calling the Lipscombs?" I asked, keeping my voice low. "Warning them?"

"Could be," Jackson said. "Not anything we can do to stop her if she is."

The woman returned a moment later with her cell phone and held it out to Detective Jackson. "Here you go."

Jackson eyed the readout and instructed me to write the numbers down as she rattled them off. She handed the phone back to the woman and thanked her. "If you happen to see them, tell them to give me a call." She gave the woman her card.

We climbed back into the cruiser and she immediately tried both cell numbers, reaching only a voice mail at each one. She left a message on both phones asking the Lipscombs to call her.

"What do you think?" I asked.

She shot me a pointed look. "I think our animal lovers may be on the lamb."

FORTY-FOUR
THE DOG DAYS OF SUMMER

Brigit

Monday morning, Brigit heard the gravelly sound of skate-board wheels tearing up the mall's walkway behind them. Megan turned and blew her whistle: *Tweeeet!*

Damn, that hurt Brigit's ears!

"Stop!" Megan hollered.

When the two boys on the skateboards sailed by without even slowing, Megan unclipped the leash from Brigit's collar and issued the order for the dog to take them down.

Gladly.

Brigit took off after the boys, her nails scrabbling and scraping on the cement. Oh, how she loved a good run. The wind in her hair, the bugs in her teeth. Such pure joy.

She leaped onto the back of the first boy she reached and grabbed hold of the collar of his shirt. The kid flew face-first off his skateboard, sending it rocketing back behind him. Luckily, the mall was nearly empty and the board crashed into a large potted ornamental tree without causing injury. The boy, on the other hand, hit the walk-way with an *oomph!* and proceeded to skid ahead on his face, palms, and chest.

"Fuuuck!" he cried.

On Megan's command, Brigit left the boy on the ground for her partner to deal with and took off after the other kid. Glancing back, he pedaled his legs like mad, trying to outrun the dog. As if the punk had a chance. If Brigit were capable of laughing, she would have.

Another leap, another *oomph!,* another kid down on the concrete. Brigit earned two liver treats for her efforts. All in all, not a bad way to start the workweek.

FORTY-FIVE
HOLE IN ONE

The Rattler

As he cruised down Colonial Parkway, he spotted that old woman who drove the green minivan. She'd pulled up next to the Dumpster at the back of the country club parking lot. The club had placed a set of weatherworn wicker patio furniture by the garbage bin for pickup. He slowed as the woman struggled to lift the love seat into her van. Might as well help her. After all, wasn't she one of the people he was fighting for? The poor? The oppressed? The underprivileged? The powerless?

He pulled his car up next to her van and climbed out. "Let me help you with that."

The old woman offered a genuine gap-toothed smile. "Thanks a bunch. My muscles aren't what they used to be."

He eased the love seat into the back of her van, then inverted the two chairs on top of it.

While he worked, she informed him of her plans. "I'm going to sand the pieces down, repaint them, and slap some new fabric on the cushions."

"Good for you," he said.

He was just about to shut the van's doors when a member of the club's executive staff stepped up, a short-range radio in his hand. He stopped on the grass ten feet away. "We need you two to move along now."

"Who's this *we*?" The Rattler shredded the man with his stare. "All I see is *you*."

The man put the radio to his mouth and pushed a button. "Security to the Dumpsters. Stat."

The Rattler snorted. *What a chickenshit.* Did the man have no balls?

The woman scurried to the door of her van. "I don't mean to cause any trouble. I'm going now."

The Rattler slithered along much more slowly, glaring at the man as he climbed into his car, started the engine, and eased slowly past, his windows down.

From off to the right came a cry: "Fore!"

Instantly the Rattler knew the perfect venue for his next strike.

A slow smile spread across his face. "Have a wonderful, terrific, ridiculously fantastic day!" he called to the bewildered-looking man on the grass.

The Rattler's first bombing attempt might have been subpar, but his next would be par for the course. Maybe even a hole in one . . .

FORTY-SIX
SLAMMER

Megan

Ricky helped me escort the skater boys to the administrative wing. As we passed the Victoria's Secret store, I caught a glimpse of the Big Dick inside, coming on to the busty blonde who managed the shop.

He held up a pink thong and ran a finger along the inside of the scooped crotch. "You wear these sexy little things?"

She snatched the panties he was fondling out of his hand and let him know in no uncertain terms she wasn't interested: "What I wear is none of your business."

The guy didn't even have the sense to be humiliated. He just laughed and said, "You ever want a sample of what I've got to offer, you let me know."

Jackson was right: I should've shot Mackey and fed him to the tigers while I had the chance.

As we passed the food stands, I spotted Aruni behind the counter at Stick People. As long as I'd been on this beat I'd never seen her working the stand. Leaving the boys under Ricky's guard, I stepped over to the counter, leading my partner on her leash. Brigit's tail began to wag in anticipation of food. Never mind that it wasn't quite lunchtime yet.

"Hi, Aruni," I said. "Are you going to be w-working here with Serhan now?"

The woman looked at me with troubled eyes, worry lines forming on her forehead. "You didn't hear? Serhan was arrested last night."

I felt my body go rigid. "What? Why?"

"Something about his visa," Aruni said, fighting tears.

An immigration issue? Now? It was too much of a co-incidence. No doubt he was being held on the unrelated charge until Fort Worth PD could put all of the clues to-gether and determine whether he was the bomber.

"I have an appointment to meet with an attorney this afternoon." She wiped a tear away with her fingers. "The police came to our house last night and went through all of our things. It was terrible. Kara cried all night for her daddy."

I had no idea what to say. "I . . . I'm sorry, Aruni. I'm sure it will all get worked out."

It would. Eventually. Either Serhan would be deter-mined to be the bomber or he'd be freed. Until then his wife and daughter would be stuck waiting and worrying.

Ricky and I sat the boys down in the security office, where we waited for Detective Jackson to come question them. She was already on-site, speaking with the people who worked the barbecue stand, trying to determine whether the meat thermometer and spatula that had been in the bomb were somehow connected to the business.

When she arrived, she asked Ricky to return in half an hour. "When I'm done with these two, I've got something I'd like to discuss with you."

He looked taken aback but nodded. "No problem."

Brigit and I stood by the door while the detective grilled the boys.

"You two ever been in trouble with the law before?" she asked as she fingered through the taller one's wallet.

They both shook their shaggy heads.

She jutted out her chin to indicate me. "Officer Luz tells me she's instructed you multiple times not to skate at the mall but that you've blatantly defied her orders. She also says you threw fireworks in the parking lot. That true?"

The two offered lame excuses.

"I didn't hear her say not to skate," said the shorter one.

"I've never even seen her before today," the taller one said, his memory, like Cuthbert's, seeming to fail him. When he looked up at the security camera mounted in the corner of the room, he changed his tune, as if realizing our interactions might have been caught on video. "Not that I remember, anyway."

I plucked my baton from my belt and flicked my wrist. *Snap!* The baton extended to its full, glorious, ball-busting length. The boys eyed it and blinked. I twirled it in my hand. *Swish-swish-swish.*

The detective finished going through their things and tossed their wallets onto the desk. "I'm not going to beat around the bush, boys. We've got camera footage of the two of you in the food court on Saturday shortly before the bomb went off. You were dancing around, acting like a couple of asshole baboons."

The two exchanged glances. *Fearful* glances. Gotta say, it felt good to see them shaken.

"If you two planted that pipe bomb," Jackson continued, "you're better off coming clean about it. The DA might reduce your sentence if you cooperate."

"What?!" cried the shorter one, his eyes popping wide.

"We didn't—" the taller one began, reflexively reaching out a hand and leaning forward in his chair.

Jackson sliced the air sideways with her index finger. "Before you say anything you might regret, you know, like a *lie,* I'm going to give each of you the chance to talk to me alone. You're looking at felony time, here. Attempted murder and whatnot."

The boys' mouths gaped, their eyes darting frantically from each other, to me, to the detective, as if reality were eluding them and they were desperate to catch sight of it before it disappeared entirely.

Jackson gestured to the shorter boy. "You. Step into the other room." She lifted her eyes to signal me to go with him.

I opened the door and stepped out, Brigit following me. The boy came out afterward. I pointed my baton at a chair on the other side of the room. "Sit over there."

He took a seat and looked up at me, terror in his eyes. "I swear we didn't—"

He jerked back as I swung my baton so close to his face it blew his shaggy bangs aside.

"Did you say something?" I said. "Because I don't think I heard you, either."

Brigit backed me up with a growl: *Grrr.* She was really starting to grow on me.

While the boy sat, quietly now, chewing his lip so hard it began to bleed, I continued to stand, twirling my baton. *Swish-swish-swish.*

I might not be a detective yet, but I knew exactly what Jackson was doing here. Utilizing the strategy of divide and conquer. If these two boys had planted the bomb, she might have a better chance of scaring a confession out of them if each thought the other might be waffling. The last to confess could be left holding the bag.

As I twirled my baton—*swish-swish-swish*—I watched

the boy in the chair. The teen who'd been so tough and cocky outside on his skateboard now seemed nothing more than a frightened, naïve child.

Five minutes later, Jackson sent the taller boy out and called the shorter one in. The taller one slid into the seat his friend had just vacated. His face bore a shell-shocked expression and his shoulders began to jerk with silent sobs. Meanwhile I continued to work my baton. *Swish-swish-swish*.

He looked up at me, tears spilling over his lids. "We didn't do it!" he cried on a breath, his voice barely more than a whisper. "We wouldn't do something like that!"

As much as I loathed the little shit, as much as I wanted to *whomp* him in his adolescent nards, I believed him. He might be a punk. He might have a rebellious streak. But he wasn't a bomb maker. His eyes bore too much sincere desperation for him to be lying.

Evidently Detective Jackson reached the same conclusion. A few minutes later, she released the two boys into the custody of their mothers, whom she'd telephoned for pickup.

"Keep a better eye on your boys," she told the mothers. "Maybe sign them up for church camp."

As the boys and their mothers left, Ricky returned.

The detective got right down to business. "After the bombing here on Saturday, I did a quick check on everyone who works at the mall. You've got a problem."

I had been the one to run the background checks and look over the paperwork, not her, but I wasn't about to debate the matter with the detective. After all, I'd been working under her direction and she'd allowed me to tag along when she'd interrogated Ulster and visited the Lipscombs' house.

When I'd returned home last night, I'd spent three additional hours finishing up the criminal background checks on the rest of the mall employees. The vast majority were clean, but my search had turned up a few interesting tidbits. One of the women who worked the cosmetics counter at Macy's had a misdemeanor prostitution conviction. The assistant manager of the men's shoe store was on probation for driving under the influence. A woman who worked at the smoothie stand had a recent conviction for possession of marijuana. Could the woman have tossed a joint in the garbage? Was that why Brigit alerted on the can? I hadn't seen the woman in the video footage, but Irving's head could have blocked the view.

Ricky's head turned slightly in alarm. "What do you mean there's a problem?"

"Where do you live?" the detective asked.

Ricky rattled off an address and apartment number. I recognized the street. It wasn't far from the mall. Just a couple exits farther west on the freeway.

She pulled out his job application and the copy of his driver's license. "Why didn't you list that address on your application?"

"When I applied for the job I didn't have my own place," he said. "I was crashing with my cousin for a while until I could find my own digs."

Jackson narrowed her eyes at him. "Your driver's license records still show your residence in El Paso. Why haven't you updated your license?"

Ricky threw his hands in the air. "I've tried. Three times! You ever seen the lines at the DMV? It takes hours to get anything done over there."

Jackson stared at him a moment longer. "You get over to the DMV and get your address updated. I don't care how long you have to stand in line. If it's not done in the next week, I'll have Officer Luz here issue you a citation."

Ricky glanced my way, an irritated look on his face.

"Get on back to work now," the detective said.

Ricky left the room without another word.

Jackson motioned to the walkie-talkie on my belt. "Call Scott in here."

I pulled the radio from my belt and pushed the talk button. "Scott, please report to the security office."

A few minutes later, he appeared in the doorway. Though his face was turned to me, his eyes darted to the detective. "You wanted to see me, Officer Luz?"

"I'm the one who wanted to see you." Jackson stood and motioned for him to shut the door. "Have a seat and let's talk."

Scott closed the door and gingerly lowered himself into the chair, perching on the edge as if poised to flee. A sheen of fresh flop sweat covered his forehead.

"I've run background checks on the mall employees," the detective said again. "We got a ding on yours."

Scott's cheeks turned a blotchy pink.

"You were arrested for criminal mischief. Want to tell us about that?"

His tight-lipped expression said *no,* he didn't want to tell us. He looked away for a moment before turning back. "I was never put on trial. The charges were dropped."

"Lucky you," the detective shot back. "Now tell me what happened."

Scott exhaled a couple of times like a snorting bull as he fidgeted in his chair. "Look, some guys in my fraternity just played a stupid prank on some guys in another fraternity, that's all."

"A prank?" Jackson asked. "What kind of prank?"

"The other fraternity had this big fountain in front of their house. You know the ones with the little boy peeing? Well, we—I mean, *some of the other guys in my frat*— snuck over there one night and drained the water out of it and replaced it with gasoline. I guess they thought it would be funny to make the statue pee fire, you know?"

He chuckled nervously. "Anyway, they tossed a match into it and things got out of control and the fire spread to the house. We—I mean, *they*—called the fire department, but everyone ran off before the truck got there."

That's as far as he went.

Jackson made a circular motion with her finger. "Keep going. How did you end up getting arrested?"

"Later that night, the cops came to our frat house and arrested a bunch of us. But then it turned out there were no witnesses who could identify the people who'd started the fire, so they dropped the charges."

"Uh-huh." Jackson stared at him for a long minute, as if trying to assess whether the young man sitting before her was merely an immature prankster or a criminal with malicious intentions. I was trying to determine the same thing.

"Where do you live?" Jackson asked.

Scott recited the address that was on his employment documentation.

"You live alone?" she asked.

Scott shook his head. "With my parents." As if realizing how pathetic that sounded, he added, "I'm only staying there until I can save up enough money to get my own place."

"Uh-huh," she said again, still staring. Finally, Jackson dismissed him. "Be sure to let me know if you see anything suspicious around here."

Scott's rigid body relaxed in relief. "I will."

After Scott left, Jackson said, "I don't trust those two."

"Ricky and Scott?"

"Yeah. They're up to something. I can feel it."

"You think they planted the bomb?"

"Maybe," she said. "Or maybe they know who did, but there's something in it for them."

"A payoff?"

"Maybe."

Blurgh. There were too many maybes and not enough certainties.

"Any word from the Lipscombs?" I asked.

"Nope. Not a one."

Although they were wanted for questioning, there wasn't yet enough evidence against the Lipscombs to order them back to Fort Worth. We'd just have to wait and hope they'd get in touch.

"The good news," Jackson added, "is that there was enough evidence to get a search warrant for their house. There's a team going through it right now."

I'd be curious to hear what, if anything, the team found.

"What do you think about the barbecue stand?" I asked. "Anything suspicious there?"

She shook her head. "Everyone seemed genuinely freaked out by what happened. None of them has a reason to suspect any of their coworkers."

"What about Vu Tran? Have you talked to him?"

"The lady who runs the bridal shop said he doesn't work Mondays. I'll be back tomorrow to question him."

"Can I be there?"

She lifted a shoulder. "Why not? Meet me there when they open at ten."

"What about the pet store? And the sushi place? And the wine shop?"

"On my 'to do' list. First I need to speak to the Stick People staff, see if they remember anyone unusual. Then I plan to talk to as many people as I can who were in the food court when the bomb went off, see if I can find any eyewitnesses. I believe that's our best bet for identifying the bomber."

"That square-headed nail. Did you figure out what kind it is?"

She snorted. "Honey, if you think all of these things get done overnight, you've been watching too much CSI. I've asked one of the techs to look into it, but these things take time. They're still cataloging and tagging all the physical evidence."

"Understood. I just thought it might be a clue." Of course the same could be said for the fishhooks, sewing needles, fondue forks, and corkscrew.

She let out a long breath. "I'm thinking the bomber put all of those strange things in the bomb to send us down bunny trails, test our moxie."

If that was the case, then the bomber was in trouble. I had moxie out the wazoo.

Her business with me complete, the detective stood to go. I followed her into the courtyard, where we bade each other good-bye. She went in search of more employees to question, while Brigit and I returned to our beat.

The Big Dick stood at the Cinnabon stand now, flirting with the redhead behind the counter, telling her what sweet, luscious buns she had and how he'd love to sink his teeth into them.

He had no better luck here than he'd had in the lingerie store. The woman rolled her eyes. "Gee. Haven't heard that one before."

Despite the lack of customers, the carousel was back in full swing today, the organ music filling the space, the horses gliding up and down in a gentle canter, the blue one bearing a corkscrew-sized hole in its side. Only one child, a pigtailed girl of about eight, was on the ride. Randy stood near his podium, practicing with his lasso. He twirled the thing over his head, then tossed it, the loop falling over the head of one of the carousel horses.

"Nice aim!" I called as I headed over.

Randy grinned and trotted alongside the carousel for a moment before hopping on and removing the lasso from the horse's neck. When the carousel came around again, he hopped down right in front of me. "Ta-da!"

"You've gotten pretty good with that rope."

He gestured at the nonexistent line of customers. "I've had lots of time to practice this morning."

I glanced up at Randy's hat. Today in his hatband he sported a Twinings Earl Grey tea bag still in the wrapper, a travel brochure for a Caribbean cruise, and a Dum Dum sucker, mystery flavored.

The girl on the horse circled by, her arms hanging limp by her sides, her cheek smushed up against the pole. She looked bored out of her skull. "Can I get off now?"

Randy glanced up at the wall clock. "But it's only been twenty minutes!" He cut me a smile with those perfect teeth of his before pushing the button to stop the ride.

The carousel glided to a smooth stop. The girl climbed down from her horse, hopped off the ride, and promptly emptied her stomach on the floor with a resounding *urp*. Her mother left the mess and tossed an irritated look in Randy's direction, as if the girl getting sick was his fault.

"I was only trying to treat the kid to some extra time on the ride!" he called. "Give you your money's worth!"

I gave Randy a pat on the shoulder. "No good deed goes unpunished." Pulling my walkie-talkie from my belt, I summoned a custodian.

An elderly grandmother with three grandkids milling about her stepped up to his podium.

"Welcome to Jism Trail Mall," Randy said. "I'm the Randy wrangler. How many tickets would you like?"

The woman's wrinkled face puckered. "Who did you say you were?"

"Randy the wrangler," he replied, giving me a surreptitious wink.

I shook my head. The guy was a hoot, but if he didn't watch it he just might find himself getting fired.

The woman looked over at me and Brigit. "Wait a minute. Aren't you that policewoman from TV? The one who got tuna salad in her hair?"

I sighed loudly. "Yes. That was me."

Though I half-expected Randy to snicker, he actually came to my defense instead. "Officer Luz saved a lot of lives. We owe her."

What a nice thing to say. I gave him a smile. "Thanks, Randy."

"You know it." He pointed both index fingers at me in a playful gesture. "That whole 'Tunabomber' thing," he added, leaning toward me. "What a stupid moniker, huh?"

I rolled my eyes. "Agreed."

I wondered how long it would take for me to live the tuna salad thing down. If anything, that stupid viral video only reinforced my determination.

Come hell, high water, or tuna salad, I'd catch that bomber.

FORTY-SEVEN
FIRST DATE

Brigit

As Megan pulled her cruiser into Forest Park, Brigit stuck her nose out the window and scented the air. *Sniff-sniff.*

Her tail began to wag of its own accord. He was here. The dog from the courtyard she'd shared the barbecue with. With any luck, maybe their partners would take them out for a nice lunch. Brigit wouldn't mind some more of that cheese-covered steak.

FORTY-EIGHT
DAMAGE UNDONE

The Rattler

He made his way across the courtyard, surprised at how normal everything looked. Amazing how quickly damage could be repaired when dollars were at stake. But when it was lives? Forget it. After all, look how long it had taken the government to react to Hurricane Katrina.

Though he had attended private schools growing up, he remembered hearing about the influx of students at Fort Worth's public schools after the devastating hurricane hit New Orleans. He'd gone with his mother and her church-lady friends to deliver bedding, groceries, and toys to the displaced families living in area shelters.

It struck him as infinitely unfair that the wealthy had been able to easily flee the deadly storm while the poor, the most vulnerable, had been left behind to face the storm head-on, to deal with the subsequent flooding. *To die.* It also struck him as infinitely insensitive and hypocritical the way his mother and her friends quoted Bible verses, offering linguistic comfort to the refugees, then turned around the instant they were out of earshot and began gossiping about and judging the very people they'd allegedly come to help. He realized then that helping others was only a by-product of, and not the purpose of, their acts of purported generosity. More than anything, the self-absorbed, image-conscious women wanted to impress one another with how much they could spare.

They did the right things, but for the wrong reasons.

Their shallowness sickened him.

It was time for people to stop worrying so much about their precious possessions, their precious images, and to start truly looking out for one another.

FORTY-NINE
LUNCH . . . DATE?

Megan

Had Seth kissed me after our dinner Saturday night, I would not have tracked him down at the Forest Park Pool today. I had never been one to throw myself at a guy, and I sure as hell wouldn't start now, no matter how many times Seth had crossed my mind in the last forty-eight hours. If you want a count, it was 83 gajillion times, give or take.

But evidently Seth and I had only a work-related relationship, and both of us had a vested interest in seeing the bomber caught. Seth would be interested to know the status of the investigation. I'd expect him to extend me the same professional courtesy.

At the end of the parking lot sat Seth's ridiculous flame-covered car. Had he kissed me Saturday, I would have instead described the car as kick-ass. Attitude affects perception, after all. But whether the Nova was ridiculous or kick-ass, I pulled up next to it, parked, and climbed out, opening the back door so Brigit could hop out, too. After giving her a chance to lap up some cool water from the pop-up bowl I carried on my belt, I led her over to the tall chain-link fence that separated the pool area from the rest of the park.

My eyes scanned the water. Kids buoyed about in the open space, splashing one another and kicking and doing handstands. An elderly woman in a bright-blue swim cap performed water aerobics with some type of hand weights. Beyond them, in the designated lap lanes, arched a strong, muscular back covered by an eagle. The eagle disappeared under the water, then reappeared as Seth swam a butterfly stroke across the pool. His rear end also popped up and disappeared repeatedly, his green buttocks teasing and tempting as they moved up in down in rhythmic thrusts.

Wow. I really needed to get some, huh?

"C'mon, girl." I tugged on Brigit's leash, leading her to the pool entrance.

The nice thing about being a uniformed cop is that you are allowed in anywhere at any time for no charge. It's like having the key to the city. The woman working the pay booth glanced up as I approached and greeted me with a cheerful "good morning" but clearly had no intention of stopping me to ask whether my business there was professional or personal or to attempt to assess the entry fee.

I walked to the end of Seth's swim lane and waited for him to wear himself out. It took longer than I expected. A full six laps. Finally, he glided to a graceful stop, put out a hand to grab the edge of the pool, and surfaced at my feet, Brigit's paws.

His eyes took in my steel-toed shoes and Brigit's fluffy feet and snapped upward. "Megan! Hey!"

For a guy who'd made no move to kiss me Saturday, the broad, surprised smile and the gleam in his eye told me his interest in me could be more than professional, after all. As my sister, Gabby, would say, he had me all confuzzled. Yeah, she says shit like that sometimes. Kinda makes me want to slap her.

I looked down at Seth's green eyes, his broad shoulders, his sexy chin dimple. On a totally unrelated note, a hot flush rushed through me. Perhaps the sun was giving me heatstroke.

"You look warm," he said. "Come in for a swim?"

"I don't have a suit."

"I've got a spare in my bag," he said. "You're welcome to it."

"Wouldn't that just be bottoms?"

"Well . . . yeah." He treated me to a naughty grin. "But you could pretend you're on a beach in France."

That would be difficult given there was nothing around that at all resembled the Eiffel Tower. The closest thing Fort Worth had was the tower at the Will Rogers Memorial Center.

"I'm here on police business," I said, as much to remind myself as to inform him. "Got an update on the bombing investigation."

Seth put his palms on the cement next to me and lifted himself up out of the pool, his pecs flexing as his muscles engaged. Even though Seth wore a regular suit rather than a Speedo, he was showing plenty of tan, sun-kissed skin. The suit dipped below his belly button, giving me a glimpse of the top of his hip bones. I felt a nearly uncontrollable urge to gnaw on one of them. Perhaps Brigit's canine ways were rubbing off on me.

As he stood up straight next to me, my temperature went up another ten degrees. Yeah, the sun was definitely causing me to suffer heatstroke.

He jerked his head in the direction of a shady area. "My towel's over there."

He led the way and Brigit and I followed. Blast stood

up from his spot under the tree he was tied to, pulled his leash out as far as it would go, and *woof*ed as Brigit approached. She barked back at him, her tail wagging so energetically her entire body wriggled as if she were working an invisible Hula-hoop. *Aloha oe*.

Seth snatched a striped beach towel off the ground and shook his head like a dog, droplets flinging from his hair.

"Hey!" I cried, putting up a hand to shield my face.

He grinned. "Payback's a bitch, ain't it?"

I supposed I had no right to complain given that I'd flicked the condensation from my margarita glass at him on Saturday. Besides, knowing that the drops of water now gracing my face had once been in contact with Seth's skin kinda got me going.

As he dried himself off with the towel, the dogs began to play. Blast bent down on his front paws, jerking left and right, while Brigit did the same.

Dry now, Seth slung the towel back over his shoulder. "I think our dogs are flirting."

I glanced at the two of them before looking back at Seth. "If they're going to get involved, I need to know a few things first. Is Blast a player? Has he had all his shots? And what exactly are his intentions where Brigit is concerned?"

Seth replied to my questions, "No. Yes. And . . ." He offered a soft smile. ". . . let's see where it goes."

All righty, then.

He put a hand up on the tree next to him and leaned against it. "So? What's the news?"

"The Turkish guy who runs the shish-kebab stand has been arrested. Purportedly it's for an immigration violation—"

"But we all know that's bullshit," Seth supplied for me.

Hmm. He wasn't going to be like Vance Ulster's wife, finishing my sentences for me, was he?

"They've also got people searching a house that belongs to two of the protestors that were at the mall Saturday. The couple have rap sheets a mile long. None of her offenses were violent, but he's got an assault charge. They seem to have disappeared and they're not answering their cell phones or returning voice mails. A neighbor says they left for a camping trip Saturday evening, but she's not sure where they've gone."

"Camping trip?" Seth gave a soft snort. "Sounds awfully coincidental."

"True." Still, coincidences happen. Just like it was a coincidence my girly parts suddenly felt rusty from lack of use. "The skateboarders have been ruled out. We talked to them this morning. The barbecue stand is a dead end, too."

Seth rolled up his towel and stuffed it into his duffel bag. "Let's talk about this more over lunch."

"Okay," I said, though, really, what more was there to say? I'd already given him all the information I had. But, you know, with this case of sudden heatstroke I was suffering it couldn't hurt to sit down inside somewhere cool.

"You got a favorite place around here?" Seth asked.

"Spiral Diner."

"Never been there."

"You'll love it."

Seth excused himself to change in the men's locker room, returning in flip-flops, wrinkled plaid shorts, and a T-shirt declaring that he'd donated blood at the fifteenth annual fire department blood drive. We rounded up our partners and headed out to the parking lot.

"Can I drive your cruiser?" Seth asked.

"No."

"Please-please-please?"

"'No' means 'no.'"

"Can I at least turn on the lights and siren? I never get

to do that on the fire trucks. They always make me hang off the back."

I wished he hadn't said that. My mind conjured up a really sexy visual of him hanging off the fire truck wearing nothing but black boots and a hard hat and swinging his big hose. "Okay, fine."

We loaded Brigit and Blast into the backseat of my patrol car. After Seth tried out the siren and lights, drawing the attention of not only everyone at the pool but also a couple of joggers, we headed a few blocks west to Spiral Diner, which sat on the corner of 6th and Magnolia.

The restaurant was a vegan place, an anomaly for a city with the nickname Cowtown. The servers were evidently hired based on their ability to tolerate body piercings and their refusal to follow fashion trends. Gotta admire that kind of courage. Normally, you'd have to drive down to Austin to find this kind of antiestablishment establishment. The décor was classic diner, with vinyl booths and chairs and Formica tables. Starburst-shaped light fixtures hung from the ceiling.

We slid into opposite sides of a booth along the back wall, our dogs taking places next to us. Seth picked up his menu and began to look it over. "What's good here?"

"Everything," I said. "But my favorite is the Cowboy Burger." Of course I'd follow it up with the Deathstar Sundae, as always. I wasn't sure whether the Force was with me, but I was pretty sure the previous sundaes had stuck around on my thighs. Maybe I should take up swimming, too.

The waitress came over to take our order. She was a wisp of a girl wearing a red bandana tied over her head and cat-eyed glasses. Her eyes went from me to Brigit. She looked back at me, squinting through her lenses. "You're the cop from YouTube, right? The one with the tuna salad in her hair?"

No sense denying it. "Yes. That's me."

"Wow! Is the fish oil why your hair is so shiny?"

"No." I didn't elaborate.

The waitress turned and called out to the other staff, "Look who's over here! The tuna cop from the Internet!"

Before I knew what was happening, Brigit and I were surrounded by a half-dozen waitstaff. Another stood in front of me, taking a photo on his smartphone. Seth watched the encounter with an amused look on his face.

They say everyone gets their fifteen minutes of fame. I hoped mine was over now, even if I'd been shortchanged by twelve minutes.

Seth and I placed our orders and sat back.

"So," Seth said, looking around the place before eyeing me across the table, "you're into organic food and stuff like that?"

I shrugged. "I try to be healthy. Reduce my carbon footprint when I can. Buy fair-trade p-products."

His upper lip quirked. "Sounds like a lot of work."

"It c-can be." Honestly, there were times I wished I could live in blissful ignorance and not worry about the consequences of my actions. It would make life so much easier. Unfortunately, I knew too much to go back. That's what I got for being curious and reading so much.

"You stutter a little," he said.

Once again I was blindsided by his bluntness. But once again I realized that such directness could be refreshing. "Sometimes," I admitted before turning the tables on him. "What are your faults?"

"You mean like a foot fetish? Porn addiction? Undescended testicle?"

"Yeah."

"I used to have trouble with the *th* sound. I called myself Seff until I was seven."

"Hmph. An undescended testicle would have been

more interesting." *Really. Where does it go? Does it play hide-and-seek behind the pancreas or what?*

"Sorry to disappoint you." Seth offered me a sly smile and took a sip of his water. "Are things back to normal at the mall?"

"For the most part," I said. "Most of the repairs are done and the shoppers are back, but some of them are avoiding the courtyard."

"Give them another day or two," Seth said. "They'll forget all about it." His eyes took on a faraway look, as if he was remembering bombs others had long since forgotten.

After a few more minutes of small talk, the waiter brought our food and we dug in.

"You were right," Seth said around his first bite. "This is delicious."

Brigit and Blast seemed less impressed with the vegan patties, sniffing their meals thoroughly and casting disgusted looks in my direction before resigning themselves to the fact that no dead animal was forthcoming.

When we were done eating, I drove Seth back to the pool so he could collect his car.

He sat in my front passenger seat, simply eyeing me for a moment. "Can I touch your hair?"

An odd question. But Seth was kind of an odd guy. I think I actually liked that about him.

"Okay, I guess." I offered a nonchalant shrug, though my heart was spinning like a baton in my chest. *Swish-swish-swish.* "As long as I can touch your chin dimple."

"Deal." Smiling softly, he reached out and fingered a tendril of my hair that had pulled loose from my bun and hung by my ear. "That waitress was right. Your hair is very shiny."

If he only knew . . .

After a moment, he released my hair. "Your turn."

I reached out a finger and placed the tip gently against the cleft in his chin. His skin felt warm and slightly scratchy, since he'd evidently skipped his shave this morning.

When I pulled my finger back, he asked, "You think it's sexy, don't you?"

Wasn't it obvious? Still, I wasn't about to be as honest with him as he'd been with me. "It's . . . unique."

"Unique, huh?" He seemed to mull that over for a moment before pulling his cell phone from the pocket of his shorts. "What if Blast wants to take Brigit out on another date? How would he get in touch with her?"

Swish-swish-swish! "He could call her on my cell."

Seth added my number to his cell phone contact list, though he input it under the name "Brigit," casting me a cocky grin when he realized I'd noticed. "He'll be in touch."

With that, Seth climbed out of my car, retrieved his dog from the backseat, and raised a hand in good-bye.

FIFTY
WILL HE OR WON'T HE?

Brigit

Despite the fact that Megan had ordered her some kind of unidentifiable, meatless slop, Brigit enjoyed lunch. Spending time with Blast had been a lot of fun. If Brigit had been capable of understanding how cell phones worked, she would have hoped he'd call soon. Given that she didn't comprehend the concept of wireless communication, she merely hoped the two of them would cross paths again.

FIFTY-ONE
DINNER AT THE CLUB

The Rattler

He followed his mother and father into the dining room at Colonial Country Club. The very man who'd shooed him and the elderly lady away from the Dumpsters greeted his parents by name with a respectful tip of his head. The man offered the Rattler a nod, too, evidently not recognizing him. Of course the Rattler was dressed differently tonight. He'd worn the damn khakis and button-down shirt and sport coat his mother had forced upon him.

He hated dressing this way. It reminded him of his days in prep school, where he'd always been the odd man out, never fitting in with the other kids, who seemed content to live as virtual clones of one another, who accepted the status quo, who never dared to think an original thought or dream of a different world.

The hostess seated the three of them at a table by the back windows, the perfect vantage point from which to watch the golfers. Not that the Rattler gave a shit about golf. But watching the men play would give him some inspiration.

His father chuckled as he gazed out the window. "What a knucklehead," he said of a man on the fairway. "He hit his ball right into the water hazard."

The Rattler smiled. For now, a shallow pond might be the biggest hazard the golfers would face. But give him a little time and he'd show them a hazard like they'd never seen before.

FIFTY-TWO
NAILED IT

Megan

Brigit and I met Detective Jackson in front of the bridal shop promptly at ten on Tuesday morning. Before we went inside, Jackson gave me an update. The search of Serhan's house had turned up the usual inventory of nails and screws found in any suburban garage but no gunpowder, no metal pipes, and no oddly shaped nails.

"So he'll be released from jail, then?" I asked.

She nodded. "The immigration issue is minor. As soon as his attorney gets the paperwork cleared up he'll be out."

"What about the sushi place and the pet store?"

"Dead ends. Nobody knows nothing. Nobody seems suspicious."

None of our leads seemed to be leading anywhere. But I supposed the fact that we could at least eliminate some people as potential suspects was some sort of progress.

We stepped inside the bridal store and were directed by the salesclerk to the rear. Vu Tran was already at work at a large table in the back room, letting out a wedding dress for a bride who, I surmised, was a nervous eater and had gained a few pounds en route to the altar.

He looked up as we stepped into the doorway.

"Good morning, Mr. Tran," Detective Jackson said. "We'd like to speak with you."

Tran said nothing, just waved us in, gestured to a couple of stools pushed back against the wall, and continued his work, using a pair of tiny scissors to snip the tight stitches along the seam.

After we'd taken a seat, the detective explained why we were there. "As part of our investigation of the bombing incident, we've run criminal background checks on all of the mall employees. We learned you were convicted of a fireworks violation and a drug offense."

"Yeah, yeah. All true." He continued to carefully cut the threads.

Jackson and I exchanged glances.

"Would you care to explain?" the detective asked.

"Vietnamese New Year." He used his fingers to pluck the severed threads from the fabric. "Setting off fireworks is tradition. Neighbors call police. They come. Find my mother's Xanax in my pocket. I had to take from her because she forgetful and maybe take too many."

"You didn't fight the charges?" I asked. The fireworks violation likely would have stood, but a sympathetic judge might have reduced the drug offense under the circumstances.

"Lawyer too expensive," Tran said. "Prosecutor say no jail if I agree and pay fine." He shrugged and set the scissors down.

"Do you know anything about the bomb?" Jackson asked. "Anyone who might have had a reason to plant it here in the mall?"

Another shrug. "I do my work. I go home."

Obviously this interrogation had been a waste of time. We thanked him and stepped out of the room.

"You get married," he called after me as we left, "come see me!"

The bridal shop having been a bust, Jackson and I made our way to the Williams-Sonoma store. Three employees were on duty, two women and one man. Jackson called each one out of the store separately, posing the same question to each of them.

"We have reason to believe there may be a link between your store and the explosion. Do you think one of your co-workers could have been capable of planting the bomb?"

I watched the staff closely, gauging their responses. None seemed to think any of their coworkers could have been involved in the incident. All three were surprised and disturbed, and all three grew fearful.

"Is it safe to work here?" one of the women asked.

Jackson let out a long exhale. "Life doesn't come with any guarantees."

If only it did.

The assistant manager was able to go back through the store's data and determine how many fondue fork sets had been purchased in the last three months. They'd sold twenty-seven sets, fifteen of them on the day of the demonstration when the chef had offered the free—*and freaking delicious!*—samples. She was able to give us card numbers on the credit and debit card purchases.

She looked at her computer screen. "Three sets were purchased with cash."

Two of those purchases had taken place the day of the demo; the other had taken place in late June. Short of watching the security tapes, there was no way of identifying those particular purchasers. Even if we watched the tapes, it would be difficult, if not impossible, to figure out which shopper had purchased the forks, given that the merchandise would have been placed in a bag. We'd have to go with what we had. See if it led to anything.

Armed with this new information, and after a stern warning to the workers at the cookware store not to discuss the data we'd requested, we headed to the wine shop.

I reached for the door, but when I pulled on the handle it didn't budge. "It's locked." I stepped closer and peered through the glass, trying to determine if the store was still closed due to the bomb or whether they'd simply forgotten to unlock the door. Both Stacy and Karla were inside, packing bottles of wine into cardboard boxes. I rapped on the glass.

Stacy stepped over and unlocked the door, opening it only a foot or two, just enough to poke her head out. "Sorry," she said. "We're closed."

Jackson stepped up to the door, subtly sneaking her steel-toed loafer over the threshold to prevent Stacy from closing the door should she try. "Closed? What do you mean 'closed'?"

"That bomb was the last straw," Stacy said. "We weren't making it before and God only knows when things will be back in full swing around here. We found a wholesaler who agreed to buy our entire inventory. We're going out of business."

"What about your lease?" I asked.

Like Tran, she offered a shrug. "Mr. Castleberry won't work with us. We talked to him yesterday, tried one last time to work something out, but he still won't budge. If he sues, he sues. Nothing we can do about it. If we stay open we'll go even further in the hole."

"We need to come inside," Jackson said. "We need some information from you."

Stacy appeared a little put out, but she stepped back and opened the door to let us in, closing and locking it behind us. "What kind of information?"

"Tell us about your corkscrews," Jackson said. She'd left the question open ended, maybe hoping that doing so would lead the women to offer some piece of information she hadn't thought to ask about.

While Karla continued to pack wine into boxes, Stacy gestured at the display. "These are the corkscrews we have in stock. The wholesaler's buying those, too."

I ran my eyes over the display. While the rack contained corkscrews with flower, bird, and cow motifs and even a wooden man-shaped one with the corkscrew extending from the groin area, it contained none of the unicorn corkscrews. Had the women sold out? Or had they used the last one in the bomb?

I had trouble believing it could be the latter. Both of these women seemed fairly pragmatic. Taking such a dramatic step as planting a bomb simply to get out of a lease seemed a drastic move. But I'd learned early on in my career in law enforcement never to make assumptions. My first week on the job Derek and I had pulled over a mother who'd been speeding to get one of her kids to band practice on time. I'd assumed she'd want to set a good example for her children. Instead, when I'd walked off after issuing her ticket she'd hurled a sippy cup, a box of tissue, and a dirty diaper at me. Luckily for me, she had lousy aim.

Jackson waved a hand at the rack. "Are these the only corkscrews you've ever sold, or did you carry some other styles?"

"I ordered the wine; Karla handled the accessories. She'd remember better than me." Stacy glanced over at her partner and called, "What other corkscrews did we have besides these?"

Karla taped a box shut and walked over, running her gaze up and down the display. "We had a cute one with a bumblebee on top. It must've sold. We also had a couple with horned frogs. Those were popular with the TCU crowd. And there was the unicorn. That was our best seller."

When Jackson asked what kind of sales and inventory system they had on their registers, Stacy reached over to the sales counter and held up a scanner. "The system tracks everything automatically."

"Great," Jackson said. "We need information on all sales of the unicorn corkscrew."

Stacy's shoulders slumped. "Does it have to be now? The wholesaler is coming by this afternoon to pick up the inventory."

I took a step forward. "I'll help Karla pack up the wine while you get the information for Detective Jackson."

The shoulders unslumped. "I'd appreciate it."

While Stacy coaxed the system into spitting out the information Jackson and I sought, I pulled bottles of moscato and pinot noir from the shelves and slid them into cardboard boxes. Brigit took advantage of the downtime to take a quick catnap in the corner.

When the information had been retrieved and turned over to the detective, we thanked the women and stepped back outside the store. Stacy turned the door's dead bolt, which slid home behind us with a resounding *click*.

Jackson held the paperwork out to me. "Have at it, Officer Luz."

I took the documentation from her. "You want me to look into this? On my own?"

"Yes," she said.

"Thanks, Detective Jackson," I said. "I appreciate this opportunity."

"Thanks, nothing," she retorted. "Chances are the fondue forks used in the bomb were bought online or at another Williams-Sonoma location. It's likely a long shot and my time would be better spent talking to the rest of the food court staff and custodians who were on duty Saturday. Still, it needs to be done."

I supposed I should have been insulted that she'd tasked me with a project she thought would be futile, but I nonetheless felt proud she trusted me to get the job done. Then again, the assignment might have only been an indication of how overworked the detectives were. She'd be a fool not to delegate the less critical snooping to an eager volunteer like me.

Jackson gave me a contact number for a lawyer at the district attorney's office who could quickly obtain a court order requiring the banks to turn over the names and contact information for the cardholders. She then gave me a quick primer on how to use the numbers to identify which banks had issued the debit and credit cards and how best to contact them for information.

I set up shop in the mall's security office. While I waited for the lawyer to get the court order, I used the data and the laptop from my cruiser to determine which banks I needed to contact. Fortunately, several of the cardholders were with the same large financial institutions, which should make obtaining the information more efficient.

Within the hour, the lawyer had faxed me the judge's order. I forwarded it on to the legal departments at the various banks, all of which promised me the requested information within the twenty-four hours required by the emergency ruling.

One of the smaller banks sent me the data via e-mail right away. They'd issued only one of the debit cards. The card was held by a Rachel Felder who lived in an apartment near the TCU campus. My quick search of the driver's license records told me she was twenty-three years old, five feet, two inches tall, and weighed 118 pounds, with black hair and blue eyes.

Using my foot, I nudged Brigit to rouse her from her napping spot under the desk. "Time to get moving, girl."

We headed out to the cruiser and drove to Felder's apartment, which was in a complex popular with the university's graduate students. Fortunately, Felder was home when we knocked.

When I asked about the fondue set, she stood in her doorway, blinking her blue eyes. "You want to see my fondue forks?"

"That's correct."

"Um . . . okay." She looked puzzled, but she didn't question my motives.

She stepped back to let me and Brigit into her place, then led us to her kitchen, which looked as if it hadn't been cleaned in weeks. Dirty dishes were piled in the sink and on the countertops. The trash can overflowed with prepackaged food boxes and take-out cartons.

She cringed, evidently embarrassed. "I've been so busy working on my master's thesis I haven't had time to clean up in days."

She opened a series of drawers, looking for the fondue forks. "I know they're here somewhere." When she struck out, she glanced up in thought, then snapped her fingers. "I had some friends over a couple of weeks ago and we made fondue. I bet they're still in the dishwasher."

She pulled the machine open and rolled the bottom rack out. The four dirty fondue forks sat in the silverware compartment, mingling with spoons, knives, and table forks.

Looked like Rachel wasn't our bomber. I'd pretty much guessed that the instant she'd opened the door wearing a faded T-shirt with the Hogwarts crest imprinted on it.

"Thanks." I pulled Brigit out of the dishwasher, where she'd been licking what appeared to be petrified scrambled-egg remnants off a plate. "That's all I need."

Rachel walked us back to the door. "Um . . . can I ask what this is all about?"

"I'm sorry," I said. "I'm not able to sh-share that information."

"Oh. Well, okay then."

I bade her good-bye and headed back to the cruiser, where I checked my e-mail. While no new information had come in from the banks, the Fort Worth PD had forwarded information about immediate overtime opportunities. Thanks to Saturday's bombing, those putting on events in the area were hiring off-duty cops in droves. Given that I had nothing better to do at the moment and student loans to pay off, I decided to sign on for an evening shift at a paint horse show at the Will Rogers Equestrian Center.

After a quick stop for dinner, I drove to the center. As Brigit and I walked through the parking lot, pickup trucks and SUVs pulling horse trailers drove in, one after another. They unloaded their equine cargo in the parking lot, leading the horses inside to rented stalls. As we made our way to the main doors, Brigit stopped to sniff a pile of fresh horse poop one of the beasts had just dropped on the asphalt.

Blurgh. I tugged her leash. "Don't be disgusting."

I kept my partner close to my side as we went into the building. The place smelled like hay and leather saddles and horses. The brown-and-white horses stood in their stalls, some munching on oats, others tossing their manes or pawing the floor, the more curious crooking their heads over the gates to check out the goings-on around them.

I made my way down a line of stalls, stopping here and there to discreetly admire a nicely built cowboy or to pat a velvety nose. Like many young girls, I'd gone through a horse phase, reading all of the *Saddle Club* books the library had. Knowing my parents couldn't afford riding lessons, I'd never bothered to posit the idea. But on a rare occasion in second grade when I'd been invited to a classmate's birthday party, I'd foregone the cake and musical chairs to take a few extra turns around the girl's backyard on the rented Shetland pony.

On seeing Brigit, one of the horses reared up and whinnied in fright.

"It's okay," I reassured the horse. "It's j-just a dog, not a bear."

Lest the beast try to bolt from its enclosure, I moved on, pulling Bright along behind me.

Three stalls down, a farrier crouched next to a horse's hindquarters, facing the back end. The horse's leg was crooked back, the shoeless hoof secured between the man's bent thighs.

Curious, I stopped. I'd never seen anyone shoe a horse before. "Mind if I watch?"

He pulled a small metal instrument from his toolbox. "Suit yourself."

The man gently pushed the horse's tail aside when it swished into his face. He proceeded to file the horse's hoof into a clean, smooth edge, like an equine manicurist sans the obligatory small talk. Positioning a metal horseshoe on the mare's foot, he pulled a long, sharp nail from the leather work belt around his waist, placed it through a hole on the curved shoe, and hammered it into the horse's hoof. Growing impatient, the horse chuffed and swished her tail again.

The man continued on until the shoe was properly affixed. The instant he released the mare's leg, she took a few steps forward as if to test out the new shoes, like a woman parading around in a pair of stilettos in the Macy's shoe department. Evidently satisfied, she stopped at her trough for a drink of water.

The man gathered up his things and stood. "Here you go." He held out one of the horse's old shoes as he stepped to the gate. "It'll bring you good luck."

I could definitely use some of that. "Thanks."

As I took the shoe from him, my eyes went to the nails grasped in his other hand.

Oh, my God.

Could it be?

"Can I see one of those?" My heart rate escalated as I pointed to the nails in his hand.

He handed one to me. "Keep it. I don't reuse them."

I looked down at the nail in my fingers. It was long and sharp, with a squared head.

Just like the nail the Tunabomber had put in his bomb.

I whipped out my cell phone and dialed Detective Jackson. The instant she answered, I blurted out, "That odd nail. I know what kind it is!"

"You do?"

"It's a horseshoe nail." I told her where I was and how I'd reached my conclusion.

"Good work, Luz."

As much as I'd like to think I deserved the praise, I knew this discovery had come not due to hard work on my part but rather through sheer dumb luck. Nonetheless, after we ended our call I racked my brain, trying to determine how this piece of information fit into the puzzle.

Had the nail been planted as a clue? Did the horseshoe nail have something to do with Michael Lipscomb's arrest at the truck stop? After all, the men he'd assaulted had been hauling horses to slaughter. Was the nail some type of symbol? Or had the bomber merely gathered up nails at random, not even realizing he'd included a horseshoe nail in the mix? Had the nail been planted with the intent to throw investigators off track or maybe to frame someone else?

There were so many pieces of the puzzle left to sort out. I could only hope we'd complete the picture before the bomber struck again.

FIFTY-THREE
MUCKETY-MUCK

Brigit

As Megan led her back to the cruiser at the end of the evening, Brigit noticed a woman using a shovel to scoop up a pile of horse poop, mucking out a stall. Brigit knew her partner didn't like picking up her droppings, but after one look at the enormous turds these animals produced Brigit thought maybe her partner should count her blessings.

FIFTY-FOUR
OF COURSE

The Rattler

It was 3:00 on the following moonless Monday morning when the Rattler sneaked onto the golf course at Colonial Country Club to scout sites for his bombs. He'd dressed all in black and wore night-vision goggles, blending in with the night.

Planting the bomb at the mall had been a no-brainer, but he'd have to be more strategic with these bombs. If he planted them too early, there was a chance a golfer might find one or more of them before the timers went off and all of his efforts could be in vain. But if he didn't allow enough time between placing the bombs and his escape, there was a greater chance he'd be apprehended.

A rustle sounded in the rough nearby, and the two glowing eyes of a possum locked on him.

The Rattler put his hands on his knees and leaned toward the animal. "If anyone asks," he whispered, "you didn't see me."

As he strolled about the perimeter of the fairway, accompanied by cricket song and using the trees for camouflage, he found his first site next to the third hole's sharply angled fairway, what golfers referred to as a dogleg. The tree stump just after the turn would provide a raised platform for the bomb, allowing for greater distribution of the bomb's contents. Of course he'd have to cover the bomb with leaves to ensure it wouldn't be visible to those shitty golfers who might hit a ball into the rough.

After a half hour of wandering the course, he'd located all five positions. In addition to the one at the dogleg, he'd place another near a water stop, a third in the sand trap by the sixth-hole green, and the fourth near the water hazard of the eighteenth hole. Of course he'd plant one in the bushes by the clubhouse so those dining at the club could participate. No sense letting the golfers have all the fun, right?

The tree-lined Trinity River would provide a perfect escape. He could easily and quickly swim across and vanish into the neighborhood on the other side.

Of course he wasn't fully prepared yet. He'd have to make some additional purchases to ensure he blended in with the golf course crowd or he might draw attention.

He slipped through the rough and out onto the street. Time to go home and make a shopping list.

FIFTY-FIVE
SECRET STASH

Megan

It was a Tuesday in the first week of September now. Just over three weeks since the bomb had exploded and exactly twenty-two days since my lunch with Seth.

He hadn't called.

I'd since written him off as nothing more than a shameless flirt whom I'd stupidly let get under my skin. Well, it wouldn't happen again, I promise you that. Still, he was like a male version of a cock tease. There should be a name for guys like that. Twat tease, maybe?

I'd spoken with everyone who had purchased the fondue fork sets and the unicorn corkscrews. I thought I'd hit pay dirt when two of the credit cards had been linked to the same address, but it turned out the cards belonged to a couple who were living together in a downtown condo. They'd still had both the fondue forks and the corkscrew in their possession.

The bombing investigation, like leftover fondue, had gone cold.

The only outstanding lead was the Lipscombs, who still had not returned from their camping trip. The team that had searched the Lipscombs' house found the couple's cell phones on the kitchen counter. Evidently the two had gone off the grid and might not even be aware the police were interested in talking with them. No incriminating evidence was found at their house.

My only hope at this point was that the bombing would be an isolated incident, a prank that the bomb maker realized had been taken too far. But since there was no way of knowing if that was the case, I couldn't completely let it go.

As I cruised Vickery, a Cadillac Escalade entering from a side street failed to yield. A minor offense that resulted in no damage, fortunately, but the driver's transgression had forced another car to swerve momentarily into the oncoming lane. Had I been feeling generous, I would have let the driver slide. Given my aforementioned twenty-two days of disappointment, you can probably guess that I was not feeling generous at the moment.

I eased up behind the man and flipped on my lights.

The man pounded his steering wheel once in obvious frustration, then pulled to the shoulder, leaving his engine running.

I stepped out of my cruiser and walked up to the SUV's driver's side window. A quick glance at the stickers on the windshield told me his registration and inspection were current.

A white man in his late twenties sat at the wheel. His brown hair was cut short, and he was dressed in a button-down and navy pants. By all accounts he was some type of business professional, other than the fact that it was 9:30 AM and he wasn't yet at work.

"Sorry, Officer." The man offered me a polite smile.

"I'm late for a doctor's appointment. I'm a little distracted. I'm worried he's got some bad news for me."

I glanced down the road at the hospital district in the distance, then back at the man, wondering what type of medical problem he suffered. I had no right to ask, of course, but from the awkward way he was sitting and the strained look on his face I'd guess severe constipation, colon polyps, or anal fissures.

I was inclined to set my personal frustrations aside and let the guy go on his way but figured I might as well check his license and registration first. After all, he was already late. Another thirty seconds wouldn't make a difference and I'd already made the effort to get out of my car, after all. Might as well do my job. I held out my hand. "License and insurance, please."

The polite smile remained on his face, but his eyes flashed with anger and frustration. He hesitated a brief moment, his eyes cutting to the road ahead, before he pulled his wallet from his back pocket and retrieved his license. He held it out to me. "No compassion for a sick man?"

I gave him my own polite smile. "We'll see."

The license indicated the man's name was John Taylor Greene. Brown eyes. One hundred and sixty-eight pounds. Twenty-nine years of age. Not an organ donor. *Hmm.* Sort of hypocritical for him to accuse me of lacking compassion for the sick, was it not?

Greene sat with both hands on the wheel, looking over at me.

"Insurance?" I repeated.

"Oh," he said. "Yeah." He reached across to the glove box and opened it with his right hand, holding it open only a couple of inches while he rummaged around with his left. *Strange.* When he found what he was looking for, he finagled it out of the narrow space. "Here you go." He flipped the door of the glove box upward, but it failed to catch and instead fell back open, dumping a tire gauge, a pack of gum, and a large wad of bills onto the passenger seat.

My eyes went from the cash to the man, alarm bells going off in my brain. "Any reason you're carrying so much c-cash?"

"Got some shopping to do. My mother's birthday is coming up."

A highly questionable answer. "Why not use a debit or credit card?"

He hesitated just a moment too long. "I don't trust banks."

I took two steps back. "Please exit the vehicle."

The man's mouth fell slack. "Are you kidding me?"

"No."

After another hesitation and glance at the road ahead, the man grudgingly complied.

I pushed the button on my shoulder-mounted radio and requested backup. I couldn't search the guy's car and keep an eye on him at the same time. The last thing I needed was him sneaking up behind me and putting a bullet in my head.

Two minutes later one of the other W1 officers, a stocky black man in his early thirties, pulled up.

I greeted my coworker as he climbed out of his car: "Morning, Spalding."

He merely lifted his chin in acknowledgment. Spalding was a man of many muscles yet few words.

While my fellow officer kept a close eye on the driver, I ran the license on my in-car computer.

Bingo.

The data indicated Greene had spent three years in the state pen for possession with intent to distribute. Given the pricey car and the wad of cash, I suspected the guy was back in business.

I stepped back over to Greene. "I see you've got a record." I angled my head to indicate the car. "Anything you want to tell me?"

He snorted. "You're not going to find drugs in my car. It's clean."

As if I'd take his word for it.

While Spalding kept an eye on Greene, I performed a quick search of the car. No drugs in the glove box. Nothing in the console but an assortment of fast-food napkins and ketchup packets. Nothing under the seats but a petrified French fry.

Short of dismantling the vehicle, there was no way for me to tell if drugs had been hidden inside. It would take precious hours for human officers to perform such an intensive search, and if no drugs were found the department risked a suit for property damage.

That's where my partner came in. With her superior olfactory capabilities, Brigit could sniff out illicit drugs in seconds.

I opened the back door of my cruiser and Brigit hopped down onto the street. It might have been my imagination, but my partner seemed smug, holding her head high, her nose angled upward, as if she knew we humans were vastly inferior when it came to searching for a hidden stash of narcotics.

Greene backed up several steps as Brigit made her way to the car, his eyes bright with fear. He must be scared of dogs. Then again, with Brigit's bulk and sizable fangs she could strike fear into the most avid animal lover.

I opened every door on the Escalade, as well as the hood and trunk. Giving Brigit the signal to sniff for narcotics, I let out a few more feet of leash so she could do her work. Still standing on the street, she started her search by sniffing the floorboards. She found no drugs there, though she did find, and eat, the weeks-old French fry. *Blurgh*.

Continuing her search, she hopped into the car and ran her nose down the dashboard. Still no luck. She spent a good deal of time sniffing the driver's seat, though she eventually moved on without alerting. A thorough sniff of the backseat, trunk, engine, and tires yielded nothing. With her belly to the ground, Brigit sniffed the undercarriage, likewise finding no drugs.

I glanced over at the men.

Spalding shook his head.

Greene crossed his arms over his chest and sneered. "Told you."

Brigit backed away and put her nose to the air, her head turning toward the suspect who stood fifteen feet away.

The sneer faded.

With me following along behind, Brigit trotted over to the suspect.

"Hold on, now!" He threw his arms out in front of him, his fingers fanned as if he were about to perform a jazz dance routine. *And-a-one and-a-two and-a-shift-ball-change!* "I don't want that dog near me."

Spalding decided to spare a couple of words. The first was "tough." The second was "shit."

As Brigit drew near, Greene kicked out at her. Brigit snarled, but I yanked her back before she could bite the guy.

I whipped my baton from my belt.

Snap!

"You kick at my dog again," I hissed, "you're losing a tooth or a nut. I'm not telling you which, so it'll be a surprise."

I almost hoped he'd do something stupid so I could whap him. Seriously. Twenty-two days? Come on!

Okay, so my irritations with Seth were carrying over into my job. Given that I was a cop and that this situation called for some bravado and trash talk, I supposed that wasn't entirely a bad thing.

I gestured with my baton. "Hands on your head."

The guy executed a couple of frustrated figure eights with his head before complying.

Spalding readied his baton, too, and stepped up closer.

I led Brigit up to Greene again. She sniffed his expensive sneakers first—*sniff-sniff*—then moved up his legs to his crotch, nuzzling the guy's nuts through his jeans.

The guy took a step backward. "Get your damn dog away from my junk!"

I brandished my baton. "Stand still."

I didn't want to admit it, but I wasn't sure where dog ended and cop began. Was Brigit sniffing his crotch as a mere dog who thought nosing around in a person's gonads was an appropriate icebreaker? Or was she a K-9 officer performing a thorough search, perhaps catching a whiff of drugs that had once been in the guy's pant pocket?

Brigit circled behind the man and he turned with her, as if they were performing a tango and Brigit were leading.

I brandished my baton again. "I said stand still!"

Muttering expletives at my partner, the man stopped moving.

Brigit went behind him and promptly stuck her nose between his butt cheeks.

"This is bullshit!" the suspect cried, thrusting his crotch forward as he squeezed his glutes together.

I put the end of my baton on the man's crotch and pushed it back. "I told you not to move."

"I can't help it!" Greene hollered. "That stupid dog's got her cold nose up my ass!"

Behind him, Brigit sat, giving her passive alert.

Oh.

Gawd.

Spalding and I exchanged looks of disgust. My partner had found drugs, all right.

A buttload.

Although "boofing" was a kayaking term that referred to raising a boat's bow during a free fall, the term was also used for the practice of hiding drugs inside one's posterior orifice. Luckily for us officers, Brigit's alert was enough evidence to haul the man into the station, where another officer would have the privilege of retrieving the evidence.

"He's all yours now," I told Spalding.

"Gee," Spalding said, taking the man by the arm. "Thanks."

The pool at Forest Park had closed after Labor Day, so I didn't bother pulling into the parking lot. I continued on to the zoo and turned into the lot.

With the children back in school now, the place was virtually empty today, only a few employees meandering about, feeding, watering, and cleaning up after the animals. It probably wasn't the best use of my time as a cop to be walking around at the zoo. With so few people around, the chances of my being needed here were slim to none. But after the unpaid overtime I'd put in on the bombing investigation I figured the department owed me. And, really, wasn't busting a guy with drugs up his ass enough for one day?

"C'mon, girl." I led Brigit to one of the newer exhibits, referred to as the Museum of Living Art. This section of the zoo contained a herpetarium that featured a number of amphibians and reptiles.

I stopped in front of the enclosure containing the critically endangered gharial crocodiles, a strange-looking species with an especially long, skinny snout. Brigit and I stood there for several moments, watching the long creatures' slow, graceful movements through the water. When one swam close to the window, Brigit put a paw on the glass and growled: *Grrr.*

"Careful, girl," I warned. "That thing could eat you alive."

As we watched, one crocodile swam up over another, latched on to her, and proceeded to engage in underwater coitus, crocodile-style. Had these crocs no shame? Given that their species was in serious trouble, it was probably a good thing they had no qualms about getting it on with an audience present. Perhaps it said more about me that I continued to watch them.

"Kinky amphibians, huh?"

I looked up to find Seth standing a few feet behind me. "Actually, they're reptiles."

"What's the difference?"

"For one, reptiles never have gills," I said. "Amphibians have gills until their lungs develop. For two, amphibians reproduce through external fertilization. The males fertilize the eggs after the female lays them. Reptiles, as you can see, use internal fertilization."

Seth's eyes squinted. "I'm glad I'm not an amphibian. Internal fertilization seems like way more fun."

Brigit betrayed me by walking over to Seth, her tail wagging. He bent down and scratched her under the chin with both hands. "Who's a pretty girl?"

She woofed as if to say, *I am! I'm a pretty girl!*

"How long have you been here?" I asked.

He looked up at me with those deep-green eyes. "Long enough to have serious concerns about your voyeuristic tendencies."

He offered a smile that would've evaporated my panties three weeks ago. Today, not so much.

Much to my partner's disappointment, Seth stood and closed the distance between us, stepping up beside me at the glass. "I was driving home from a shift when I saw your cruiser. Figured I'd say hi."

Damn, but he had me feeling confuzzled again. He was dressed in civilian clothes, his ticket stub sticking out of the breast pocket on his T-shirt. What did it say that he'd dropped $12 on the zoo's admission fee just to follow me in here? I wasn't sure. I was afraid to read anything into it, to set myself up for more disappointment. The guy was too unpredictable.

I turned to watch the crocodiles again. In my peripheral vision, I noticed Seth stare at me a moment longer before he, too, turned to the glass.

"Something's wrong with that one," Seth said, pointing at the male, who had a bulbous growth at the end of his snout. "His nose looks weird. What the hell is that?"

"It's called a ghara," I said. "It amplifies their hisses."

"How come he's the only one who's got it?"

"The other croc's a female. This species is sexually dimorphic."

Seth grunted, as if annoyed by my use of jargon. "Meaning?"

"Meaning the males and females have visible differences other than their sex organs."

"How do you know all this?"

I gestured to the informational plaque nearby.

"You read all that?" he asked.

"Yeah."

He flashed me a grin. "Nerd."

Evidently bored now that their mating was over, the male swam off, leaving the female in his wake. I supposed I should say something to Seth, but I wasn't sure what. Couldn't go wrong with updating him on the investigation, though, right?

"Serhan was released from jail," I said, still looking through the glass, "but the Lipscombs are still on the loose."

Someone from Animal Control had seized their snake, leaving a note behind letting them know where they could claim him if they returned to their house.

"They can't hide forever," Seth said.

It was little consolation. After all, Osama bin Laden had managed to hide out for nearly a decade. Besides, we weren't even sure the Lipscombs had anything to do with the bombing. We might be waiting on nothing.

My radio crackled, Dispatch asking for an officer to respond to a fender bender on University. I pushed the talk button. "Officer Luz responding." I released the button and turned to Seth. "Gotta go. Duty calls."

"I'll walk you out."

Seth walked alongside me as we made our way to the exit.

As we approached my cruiser, he said, "Blast has been wanting to see Brigit again. Can he take her to the dog park Friday night?"

I'd wanted a sign of interest from Seth, but after he'd made me wait three full weeks I wasn't about to jump on it. He'd tortured me. Why not return the favor? "Sorry. She's busy Friday night."

Disappointment registered in his eyes. He hesitated a moment, as if he was trying to get a read on me. About time he read something, huh?

He pulled the ticket stub out of his pocket and appeared to be examining it, though I think it just gave him something to look at other than me. It was an insecure gesture, not one I'd expect from a guy as attractive as him. I was beginning to think there was far more to Seth than met the eye.

He fiddled with the corner of the ticket. "What about Saturday night? Is she free then?"

I looked up, pretending to consult my mental calendar, which was, as always, entirely open. "That would work."

His face brightened, though from his forcibly relaxed posture it was clear he was trying to play it cool. "Seven o'clock?"

"Okay."

I loaded Brigit into the back of my cruiser and climbed into the front, unrolling my window. "See you later, alligator."

Seth smiled. "In a while, crocodile."

The next few days were relatively uneventful. I responded to two false alarms at residences in Mistletoe Heights, issued five speeding tickets, and helped the mall security team deal with an unruly shoplifter armed with pepper spray. As she held the team at bay, I'd snuck up behind her and knocked the canister out of her hand with my baton. *Swish-whack!*

On Friday afternoon, the Lipscombs returned.

Detective Jackson gave me a call and told me the news. "I'm heading out to visit with Sherry and Michael. You wanna join the party?"

Hell, yeah! "On my way."

I met the detective at the station and we rode over together in my cruiser. When we arrived at the house, the couple met at us the door. Michael's expression was equal parts bewildered and incensed. Sherry's was equal parts befuddled and frightened. Nonetheless, they invited us inside. As Brigit and I passed the aquarium, the snake that had newly been returned to his home looked up from where he lay coiled on a flat stone, raised his head an inch or two, and gave us a silent, forked-tongue raspberry. Brigit replied with a growl: *Grrr.*

The couple led us into their kitchen, offering us seats around their cheap dinette set.

Michael stared pointedly at Jackson across the table. "You had no right to search our house and seize my snake."

Jackson waved a dismissive hand. "We had every right to do what we did. Your snake is fine. We made sure the thing got fed. Besides, you've got him back now." She set her briefcase flat on the table and snapped open the clasps. "Where the heck did you get a rattler, anyway?"

"We intervened in a rattlesnake roundup a couple years ago," he said. "The snake had been injured, but he managed to slither away from the crowd. We rescued him."

I'd heard about those roundups. Frankly, they sounded like nothing more than an excuse for a bunch of bloodthirsty rednecks to get together and commit a mass slaughter in the name of family fun. *Here, little Cindy. Take this hoe and let's hack this snake to pieces together. Watch your toes now, honey pie! Ain't this fun? Woot-woot!*

Michael folded his hands on the table and leaned toward the detective. "You want to tell us what this is all about?"

Jackson cocked her head. "We suspect you might be involved in the bombing at the Chisholm Trail mall."

"What?!" Sherry cried.

"That's bullshit!" Michael said. "We'd never do anything like that!"

"But you *would* assault two men," Jackson said, pushing a copy of Michael's rap sheet across the table.

On the drive over, the detective had told me she'd tried to get details on the incident, but since the matter had not gone to trial the records had been woefully devoid of details. The police report was vague and the assistant DA who'd handled the case no longer worked at the prosecutor's office. Jackson hadn't bothered following up on the couple's nonviolent convictions. Too many pending cases, too little time, and since the nature of the crimes was dissimilar she didn't think any information that could be gathered would be of much use in the bombing investigation.

Michael looked down at his criminal record and snorted.

"I poked a couple of truck drivers in the chest with one of those plastic souvenir back scratchers I bought at a truck stop. They were hauling horses down to the slaughter-houses in Mexico and a group of us were trying to stop them. The pussies got their panties in a bunch and filed charges on me."

Jackson and I exchanged glances. His story made perfect sense.

Jackson laid a copy of Sherry's criminal record on the table now, too, tapping it twice with her index finger. "Fill me in, Mrs. Lipscomb."

Sherry offered up information willingly. The theft charge related to a pair of registered poodles she'd stolen from a breeder running a puppy mill. Sherry had gone on to vandalize billboards promoting a substandard roadside zoo with a history of negligence. Most recently, she'd pled guilty to slashing tires on the 18-wheelers driven by the truck drivers Michael quote-unquote "assaulted."

"Look," Michael said, calmer now. "We're all about compassion. Planting a bomb that would hurt or kill innocent people isn't how we swing."

Jackson looked from Michael to Sherry. I could tell from the detective's expression that she believed them. I did, too.

The detective gathered up the reports and slid them back into her briefcase. She stood and held out her hand. "Sorry for the trouble."

After conciliatory handshakes were exchanged, Jackson and I headed back to my cruiser.

"What now?" I asked after we'd climbed in.

"I'm out of ideas," she said, "and I'm out of suspects. I suppose the only thing we can do now is hope for a break before another bomb goes off."

I didn't like that plan. I didn't like that plan at all.

* * *

As I drove home from work on Friday, I passed by Honey-suckle's house. She sat on her stoop in her overalls and Keds, her arms wrapped around her tiny knees and her refurbished wares on display about her small yard, wait-ing for potential purchasers. Noting the bookcase on her lawn, I circled the block and pulled up to her curb.

She stood and waved. "Hello, Officer Luz! Hello, Ser-geant Brigit!"

We climbed out of my tiny car and met her under the tree.

I ran a hand over the bookcase. "Wow. This looks as good as new."

Honeysuckle beamed. "Sanded it. Re-stained it. Fixed the shelf and the support on back."

"I'll take it."

A wicker patio furniture set caught my eye, too. The set was painted a golden yellow and included a love seat and two chairs with sunflower print cushions. I had no room for it in my apartment, but it would look nice out by the pool.

Honeysuckle and I agreed on fifty dollars for the patio furniture, twenty for the bookcase, and another ten for her to drive the pieces over to my place in her van. Both of us were pleased with the deal. Me because I'd finally have a place to shelve the stacks of books sitting on my floor and a place to sit by the pool. She because she now had enough money for her next week's groceries.

I loaded the pieces into the back of her van and she fol-lowed me to my place. When we arrived, I pulled them out and set them in the parking lot.

"Thanks, Honeysuckle!" I called to her after I shut the back doors.

She beeped her horn and raised a hand out the win-dow. "Enjoy your new furniture, dear!"

Another five dollars paid to Rhino got the bookcase up

to my apartment. The love seat and chairs I carried myself, positioning them inside the small fenced area while
Brigit swam around in the pool, lapping up water as she
swam, her leash trailing behind her.

Grigsby yanked his door open and stormed over to the
fence. "What do you think you're doing?"

I straightened the cushions on the chairs. "Making this
place look like less of a shithole." Hey, that would make a
great marketing slogan, wouldn't it?

"If you expect me to pay you for that furniture,"
Grigsby spat, "you've got another thing coming."

"Trust me." I shot the man a look. "I had no such expectation."

"And get your dog out of the pool." He swung his arm
like an umpire calling a batter out. "Her fur keeps clog-
ging the drain."

"If you've got a problem with Brigit," I said, "you'll
have to take it up with the police chief."

Grigsby scowled. He'd never call the chief. Too many
building-code violations around this place to risk getting
someone higher up at the department involved. Cowed,
Grigsby stormed back to his apartment.

Rhino flopped back on the love seat with his bass guitar and a can of Bud.

My yellow-toenailed neighbor descended from his
usual spot on the stairs and settled in one of the chairs
with a cigarette. "Ahh." He expelled a stream of smoke
into the air. "*This* is living!"

FIFTY-SIX
BEST IN SHOW

Brigit

Brigit wasn't sure what was going on, but she knew it must be something special. They'd spent their entire day off preparing. Megan had given her a bath this morning. Afterward, Megan had taken her to a salon, where they'd both had their nails painted a pretty shade of red. Megan had bought her a new collar, too, a pink one with rhinestones. She'd even given Brigit's coat an extrathorough brushing and clipped a flowered barrette in her hair.

A knock sounded at the door. Brigit trotted over and put her nose to the threshold to see if she could identify who stood outside. She recognized the scent in an instant.

Blast!

FIFTY-SEVEN
PACKING UP

The Rattler

He had everything he needed ready to go. The bombs, fully assembled and waiting to be placed. A set of secondhand golf clubs and bag he'd bought at a garage sale forty miles away in the town of Granbury. A new golf glove. Not only would it make his disguise more authentic; it would also help prevent him from leaving fingerprints.

He could hardly wait until tomorrow.

FIFTY-EIGHT
DOUBLE DATE

Megan

Seth stood at the door, Blast at his feet, the two wearing matching green bow ties. I'd planned to act cool and aloof, but they looked so damn cute I couldn't help myself. I smiled.

Seth glanced down at Brigit, then up at me, his eyes roaming over my loose hair, the silver dangly earrings, the black halter top. "Brigit looks really pretty tonight." The gleam in his eyes told me the compliment extended to me, too.

"Thanks."

I locked up my apartment and we went down the stairs to his Nova. Rhino was sprawled on the sunflower love seat by the pool, one leg crooked under him, his guitar and a beer in his hands. He raised his can in greeting as we passed by.

Seth opened the passenger door. Brigit and Blast hopped in and over the seat back. I slid inside after them.

In fifteen minutes, we were at the Fort Woof dog park.

An unusual place for a date, but not a bad one, necessarily.

Seth grabbed a soft nylon throwing disk, a tennis ball, and a blanket from the trunk of his car. After a quick look right and left, he pulled a bottle of red wine out of the trunk, too, and slid it into the front pocket of his loose-fitting shorts, pulling his shirt down over the mouth to hide it.

"What are you doing?"

He pointed to a nearby sign that listed the dog park rules: No Alcohol.

"Ah," I said. "You're a bad boy, Seth Rutledge."

On hearing the words "bad boy," Blast looked up, his furry forehead furrowed in worry.

"Not you, Blast." I ruffled his ears. "I was talking about your daddy."

We headed through the gates, unclipping the leashes from our dogs' collars once we were inside. Brigit and Blast took advantage of their freedom and bounded off together, making the rounds to meet the other dogs hanging out tonight. While Blast sniffed the back end of a fluffy red chow, Brigit did the same on a Dalmatian before the two switched places. A Shar-Pei puppy trotted up, looking like an old man even though he could be no older than six months. A bowlegged basset hound stood on the edge of the group and began baying, as if feeling left out. When Brigit circled around from behind and mounted him, he stopped baying and instead put his efforts into crawling out from under her. Blast stood nearby, watching and looking perplexed and concerned.

"She's so embarrassing." I put my hand over my eyes. "Tell me when it's over."

"It's okay now," Seth said after a few seconds. "The basset hound got away."

Seth and I walked around the perimeter of the park.

"Do you bring Blast here a lot?" I asked as we made our way along the fence line.

"At least once a week. He loves it here. It gives him a chance to sow his wild oats."

I glanced over at Seth's canine partner. "Looks to me like you've had his 'wild oats' removed."

"Yeah," Seth said. "Didn't want some skanky poodle showing up with a litter claiming Blast was her puppy daddy."

I'd never been to the dog park before, but seeing Brigit frolicking with her furry friends I knew the place would become a regular hangout for us.

As Seth and I made our way around the park, Blast and Brigit routinely checked in with us, darting over to see what we were up to, then running off to see who'd just come in the gate.

"Hey, boy!" Seth pulled out the Frisbee, held it up where Blast could see it, and sent it sailing through the air. Blast took off after it, with Brigit on his heels. As the disk began to descend, Brigit bolted past Blast and rocketed into the air, snatching the Frisbee before Blast had a chance.

"She's good," Seth said. "You teach her that?"

"No. I didn't even know she could c-catch a Frisbee."

My partner was full of surprises.

Brigit loped back our way with the disk in her mouth and dropped it at my feet. I picked it up and hurled it into the air. She took off after it again. With the Frisbee now shanghaied, Seth threw the tennis ball for his partner to retrieve. Blast galloped after it, snatched it up midbounce, and returned in record time.

As we walked, Seth mentioned that he'd spent the previous weekend at the joint reserve base west of town, fulfilling his required one-weekend-a-month Army reservist duty. Knowing he hadn't been free made me a little less annoyed that he hadn't called. Of course that didn't explain why he hadn't called during the two weeks before. Was he seeing someone else? Busy with previous commitments? Unsure whether I was worth the trouble? I was dying to know, yet I knew asking would only make me appear desperate and needy. Besides, we were here together now. Better to look forward, right?

When we reached a relatively private spot in the back corner, Seth stopped and spread the blanket out on the ground. While I settled on the spread with the now worn-out dogs, Seth knelt down, pulled the wine from his pocket, and used the corkscrew on his Swiss Army knife to remove the cork from the bottle. *Pop!*

"Uh-oh," he said once he'd gotten the bottle open. "I forgot glasses."

"We'll make do." I took the bottle from his hand, took a drink straight from the mouth, and handed it back to him. "That's some good stuff."

"For three-ninety-nine it better be." He cast me a grin before taking a swig himself.

We chatted as we passed the bottle back and forth, eventually finding ourselves on our backs on the blanket with an empty bottle between us and two softly panting dogs at our feet.

The sky had grown dark with dusk and virtually everyone at the park had gone. Other than the chirping crickets and buzzing cicadas, we had the place to ourselves.

Seth and I chatted about various things as we lay there. I asked about his time in the Army and he told me about basic training and ordnance school in Fort Sill, Oklahoma. He described the devices they'd used to detect and dispose of bombs. Heat sensors. Metal detectors. Even remote-control cars.

"We had these big minesweeper machines that we'd drive through areas where we suspected IEDs had been planted," he said "That was a trip. You never knew when you'd hit something. It was like driving a bumper car with your eyes closed."

He went on to tell me that bombs could contain not only dangerous, flesh-shredding shrapnel but deadly chemicals as well. "We had to be prepared for anything. And you always had to think three steps ahead. One wrong move and it could be your last."

It sounded like a sick and twisted game of chess. He must have had to maintain a cool head to do the job. I'd never be able to do it. I was too hotheaded.

He went on to tell me that knowing the explosive ordnance disposal specialists would attempt to disable the bombs they found, the enemy would sometimes booby-trap the bombs, burying one under a more visible decoy explosive or secreting a trip wire nearby.

Seth looked up at the sky as if searching for something among the faint stars. "We had to learn to think like killers."

We lay there quietly for a long moment, his words hanging heavy in the warm evening air. I wanted to reach out and take his hand, to let him know that, to at least a small degree, I understood, yet I didn't want to be the one to make the first move. Fortunately, Seth remedied the problem.

"You know what would be more fun than talking about bombs?" Seth said, rolling toward me and propping himself up on his elbow.

"What?" I turned my head his way and looked up at him.

"This." He leaned in and softly pressed his lips to mine.

Seth's kiss was sweet and gentle and warm and wonderful and exactly what I needed.

He pulled back slightly, opening his eyes as if to assess my response. My heavy-lidded gaze told him not only that his kiss had been welcomed but also that he better keep 'em coming.

When he leaned in to give me another, my hands found their way over his broad, strong shoulders and around the back of his neck, capturing him. If he thought he'd get away this time, he was sorely mistaken.

The kiss deepened, detonating a warmth in my core. I found my heart pumping so hard and loud inside me I could count its beats, like a time bomb ticking down. I only hoped that this timer would go on for eternity. I didn't ever want this to stop.

A minute or so later, movement at our feet demanded our attention. I released Seth and we sat up to find Blast humping Brigit now. She stood there, putting up no fight. In fact, she closed her eyes and leaned back into it.

"Brigit, you slut!" I cried. "You should be ashamed of yourself. This is only your second date!"

FIFTY-NINE
DO THE MATH

Brigit

Brigit didn't know why Megan was so upset. After all, two dates is like fourteen in dog years.

SIXTY
THE MEAN GREENS

The Rattler

He bent down behind the clubhouse, leaning his bag of battered clubs against the wall as he pretended to tie his golf shoe. Not easy to do with the golf glove on. He hadn't thought this through well enough, apparently, and hoped his actions didn't seem strange.

With a brown ball cap on his head and dark sunglasses over his eyes, he'd be hard for anyone to identify, especially since he'd purposely worn drab-colored clothing to be inconspicuous. The sage-green shorts and beige golf shirt were easily overlookable, easily forgettable, and would blend in nicely with the greens and browns of the rough.

It was barely 7:00 AM, but already people were out on the course, probably trying to get a game in before the heat of the day set in. Still, he knew the club would later be teeming with the after-church crowd, stopping by for a nice lunch after worshiping one version of a deity or another, none of whom seemed to give a shit about the world they'd purportedly created or the creatures who populated it.

When he was sure nobody was watching, the Rattler snuck the first bomb out of the side pocket of the golf bag. Wrapped in a green plastic leaf bag, the bomb wouldn't be noticeable under the bushes. He slid the bomb into place and set the timer for six hours.

He slung the golf bag back over his shoulder as he stood and headed to his second location. He had to be careful. The golf marshals kept a fairly close eye on the course to make sure nobody was sneaking on to play and that things were running efficiently.

He managed to cut through the rough and plant the second bomb without seeing anyone. As he planted the third, two men on a cart careened up the path a hundred yards away. He crouched down and hid among the trees until they'd played through. Luckily for him, they were good golfers who kept their balls on the fairway. His balls, on the other hand, had threatened to crawl up inside him. It was one thing to shove a bag into a trash can in a crowded food court where detection was unlikely. It was another thing entirely to be slinking around on a private, supervised golf course with a bag full of explosives. Still, he wouldn't let his trepidations keep him from his mission.

He was crouched next to the water hazard, planting his fourth bomb, when *plop!* A ball dropped into the pond a mere ten feet from him. His nerves were so on edge he very nearly shrieked with the surprise. Forcing himself to move slowly and casually, he stood and walked down the path, hoping nobody would question why he wasn't driving a cart.

His nerves were frayed now, but he had to finish the job. He hadn't come this far to chicken out now.

Keeping to the outer perimeter of the course, he set the

last bomb in place and scurried through the brush to the
bank of the Trinity River. Stripping down to his shorts, he
shoved the shirt, shoes, socks, and cap into the golf bag.
He picked the bag up and flung it with all his might out
over the water. It splashed into the water thirty feet from
shore, bobbing for a moment before slipping beneath the
dark surface.

Easing himself into the water, the Rattler swam south
along the shoreline, hidden from the golf course by the
trees. Once he'd cleared the southwest end of the course,
he removed the glove, dropped it in the water, and struck
out over the river, pulling so hard with his arms his muscles felt like they'd tear.

He reached the other side in record time and found the
dry clothes and towel he'd hidden in a hollowed-out part
of a tree. In less than two minutes he was dry and dressed,
no longer a bomber but simply a jogger taking a leisurely
run through the sleepy, peaceful neighborhood.

Enjoy it now, folks, he thought.

At 1:00, their peace would be shattered.

SIXTY-ONE
EXPLOSIVE RELATIONSHIPS

Megan

For the first time in weeks, I was able to set aside my obsession with the bombing and focus on something else.

Seth.

Our date at the dog park last night had been casual and fun, giving us a chance to get to know each other without too much pressure. He'd asked to see me again today. After those mind-blowing kisses he'd given me last night, how could I refuse?

He arrived at my apartment at noon, dressed in sneakers, jeans, and a striped dress shirt under another vest.

I eyed his clothing. "You have an unusual style." *Kind of like a male Ellen DeGeneres,* I thought, though of course I'd never tell him that.

"My grandmother made these vests for my grandfather when they were first married. They remind me of her."

"Are you two close?"

"We were," he said. "She's dead now."

He didn't elaborate and I certainly wasn't going to force

him to talk about anything he wasn't ready to share with me. We weren't in any hurry, after all. There wasn't a clock ticking down on this relationship. Still, I found it intriguing how he was so open about some things and so closed about others. I'd noticed his family seemed to be one of the closed topics. He had no qualms letting me in on all the goings on at the fire station, though. They'd suffered two layoffs thanks to the budget cuts. One of the firefighters who'd been cut was often late for his shifts and didn't chip in for the groceries they shared at the station. The guys weren't sorry to see him go. The other, however, was a newer firefighter with a young wife and new baby. That one had been much harder to take.

"What would you like to do?" Seth asked. "Movie? Bowling? Go back to the zoo and watch those sexually ambivalent crocodiles get it on?"

"Sexually *dimorphic*."

"Whatever."

"How about the Perot Museum?"

"Is that the place in Dallas? The one with the science and stuff?"

I nodded. "I had planned to go the day after the bomb went off in the mall but didn't get the chance." I'd been too busy assisting Detective Jackson that day.

He frowned slightly.

"Problem?" I asked.

"I don't really want to go to the museum," he said after a brief pause. "But at some point I'd like to get you naked. I'm thinking my odds of getting you naked are better if I agree to go to the museum."

There was that no-holds-barred banter of his. Might as well return it in kind, right?

"Taking me to the museum is a necessary but not sufficient condition of getting me naked."

He just stared at me for a moment.

"In other words," I said, "if you take me to the museum,

you stand a chance of one day getting my clothes off. If you don't take me to the museum, it'll never happen."

"I knew what you meant." His mouth spread in a cocky grin. "I was just trying to decide if it was a good trade-off."

I snatched my twirling baton from its spot on the wall and held it up over my head, poised to give his skull a good *whap*. "Does this help with your decision?"

His eyes traveled the length of my baton. "The museum it is!"

I left Brigit in the apartment with a new rubber chew toy. It was a cute one shaped like a chipmunk, with a squeaker. The designers had positioned the squeaker between the chipmunk's hindquarters, like a whistling plastic asshole. At any rate, the toy should keep her busy while I was gone.

Seth and I headed east on the interstate to Dallas. Despite sitting only thirty miles apart, the cities of Dallas and Fort Worth couldn't be more different. Fort Worth, on the one hand, clung to its Western roots and proudly boasted its cowboy heritage. The city's historic stockyards area on the North Side was a popular tourist attraction with Old West barrooms, a vintage train, a rodeo venue, and Billy Bob's, which touted itself as the world's largest honky-tonk. Dallas, on the other hand, tended to embrace all things modern, expensive, and pretentious. From its signature skyscrapers, to its exclusive shops, to its national sports teams, Dallas was the city slicker to its country cousin to the west. Living in the area gave residents the best of both worlds.

In half an hour we exited the freeway and made our way up the surface streets to the museum. The Perot Museum of Nature and Science was housed in a modern gray square building with a rectangular glass structure that jutted outward and upward from its center, as if the building had an architecturally designed boner. Fortunately, Seth and I were among the first to arrive and were able to snag a close parking spot.

We made our way inside. Seth paid for our tickets at the booth and turned to me. "Where to first, nerd?"

I might be offended by the term, but it was clear he was only teasing me, flirting. Besides, I liked that he recognized my intelligence. Not many people had ever gotten to know me well enough to realize how smart I was. I looked over the brochure. "The Expanding Universe Hall."

I'd always enjoyed astronomy, though I had to admit I never could grasp the concept of black holes. How could a small mass deform spacetime? And if a black hole sucked light into it, why was it dark instead of light? Why weren't they white holes? It was beyond my comprehension.

We made our way to the exhibit. We spent several minutes viewing images taken by the Hubble Space Telescope before moving on to the display about the light spectrum and how it was used to classify stars.

Seth glanced my way. "Do I look smarter yet?"

"Infinitely."

I gave him a smile and he took my hand as we walked to the next display. At my age I probably shouldn't have gotten so excited about a guy holding my hand, but I couldn't help myself. It felt wonderful to feel connected to someone. I guess I hadn't realized just how lonely I'd been. When you feel a certain way all the time, it becomes normal.

We'd just finished watching a 3-D animation of the big bang when Seth's cell phone vibrated, bringing him information about another big bang.

He checked the readout and accepted the call. "Hey . . . What? . . . Oh, shit!"

His choice of words earned him a dirty look from a mother with a young son who stood next to us.

"Any injuries?" Seth listened intently, his free hand going to his head in alarm. "All right. I'm in Dallas. I'll be there as soon as I can."

SIXTY-TWO
CHEW TOYS, SHOE TOYS

Brigit

Megan hadn't learned her lesson last time, had she? Although she'd left Brigit with a chew toy, the dog had made short work of it, shredding the cheap rubbery toy in mere seconds. And what idiot thought it would be a good idea to put a squeaking device in a dog toy? Didn't they know the high-pitched sound hurt a dog's ears?

After littering the floor with rubber chunks, Brigit walked over to the closet and lifted a paw to push down on the lever. Although she heard the *click* of the door unlatching, the door opened only a fraction, held in place by the hook and eye Megan had installed. Of course a small hook screwed into cheap wood trim was no match for Brigit. A claw hooked in the gap and a few forceful nudges of her nose were all it took to yank the hook out of its mooring.

Brigit scanned the shoe offerings, sniffing each pair in turn.

A pair of canvas rubber-soled sneakers. *No, thanks.*

Cheap sandals with wooden bead accents. *Nope. Not real leather.*

A pair of sleek, high-heeled boots. *That's the ticket.*

The dog took one of the boots in her teeth and dragged it to the middle of the floor. *This is living!*

SIXTY-THREE
BOOMTOWN

The Rattler

He lay on a chaise lounge next to the backyard pool, ostensibly napping, though in actuality he was listening intently for the final explosion.

The first had gone off precisely at 1:00. A half mile away as the crow flies, he heard only a faint *poom,* though those at the country club had surely been temporarily deafened by the sound.

The second blast, which took place a minute later, was slightly louder. *Kaboom.* The birds lifted off from the trees in the yard, their wings *whap-whap-whapp*ing as they took flight. He fought to keep a smile from his face.

Another minute of relative quiet, then a much louder *kaboom!*

His mother opened the French door that led out on to the patio. "Did you hear something?"

He'd pretended as if she'd woken him, feigning grogginess as he sat up in the padded chair. "Nah," he said, using the casual language he knew drove her crazy. "I didn't hear nothin'."

She frowned disapprovingly. How many times had he seen her wearing that same expression?

"Never mind." She huffed in annoyance and yanked the door closed.

He chuckled to himself. *Bitch.*

Sirens sounded in the distance, the fire department on its way. For their own sake, they might want to slow down a little. This party wasn't over yet.

The fourth blast a minute later was another faint but effective *kapow.*

Finally, he heard the last bomb explode: *BOOM!*

Just for kicks he'd loaded that one with an extra funnel's worth of gunpowder.

His mother yanked the door open again. "I know I heard something that time. It rattled the windows." She tilted her head. "I'm hearing sirens now, too."

North Texas was no stranger to explosions. It wasn't long ago that an estimated two hundred tons of ammonium nitrate had exploded at a chemical plant in the town of West, an hour south of Fort Worth. A multitude of people had been injured and fifteen people had been killed, including a number of firemen who'd responded to the initial fire. Property damage was extensive, with over 150 buildings damaged or destroyed, including a nursing home and an elementary school. A gas well had exploded near Cleburne four years ago or so, creating a massive fire and cloud of smoke, and killing one worker. And of course there was that fateful Saturday morning in 2003 when the Space Shuttle *Columbia* had exploded in the atmosphere over the state, leaving a debris field that expanded from south of Fort Worth east into Louisiana. The Rattler had been only a kid then, riding his bike up and down the street alone when he'd heard the explosion. He'd pedaled home as fast as he could, dropped his bike in the driveway, and rushed inside.

"Did you hear that?" he'd asked his parents, who sat at their kitchen table drinking their morning coffee in their plush designer bathrobes. "I think something blew up!"

His father didn't bother to lower the newspaper he was reading or to respond. The child might bear his name but wasn't his responsibility. Child rearing was his wife's job. After all, he worked fifty hours a week helping the movers and shakers of Fort Worth strategically plan their estates so as to keep as much of their amassed wealth as possible within their families and pay as little as possible to Uncle Sam. He couldn't be expected to pander to a pesky child, too, could he?

The Rattler's mother merely glanced his way and said, "I didn't hear anything," before returning her attention to a decorating show on one of their home's seven televisions. "Look at those floors, hon," she'd said to his dad. "Maybe we should redo ours."

Nonetheless, today the Rattler climbed off the chaise, strolled past the pool, and entered the door his mother had left open. "Let's check the TV. Maybe they'll have some news."

SIXTY-FOUR
THE TUNABOMBER STRIKES AGAIN

Megan

Seth drove so fast back to Fort Worth I wouldn't have been surprised to see actual flames shooting down the sides of his car.

He screeched to a stop in front of a small house a few blocks east of I-35 in the Morningside neighborhood. The house was an unattractive patchwork of building materials, with gray wood siding on the main part of the house and chipped orange brick walling in the converted one-car garage. Rusty air-conditioning units took up the bottom panes of the three windows spanning the front of the house. The roof had been patched in several places with mismatched shingles. An overgrown live oak tree in the front yard robbed the ground of sunlight, making it impossible for grass to grow and leaving the yard little more than bare dirt and a persistent weed or two poking up here and there. But I supposed such qualities were characteristic of a bachelor pad. And who was I to judge given the crap hole I lived in?

"Stay in the car," Seth ordered. "I'll be right back."

I remained in the Nova as he sprinted to the porch and pulled open the screen door. He unlocked the regular door and disappeared inside. He reappeared a half minute later with a duffel bag over his shoulder and Blast's leash in his hand. I opened my door to let Blast into the car while Seth stashed his bag in the trunk.

Kicking up dust, he tore away from the curb and headed west to Colonial Country Club.

As we approached, an ambulance pulled out of Colonial Parkway, its lights flashing and siren screaming. It turned and headed past us, carrying injured to the emergency room. Seth's grip tightened on his steering wheel. Like me, he must have been wondering who had been injured and how badly, what horrors we would find when we arrived at the country club.

My stomach felt sick, my head airy. A part of me wanted to beg Seth to pull over and let me out of the car. After all, I hadn't been summoned to the scene. But I knew I had to go with him. We'd have to face—*and fight*—this thing together.

We turned onto the parkway and sped to the clubhouse driveway. A number of fire engines were on the scene, as well as three ambulances and a half-dozen police cruisers. EMTs performed triage on a dozen bloody people who'd been injured to various degrees.

When I saw the carnage, a sick sensation overwhelmed me and a coppery taste flooded my mouth. I fought down a rising gorge.

Clusters of country club employees and patrons gathered on the other side of the street. Many of the women were crying, their husbands or coworkers doing their best to comfort them. Not an easy task when the men barely had a grip on their emotions.

Just beyond the groups of dazed, stunned people, an old green minivan sat at the curb. The van was empty.

"Oh, my God," I breathed. "Honeysuckle!"

Seth and I leaped from the car and ran to the make-shift command center in the club's circular drive. Two paramedics hurriedly wheeled an unconscious man in torn, blood-drenched golf clothes toward one of the waiting ambulances. Another man with blood spatter on his golf shirt followed them. His eyes were glazed and expressionless with shock.

My head turned in every direction as I frantically searched for the sweet old woman who'd only days ago sold me a refurbished bookcase and patio set. But there was no sign of Honeysuckle. Trish LeGrande and her cameraman had arrived, though, and were preparing to make a live report. The woman gazed into a mirrored compact, checking her lipstick and fluffing her butterscotch hair as if about to report on a high school homecoming parade rather than an act of senseless violence.

While Seth and Blast gathered with their team, I ran over to Derek Mackey and the chief, who were huddled in the shade speaking with Officer Spalding and Detective Jackson.

I forced my way into the circle, frantic. "What happened?"

The chief and Mackey replied only with frowns, but the detective was more informative.

"Five bombs," she said quietly, "timed to go off a minute apart."

Five bombs? I'd seen the damage a single bomb could do. Five could cause widespread devastation and horrific injuries.

Or worse. . . .

Had everyone been accounted for? Could there be more bodies in the clubhouse or out on the course? When I asked the detective she simply said, "The search and rescue is still in progress."

My hand lifted of its own accord, indicating the way the ambulance had gone. "I saw an ambulance. . . ."

Jackson drew a deep breath as if to steel herself. "There was a woman near the Dumpsters gathering up some wedding decorations that had been thrown out. She took a direct hit. We haven't been able to identify her yet."

Hot tears blurred my vision, turning Jackson, the chief, and Mackey into a wavering mass of undifferentiated colors. "I think I know who she is."

As I told the detective about Honeysuckle, Seth and Blast strode quickly past. Seth had changed into his bomb suit. The two were at work now, Blast's nose to the ground as he sniffed for any explosives that had not yet detonated.

I watched them go, wondering if it might be the last time I'd see them alive.

Hours later, dusk had set in, the bomb squad and their dogs returned to the clubhouse, and the country club was declared free of explosives.

Seth said little as he settled Blast in the back of his Nova and stripped out of his gear.

"Are you okay?" I asked.

"I'm fine."

The flat tone in his voice and the fact that he didn't look at me told me he was anything but. I felt the urge to wrap my arms around him yet wasn't sure how he'd take it. Despite the kisses we'd shared last night, we barely knew each other, really.

Detective Jackson stepped out of the clubhouse.

"I'll be back," I told Seth. I rushed over to the detective, eager to hear what evidence had been uncovered.

"The crime scene techs found a golf glove washed up on the banks of the river. It may or may not have anything to do with the bombs. Unfortunately, they weren't able to get any good fingerprints from it. There doesn't appear to have been any fishhooks or corkscrews or utensils in this bomb. It was mostly nails and screws with a bunch of razor blades and some of those Chinese throwing stars. Get this: One of them was shaped like a butterfly."

Unbelievable. Who would even think to make such a thing? "What about horseshoe nails?"

"Too soon to tell. The techs are still gathering the evidence. We're going to have some lights brought in, but it will probably be sometime tomorrow before we'll have everything collected."

"Is there any video footage?"

She shook her head. "There are no cameras on the golf course and only interior cameras at the clubhouse."

"Any suspects?" I asked.

"The club's manager told me he'd recently fired a groundskeeper who'd been caught smoking dope while mowing the thirteenth hole. He'd been belligerent and had to be escorted off the grounds by the club's security team. Evidently he'd vowed revenge."

While Jackson hadn't come right out and said so, I surmised she thought it was possible that the bomber at the country club might have been a copycat rather than the same person who'd planted the bomb at the mall. If so, we were dealing with two bombers rather than just one. The thought made my worries double.

Seth drove me back to my apartment in silence. I fought back tears the entire way, wiping away the occasional drop that broke free to roll down my cheek. Though he walked me to my door, he made no move to kiss me tonight. He merely reached out, gave my hand a squeeze without looking at me, and left.

I went inside to find my favorite boots chewed to pieces. Brigit lay on the futon, her head down and her ears back as if ready to be chastised. It was her lucky night. I didn't have the strength to be angry with her. I was too upset about Honeysuckle, about the golfers, about the fact that such pure evil could exist in this world and that the rest of us seemed powerless to stop it.

I no longer fought the tears. I let them flow free.

I was assigned to work the swing shift for the next few days, which left me open Monday morning to visit Honeysuckle in John Peter Smith Hospital. She lay in intensive care, looking even tinier than usual in the long bed. I carried a vase of yellow roses interspersed with baby's breath over to the table next to her bed.

A bandage was wrapped at an angle around her head, completely covering her left eye. Her left arm was bandaged from her shoulder to what remained of her fingertips.

Honeysuckle looked up at me with her one remaining eye. "Hi, Officer Luz."

My lip quivered so badly I couldn't speak. Honeysuckle reached out with her right hand and gave my upper arm an affectionate squeeze. I felt horrible. I'd come to offer her support and consolation and instead she was the one comforting me.

"Don't you worry," she said. "I'm going to be just fine. I'm a survivor."

I admired her fight. She'd need it over the next few weeks as she adjusted to the changes her injuries would force upon her.

She reached for the cord and pushed the button to raise the top half of the bed. Upright now, she asked, "What do you know about the others who were injured?"

I gave her an update. The golfer I'd seen being loaded into the ambulance yesterday was in intensive care, too, with severe injuries to his chest and abdomen. He'd lost untold amounts of blood before anyone had been able to get to him. It was uncertain whether he'd survive. Three others were still in the hospital with serious injuries but were expected to eventually make full recoveries. The others who'd been injured had been treated and released.

Honeysuckle blinked her eye, which had grown misty. "Do you know who did this? Has he been caught?"

I shook my head. "No, Honeysuckle. We haven't figured out who did this. Not yet."

"You'll get him, Officer Luz," she said, raising an encouraging fist. "I just know you will."

How I wished I could share her confidence.

Brigit and I arrived at the W1 station at 5:00 to begin our shift. Whipping out my baton, I gave the rubber testicles hanging from Mackey's truck a swift *whack* as my partner and I headed to our cruiser.

I loaded Brigit into the patrol car, climbed in, and eased out of the space, circling around by the station's main doors. Mackey walked out of the building, spotted me heading his way, and stepped right in front of my cruiser. I had to slam on the brakes to keep from running him over.

Screeech!

My seat belt yanked me back, but Brigit wasn't so lucky. She slid forward, smacking into the metal barrier. Good thing I hadn't been going very fast or she might have been hurt.

The Big Dick stood at my front bumper, glaring at me.

I mashed down on the horn. *Hoooonk!* The Big Dick made no effort to move.

I unrolled my window. "What's your problem?"

He stepped around to the side of my car. "You are, Luz-*er*. You keep butting in where you don't belong."

"What the hell are you talking about?"

"The bombing investigation. It's none of your business."

I rolled my eyes. "We're cops. It's all of our business."

"You know what I mean."

Why the hell did he care what I was doing?

Wait. . . .

Did the Big Dick want to be a detective, too? He did, didn't he? That's why he kept acting so pissy about Detective Jackson taking me under her wing.

Now that I'd surmised this tidbit of information, the only question was, what should I do with it?

Why, I think I'll torture him with it, that's what.

I stepped out of my cruiser and got in his face. He didn't back up, and he didn't blink.

"I'm going to figure out who the bomber is," I snapped. "And I'm going to bring him in."

False bravado, sure. The chances of me being the one to solve the case and apprehend the bomber were about as good as my chances of winning the lottery. And I never played the lottery. Still, mere mathematical improbability would not prevent me from lying through my teeth to get under Derek's skin.

"You're full of shit," he snapped back. "There's no way you'll be the one to catch the guy."

"Wanna bet?"

He chuffed. "Sure. If someone else nabs the bomber, you owe me a steak dinner."

"Okay. And if I snag the bomber, you give me your balls."

His nose scrunched. "The fuck you say?"

I whipped out my baton—*snap!*—and pointed it at the rubber testicles hanging from his truck across the lot. "Your balls."

At her back window now, Brigit backed me up with a bark: *Rrruf!*

Derek chuckled. "All right, bitches. It's on!"

Mackey moved aside, I climbed back into my cruiser, and Brigit and I headed out on our beat.

* * *

I didn't like working the swing shift. While there were fewer people about and thus less to do, the crimes that were committed in the dark, wee hours tended to be more senseless and disturbing. Bar fights. Sexual assaults. Armed robberies. Also, there were far more drunks on the road. As I'd learned in the police academy, one out of every seven drivers on the road after midnight was legally drunk. Knowing I'd be driving about in such company didn't exactly give me the warm fuzzies.

Detective Jackson called me in the early evening to inform me that a horseshoe nail had been found among the various projectiles in the golf course bombs. That pretty much ruled out the possibility of a copycat. What were the chances that two separate bombers would include a horseshoe nail in their devices?

But what did it mean? If the Lipscombs hadn't been the bombers, what was the connection between a horseshoe and the bomber? Was the bomber someone who rode horses? Bred them? Raced or bet on them at the nearby Lone Star Park in Grand Prairie? Could the bomber have been someone associated with the paint horse show at the Will Rogers Equestrian Center, maybe even the very farrier I'd spoken with? Or was the nail a mere ruse? The possibilities seemed innumerable.

At eleven o'clock, after handling a couple of minor traffic issues and responding to yet another false house alarm, I stopped at a gas station to refill my travel mug with coffee. Adjusting to a new shift was never easy, especially the first night or two. Though I'd taken a nap earlier in the day, I hadn't been able to stay asleep for more than an hour, even with encouragement from two fingers of Baileys Irish Cream. On the bright side, at least nothing creepy had happened so far tonight.

I drove past Colonial Country Club, noting a car from

a private security company parked in the front drive. Looked like they'd hired additional outside help.

As I weaved my way slowly up and down the streets, I spotted a pink Cadillac in the drive at one of the houses. While a late-model Cadillac was not unusual for the upscale neighborhood, an older pink one was an anomaly. Could that be Randy's car? The one I'd seen him drive to the mall?

Curious, I pulled to the curb and ran the plate on my laptop. Sure enough, the car was registered to a Timothy Randall Dunham III. The "William" was missing, but there probably wasn't a space on the registration form for a second middle name. Of course most people only had one middle name, so few Texans other than Randy and the former president George Herbert Walker Bush were likely affected.

I ran the property data next, learning that the house was owned by Timothy Randall William Dunham Jr. and his wife, Elise. Randy's parents, evidently. If Randy had grown up in this neighborhood, that would explain why he had such nice teeth. Surely his parents had sent him to an orthodontist. But it didn't explain why he was working such a menial job. You'd think a kid from a place like this would have had all the advantages to establish himself in a professional career. Given that he'd attended SMU for two years, it appeared that he'd started out on the typical path. But I supposed it wasn't surprising that it hadn't worked out. Randy definitely marched to the beat of his own drum. I might not understand all of his choices, but I respected him for being himself. Not everyone had the guts to do that.

I wondered whether Randy had been home when the bombs went off. Living this close to the club, he surely would have heard the explosions here.

My curiosity about the car now quenched, I left the

country club area and cruised south through TCU and University Place, working my way west to the Ryan Place and Fairmount neighborhoods.

Nothing.

Going.

On.

If I didn't think I'd get fired, I'd pull down a side street and take a nap in the backseat.

With just under an hour left in my shift, I found myself yawning and nearly nodding off at the wheel. I decided a brisk walk might wake me up. Besides, Brigit needed to take a potty break.

It was 1:18 AM when I pulled into the parking lot at the Shoppes at Chisholm Trail. I gunned the cruiser's big engine as I sailed over the lot: *Vroom*. Given that the lot was empty, there was no need to park in my reserved spot. I pulled into a place near the end of the northeast extension. I climbed out, took Brigit's leash in my hand, and headed down the dark wing.

Without lights and people, the mall felt odd and eerie. A single cricket chirped from its hiding place somewhere along the way, but the only other sounds were the soft padding of my rubber-soled loafers, the click of Brigit's nails on the concrete, and the tinny tinkle of her tags.

When we reached the courtyard, I took a quick glimpse inside. At first, the only thing I saw was the vague reflection of my own eyes looking back at me. A little unnerving, even if it was my own self. But then I noticed something: two small, round spots of light moving on the other side of the courtyard, on the southwest extension.

Flashlights.

While the mall employed a team of security guards during the day, the management relied on the building's extensive alarm system to provide security at night. What's more, the janitorial staff worked only until midnight. Nobody should be here now. Had these people come here on foot? I hadn't seen any cars in the lot, but then again, I hadn't circled all the way around the building, either.

My heart began to pulse so frantically it threatened to break my ribs.

Was the bomber back, planting more timed devices? Given that there were a couple of flashlights, were two people involved? So help me God, if I found the Lipscombs or the skater boys planting explosives after we'd cleared them from suspicion I would beat them to death with my baton. And there'd be no need to feed their dead bodies to the tigers. I'd eat them myself.

No one plays me for a fool.

I pushed the button on my shoulder-mounted radio. "Backup needed at Chisholm Trail mall."

Once the dispatcher confirmed my request I turned the volume down low so as not to alert the intruders I was coming for them. I yanked my baton from my belt and gave my wrist a quick flick.

SNAP!

The sound might as well have been a gunshot in the silence. I stood stock-still for a moment or two, watching through the glass, waiting to see if the persons on the other wing had heard the sound.

Evidently not. They continued to move down the walk with their flashlights.

As quietly as I could, I led Bright back down the wing at a fast trot. We circled around the adjacent extension and stopped at the end of the next row. I crouched down beside her and peered around the corner of the building.

The people with the flashlights had disappeared, but one of the doors to Macy's had been propped open. Were the men inside, hiding bombs inside rounder racks or soup tureens? Or were they up to something else? And why hadn't the burglar alarm gone off? The air should be filled with an eardrum-shattering *woo-woo-woo* right now.

In the quiet night, my nervous breaths sounded quick and loud. The only way I knew to calm myself and maintain my focus was to twirl my baton, so I rotated my wrist and set the thing in motion. *Swish-swish-swish.*

A minute later the door swung open and two men emerged, one on each end of an enormous big-screen television still in the box. They supported the huge box from the bottom, the upper part leaning back against their shoulders. With the odd positioning, they could only waddle at a slow pace.

I squinted in the darkness, trying to make them out. I had no idea whether these burglars were armed and didn't want to take any unnecessary chances. But I didn't want them to get away, either. Having had no success tracking down the bomber, I needed a big arrest to restore my faith in myself.

They headed toward me on the opposite side of the walkway. I readied both my flashlight and my baton. When they reached the end and were about to turn the corner, I extended my arm out as far as I could to my side like they'd taught us in the academy and switched on my powerful Maglite. If the burglars had guns and tried to shoot me, they'd aim for the light and, with any luck, miss me entirely.

I took a breath and belted out, "Stop right there!"

The beam illuminated the two men like a spotlight, blinding them. Instinctively they dropped the television and threw up their hands to shield their eyes. The box flopped forward and fell flat on the sidewalk with a *fwump*.

"Ricky?" I took a step in their direction. "Scott?"

Detective Jackson had been right. These guys had been up to something. Planning to rip off the mall.

The two exchanged looks and took off running.

Brigit and I ran after them. They headed to a pickup idling at the curb, its headlights off. At the wheel sat a third man, probably a friend they'd recruited to drive the getaway car.

I grabbed my whistle from where it hung at my chest and blew it: *TWEEEET! TWEET-TWEET!*

"Stop right there!" I hollered.

But did they listen? No, they did not.

"You're up, Brigit!" I unclipped her leash and gave her the signal to take the men down.

My partner scrabbled on the sidewalk, closing the distance between herself and the men in three seconds flat. She bypassed Scott and went straight for Ricky, who'd taken the lead. Smart move. She leaped onto Ricky's back, riding him down like a surfer hanging ten on a long board off Maui. Ricky threw out his arms as he fell, taking Scott out at the knees. Both tumbled to the cement, Ricky sliding forward a few feet, Scott rolling gracelessly to the side.

The guy in the pickup punched the gas and squealed away from the curb. But he was too late. My backup had arrived and quickly cut him off, illuminating the cruiser's spotlight. Blinded now, too, their friend swerved to avoid the cruiser and drove directly into the concrete mooring of a light pole. His bumper and hood crumpled with a satisfying *crunch* while his air bag deployed an instant later with a *whoosh!*

What a bunch of dumb asses.

SIXTY-FIVE
TWO FOR ONE SPECIAL

Brigit

The dog was feeling quite proud of herself. With one leap, she'd taken down two men. Not bad. Now maybe Megan would forgive her for chewing up the boot. Brigit really shouldn't have done that. Sometimes she just couldn't help herself.

SIXTY-SIX

MANIFESTO

The Rattler

He'd watched all of the news reports and learned that the old lady he'd helped with the wicker chairs a few weeks ago had been injured. While he regretted that she'd been hurt, some collateral damage was to be expected. No good battle was fought without losing a soldier or two along the way. Besides, it was her own fault she'd been injured. What had she been doing back at the club? The manager had shooed them off in no uncertain terms the other day. The Rattler supposed she'd been so desperate to earn an extra buck or two that she'd been willing to risk venturing onto the club property again.

But how the hell did one of his bombs get into the Dumpster? He hadn't planted one there. More than likely someone had found one of the green plastic lawn bags the bombs were hidden in, assumed it contained trash, and tossed it into the receptacle. Whoever it had been was lucky the bomb hadn't blown up in his or her hands.

While all of the news reporters speculated on the

connection between the bombings at the mall and the country club, not one of them got it right. One station suggested the attacks might have been carried out by an Occupy Wall Street type group. Another suggested it might have been some type of protest by homeless in the area. *Idiots.* What's more, despite the fact that no fish had been involved in the country club bombing, the reporters still referred to him as the Tunabomber.

He'd have to set them straight.

The Unabomber had written a manifesto. So had Karl Marx. If it was good enough for them, it was good enough for the Rattler.

He sat down at his brand-new laptop and began composing his missive.

SIXTY-SEVEN
HORSING AROUND

Megan

My turn on the swing shift was over. I was glad about that. I was also glad that Honeysuckle had been released from the hospital. She left with one less eye and three fewer fingers than she'd entered with, but she was already back at work, collecting a sagging rocker from a curb. I spotted her early Friday morning and stopped to help her load it into her van.

The golfer who'd been severely injured had survived, though he was still in the hospital. According to Trish LeGrande's news reports, he was expected to be released in another day or two. I had to admit, for a woman who looked like a total bimbo she sure could dig up information.

While I was happy about the good news, I was not happy at all that Seth had failed to call me since we'd parted ways last Sunday. I was getting damn tired of him treating me like a yo-yo, pulling me in, then pushing me away. I didn't get it. I'd thought the two of us had hit it off. I guess I'd been wrong.

Maybe I wasn't as smart as I'd thought I was.

Early Saturday evening I sat in one of the wicker chairs by the pool, my eyes closed as I listened to Rhino fool around on his bass guitar. Brigit lay at my feet, refreshed and relaxed after dog paddling around in the pool for the last half hour.

My ears picked up the sound of a car pulling into the lot. The driver cut the engine and engaged the parking brake.

"Your boyfriend's here," Rhino said.

"That's impossible," I said, forcibly keeping my eyes closed now. "I don't have a boyfriend."

A boyfriend would have realized how upset I'd been after the bombing at the country club and offered me comfort. A boyfriend would have opened up to me about his feelings, too, let me offer him some comfort in return. A boyfriend wouldn't have left me feeling more alone and lonely than I'd ever felt in my life.

The gate creaked open and swung closed, rattling as the latch engaged. A moment later I heard the click of dog claws and a rustle as Brigit stood, followed by Seth's voice saying, "Hi, pretty girl."

He had a lot of nerve showing up here uninvited and unannounced. What if I'd been out? What if I'd been expecting another date or had a guy at my place? What if I kicked Seth in the balls?

I had no choice but to open my eyes now. To continue to ignore Seth would only show that he'd hurt me, and I didn't want to give him the satisfaction or power.

I looked up at him, feeling a surge of anger when my heart betrayed me by responding with a pitter-patter. "Hey, Seth."

Our two dogs stood between us, wagging their tails and sniffing each other, getting reacquainted. It took them only a moment to pick up where they'd left off, and they began to chase each other around the small enclosed area.

Maybe I should take a lesson from them and just enjoy my time with Seth for what it was. I could be just as casual as he could about whatever was going on between us. So what if it was just an occasional thing that wasn't going anywhere? No strings, no expectations, no hassles, right? And, really, what was I getting so worked up about? It had only been six days since we'd last seen each other. That wasn't such a long time, was it?

Seth grabbed the other wicker chair, carried it over next to mine, and plopped down into it. "How ya been?"

Lonely. Frustrated. Worried. "Busy."

"Eaten yet?"

I'd had a bowl of granola cereal earlier, but I wasn't one to pass up a free dinner. Whatever I didn't eat tonight I could bring home for lunch tomorrow.

"No," I lied. "I haven't eaten."

"Want to grab some dinner?"

I shrugged. "Okay."

A half hour later we were seated at Sapristi's. The waitress set a steaming bowl of penne in front of me and another filled with shrimp linguine in front of Seth. Seth had let me choose the wine. I'd picked a bottle of Domaine des Baumard chenin blanc, partly because it was described as having notes of honeysuckle but mostly because it had a $45 price tag. I wasn't about to let Seth off easily with one of the lower-end bottles. Besides, I was worth it.

We made small talk over dinner. He, on the one hand, told me about a string of roadside fires presumably caused by motorists tossing cigarette butts from their car windows.

Dried grass and smoldering tobacco were a combustible combination. He also told me about a recent fire he'd worked at a small hotel in which arson was suspected. The run-down place had been in the red for years, and investigators suspected the owner had torched the place for the insurance money. I, on the other hand, told Seth about me busting the security guards at the mall. But I did *not* tell him about the horseshoe nail in the bomb at the golf course. Withholding this piece of information was a bit titillating. It gave me a sense of power and control.

When we'd finished our dinner, we returned to my apartment. It was dusk now, and the complex was dark. Someone had thrown a rock and taken out the streetlight in front, so the place was even darker than usual. Warm, too. Indian summer had set in.

We made our way up to my apartment, where we found Blast and Brigit entwined on the carpet, licking each other's mouths in a canine make-out session.

"Careful, buddy," Seth said, nudging Blast's butt with his toe, "or you may have to marry her."

I supposed it was a funny comment, but it rankled nonetheless. Was committing to someone you cared about such a bad thing? I supposed being tied to another person would come with limitations. But spending a lifetime alone sounded so much worse.

"How about a swim?" Seth asked.

"Pool's closed after dark," I said. The underwater lights hadn't worked since I'd moved in, and Grigsby was too cheap to have them repaired.

"What's the manager going to do?" Seth said. "Call the cops?"

"Point taken," I said.

Seth took Blast and Brigit down to the pool while I changed into my bikini, pulled my hair up in a ponytail on top of my head, and grabbed a couple of towels.

When I made my way down the outside steps and into the pool area, I found Seth's shirt, shoes, and socks in a heap on the ground and Seth himself puttering around in the water in his shorts. Brigit and Blast lay side by side on the love seat, panting mildly in the warm night.

I draped the towels over the back of a chair and went to the ladder. Seth met me there, looking up at me like a wolf eyeing his prey. "*Damn,* girl. Are nerds allowed to look like that in a bikini?"

Flattered, I nonetheless responded by using my toes to kick water into his face.

He chuckled and eased back to give me space.

I bent down in the water, wetting myself up to my neck.

We were the only ones outside tonight. The place was private and dark and quiet, the only sound the steady, rhythmic thrum of the pool filter. We swam around for a bit in silence, working off our dinner and wine.

After a few minutes, Seth stopped swimming and waited at one end, watching me as I approached. When I drew close enough, he reached out and grabbed my wrist, pulling me through the water toward him. I stood in front of him now, the water up to our chests, swirling softly around us, caressing our bodies.

We stood there for a moment, mere inches apart, staring into each other's eyes. His pupils flashed with desire as he reached up a hand and tugged my ponytail loose, letting my hair fall around my face.

"That's the way I like it," he said, his voice husky.

He cupped his strong hands on either side of my chin and covered my mouth with his. His kiss was warm, wild, and wonderful, his lips and tongue teasing and tempting me.

My arms wrapped around his neck as the kiss deepened. Seth moved his arms to my back now, pulling me toward him until my wet chest pressed against his. After a few intense, sensuous moments, his mouth released mine, moving to my neck.

Seth turned us around as one now, pushing me back against the pool wall, pressing himself against me.

I enjoyed it for a brief moment before pushing him back. "Slow down, cowboy. I'm not that easy."

Seth issued a groan of frustration that was immensely rewarding. Looked like I had the upper hand for the moment.

A stray cat darted past the fence and Brigit and Blast leaped off the love seat, rushing to the fence and barking their heads off. *Woof-woof-woof-woof-woof!*

Before we could quiet them, Grigsby's door flew open.

"Shut those dogs up now!" Grigsby shouted.

The moment spoiled, Seth and I shushed our partners and gathered up our things.

As we parted ways at the gate, Seth gave me a soft smile. "I'll be in touch."

Something told me he meant it this time.

SIXTY-EIGHT
A LITTLE BIRDIE
TOLD ME

Brigit

A few days after she and Blast had been left alone in the apartment, Brigit and her partner were back on the beat, making the rounds of the mall. After lunch from the shish-kebab stand, Megan led Brigit over to the carousel. As they approached the man who worked the ride, Brigit scented something.

A bird.

Had a pigeon flown into the courtyard? It had happened before. Brigit had seen the maintenance men and custodians chasing it with a net, trying to shoo it out the doors.

Her nose lifted to the air and twitched. No, this wasn't a fresh bird scent. It was faded and old. And it was coming from the bright-red feather stuck in the smiling man's hatband.

SIXTY-NINE
TRICK OR TREAT

The Rattler

Sundance Square in downtown Fort Worth teemed with swaggering, self-indulgent people in costumes traipsing from one bar or nightclub to the next. Witches. Zombies. An oversized banana. A big-breasted saloon girl in fishnet tights. Three gay men and their straight girlfriend dressed as Dorothy, the Tin Man, the Lion, and the Scarecrow from *The Wizard of Oz*. Fitting, he supposed, given that once his bombs exploded tonight they'd be flying somewhere over the rainbow. The Tin Man might even be able to find a spare heart, the Scarecrow a brain—assuming he could beat the zombies to it.

Dressed in his wrangler outfit, he'd blend right in. As soon as he could find a parking spot, that is. Every lot seemed to be full, every spot at the curb taken.

He cruised the block in his father's car. He'd left his pink Cadillac at home, knowing it might be too memorable. But a black Lexus? These cars were designed to be tastefully demure.

Mere minutes ago, he'd slid the envelope containing his manifesto into a box at the downtown post office on Taylor Street. The envelope was addressed to the managing editor of the Fort Worth *Star-Telegram,* sometimes jokingly referred to as the *Startle-Gram.* The editor would certainly be startled when the manifesto landed on his desk in the next day or two.

It hadn't taken the Rattler long to craft his manifesto. After all, his principles were straightforward and simple. Unlike "Unabomber" Ted Kaczynski, the Rattler had no intention of rambling on for thirty-five thousand words. *Seriously, dude, get to the fucking point already. It's not like they pay by the word.*

WOOooo.

Holy.

Shit.

The Rattler had been so caught up in his musings and his search for a parking place that he'd run a red light—a light with a cop sitting in an alleyway just past it, waiting to snag someone for a traffic violation.

Given the bedsheet and bombs in his trunk, the Rattler's first impulse was to floor the gas pedal and attempt to flee, but he knew such an attempt would fail. Cruisers had powerful engines, and even if he got away from this particular cop the officer would call for backup and have a helicopter on him in seconds. Besides, the cop had seen the license plate on his father's car. They'd identify the Rattler in no time. No way would he spend the rest of his life behind bars.

He'd rather die.

His heart pumping so loud it virtually rendered him deaf, the Rattler pulled over, stopped the car, and unrolled his window. It seemed like an eternity before the cop climbed out of his cruiser and came to the Rattler's window.

Shit. Again.

It was that dickhead with the red hair, the one who worked the mall beat, constantly tugged on his pants to rearrange his nuts, and came on to every woman in the place. Officer Mackey. The Rattler had watched him. What a supreme asshole.

The Rattler knew Sundance Square wasn't part of Mackey's usual beat, but given the drunken hordes here tonight he guessed that officers from other districts had been assigned here to help with crowd control.

The prick bent down to the window, blowing onion-scented breath in the Rattler's face. He looked the Rattler's costume over and issued a grunt of amusement. "Howdy, pardner," he said with no sign of recognition. "You just ran a red light."

"I'm sorry," the Rattler said. "I was distracted by that woman in the saloon girl costume."

"Can't blame you there." Mackey emitted an onion-fumed chuckle. "Nice rack on that one, huh?"

"You know it!"

The two nodded their heads in unison, agreeing that yes, breasts were awesome.

Wow, am I actually going to get away scot-free?

No such luck. Mackey whipped out his pad and wrote Randy a ticket, tossing it through the window. "Keep your eyes off the tits and on the road."

SEVENTY
BREAKING UP ISN'T HARD TO DO ... FOR SOME PEOPLE

Megan

Seth and I had so much fun on Halloween it should have been illegal.

I'd worn a black cat costume complete with a bendy tail. Seth had dressed as a pirate, with an eye patch, a plastic sword at his waist, and a stuffed parrot on his shoulder. While our dogs had a date on my couch, we'd barhopped at Sundance Square, drinking and dancing until the wee hours of the night.

With all the stress we'd been under with the bomber on the loose, it felt great to set our troubles aside for a few hours and enjoy life and each other's company.

I'd been concerned that the Tunabomber would take advantage of the holiday to plant more bombs. After all, on a night when everyone was in costume and carrying props it would have been easy to do so without anyone noticing. Fortunately, he must have had other plans that night. Halloween came and went without a single explosion.

When Seth brought me home that night, he not only gave me a warm kiss, but he also held me gently in his arms, bending down to press his forehead to mine in a soft, sweet gesture, as if trying to read my mind and learn everything about me by osmosis.

He wanted to be closer to me. That much was clear.

For the first time in a long time, maybe even ever, the loneliness completely left me.

Three days after Halloween, Detective Jackson summoned me to her office and gestured for me to take a seat. She handed me a single sheet of paper. It was titled "A Warning Rattle" and read:

Priorities must change. Excessive self-interest can no longer be tolerated. The material means nothing. Equality and justice are required now. Until everyone takes this message to heart, I must continue my efforts to instigate change. Think about this as you contemplate the recent events at the mall, the country club, and Sundance Square. And for fuck's sake, lose the "Tunabomber" moniker. It demeans us all.

The Rattler

Oh, my God. The letter was from *him.* The bomber.

I looked up at the detective, so many questions running through my mind but none coherent enough to escape my gaping mouth.

"The letter was mailed to the newspaper on Halloween," she said. "Given the reference to Sundance Square, we believe he may have made an attempt to place explosives there but was thwarted somehow."

The thought that Seth and I could have crossed paths

with the bomber caused my spinal fluid to freeze. When I could finally get my words out, I asked, "Were there any fingerprints on the letter or envelope?"

"None."

"What does this name mean? The Rattler."

"Hell if I know. You got any ideas?"

"The Lipscombs had that rattlesnake."

"We've ruled them out, remember?"

"Think we should rule them back in?"

The detective exhaled sharply. "Again, hell if I know."

"Do we know where the letter was mailed it from?" I asked. "Is there any video footage of the bomber sticking the letter in the box?"

"He mailed it from the downtown post office. The video feed shows a letter being mailed by a person wearing a white bedsheet with holes cut out for the eyes. You know, like Charlie Brown in that *Great Pumpkin* show."

Coincidental, probably, but the tone and angst in the Rattler's letter reminded me of Charlie Brown's consternation in the Christmas special, when the poor kid tries to find meaning in the holiday beyond the artificial trees and the gifts and the greed and the supercolossal lights and display contests. No matter how many times I watched the show, I always found it heartbreaking when Charlie lamented the fact that even his baby sister and dog had "gone commercial."

Something niggled at me, though. There was something about the letter that seemed familiar somehow, but I couldn't quite put my finger on it.

"What now?" I asked the detective, returning the paper to her.

"We've got a profiler working on it," she said. "The only thing he's come up with so far is that it's likely a young white guy."

"Why's that?"

" 'Cause with this crazy-ass shit," she replied, "it's always a young white guy."

Fall marched on with no progress in the bombing investigation. Frustration and fear were my constant companions. No doubt the bomber would strike again. But when? And where?

It was Sunday of the second week in November now, and Thanksgiving loomed. Seth and I had met for lunch a couple of times recently, but between me being assigned a two-week round of night shifts and his reservist weekend coming up again, we'd had no time for real dates. At least I was back on the day shift again now. Those night hours threw my biorhythms for a loop.

Seth had mentioned that he had today off from work and, on a whim, I decided to surprise him by popping by his place on my lunch break. I couldn't remember the street or house number, but I recalled what the house looked like. I spent ten minutes rolling up and down the streets of the Morningside neighborhood before I spotted the house.

Gray paint. Ugly orange brick. Mismatched shingles. And Seth on a ladder, shoeless and shirtless, cleaning out the gutters.

He scooped handfuls of leaves and twigs out of the channels and tossed them into a garbage can below. Damn, but the guy made housework look sexy.

Given the unseasonably warm weather, quite a few people were working on their yards today. Seth's next-door neighbor was trimming limbs with a chain saw as I pulled up, the *bzzzzz* masking the sound of my cruiser's engine.

I unrolled my window, cut the motor, and simply watched Seth for a moment, savoring the chance to observe him in his natural state, unnoticed. The neighbor finished with his chain saw and disappeared inside his garage.

As I watched, the screen door to Seth's house flew open and an elderly man in wrinkled pants and a blue pajama shirt stormed out onto the porch. Well, perhaps "stormed" was too strong a word given that he pulled a wheeled oxygen tank behind him.

He looked up at Seth. "What did I tell you?" he hollered. "You can't just toss that shit into the yard!"

Seth didn't bother looking down. "I'm not. Look. I'm using a garbage can."

The man waved an arm around. "It's blowing all over the place!"

Though Seth spoke slowly, the tone made it clear he was on the edge of snapping back at the old man. "I'll clean up the yard when I'm done up here, Grandpa."

"You'd better, you dumb bastard!"

With that, the man marched back inside, the screen door slapping shut behind him.

I sat there, stupefied. What, exactly, had I just witnessed?

Seth crooked an arm over the edge of the roof now and rested his forehead on it, obviously frustrated. Part of me felt I should leave, let him have this private moment to himself. But another part of me wanted to understand what the hell had just happened and to offer him some type of support.

Dumb bastard?

What kind of grandfather calls his grandchild such an awful name?

Of course here in Texas men called one another bastards and sons of bitches all the time, but they did so with a jesting grin and followed it up with a companionable handshake or slap on the back to make it clear the term was being used ironically. Seth's grandfather had done nothing of the sort.

When a squirrel skittered up the trunk of a nearby oak, Brigit sat up on the backseat and emitted a loud and unexpected bark, causing me to nearly jump out of my skin and Seth to look in my direction.

He didn't look happy to see me.

Uh-oh.

I raised a hand and called out the open window, "Hey!"

Without responding, he climbed down the ladder and stepped over to the car. A light sheen of sweat covered his chest and shoulders, and specks of dust and leaf particles had stuck in the sweat. Still, the effect only made him look more manly, like a force of nature.

"What are you doing here?" His voice was dull, lifeless, like it had been after the bombing at the country club, as if something in him had shut down.

"I'm on my lunch break," I said. "Thought I'd see if you wanted to grab a bite to eat."

Again he failed to reply, but he circled around to the other side of my patrol car and climbed in. I glanced over at his dusty bare feet and shirtless chest. Looked like we'd have to pick up something at a drive-thru and eat in the car. I'd been hoping for a real lunch at a table with a plate and a fork, but no sense being inflexible.

I pulled away from the curb and we drove to a Sonic a mile away. There was little on the menu that met my healthy-eating requirements, so I settled for an iced tea, ordering a burger for Brigit. Seth leaned across me to call his order into the intercom, getting a burger for himself, as well as fries and a frozen drink.

While we waited for our food, I decided to take a chance and break the ice. "You live with your grandpa?"

Seth stared straight ahead. "Yep."

I wondered why he'd never mentioned it. "Is he always like that?" I asked.

"Like what?" Seth asked, still fixated on the windshield.

"I don't know . . . *mean*?"

I'd meant my words to show concern and support, so I was shocked when Seth said, "Don't go there, Megan." His harsh tone carried an unmistakable warning.

Confused, I sat in silence until the waitress arrived with our food.

"That'll be twelve-sixty-seven," she said.

Seth looked down as if realizing for the first time that he wore only a pair of shorts. "Ah, shit. I don't have my wallet."

"No problem." I pulled a twenty from my purse and handed it to the girl. I gave her a two-dollar tip and dropped the rest of the change in my purse.

Brigit and Seth ate while I quietly sipped my tea, picked at the bun from Brigit's burger, and wondered why I suddenly felt worlds apart from the very man I thought I'd been growing closer to.

When Seth finished his lunch, he gathered up his trash, climbed out of the car, and carried it to a can along the wall. He returned to my cruiser but didn't get back inside. Instead, he rested his elbows on the open window and leaned in. "Look, Megan. I just . . . I don't . . ."

He shook his head as if angry with himself that he couldn't get the words out. Hell, I could relate to that.

He looked at me for a split second, a darkness in his eyes, before shifting his focus off to his left. "This isn't going to work out."

KABOOM!

That was the sound of my heart exploding. They'd probably heard it all the way to Oklahoma. It actually felt as if there were a ragged hole in my chest. It was all I could do not to burst into tears.

But after the initial shock wore off, it took everything in me not to whip out my baton, beat him with it, and demand answers. *Why wouldn't this work out? What changed your mind? Is there someone else? What kind of game are you playing here? What the hell do you want from me?*

But I would not grovel. I would not point out that he owed me eight bucks for his lunch, either. That would just seem petty. But I couldn't pretend as if this meant nothing at all. At this point, saying, *No biggie,* or, *It wasn't working for me, either,* would only underscore my hurt and let him know I'd cared more for him than either of us had realized until now.

Biting my lip to put an end to its quivering, I looked over at him. Despite having just broken up with me, he had not backed away from my car. He still leaned in, though his eyes were now locked on my steering wheel instead of my face. *Asshole.* The least he could do was have the balls to look me in the eye as he crushed me.

"Okay. Take c-care, S-Seth."

I hit the button to roll up my window, forcing his arms off the sill. He took a step back but made no move to go, instead watching as I backed up and drove off.

I hoped he enjoyed his barefoot walk home, the *dumb bastard.*

SEVENTY-ONE
CHEER UP, MEGAN

Brigit

Her partner lay curled up on the futon and cried most of the evening. Brigit did her best to lick the salty tears away, but it didn't seem to help. They just kept coming.

Brigit tried distracting Megan by doing some of her tricks. Walking on her hind legs. Rolling over. Playing dead.

Nothing.

As a last resort, she opened the closet and latched on to a pair of sneakers, dragging them out into the middle of the floor. Surely that would give Megan something else to think about. But Megan didn't seem to care. She just lay there, her wet eyes staring off into space.

Finally, Brigit climbed onto the futon next to Megan and lay down, resting her nose next to Megan's face.

Sometimes a person just needs to know she's not alone.

Megan put her arms around Brigit and gave her a sad kiss on the forehead. "I really don't deserve you, do I?"

SEVENTY-TWO
AULD *BANG* SYNE

The Rattler

Christmas would arrive in a matter of days. The mall bustled with shoppers loading their bags with more things they didn't need and spending money they didn't have, the holiday fueling and excusing their insatiable greed and lust for possessions. The shopping-mall Santa sat on his sleigh-shaped throne, the commercial icon encouraging children to tell him everything they wanted for Christmas.

Greedy little shits.

The Rattler sat on his stool next to the carousel, a smile plastered on his face for the sake of the children and their parents in line. But inside, he fumed.

They still didn't get it.

He'd sent his manifesto to the newspaper and it had been printed, uploaded to the Internet, and reported on every news channel. Yet, obviously, it had made no difference.

Well, fuck it.

Fuck them.

He'd set his next bomb just for the fun of it. And he'd

put it somewhere guaranteed to have maximum impact. Then he'd make that move to the coast.

Officer Luz walked up with that fluffy-ass dog of hers. "Hi, Randy."

As always, she eyed his hatband. Today it sported a Hannah Montana Valentine's card, a button that read: I am the Man from Nantucket, and a glitter-encrusted snowflake he'd made in kindergarten. To this day he could remember how carefully he'd cut the paper, the painstaking way he'd applied just the right amount of glue and sparkles so the snowflake would be perfect. He'd even convinced his teacher to let him skip recess to work on it. The day after he'd proudly presented it to his mother to hang on their Christmas tree, Randy had found it in the trash can. Apparently, his silly paper snowflake wasn't worthy of hanging with her collection of Waterford crystal ornaments.

"Nantucket, hmm?" Megan chuckled. "Better be careful or all the ladies will want to sit on *your* lap instead of Santa's."

It was the first time in weeks Randy had seen even a hint of a smile on her face.

"All ready for the holidays?" she asked.

"Sure am," he said. Given that he did precisely nothing to acknowledge them, he was always ready.

"Big plans?" she asked.

"Just the usual for Christmas," he said. "You know. Hanging with the folks." He offered a cringe for authenticity. "I'm working New Year's Eve, but as soon as the mall closes I'm heading up to Billy Bob's." He tossed his lasso into the air for emphasis. "I'm gonna bring in the new year with a bang!"

She smiled. "Sounds like fun."

If she only knew . . .

SEVENTY-THREE
RESOLUTIONS

Megan

The profiler had elaborated on his description of the bomber as not only young, white, and male but also of above average intelligence and with sociopathic tendencies. Alas, the profile did nothing to help us identify which young, white, intelligent male with sociopathic tendencies it was. There were probably hundreds in the area. Thousands, even.

Detective Jackson had hoped that publishing the Rattler's manifesto would bring in some tips, but the few that had come in hadn't panned out. Given that the second bomb had also contained a horseshoe nail, she'd looked into criminals with ties to the local horse breeding and racing industries to see if she could generate any leads. While there had been some gambling violations and illegal doping, nothing she found seemed to connect anyone to the bombs in any apparent way. The case had hit yet another wall.

Ricky and Scott had pleaded out their attempted-theft

charges, receiving a year's probation each. Last I heard they were flipping burgers at a place on Hulen. Working at minimum wage now, they'd never be able to afford that big-screen television.

The holidays had been the same as always. Loud, boisterous affairs at my parents' house.

At Thanksgiving, all seven of us had crowded elbow-to-elbow at the kitchen table, fighting for what little oxygen remained in the room and the last piece of pumpkin or pecan pie. I'd fixed Brigit a plate of turkey, dressing, and mashed potatoes. Brigit had eaten every last bite, then curled up on the couch to nap with my father and Joey, displacing the orange tabbies who hissed and spit and gave her what-for.

Gabby's crush, T.J., had stopped by in the early evening when we'd all fixed ourselves a plate of leftovers and gathered around the television to watch football, fighting again over the limited seats. I'd ended up sharing the ottoman with my mother. I took the whole thing over when she got up to fix T.J. a plate.

He was a cute kid. Clean. Mannerly. And clearly totally smitten with Gabs.

Why couldn't I find someone who felt that way about me?

Christmas was much of the same. More cramming our oversized Catholic family into a house built for Protestants. More food. More afternoon naps in the living room. Another visit from T.J., who scored extra points by showing up with a tin of his mother's holiday fudge.

I worked the swing shift on Christmas and spent the evening and early hours of the night arresting drunks who'd indulged in too much wine and eggnog and responding to a seemingly endless series of domestic disturbance calls. There is such a thing as too much togetherness. Really, the city council should enact an ordinance forbidding any family from spending more than four consecutive hours together. It would make my job so much easier and prevent at least a dozen attempted homicides.

The Big Dick had been making noises about the steak dinner he believed I owed him for failing to nab the bomber. When I reminded Derek that we had not put a time limit on our bet he'd pushed for a date. We'd agreed on January 1. Given that it was now New Year's Eve, I wished I'd padded the time period a little more, stretched it out to St. Patrick's Day. Maybe Mackey would've agreed if I'd upped the ante with the promise of green beer, too.

At 8:00, I was curled up on my futon with Brigit, watching the festivities from Times Square on television, feeling sorry for myself, and wondering what Seth was doing tonight.

Did he have a date? Someone special to kiss at midnight?

Blurgh. Dealing with drunks was a pain in the ass, but I almost wished I'd been assigned to work tonight. At least then I wouldn't have been alone.

After a half hour watching the revelers and pop bands on television, I couldn't take it anymore. I threw on a sweater, jeans, and the new boots my mother had bought me for Christmas to replace the pair my partner had chewed up. I moved Brigit's cage over in front of the closet door to keep her from getting to the few remaining shoes inside and gave her a scratch on the head. "Be a g-good girl, 'kay?"

Grabbing my purse and keys, I headed out.

It was after closing time at the Chisholm Trail mall when I strolled down the walkway, contemplating my New Year's resolutions. So far I'd come up with:

1. Stop moping around wondering why Seth broke things off.
2. . . . .

I hadn't come up with a second resolution yet, but I'd keep working on it.

The courtyard was dark when I entered, the overhead lights turned off. I'd forgotten that the mall planned to close earlier than usual for the holiday. It looked like everyone had moved on, employees included. *Damn.* I'd been hoping to catch Randy, to see if he'd mind me tagging along with him to Billy Bob's. Country music wasn't really my thing, but it beat sitting at home like some pathetic loser. Besides, the guy amused me. I could use a laugh about now.

When I found the courtyard empty, my first impulse was to turn around and go. But a moment later something drew me to the quiet carousel. I walked around it in the dim light, eyeing all of the horses just as I'd done as a child, looking for the prettiest one. I bypassed the one with the corkscrew hole and continued my search.

There he was.

A black stallion rearing up on his hind legs, his silver saddle bejeweled with fake rubies.

Leaving my purse on Randy's podium, I stepped up on the platform and climbed onto the horse. I was lost in thought when a voice came from behind me.

"Riding off into the sunset?"

I turned to find Randy walking toward me. He must've come from punching the clock in the employee break room.

I offered him a smile in return. "Thinking about it."

He was still dressed in his wrangler's outfit, his lasso at his waist. Heck, he could probably wear the costume to Billy Bob's. He'd fit right in.

A security guard poked his head in one of the courtyard doors. "Hey, you two. I'm heading out. The custodial staff is off tonight for the holiday, so just make sure the door lock catches when you leave, okay?"

"No problem!" I called.

Once the door had closed, Randy hopped onto the carousel platform and made his way toward me. "No plans tonight?"

I sighed. "No. Any chance I can tag along with you to Billy Bob's? I can be your wing woman, help you pick up girls."

He chuckled. "I don't need any help with that. Girls love the Randy wrangler. I have to beat them off with a stick."

"Darn," I joked, giving a finger snap. "Should've brought my baton."

Randy leaned back against the horse next to me, reaching up with his hand to grasp the pole. As he did, the pearl snap at the wrist of his Western shirt popped open. The cuff slid down his arm an inch or two, revealing part of a tattoo—the head of a diamondback rattlesnake, its mouth open to reveal a forked tongue and a set of fangs ready to sink into the flesh of an unwitting victim.

Randy looked up at his wrist, then back at me, his wide-set eyes that usually glimmered with humor now cold with hate.

In that instant I knew.

Randy is the Rattler.

Oh, God! Why hadn't I seen it? So many things now made sense.

His car in the driveway of his parents' house near the country club. No doubt he knew the area and could easily sneak on and off the golf course without detection.

Why the manifesto had rang a bell in my head. Randy had used the unusual word "moniker" both when speaking to me and in his manifesto.

His actions shortly before the bomb exploded in the food court. He'd been looking down at his cell phone, probably watching a timer to see how many seconds remained before he'd need to excuse himself from his post, leave the courtyard, and escape to safety.

The horseshoe nails in the bombs. An inside joke with himself, as he waited to see if Fort Worth PD would make the connection between the nails and the carousel operator. We hadn't.

Yes, in that instant I knew.

But in that instant Randy also realized I knew.

"Well, well." A sick smile slithered across his lips. "Looks like you're not as stupid as I thought."

Fear seized me with a frozen grip. If I'd had my baton with me, I'd have delivered a skull-cracking *whack* to his head. As it was, I had no weapons.

Not my baton.

Not my gun.

Not my pepper spray.

My best weapon, Brigit, was back at my apartment, probably eating the couch cushion since she couldn't access the shoes in the closet.

My fight-or-flight instincts kicked in and I slid from the horse, leaped off the carousel platform, and took off running as fast as I could across the courtyard, which wasn't fast at all. *Damn it!* Why had I worn these new high-heeled boots?

A shadow fell over me a split second before Randy's lasso came down over my shoulders. I was yanked backward as Randy jerked the rope tight around me. It hurt like hell when I hit the tile floor. Can a person break her ass?

Randy pulled on the rope, singing as he tugged me toward him. "Come a-ti yi youpy youpy yea youpy yea, come a-ti yi youpy youpy yea."

He jerked me inch by inch, toying with me as I squirmed and struggled, trying to break free from the impossibly tight binding cutting into my skin. As he pulled me close, he hissed, "You didn't think I'd let you get away now, did you, little filly?"

Minutes later, and despite my best efforts to fight Randy off, my legs were tied to the black stallion I'd been sitting on earlier, my hands and feet were bound tightly to the metal bar on which the horse was mounted, and a bomb was strapped to my chest.

Looked like I'd be bringing in the new year with a bang, too. At least I hadn't wasted a lot of time making resolutions I wouldn't be able to keep. I'd managed to get a few kicks in, too, temporarily disabling Randy with a spike heel to the nuts. Frankly, I was surprised he hadn't used the rope to strangle me for that.

"Don't do this, Randy!" I pleaded. "Please!"

He reached out a finger and stroked my cheek, causing me to flinch. "You're sexy when you beg."

My stomach clenched tight in terror, my lungs soon following suit. Even as I gasped for air, hyperventilating in pure panic, my mind raced, thinking back to my criminal psych classes and everything the instructors had taught us about sociopaths.

They have no emotional connections to others, no moral compass.

They lie with ease. Manipulate.

They're egotistical, hypocritical, controlling.

And, above all, they want to win.

"You've already won, Randy!" I cried, attempting an appeal to his sense of self-preservation while trying to get my emotions under control. "You've proved that you can outsmart the rest of us. Killing me will only make the department more determined to bring you in!"

He eyed me for a moment as if thinking over my words.

I tried my best to persuade him: "You don't have to let me go, Randy. Just turn the bomb off!"

"Maybe you're right." He stepped toward me, his hands reaching out to the device on my chest. "I could escape before anybody knows you're tied up here."

Thank God! I sobbed in relief, my shoulders heaving.

Just as his fingers touched the bomb he jerked them back, laughing. "Pysch!"

Rage overtook my fear now. I attempted again to kick him to no avail. My legs and feet were tied too tightly.

He reached out to activate the timer on the bomb. "I'll set this one for eleven thirty. That way the bomb squad will be here when the real show starts at Billy Bob's at midnight."

I'd merely be the warm-up. I supposed it was odd to be insulted by that fact, but nevertheless I was. The least he could have done was set my bomb for midnight, too, so that I could count down to the new year before going up like a firework.

Randy hopped off the platform but turned back to look at me one last time. "I better get going. Time's a-wastin'." He gave me an exaggerated wink and gestured to the timer on my chest.

According to the readout on the timing device, the bomb would go off in one hour, twenty-nine minutes, and fifty-three seconds.

He stepped over to his podium and turned the key to start the carousel. The organ music kicked in with "Happy Trails," the platform began to rotate, and my horse began moving up and down.

"Randy, no!" I screamed as he made his way across the courtyard. "Get back here! Please!"

I was tempted to cry, *Why me?* After all, I'd never done anything mean to him. But neither had Honeysuckle or the golf player. For sociopaths, it didn't matter. Everyone was the enemy.

The door swung shut behind him, sealing my fate. The timer continued to count down, at one hour and twenty-eight minutes now.

As the carousel circled, I screamed and shrieked and wriggled and squirmed and tried to free my limbs. It was no use. Randy had tied me tighter than a calf at the rodeo. The only thing I managed to do was dig the rope deeper into my wrists, drawing blood that seeped into the wrist-bands of my sweater.

An hour later I was exhausted and delirious with horror, had only twenty-seven minutes left to live, and was singing along with the organ music at the top of my lungs.

"Oh, come along, boys, and listen to my tale,
I'll tell you all my troubles on the ol' Chisholm
    Trail.
Come a-ti yi youpy youpy yea youpy yea,
Come a-ti yi youpy youpy yea. . . ."

A loud rap sounded at the window of the courtyard. I looked over to see the Big Dick standing behind the glass, his flashlight in his hand. Although the carousel music was too loud for me to hear his words, I was able to read his lips.

What the fuck?

Who would have thought I'd ever be happy to see that guy?

He spoke into his shoulder-mounted radio. In three minutes the fire department had arrived and used a battering ram to break through the glass. Two men in bomb squad uniforms stepped through the jagged space and came inside, one leading a black Lab, the other leading a yellow Lab.

Seth.

Wonderful. Could anything be more humiliating than having to be rescued by the man who'd dumped you without explanation?

Mackey stuck his head through the hole in the glass but didn't come inside.

"Derek!" I screamed. "Get officers up to Billy Bob's! Randy's there now!"

"Who's Randy?"

For God's sake, Mackey, get a clue! "The skinny guy who runs this ride! He's the bomber!"

Derek backed away to make the necessary calls to Dispatch. *Damn.* He'd get credit for bringing Randy in. I was going to have to buy that asshole a steak, wasn't I?

Seth rushed over as fast as he could in his gear and stepped onto the carousel platform. My eyes met his through the clear faceplate of his helmet, his intense, pained gaze carrying a load of turmoil and regret. "Megan, I—"

"It's okay, Seth. Really! You have nothing to feel bad about."

Actually, I thought he should feel like a total shit for the way he treated me. But the last thing I needed right now was for him to be distracted trying to obtain a last-minute absolution from me to clear his conscience.

Seth didn't look like he was buying my story, but nonetheless his focus went from my face to the explosive device on my chest. His eyes popped wide when he saw that only nineteen minutes remained on the timer.

His eyes narrowed as he cocked his head one way, then the other, evidently assessing how best to dismantle the bomb without blowing both of us to bits. He looked up at me one final time before he reached out with trembling hands to slowly and methodically begin pulling the bomb apart.

While Seth worked on me, the other tech made his way around the large room with Blast and the black Lab, the two dogs sniffing around the furniture and fixtures, searching to see if Randy had planted more bombs. I doubted they'd find any. The one he'd strapped to me was definitely impromptu, part of the stash he'd planned to take up to the stockyards. Still, it couldn't hurt to be extra-cautious.

The timer continued to count down. It was at ten minutes now.

Then nine.

Worry lines creasing his forehead, Seth continued to pull the bomb apart. I mumbled incoherent, frantic prayers and tried my best not to wet myself.

Eight.

Seven.

Time was running out and Seth still wasn't done. My head felt as if it were full of air and spinning like an out-of-control carousel. With any luck, I'd faint from fear before I was blown to smithereens.

Six.

Five.

A drop of sweat ran down Seth's cheek.

Four.

Three.

Two.

When the timer hit one minute, a cry burst from my lungs.

This was it. My life was over.

I'd die without ever marrying or having kids or even an expanded cable package. Brigit would be assigned to a new partner and probably forget all about me. How would my family achieve closure without a body to bury? All that would be left of me would be chunks of flesh, maybe a limb or two. My new boots would be ruined.

My mind went woozy. Whether it was from fear or from the fact that I'd stopped breathing I wasn't sure. I only knew I couldn't seem to hold my head up straight anymore. It lolled about on my limp neck, rolling from one shoulder to the other.

Seth's voice broke through the fog in my head: "Hang on, Megan! I'm almost there."

With only seconds remaining, Seth was inside the bomb now, separating the fuse from the ignition source. He took a deep breath and gingerly eased the fuse from the casing.

When no *KABOOM* followed, he released a breath of warm air that steamed the inside of his helmet and his body visibly relaxed. He looked up at me. "You're safe now."

My lungs gasped for air as I looked down at the timer. Only three seconds remained, yet Seth hadn't abandoned me even when facing his own possible death. The guy was either a hero or nuts. Maybe both.

Seth stood, removed his helmet, and shouted, "All clear!"

He reached up now and attempted to untie my arms but had no luck with the tight knots. He turned and hollered to his fellow firefighters at the door, "Someone bring me a pocketknife!"

One of the men ran over and handed him a small switchblade. Seth sawed at the rope and freed my hands, then moved down to cut away the bindings on my legs.

"We've got to get to Billy Bob's!" I said, jumping down from the horse. "Now!"

We ran to his car, Blast pounding the pavement alongside us. Tires squealing, we peeled away from the curb in Seth's Nova. He put the pedal to the metal to my apartment, where I grabbed my ballistic vest, sneakers, and tool belt and rounded up Brigit. She had somehow moved the cage away from the closet door and chewed on my rubber rain boots, but no way would I leave my partner out of this bust, not after she'd taken a nail to the hip. Heck, her shaved fur had only recently grown back. She deserved to be a part of this.

We streaked up Northside Drive and hooked a quick turn onto Main. Brigit and Blast slid across the backseat as the car fishtailed.

It was a mere three minutes before midnight when we pulled up to the parking lot of Billy Bob's. Two fire trucks and a dozen police cruisers had surrounded the lot, their lights flashing and spinning on top of their cars, lighting up the night as if this were some kind of party. Officers hunkered down behind their automobiles, guns drawn and aimed at Randy, who stood in the center of the parking lot, an enormous bomb strapped to his own chest now. The bright-red LED display indicated two minutes and fifty-seven seconds remained before the bomb would detonate.

Seth pulled to the curb and the two of us slipped out of his car, bringing our dogs with us. Crouching low for safety, we scurried over behind the open door of the Big Dick's cruiser and took places next to him.

His gun aimed at Randy over his hood, Derek glanced my way. "I hope you've been saving up," he said, "because I'm going for the blackened buffalo rib eye at Reata."

"And I hope you're ready to turn your balls over to me," I spat back.

Seth's lip quirked. "Am I missing something here?"

A negotiator stood near the chief and Detective Jackson. He spoke in a soothing voice through a bullhorn, urging Randy to disable his bomb and give himself up. "Remove your bomb, Randy, and let's talk. It's not too late. You haven't killed anyone yet."

Randy merely laughed and raised his middle finger. "Yes, I have! Didn't you hear? I got that dumb bitch cop at the mall! Blew her ass to bits!"

Not quite.

Of course Randy hadn't noticed me yet. For all he knew I was now nothing more than a bloody splatter covering the mall's carousel. If not for Seth, I would have been.

As the readout ticked down to 2:13, Randy stalked toward a line of cruisers to our right. The officers scrambled backward away from their vehicles rather than firing at Randy. There was no way of knowing whether the bomb would detonate if they shot him or how much protection their ballistic vests would provide against an explosive of this size.

"Chickens!" Randy hollered, rocking back on his heels, flapping imaginary wings, and cackling with laughter. "Squawk-squawk!"

The commanding officer on-site attempted to establish a larger perimeter to allow officers the potential to get a clean shot at Randy without the risk that the bomb would cause extensive injuries to law enforcement. Unfortunately, Randy seemed to know such would be the strategy. As the officers moved back he moved right with them, maintaining a spread of only ten feet.

Much too close for comfort.

As the readout hit one minute, the negotiator issued a final plea to Randy. "You don't really want to die, Randy. Turn that timer off. We'll get you some help."

"Help?" Randy shrieked. "I'm not the one who needs help!" He pointed his index finger and made a broad sweep of his arm to indicate everyone gathered about. "You are the ones who need help!"

The negotiator lowered the bullhorn. There was nothing

else to be done. Randy was intent on blowing himself up and taking as many cops as he could with him.

Randy looked down at the timer on his bomb, then looked back up, his eyes catching mine though the window of Derek's cruiser. Surprise registered on Randy's face. Obviously, he hadn't expected to see me here. Well, he'd thought wrong, hadn't he?

"Ten!" he cried, beginning the countdown to both the new year and the inevitable explosion.

His gaze still locked on me, he took a step in my direction. "Nine!"

A group of rowdy, drunken cowboys and their dates stood behind one of the sawhorses the police had set up to keep the crowds back. They raised beer bottles and began to count down with Randy as if this were some kind of party. The officers nearby ordered them back, but they didn't listen.

Randy stalked toward me. "Eight! Seven!"

As he approached Derek's police cruiser officers scattered like ants from a mound. The Big Dick turned and scrambled between cars parked on the street. Seth and I followed suit, our canine partners scrambling along with us.

"Six!"

At this point, Randy reached Mackey's cruiser and hopped onto the hood.

"Five! Four!"

He stepped onto the roof of the patrol car now, the flashing lights at his feet illuminating him standing tall while everyone else cowered. Crouching next to me, Brigit growled: *Grrr.*

"Three!" Randy and the drunk cowboys yelled. "Two!"

Seth, still dressed in his bomb squad uniform, pushed me up against the car for safety and covered me with his body.

I peeked out from under Seth's chin to watch Randy. Despite everything that had happened over the last few months, I still somehow couldn't believe it had come to this.

"One!"

The countdown complete, Randy spread his legs and threw his hands in the air.

Instinctively I covered my face with my hands, as much to protect myself as to block out the image of a deranged young man blowing himself to bits.

But the explosion never came.

A moment later I opened my eyes to see Randy looking down at the bomb on his chest. He made a fist and beat it against the device.

Nothing.

He glanced up now.

"Holy shit," Seth said on a breath. "It's a dud!"

That was all the Big Dick, Brigit, and I needed to hear. The three of us ran out from behind the car we'd used for cover and rushed the Rattler. A bold move, sure, but there was a rib eye and rubber testicles at stake.

Footsteps and jingling from behind told me that Seth and Blast had joined in our chase.

Randy's eyes popped wide when he saw two armed cops, two dogs, and a bomb squad officer hurtling toward him. He turned and leaped from the top of the patrol car. He landed first on the hood of the cruiser, which gave in a few inches with a resounding *kadunk!* His second leap took him to the ground.

He took off in the other direction. The cops on that side were unaware the bomb was a dud and ran off to the sides, clearing a way through. The five of us ran after Randy. I found it ironic that he was running for his life now when he'd been so willing to end it only a moment ago. Evidently he'd wanted to go out on his own terms.

Well, tough shit.

He'd be going down on mine.

Despite breaking my own personal speed record, Derek and Brigit were gaining on Randy and leaving me behind. I know I'd said I wanted Brigit to be involved in the bust, but I didn't say I wanted her to actually take Randy down. No, after getting screwed in the ass and humiliated on the Internet, I think I deserved that privilege.

I yanked my baton from my belt and flicked my wrist. With a crisp *SNAP*, the baton extended to its full, glorious length. Raising my arm, I pulled my baton back over my head and hurled it with every ounce of strength I could muster, sending it spinning end over end toward Randy's skull.

Swish-swish-swish-swish.

The baton sailed over Brigit and past Derek, finally meeting its target.

Whack!

Randy's head snapped forward, then back. His body went limp, momentum carrying him forward several more feet as he crumpled to the cold asphalt like a marionette whose strings had been cut.

Those of us in pursuit were on him in an instant. Brigit yanked at the back of his collar. The Big Dick and I bent over him, shouldering each other aside as each tried to be the one to cuff the Rattler. Seth stood at Randy's head, his fists clenching and unclenching as he seemed to be fighting the urge to pound the guy's face into the pavement. Blast circled and lunged around the perimeter, barking.

"Who's the dumb bitch now?" I yelled at the prone man at my feet. A moot point. The guy had been rendered unconscious by my baton and thus would be offering no response.

Men might have better upper-body strength, but women

had some pretty powerful bones and muscles just below our waists. I hip-checked Derek, sending him careening off balance to the side. He scowled as he struggled to regain his footing. When he did, he simply stood rather than jumping back into the fray. A wise choice. I'd recovered my baton and would be more than happy to use it again.

I brandished the stick at him. "Do I get your balls?"

Derek shoved my baton away and let out a long, resigned breath. "Yeah, Luz. You got my balls."

"Okay, then." I backed away from Randy and put the end of my baton in the palm of my left hand, pushing it closed. "He's all yours now."

On New Year's Day, in the parking lot of the W1 station, in front of a dozen witnesses, Derek "the Big Dick" Mackey removed his rubber testicles from his pickup truck and attached them to the rear axle of my smart car. To both my surprise and relief, the car did not fall over backward.

The assistant DA who'd been assigned to prosecute Randy's case was among the spectators. He'd swung by the station after a quick meeting with Randy and his attorney at the hospital. Though Randy's attorney hinted he'd be going for some type of insanity defense, the DA assured us it would never fly. "Multiple explosives? Serious bodily harm? Attempted murder? This guy's going away for fifty to life."

Sounded like a great plan to me. Maybe Randy could complete his philosophy degree in the pen or start up a theater group, revise his role as the male lead in *The Best Little Whorehouse in Texas*. I could only imagine the inmates who'd be willing to play the female prostitutes.

I climbed into my car and drove off, dragging my newly acquired balls behind me.

So where was I headed? To a pancake house to meet Seth. After the bust last night, he'd said he wanted to talk and asked if we could meet for brunch. Heck, I was never one to turn down a free meal.

As far as Seth goes, we'll see. . . .

Don't miss the next Paw Enforcement novel by

Diane Kelly

"Kelly's writing is smart and laugh-out-loud funny."
—Kristan Higgins, *New York Times* bestselling author

PAW
AND ORDER

Now available from St. Martin's Paperbacks